SEVEN GIRLS GONE

SEVEN GIRLS GONE

ALLISON BRENNAN

mira

mira™

ISBN-13: 978-0-7783-3347-0

Seven Girls Gone

For questions and comments about the quality of this book, please contact us at CustomerService@Harlequin.com.

Mira
22 Adelaide St. West, 41st Floor
Toronto, Ontario M5H 4E3, Canada
BookClubbish.com

Printed in U.S.A.

Recycling programs for this product may not exist in your area.

To the woman behind the curtain, Kimberley Howe.
An author, a leader and a friend.

SEVEN GIRLS GONE

1

Friday started at 12:57 a.m. for St. Augustine detective Beau Hebert. Two hours' sleep was going to have to be enough.

A homicide at the Magnolia Inn wasn't a surprise. Not the first time he'd been called to a crime scene at the brothel that fronted as a bar—wouldn't be his last. The Magnolia Inn had been the hub for drugs, prostitution and violence longer than Beau had lived in Broussard Parish, the heart of the Louisiana bayou.

Untended fields overgrown with weeds and prickly blackberry bushes surrounded the tired, rambling Inn. A small house owned by the Inn's manager, Jasper "Dog" Steele, was the only other structure on the gravel road. The Inn was more for local use than travelers—unless the purpose of the travel was sex and drugs.

The original building was more than two hundred years old and had once been a grand Southern-style home—wide veranda, stately pillars, carved double-doors. Beau's grandmother said when she was a little girl, the family had moved out in the middle of the night and no one knew what happened to them. The house was vacant for a time, then seized by the parish for unpaid taxes and sold at auction. It went through a series of business ventures including an antique warehouse and a stint as a bed-and-breakfast in the seventies whose claim to fame was a double murder-suicide when a woman walked in on her husband in bed with the owner.

Beau supposed sex and violence were built into the foundation.

Over the years, ill-fitting additions had been built onto the main house and now the place was owned by an LLC whose sole signatory was Jasper Steele. Jasper was no saint. Twice arrested for felonies, but charges were never filed and he walked.

That was St. Augustine in a nutshell, even before corrupt Chief of Police Richard Dubois took the helm three years ago. Regular folk turning a blind eye to crime. Might as well put those three so-called "wise" monkeys up on the town sign because no one saw, no one heard, no one said a damn thing to put criminals like Jasper behind bars for good.

Beau walked up the stairs to the main house, which pretended to be a hotel. If an unsuspecting traveler ventured off the interstate and needed a place, the Inn could accommodate them with one of four marginally maintained rooms upstairs, holdovers from the ill-fated bed-and-breakfast. But rooms generally rented by the hour allowing prostitutes to trade sex for money or drugs or both.

The main floor of the house was a bar and lounge that served food when they had something in stock and the chef wasn't on a bender. Beau didn't know if the health department even knew the place existed or if they cared. He'd never seen anyone eating anything but po'boys and fried oysters.

As soon as he stepped inside, the smell of marijuana assaulted him. Pot wasn't legal in Louisiana, but no one did much about it unless someone was caught dealing. And then? It just depended on who was arrested and who they knew whether they did a day in jail or faced arraignment.

Most weren't arraigned.

"Didn't know you were coming in, Beau," Officer Joey Kinder said when he saw Beau walk in.

"Got the call."

Beau was one of three detectives in the town of 9,500 people. Perry Hebert (no relation), was fifty-nine and waiting for retirement and his pension. Perry rubber-stamped anything an officer said or did, simply marking the days until he could claim his pension—literally, with a big red X on his desk calendar.

Andre Armand was the other detective. Came in a year after Dubois was appointed, but Beau didn't have an angle on him. Originally from NOLA, Armand was thirty, quiet, lived alone. He was competent but didn't put in extra hours. Beau had seniority, so kept most homicides on his desk, passing along property crimes and vandalism to the younger detective.

He glanced at Joey Kinder. Mostly a good cop, but Beau still didn't know if he could trust him. He'd transferred from Baton Rouge nine months ago and didn't have longtime allegiances, but Kinder might not want to take on Beau's cause. Beau had been accused of tilting at windmills—when he wasn't outright threatened to drop an investigation.

"What happened?" Beau asked Kinder.

"Witnesses state Jean Paul LeBlanc shot Jake West. Jake is dead."

Beau knew the bartender. Jake was edgy, always seemed to be circling around illegal activity, but nothing stuck to him.

"Dead on scene," Kinder continued. "Paramedics confirmed,

already left. Coroner on his way." Kinder glanced at his watch and cleared his throat. Doc Brown or his assistant would get here when they damn well felt like it.

"Show me," he said to the uniformed officer.

All eyes were on them as they walked toward the bar counter. A jukebox played country twang, turned low.

Crystal Landry, cousin to Broussard Sheriff Bobby Landry, was sitting with Gray Cormier. Crystal ran the bar—probably managed the girls, though Beau didn't have evidence of it. She rarely worked nights. Gray worked for his half brother Preston. The two lowlifes were St. Augustine's resident drug dealers, but Preston was the brains of the operation. Beau would love to see him in prison, but nothing had stuck.

Then he saw Ernestine.

Well, crud.

Ernestine was sitting alone in the far corner biting her thumbnail. When she caught his eye, she looked down, her dark face etched with worry.

Beau had told the young woman to steer clear of the Magnolia Inn, especially since she had been talking to him. He didn't want her to get hurt. Or worse. Yet here she was, possibly a witness to murder, at the number one hub for violence in St. Augustine.

"Brown give you an ETA?" Beau asked Kinder.

Kinder shook his head. "He was called more than an hour ago."

Dr. Judson Brown was the coroner of Broussard Parish. He had been elected eight times, now serving more than thirty-two years. He was in his seventies and Beau didn't think he was corrupt, just incompetent.

He could be wrong. Brown could be corrupt *and* incompetent.

But when your family lived in the parish for more than two hundred years, people voted for you, no matter how ill-qualified you were or how many mistakes you made.

Beau didn't step behind the bar, though it was clear others

had—the paramedics had left gauze and other supplies, bottles that should have been on the bottom shelf had been pushed to the back and sides, as if someone had squatted to inspect the corpse. Jake West had a hole in his chest, half his head shot off. His one remaining eye open and glazed. Why the paramedics went to check the pulse of a guy with half a head, Beau couldn't fathom.

But even if the evidence was compromised, at least there were two eyewitnesses, according to Kinder.

"Witnesses?" Beau asked.

"Gray and Crystal."

Drug dealer and cousin to a cop. Bobby Landry was probably as corrupt as Chief Dubois, but nicer about it. Everyone loved Bobby, which was why he'd been elected three times—twice unopposed—and would have the job as long as he wanted it.

Beau walked over to the two. "Cormier. Crystal."

"Sit down, Detective," Crystal said. All charm. "Can I get you a beer? Something stronger?"

"Working," he said. "Officer Kinder said you both witnessed the shooting."

He'd made plenty of waves of late investigating a string of murders, so he wasn't going to add fuel to the fire antagonizing the sheriff's cousin by asking that he interview Crystal separate from Cormier.

"I didn't think you worked nights, Crystal," Beau said.

"It's Danny's poker night." Crystal lived with her brother Danny, whose raucous Friday night poker parties were well-known.

"You witnessed the shooting?"

"Jean Paul. He'd been drinking half the night. Jake cut him off, they had words, Jean Paul pulled out a gun and shot him. Twice."

Though he knew the answer, he clarified, "Jean Paul LeBlanc?"

"Yep."

"He shot Jake because Jake cut him off?" That seemed odd for a multitude of reasons. First, that Jake would cut anyone off seemed farcical, and second, that Jean Paul would shoot him over it. "Was Jean Paul tweaking?" If he was drugged out—a distinct possibility—that might make sense.

She shrugged. "Don't know. I thought Nellie kicked him out again, that's why he was here so late."

"What time did the shooting occur?"

"Eleven twenty? Eleven thirty? Thereabouts."

Over an hour before Beau was called. He turned to Cormier, concealed his hatred of the man. Barely.

"You saw the shooting?"

"Yep, what Crystal said."

"Did you hear what words were exchanged?"

"Nope."

Beau didn't believe him.

"Neither of you heard what Jean Paul said before he shot Jake?" Beau repeated.

"Just—nothing. Nothing that made sense," Crystal said.

"But he said *something*."

Crystal hesitated as if she was debating telling him the truth, then said, "I didn't hear most of it, except right before Jean Paul pulled his gun, he said, 'Fuck you.'"

"Yep," Cormier said.

Beau didn't believe either of them.

The murder was likely drug related—most of the murders in St. Augustine were—but the boldness of shooting a man in cold blood with witnesses just didn't feel right.

"How far away was Jean Paul from Jake?" he asked.

Crystal got up, walked over to the bar—stood right in the middle, five stools to the right, five to the left. "Jake was there, pouring a draft," she said, gesturing behind the bar to where two taps—both now decorated with blood—came out of the counter. "And Jean Paul stood…" she walked four, five, six steps from the stools "…about here."

Eight to ten feet. Even if someone was high, they probably wouldn't miss at ten feet.

"Did anyone else witness the shooting?"

"Nope," Cormier said.

That was unlikely with a half dozen people still here.

"Crystal," Beau said, "did anyone leave?"

"Excuse me?"

"You know what I mean."

She was going to lie to him. He could tell because she hesitated again, then she said, "I shouldn't say."

"Say."

"Well, Tex was here, he didn't see anything, but his wife doesn't like it when he comes down."

Really, Beau thought, Tex's wife didn't like when he visited a brothel? Wonder why.

"Don't go causing trouble for him. Mags is a ball-breaker, you know that, and Tex is my kin."

Tex Landry was Crystal's cousin. There were a lot of Landrys in St. Augustine. Beau suspected that 10 percent of the parish had Landry blood going back a dozen generations or more.

So Tex Landry was screwing one of the prostitutes when Jean Paul shot Jake West. Slipped out so his wife wouldn't find out.

"Anyone else?"

"No," she said.

Fifty-fifty she was telling the truth.

Beau got up and walked over to the larger group of men and women sitting in the corner. He asked if anyone had witnessed the shooting; no one admitted they had. He asked if anyone heard what the argument between Jake and Jean Paul was about; no one had heard a word.

"Where was Jean Paul drinking?" Beau asked.

They looked at each other, shrugged.

He turned to Crystal and called across the room, "Where was Jean Paul sitting?"

She pointed to the end of the bar.

That's when Beau noticed the entire bar was cleaned off. No glasses or ashtrays. Completely wiped down.

"Did you clean the bar after the shooting?" he asked.

"I put the glasses in the sink."

"Well, dang it, Crystal, it's a crime scene."

"I'm sorry, Beau, I didn't think about that," she snapped without remorse. "Force of habit."

"And the gun? Did you clean up the gun, too?"

"Gun?" She shook her head. "He took it with him. Shot poor Jake and walked away."

"What time did Jean Paul arrive tonight?"

"Nine or ten."

"He sat at the end of the bar for more than two hours?"

"Yep."

"Visit next door?" Meaning, did he get laid.

"No, sir."

"How much did he drink?"

"Couple double shots of bourbon, a couple drafts. I wasn't bartending. I was catching up on paperwork in the back most of the night. And he could have been high when he came in here, I don't know. You know Jean Paul."

Beau had arrested Jean Paul twice for drug possession and neither arrest stuck. Released within twenty-four hours. Nice guy to chat with when he was sober, and generally a "happy" drunk. Not known to be violent, but could get moody when he was high.

Beau talked to two guys in the corner who were part of Cormier's crew (they had nothing to add), then he approached Ernestine. She was chain-smoking, a half dozen cigarettes stubbed out in the small ashtray in front of her. He had to talk to her, otherwise it would appear suspicious, and he didn't want to do or say anything that would put Ernestine on Cormier's radar.

"Did you see the shooting, Ernestine?"

"No, Mr. Beau. I was just sitting here talking to people."

"Who'd you talk to?"

She shrugged, bit her bottom lip. "Whoever wanted to talk."

He spoke quietly, mindful of who might overhear. "You shouldn't be here, Ernestine. You know that, right? Remember?"

Remember what we talked about? Remember what I told you when you came to me in April and said you wanted to help find out what happened to Lily?

He couldn't say any of that, and he wasn't certain Ernestine would put two and two together. She was a sweet girl, but developmentally disabled. She didn't have a mean bone in her body, and people used her because of it. He hadn't wanted her help, but she kept tracking him down, wanting to talk to him about Lily, who she called her "best friend." He'd finally relented, talked to her in private when her no-good father was at work one day. Listened, then told her to call him if she heard anything. And every single time she called him, whether the information was valuable or not, he reminded her not to tell anyone she had talked to him.

He already had one dead girl on his conscious—one girl who wanted to do the right thing and ended up strangled and half-naked in the bayou. He didn't want Ernestine dead, too.

"Yeah, okay, Mr. Beau. If I saw anything, I'd tell you."

He walked away before she said anything that Cormier or his goons might overhear.

He said to Kinder, "Wait for the coroner. I'm gonna go find Jean Paul."

"Need backup?"

"Nope. If he's where I think he is, he'll come in without incident."

On the surface, Jake West's murder appeared cut and dried.

But like most everything in St. Augustine, nothing appeared as it seemed.

Which was why he had five unsolved murders on his hands. And each dead girl had a connection to the Magnolia Inn.

2

Beau headed east, to the edge of town where the swamp began, where Jean Paul lived with his girlfriend Nellie and her kid in a trailer that had seen better days.

Not surprised to find Jean Paul sitting on the sagging steps smoking a cigarette, Beau got out of his car. Though it was after two in the morning, the thick air weighed on him. Least it was a mite cooler, but as soon as the sun came up it would feel like a sauna.

Beau walked over to the man, stood ten feet away. He didn't consider Jean Paul a threat, but you never knew. Crystal said he had kept the gun. Beau put his hand on his holstered weapon, just in case.

Five foot eight, skinny—if he weighed a buck fifty, Beau would eat his hat. Not even thirty, the years of hard living made him look closer to fifty.

Jean Paul took a long drag on his hand-rolled cigarette.

"Beau."

"Jean Paul. Where's Nellie and the kid?"

"Sleepin'."

"Keep your hands where I can see them."

Jean Paul nodded.

"There was some trouble at the Magnolia," Beau said. "I need to bring you in for questioning."

"Yep."

"You know what it's about?"

"I might."

"Do you have a weapon on you?"

"Nope."

"I'm gonna have to search you."

"If you must." He didn't make a move to get up. "I hear you're the last good cop in the bayou?"

He said it like a question. As soon as Beau read him his rights, Jean Paul wasn't going to talk. This wasn't his first rodeo.

"I might have some information," Jean Paul said when Beau remained silent. "If you walk away."

"Can't do that."

Jean Paul knew the St. Augustine drug trade. He had once been tight with the Cormiers, though Beau heard through the grapevine that Jean Paul may have been cut out. Was that the reason he killed Jake West?

If Jean Paul had evidence that Beau could take to the state police, something big enough that it couldn't be ignored, maybe they could deal…but he couldn't just let the man go. That would make him no better than the cops he was fighting.

"Shit, Beau, I should be given a fucking medal for whacking Jake West."

"Why?"

"You don't know?"

"Rumors that no one has been able to prove."

"Which is why he deserved a gut full of lead." Jean Paul half smiled.

Rumors that Jake liked underage girls were likely true. But someone had to file charges. Someone had to come forward. A parent, a teacher, anyone. Without evidence, rumors were just rumors. Word was he liked them fourteen to eighteen. Underage, but fourteen was the special circumstances cutoff. Didn't make it right, but that was the law, and not much Beau could do about it unless one of the parents wanted Jake on statutory rape or a girl came forward claiming he raped her.

As it was, Beau suspected Jake sweet-talked himself into their pants. Didn't make it right, didn't mean he didn't deserve a good beating—and Beau could have walked away from that—but not cold-blooded murder.

"Can't say I disagree with you, but you can't take the law into your own hands."

"What I know, it's worth something."

"Don't even try to offer me a bribe."

"Not money, information. It's big, Beau. Real big." He inhaled his cigarette until it damn near vanished. Jean Paul pinched the end between his thumb and forefinger and flicked the stub away.

"Multiple witnesses saw you shoot Jake West in cold blood. I can't let you take a pass on this one."

If he had information about the chief...

"But," Beau continued, "you give me something I can follow up on, I'll go outside the parish, get you relocated."

Jean Paul shrugged. "You didn't fall off the turnip truck yesterday, Beau. I'm a dead man unless I run."

"We have to do this by the book."

"Suit yourself."

Beau needed *someone* to talk. For far too long he'd been up against corruption. Witnesses recanted, evidence went missing, people who talked turned up dead.

He'd considered leaving St. Augustine, but he couldn't just up and leave his grandmother after his granddad died, and she refused to move with him to Baton Rouge where her son—Beau's dad—lived. So Beau stayed. There was a lot to love about the small bayou town. And a lot to hate.

No matter what Jean Paul knew, it wasn't worth letting a killer walk. That was crossing a line Beau wasn't ready to cross.

"Get up, turn around," he said. If he didn't stand for something, he stood for nothing.

Beau read Jean Paul his rights, searched him—he wasn't carrying, didn't have drugs on him—and called in the arrest. A patrol would be out in ten to fifteen minutes.

"Where's the gun, Jean Paul?"

"Tossed it."

"Where?"

"Out my truck window when I turned onto Oak Mill."

They might be able to find it. He'd send a team out to look—Beau wouldn't want a kid to find it. But if it was in the river, it was buried in the muddy bottom.

"Why'd you kill Jake?"

He shrugged. "Didn't like him."

It just didn't ring true.

"Now's the time, Jean Paul," he said. "Tell me what you know."

"Everyone knows you're trying to nail Cormier. You never will. Dubois protects him."

Knowing the chief was corrupt and proving it? Two different things.

"If you have proof, I'll get him. Make a statement, I can work with you—"

Jean Paul laughed again. "Lordy, Beau, you're a funny dude. Nuttin' going anywhere."

"Give me something I can prove."

Again, silence. "I saw Tanya Ewing getting into a patrol car with Jerry Guidry the night she was last seen."

Beau didn't expect that. He was expecting intel on Cormier's drug trade, not information about a murder.

Tanya was the third of six dead or missing prostitutes over the last three years. If Beau could get Guidry on murder? That was...well, he wouldn't let Jean Paul go, but he would walk over hot coals to get him transferred to another jail.

"She didn't seem to be in no distress or nuttin', so I didn't think twice," Jean Paul continued. "I'd seen her with Guidry before. And a couple of your other guys."

Beau had long suspected that some of the cops took advantage of the prostitutes in town. One of the perks of being an officer in St. Augustine were the free blow jobs, he'd once heard Guidry boast.

Made him sick to his stomach.

"You're sure it was April 2nd, last year?" Beau asked.

"I don't know about the date, just that it was the last night anyone saw her."

"Where did you see Tanya get into Guidry's car?"

"Outside the Inn. I'm pretty sure I wasn't the only one who'd seen her."

During Beau's investigation into Tanya's disappearance and subsequent murder, Jake West said that Tanya left the Inn at 10:55 p.m. the night she disappeared. Allegedly, her brother's friend drove her home, but later, she left on foot after she and her brother argued. After that, no one claimed to have seen her.

The tidbit about Guidry was something he could follow up on, but it wasn't enough, and he told Jean Paul that. "What time did you see her? Before or after eleven?"

"Couldn't say," he said. "I also knows something about Lily Baker."

The bright lights of a patrol car could be seen as it turned down the long, narrow gravel road that led to the trailer park.

Beau held his breath, at first not expecting Jean Paul to speak. Lily Baker had been missing for four months. The other five girls had all been found dead within days of their disappearance.

"She was pregnant."

That was news. "Are you certain?"

He shrugged. "Yep."

"How?"

He didn't say.

"Did she know who the father was?"

Jean Paul cleared his throat. "Don't know. But you know who might've known? Crystal."

Great, Beau thought. Just what he needed: the sheriff's cousin as a potential witness.

Or potential suspect.

Hell, everyone's a suspect in this town, guilty of something.

Jean Paul said one more thing, though his eyes were on the approaching police car.

"Someone dumped her out in the bayou, just south of Lantern Gate."

"How do you know that?" Beau snapped. "Were you there? Did you witness it?"

Jean Paul didn't answer the question. "Don't know if she's still there, but she might be. I don't think it's right, her mama not having a body to bury. I hope you find her." He paused as the patrol car stopped next to Beau's truck. "But don't say it came from me."

3

Beau hadn't slept more than an hour on Friday after booking Jean Paul into the St. Augustine jail. When his alarm went off at five thirty, he showered, didn't shave, and headed to meet Addie Benoit for breakfast forty minutes away in Lake Charles. They always met in Lake Charles, not just because it was a larger city, but because it was two parishes away.

He arrived first and sat in the corner with a good view of the door, flipping his mug over to signal he would like coffee. The waitress brought over a carafe, filled his cup and put the carafe on the table. He liked that. He could keep the caffeine flowing until he felt marginally human.

The diner was a chain, generic, nondescript. Could have been located anywhere in the US from Washington to Florida, and the only telltale sign that they were in the South was that grits was a standard menu option. Catered to tourists and old people, and the chances that anyone from his life in Broussard Parish would walk in were slim.

But never none.

It would put both him and Addie at risk to be seen with their heads together, but mostly Addie. Beau thought it was ridiculous that a cop and a prosecutor had to be careful when meeting, but that's where they were.

Addie walked in not five minutes after him. He laid eyes on her, a petite and rounded Southern belle, only seconds before she saw him.

She still took his breath away.

Addie had no hard edges. Light brown hair, tawny skin, warm hazel eyes that sparkled when she laughed. The extra pounds she carried just made her more huggable. She always dressed professional—pencil skirt that hugged her wide hips, a blouse or a modest camisole to go with whatever blazer she wore on any given day. Low-heeled, comfortable shoes. Simple but classy jewelry. She was in her midthirties, never married. He didn't know her whole story, but he wanted to.

They hadn't known each other long, other than in passing at the courthouse, but she'd been assigned to one of Beau's cases last year—a drug dealer who ended up having the charges dropped by the DA against Addie's advice—and they realized that they were kindred spirits, stuck in a corrupt jurisdiction.

It was with Addie that he'd put together more information about the five dead prostitutes, and the missing Lily Baker. When they began to make connections between law enforcement, the district attorney and the drug trade—all centered around the Magnolia Inn—they realized they needed to be extra careful.

Especially when they layered in the dead. It went beyond five prostitutes, and beyond the borders of St. Augustine, oozing out into all corners of Broussard Parish. Beau didn't know how he was going to stop the corruption.

But he couldn't live with himself if he didn't try. Especially since the most recent victim was dead because of him.

Addie walked over, sat down across from Beau and touched the back of his hand. "You okay?"

"Yeah, why?"

"You look tired. Sounded worried when we spoke."

"I'm always tired and worried these days."

They ordered because they both had to be at work before nine. She feared for her job—the DA was watching her closely, and she didn't want to give him any excuse to fire her. Beau feared for her life. He'd been subtly threatened, but he took precautions. Being a cop as well as former military gave him the skills and instincts to be careful. As long as no one knew Addie was working with him, she should be safe.

As soon as their food was delivered and the waitress was out of earshot, Addie said, "Tell me."

"Jean Paul LeBlanc killed Jake West last night. In front of witnesses at the Magnolia."

Addie crossed herself. She was one of the few young people he knew who went to church and meant it. "So he did it? Good witnesses?"

In St. Augustine, being arrested didn't always mean you were guilty. And being released didn't always mean you were innocent.

He shrugged, told Addie what he knew, who the witnesses were.

"Cormier," Addie said with distaste. He was the reason Beau and Addie had gotten to know each other in the first place— Gray Cormier was the drug-dealing dirtbag who had been let go for "lack of evidence" when the evidence went missing. But Gray's half brother was worse. Preston Cormier could charm the wings off an angel, but he was the brains of the brothers' drug enterprise.

"When I went to Jean Paul's place to arrest him, he didn't deny it. Didn't even argue with me."

"Why did he do it?"

"Hell if I know. Could have had a reason, could have been having a crap day. Jean Paul said he didn't like him, that he should get a medal because Jake seduced underage girls."

"Maybe Jake slept with the wrong girl."

Beau hadn't thought about that. "And a father didn't beat Jake into a pulp, yet convinced Jean Paul to kill him? I don't know. Maybe—it's worth looking into. But then why wouldn't Jean Paul tell me that? It wouldn't get him off from murder, but if it was for hire, he would shave off some years. Hell, in this place, with Jake's reputation? You never know what will happen if he goes to jury trial."

"You believe Crystal?" Addie asked.

While Beau didn't trust Crystal, especially since she ran prostitutes and likely drugs, she'd mostly been straight with him over the years.

"I don't think she's lying about this," he said.

"I hear a *but*."

"It's Crystal. I think the facts she told are accurate, but she's leaving out details. Do they matter? Don't know. I asked specifically if anyone left after Jean Paul shot Jake. She hesitated just a few seconds too long, then said her cousin Tex."

"Well, anyone who knows Mags knows that she would hit him upside the head with a hot frying pan if she found out he was at the Magnolia."

"I think someone else was there, but no one said a peep."

"They wouldn't, not around Cormier."

"Maybe if I heard different from Jean Paul, I wouldn't be getting that itch that this is bigger than a struggling addict shooting a pervert bartender he's known for most of his life just because the addict was cut off from his bourbon. And I've never heard the Magnolia cutting anyone off from anything."

There's a line from an old movie that Beau always watched if it came on television. *Perhaps you have already observed that in Casablanca, human life is cheap.*

Damn movie could have been written about St. Augustine. But instead of World War II and Nazis and politicians swaying whichever way the wind blew, you had the drug war, prostitutes and cops that looked the other way. Or worse.

Beau glanced around, then leaned forward just a bit. He didn't recognize anyone in the diner, but he didn't want anyone to overhear. He quietly told Addie everything Jean Paul told him, including Tanya Ewing last seen getting into Jerry Guidry's police vehicle.

Her eyes widened. "No hint of it before?"

He shook his head. Jerry Guidry had been hired by the chief when Dubois was appointed three years ago by the new mayor, and was the only cop that Beau was positive was dirty, other than the chief. Beau suspected the other cops simply turned a blind eye to the corruption, but he couldn't be sure. Once you made a conscious decision to not *see* bad, it was only a hop, skip and jump to *doing* bad.

"Will he go on record?" Addie asked.

"You know as well as I that a drug addict like Jean Paul isn't going to have any fuc—damn credibility. That was our biggest problem in the Cormier case, every witness was unreliable. Just because I believed them doesn't mean a jury would believe them, and unless we can get the case sent to another jurisdiction, we're screwed."

"You don't have to tell me that," Addie said, slightly defensive.

"I'm sorry." He breathed deep, forcing himself to calm down. Addie had to deal with this bullshit every day as a prosecutor. Her boss Alston Gary was tight with both Sheriff Landry and

Chief Dubois, and if a case wasn't airtight with a priest and a cop as witnesses, they only got prosecuted if Alston didn't like them.

"Anyway, Jean Paul said that Lily Baker is just as dead as the others and he implied it wasn't because she was a prostitute." He paused. "He wouldn't tell me how he knew, but he claimed that Lily was pregnant. Implied Crystal knew who the father was, and gave me a location as to where her body was dumped."

Beau loved being a cop—but he hated his job at the same time. He knew how it was in towns like St. Augustine. Many of the young women didn't have many options. If they didn't start using drugs, they generally did okay—married, had a couple kids young, worked at the five-and-dime or one of the interstate restaurants that catered to travelers. And some got out of the cycle—Beau had helped one young woman enlist in the Navy when she graduated high school. He got regular emails about her time on the *USS Gravely*. He spoke to the high school every year about career opportunities in the military because he'd served for nearly twenty years, but Jenny was the only one who had followed up with him.

Unfortunately, family and peer pressure kept many kids trapped in a cycle of poverty and drugs. As soon as they started using, drugs became their life. They didn't see a way out. Selling sex was a means to get more drugs, a cycle that almost always ended in early death: murder or an overdose.

"Lily's body—you don't think it's still where he says it is." It was a statement. He shrugged. The bayou had a way of disappearing bodies. That made the marshy waterways a good place to leave the dead you didn't want anyone to find. The eastern boundary of the parish was a meandering river that could be taken all the way to the gulf if you had the time and patience and could navigate when the swamp took over.

"Four months? I doubt we'll find her remains. But I have to try. I need to go out there alone, not tip my hand with Dubois. Even if the body is destroyed, there could be bones, clothing, personal effects." He paused then said, "I think Jean Paul knows a lot more. I just need that one hard piece of evidence. Is there any way, for any reason, you can get him transferred to state or federal custody? Maybe an old crime? A warrant in another state?"

"You think he's in danger?"

"Yes. I need him alive, and I need him talking. If I can get him into state custody, I hope he'll talk to me."

"We don't make deals until we know what we're getting, but in this case, I might have an idea. I'll call a friend in the state attorney's office. We were in law school together, and she was always the one who came up with unique solutions to legal problems. Maybe, if he knows something big, we can bring in the US Marshals. Move him to a federal prison, different state."

"Getting him out of St. Augustine is a start. Thanks, Addie."

"Don't thank me yet. I have to do this behind Alston's back."

Alston Gary, just one more corrupt cog in the wheels of injustice. "Be doubly careful, Addie."

"You're the one who has to be careful, Beau."

She didn't have to remind him. Though the threats were subtle, they had come from the chief. Things like, *Be careful out there, Beau, it's hunting season.* Or, *You sure you want to go looking at so-and-so for drugs? I'd stand down, if I were you. Just some friendly advice.* Similar comments that could be taken two ways because the chief never got his hands dirty. So everything Beau did he did with great caution and reserve. Yet, he couldn't shake the feeling that his days were numbered. That his pursuit of this killer was going to seal his death sentence.

"Call me as soon as you know anything, okay?" he said to Addie as he put cash on the table for their meals. "We need to move Jean Paul sooner rather than later."

Beau searched for the gun where Jean Paul said he'd tossed it, but after an hour couldn't find any sign of it. He informed the chief, who said he'd send out a couple officers to look in a wider area.

Maybe Jean Paul lied. Maybe Beau missed it. Maybe he threw it far enough that it hit water. The ground was soft enough that the gun could have sunk out of view.

He tried to talk to Jean Paul in jail, but the guard said he lawyered up and no one could question him until after his arraignment Monday. That was bullshit—he just needed his lawyer present—but the guard didn't budge.

The chief heard the conversation and called Beau into his office. He closed the door behind Beau so they were alone.

"I read your report on LeBlanc," he said. "Good job tracking him down so quickly. He confessed?"

"It's all in my report."

"Did he say anything else?"

"Everything he said, I wrote down," Beau lied.

"So you think Jean Paul grew a conscious? Killed Jake because he liked girls who were too young?"

"Honestly, I have no idea. Jean Paul has done a lot of drugs in his thirty-some years." As if that was the answer to everything.

"Hmm. Okay. Did you know there was an active warrant for him in Baton Rouge?"

Beau shook his head. "For what? And why didn't we know about it?"

"I asked—they said there was a glitch, it didn't get uploaded, but when his arrest went into the system someone flagged it. A bench warrant, missed a court hearing on a drug charge two years ago." Dubois paused, looked square at Beau. "It's odd."

Beau knew this development was Addie's doing, but kept his face impassive.

"We get him first," he told Dubois. "Homicide trumps drugs."

"It does. I'll let you know what happens."

"Thanks."

Beau left and as soon as he was in his car and on the road—

even though he had no place to go—he called Addie. "Did you get a bench warrant put into the system? For LeBlanc?"

"Yes," she whispered. "It was all I could do on short notice. I called in a favor. I really hope no one digs too deep—it won't hold up to scrutiny. But this buys us time."

"So he's being moved out of St. Augustine, right?"

"I'm doing everything I can, Beau. My goal is to have a patrol from Baton Rouge pick him up, process him there. I'll let you know when it's set up."

"I had to play the game, tell the chief that homicide wins over a drug charge, otherwise he'll know exactly what I'm doing, and it might come back on you." Though he didn't know how, if she had a third party work through the fake warrant.

"It's a long shot, but we have a chance."

"Thanks, Addie."

He hoped it was today. The longer Jean Paul remained in St. Augustine, the more danger he was in.

Beau drove out to Lantern Gate and walked the hundred yards from the road to the river. Looked around, walked up and down the shoreline. It was steep with lots of brambles and blackberry bushes, so he couldn't get down to the water. But he didn't see—or smell—a body.

It's been four months. There's nothing of her left.

Frustrated, Beau headed back to the car. It was getting dark, and he had to figure out how to protect Jean Paul.

4

The chirping cell phone pulled Beau out of a deep sleep. He opened one eye in search of his clock while his hand fumbled around for the phone: 11:17 p.m. Well, damn.

He'd been up since one in the morning with not much more than a couple thirty-minute catnaps. Then spending half the day on the river near Lantern Gate looking for Lily Baker's body or evidence of her murder had worn him out and given him a pounding headache, only slightly dulled by his double shot of whiskey before bed. Now, less than two hours after he put his head on his pillow, he was awake.

"Beau," he said into the phone. He coughed, cleared his

throat, his head still throbbing. All he'd wanted was to bunk for four solid hours.

"Mr. Beau? It's me."

Me? Who the hell was "me"?

"I reckon I made a mistake."

Ernestine.

He sat up in his bed, swung his bare feet over the edge. His room was sweltering, even with the windows open and the whole-house fan he'd had installed last year running through the night.

"Where are you?"

"Walkin'."

"Where? Where *specifically* are you, Ernestine?"

Beau turned on the lamp next to his bed, switched the phone to his left hand and reached for his jeans on the chair in the corner.

"Lake Pierre Road."

That road cut diagonally through St. Augustine, nowhere near where Ernestine lived.

"Where are you going?"

"Dunno. Just thought I should leave."

"Leave where?"

He zipped up his pants and put Ernestine on speaker while he strapped his shoulder holster over his white T-shirt and clipped his badge to his belt. Talking to Ernestine, especially over the phone, was a challenge. She did much better communicating face-to-face. She didn't realize that she had put herself in the middle of danger months ago when she talked to him about her missing friend Lily Baker. He had done everything he could to protect her, but she didn't understand that her life was in jeopardy.

She should never be walking around in the middle of the night.

Especially after witnessing Jake West's murder last night.

"Ernestine? Where were you tonight?"

"Magnolia. The Fat Catfish."

Well, shit.

Why'd she go back to the Magnolia Inn? He'd told her to lay low. Maybe she hadn't understood him.

Tammy Bergeron, Ernestine's aunt, managed The Fat Catfish, generally called Fat Cat or Catfish or just The Fish, depending on who was talking. No matter what the name du jour, it was a dive bar—and not the good kind—where half the drug trade was centered, a dangerous hangout on its good days. Five of the six dead or missing young women had been to either The Fat Catfish or Magnolia within twenty-four hours of their disappearance. And sometimes both. Beau suspected they'd seen or heard something that put them in danger, but couldn't prove squat.

He had told Ernestine multiple times to keep a low profile, but her memory was sketchy, especially when her friends gave her drugs.

"Ernestine, listen to me."

Silence.

"Are you there? Talk to me."

"I'm here, Mr. Beau."

"I'm coming to get you." He slipped on his boots, quickly laced them up. "Can you tell me exactly where you are on Lake Pierre Road?"

"Ummm… I walked past the old oak tree that was hit by lightning last year."

He knew the one. Corner of Mills and Lake Pierre. What was she doing way out there?

"Did you walk there from The Fat Cat?" It was a couple miles. Ernestine didn't drive. It was possible, but why would she go way out there?

"Yeah?"

Why did she answer in the form of a question?

"Are you close to that oak tree? Can you go and sit under the oak tree right now? I'll be there in ten minutes."

"Okey dokey."

"Ernestine, don't hang up—"

But she was gone.

Dammit. He holstered his gun, grabbed his keys and ran to his truck. He tried calling her as soon as he was driving, but she didn't pick up her phone.

She *never* answered her phone, but this time he was worried.

What mistake had she made? Who had she talked to? He didn't want to pull another young woman out of the swamp.

He made it to the oak tree in nine minutes and jumped out of his truck, leaving it idling on the two-lane road.

"Ernestine!" he called out.

She didn't answer. He didn't see her sitting under the tree. He looked everywhere near the corner. No houses here—the closest was Faye Jennings, who lived with her sons at the end of a dirt road, quarter mile down.

He drove slowly up and down both Lake Pierre near Mills, then both sides of Mills. She'd be wearing a bright, flowered dress—it's all she wore. She would stand out, even at night.

When he found no sign of her, he headed over to her house, though he had no plans to knock on her door. Her father, Nels Bergeron, was an alcoholic. Nice as a Labrador when sober; an angry pit bull when drunk. Which was most nights.

There was no sign of Ernestine.

His phone rang and he grabbed it.

"Ernestine?"

"Detective Hebert?"

Not the girl. "Yes. This is Beau Hebert."

"Hi, Beau, it's Margery at the station. Jean Paul LeBlanc committed suicide tonight. Chief Dubois thought you'd want to know."

Beau didn't know what he said, if anything, before he ended

the call with the dispatcher. He stared into the dark. There were no lights out here, just reflective markers on the road and along the side, to make sure people didn't drive into a ditch.

Jean Paul had told Beau he would be dead if Beau arrested him; now he was dead.

Suicide my ass.

Shit! He didn't know what to do at this point. Had someone seen Beau looking around Lantern Gate? Did someone learn the warrant out of Baton Rouge was falsified? Or maybe they didn't want to risk Jean Paul leaving their control.

Who the hell are they? Who's behind these murders?

His phone rang. Unknown caller.

"Hebert," he answered.

"Stop stirring the shit," a whispered voice said. Beau didn't recognize it, but the caller spoke low to avoid recognition. He thought man, but couldn't be positive.

"Who is this?"

"More people will die if you don't back off."

The caller hung up. Beau didn't know if this was a direct threat from someone who didn't want him looking for fear of imprisonment, or if it was a threat from someone who feared what he found would get more people killed.

Either way, Beau wasn't backing off now. But he could no longer do this alone. He called the only person he could trust, and hoped his old friend didn't want to pummel him for calling after midnight.

"Hello?"

"Did I wake you, GQ?"

"Is this LC?"

"The one and only."

"Well I'll be—is everything okay?"

"No, no it's really not. Michael, I need your help. I have no one else to turn to."

SUNDAY

5

Kara Quinn stared out the passenger window at the thick growth of shrubs and trees that lined the country road north of the interstate. Her eyes narrowed as she contemplated what dangers lurked in the shadows.

"Do not tell me there are alligators in there," she said.

"It's a swamp. There's gators."

"I said don't tell me."

FBI special agent and all–American good guy Michael Harris glanced at her with a grin. "So you're actually afraid of something."

"I'm afraid of a lot of things."

"Don't act it."

"Rattlesnakes, spiders, alligators top the list."

"No rattlesnakes in Louisiana."

"Good."

"There are water moccasins. I've heard they're more dangerous than rattlers. They swim. And they climb trees, drop right down into your boat."

"That's just wrong." She hoped she didn't have to take a boat anywhere. They were in the middle of the bayou, practically surrounded by water. "Snakes should not be able to climb anything."

Michael looked at his phone, from which he was navigating. Swamp to the east, farmland to the west. He turned left onto an unpaved road. The sign said Hebert Lane.

"Your buddy has a road named for him?" she said. "Pretty cool."

"His grandparents—probably also his great-grandparents and beyond—used to own a bunch of land, couple hundred acres. They have ten left, half of it swamp."

They passed small, fenceless houses, all set far apart. Some were clearly abandoned. Some had toys and cars in the front. They were built on foundations at least two feet above ground. But based on the history of the area, they had all flooded a time or ten.

Beau Hebert lived at the end of the road, though Kara wouldn't call the gravel lane liberally dotted with potholes a *road*. Thick shrubs and vines so dense she wouldn't be able to walk among them meandered along the western edge of the property. Michael pointed in that direction as he parked the car next to the main house. "More swamp."

"Alligators? Water moccasins?"

He shrugged. "Your guess is as good as mine. But those are cypress trees, which can grow in the water, so watch your step."

There were two houses, a barn, and a couple smaller buildings that Kara might call sheds if she was being kind. One leaned heavily to the right and she was surprised it still stood.

The two-story farmhouse must have been built at the turn of the century, she figured. The wide porch was quaint and inviting. The house needed paint, and four of the eight front steps to the porch had been replaced with fresh wood, awaiting stain. A new roof was out of place over the tired home.

Even with the sad appearance, the house felt well loved. Potted flowers on the porch. Wood chairs and a porch swing that actually looked like people sat on it. A sign above the front door with a hand-carved bible verse—Matthew 25:35—that Kara assumed was a kind of welcome, but she wouldn't have been able to even guess what it might be.

A smaller house was across the way, next to the rickety barn. It looked even older, if that was possible. It did not boast a new roof, but had rusting, corrugated metal—tin?—to protect the inhabitants from the elements. Definitely not as homey as the main house, even though it had a couple of chairs on a narrow deck.

"Brace yourself," Michael said.

"For what?"

He grinned, turned off the engine, and opened his door. A wave of hot, wet air assaulted her. Her armpits were immediately soaked.

"Shit," she said. "We're in a fucking sauna."

Michael laughed, his voice deep and warm. "I warned you." Already, she could see sweat beading on his dark skin, damp circles in the armpits of his white dress shirt.

Kara couldn't remember ever being in this kind of oppressive humidity, but the last time she'd been anywhere in the South was when she was a kid. She distinctly remembered a trip to Orlando, Florida, before her father was arrested. That trip was to scam tourists—her parents' favorite pastime. She tried to forget the years before she turned fifteen and moved in with her grandmother.

"I'm drowning," she groaned as she followed Michael up the steps to the main house.

"I could lie and say you'll get used to it."

She hit him on the bicep and he smiled again.

The door opened before they reached the top step.

"Damn, GQ, it's good to see you."

A man a few years older than Michael, aka GQ, stepped onto the porch, the screen door slamming shut behind him. She figured this must be Detective Beau Hebert, the man they'd come to see, Michael's military buddy from the Navy. Graying brown hair that curled at his collar, two days' growth of beard that had more red than gray, and sharp pale blue eyes.

He was a couple inches shorter than Michael's six-two, and skinnier, but he had sinewy muscles that rippled under his tanned, leathery skin.

Michael wrapped his arms around Beau and slapped him on his back. "Don't they have any gyms around here? You're soft."

"The bayou just saps the energy right out of you," Beau said. "I still outrank you, so watch your mouth." He stepped toward Kara and extended his hand. "Kara Quinn? The detective. You look like you have an interesting story."

"A couple good stories," she said and took his hand.

"Beau! Come help me with the tea!" a woman's voice called from inside.

"Word of warning—no shop talk around my grandmother. Feel free to sit." He motioned to a small round table at the corner of the deck where it wrapped around the side. "Believe it or not, it's nicer out here than inside. Mimi's been baking all morning when I told her we were having guests. The house is hotter than six shades of hell."

He went inside and Kara turned to Michael. "Well. Guess we're on vacation." She hooked her arm around Michael's.

He glanced at her and shook his head. "You have an odd sense of fun."

"If we can't have fun with our job, why the hell do it? So do we need a cover or what?"

"I'd like to talk more to Beau about what's going on, and I don't think we have enough time to create anything." And, Kara knew, anything that required Michael to lie or pretend he was someone he wasn't made him extremely uncomfortable.

"Nothing that'll hold muster." Kara had been an undercover cop for twelve years. She preferred having a solid identity before she walked into a situation, but she had created one or two successfully on the fly. "Still, remember that the best lies are always based in truth. You have to tell Beau's grandmother something."

"Beau can lie to his grandmother, not me," Michael said as he sat down at the table. "Besides, it's not like we can hide the fact we're feds."

"*You're* the fed, not me."

"Close enough."

"Bite your tongue."

Kara moved her chair so it backed to the house, sat, leaned back. One eye on the swamp, looking for pesky gators who might want to take a bite out of her ass.

Technically, Kara was still on the payroll of the Los Angeles Police Department, temporarily on loan to the FBI. Her last undercover assignment had resulted in multiple arrests, but the human trafficker who ran the sweatshop she shut down put a hit out on her. She hoped that after the trial—when he should be convicted—she could return to her old job, but that was still up in the air.

Not knowing made her antsy.

Kara pulled her damp T-shirt away from her skin, but it just flopped back down. She didn't know she had that much sweat in her body. She swatted at a gnat. "Don't you have other friends who need help? Maybe someone who lives in like, I don't know, Alaska? Maine? Montana is probably real nice in August."

The door opened and Beau held a tray with two large pitchers of iced tea, thick condensation visible on the glass decanters. He held the screen door open for a white-haired woman shorter than Kara—Beau's grandmother wasn't even five feet. Maybe four-ten if she stood straight. The tiny old woman carried a tray of cookies and mini-sandwiches in shaking hands. Michael immediately jumped up and took the tray. "Let me get that, Mrs. Hebert."

"Such a sweet boy," she said.

"These look delicious, ma'am."

Beau mouthed *kiss ass* over the head of his grandmother and Kara grinned.

"Beau has told me so much about you, Michael, I feel like I know you."

Beau put the tray down and said, "Sweet," he pointed to the pitcher on the right. "Unsweet," and pointed to the left.

There were a couple water bottles on the tray as well.

"You need to stay hydrated down here or the humidity will suck the life out of you," Michael said.

"It already did." Kara poured herself some sweet tea. Sipped. Supersweet, but she figured the sugar would give her a rush.

Michael stuck with the unsweet and picked up a sandwich.

"Mimi, you remember Michael—I might have called him GQ—from my stories," Beau said. "And this is Kara Quinn, a friend of Michael's. This is my grandmother, Toni Hebert."

"Call me Toni," she said. "Or Mimi, I'm not picky."

"Mimi means grandmother," Beau explained.

"Don't matter," Toni said. "Half the kids in these parts call me Mimi."

She eased herself into a cushioned seat and sighed. Kara wondered how old she was. She figured Beau was in his early forties, so Toni was probably in her eighties. Older than Kara's own grandmother.

"You have a lovely home, Toni," Michael said. "This porch is very inviting."

She nodded with a half smile. "Been through a rough patch now and again, but she has good bones. Beau put on the roof just last year, and in the nick of time. Don't think it would have made it through the last big storm."

"Place still needs a lot of work," Beau said, "but I do what I can when I have a day off."

Toni scoffed. "Day off? You haven't taken a day off in weeks, until today, and only because Michael was coming for a spell."

"Maybe I can help with whatever you need," Michael said. "I'm pretty good with my hands."

"Best damn munitions expert I know," Beau said.

Kara opened her mouth to tell the story about how Michael saved her life last month when he disarmed a bomb she'd accidentally picked up, but then simply grabbed a cookie and shoved it in her mouth. Better to keep the details to a minimum around the grandmother, she figured.

"These are amazing," she said honestly, her mouth still full. She drank half the sweet tea in a gulp and took another cookie. "You made these?"

"Of course I did, those store-bought cookies are garbage. Recipe from my grandma, God rest her soul. My own mother couldn't devil an egg. Guess it's true that talent skips generations. Beau here, he's a mighty good cook. Even worked as a sous chef in N'orlins right out of high school, before he joined the Navy."

Michael grinned. "I'll never forget the weekend you made a huge pot of gumbo in a slow cooker in the bunkhouse. Thought Sergeant Tucker was going to blow a gasket."

"Till he tasted my creation," Beau said. "Then he let me take over the kitchen once a month to whip up something better than the slop they fed us."

"Good ole days."

They swapped a few stories and Kara soaked up their friendship. She rarely saw Michael so relaxed; she liked it.

A bit later, the phone rang and Beau jumped up to answer,

but Toni waved him down. "House phone ain't never for you, dear. Probably Midge wanting to know why I didn't come to bingo after church this morning."

Toni shuffled into the house, the wood-framed screen door slamming shut behind her.

"I like your grandma," Kara said.

"Everyone loves Mimi. She talks about my granddad a lot, so if you hear about Carl doing this or that, that's my Pop. I tried to get her to move to Baton Rouge with me when he died two years back, but no luck. She's stubborn as a mule. Said she's going to die here when she's good and ready."

"You would have quit the force?" Michael asked. "Moved back home?"

He nodded slowly, turned one of the cookies over and over in his hand, but didn't eat. "When I left the Navy and moved here five years ago, I was really looking forward to the quiet country life. There's a lot to love about St. Augustine and the bayou, and I came wearing rose-colored glasses, ignoring my dad's warnings. He told me I would detest the place, and he was right—though his reasons are different than mine. I don't know how Dad came from down-to-earth Toni and Carl, since he's practically an elitist. He looks down on the people here, and I don't understand that. These people are salt of the earth. Most of them. They look out for each other, take care of the community, everyone knows everyone else. No one is in a rush. To be honest, I needed the peace for a time. That's what I love about St. Augustine."

"And now?" Kara asked.

"Drugs and corruption. They were here five years ago, to be sure, but not like now. Chief Dubois was hired by the town council three years ago after we elected a new mayor. Before him—it wasn't as bad. It wasn't good—Preston Cormier was still running drugs back then, and the Magnolia Inn was still a brothel. But it's gotten worse, and I think it's directly related to a couple cops Dubois hired. I can't say how deep the corruption goes, but I have five dead girls, two more missing who I fear are dead. And the main reason I called you—a potential witness who died in custody."

"Have you reached out to the county? The state?" Michael asked.

"We call them parishes in Louisiana," Beau said. "The sheriff of Broussard Parish isn't going to come in and do squat. Landry lets every town pretty much run autonomously. And the state police?" He laughed, shook his head. "They won't do anything. They don't get involved in local crime, even if it's drug running, murder or corruption. They don't care. The feds are hamstrung. Before I was here, the FBI worked an investigation in the parish next door—bribery, political corruption, I don't know the details. After a two-year investigation? Nothing. Not one consequential indictment. I think a couple people went to prison for crap. Waste of time and resources. No one will talk to the feds. Everything you've heard about Louisiana politics and corruption? It's worse."

"You think the police chief had something to do with the in-custody death of Jean Paul LeBlanc?"

Michael asked exactly what Kara was thinking. Beau was talking around it, but Kara suspected he believed that the chief of police himself, and others under his command, were responsible for the dead and missing women. Kara wasn't as ready as Michael to jump on the bring-in-the-cavalry bandwagon. Corruption was damn difficult to prove, and often took months of painstaking investigation. If the state or feds walked in? People would keep their mouths shut, evidence would disappear and nothing would be solved.

Kara was definitely more the cynic than her partner.

"I didn't want to say too much over the phone," Beau said, standing. "And I don't want to say too much here, where Mimi might hear. But I want to show you something. Then, maybe you'll understand what I'm up against."

Michael also rose from his seat, clapped his hand on his friend's back. "What *we're* up against."

6

Kara grabbed her sweet tea—it was really good—tucked a water bottle under her arm, then picked up the tray of cookies and mini-sandwiches before she followed Beau and Michael across the wide gravel drive to the smaller house with the tin roof.

"This was the first house on the property," Beau said. "You'd think it would have fallen apart decades ago, but my great-great-grandpa was a carpenter. Built this place himself, and it's stood the test of time."

It looked ancient, but it was standing straight, unlike the shed next door.

Beau had two locks on the door. "We rarely lock the main

house, but I don't want anyone seeing what I have in here. Not that someone can't break in, but at least I can delay them."

The door opened into one large room. A couple recliners, a small couch, a desk and chair, and a wall half covered with a mounted whiteboard. To the rear was a small kitchen, and to the right a short hall that led to a bedroom. "You live here?" she asked.

"Used to," he said. "But when my Pop died, I moved into the house so I could hear if Mimi falls or needs something. Michael, you can stay in here, I have a guest room for Kara in the main house."

"I'll take this place," Kara said. She hoped she didn't overstep. "Trust me, I rarely sleep more than a couple hours, you don't want me roaming the house in the middle of the night."

Beau hesitated, but Michael intervened. "Fine by me."

He winked at Kara, and she appreciated his understanding. She and Michael made a good team, and she was glad she didn't have to explain that she needed privacy.

"Sure," Beau said. "Whatever you want. Come over here, I'll show you what's been going on."

They walked over to the board. Across the top he had attached seven photos of young women, their names and vitals beneath the photographs.

Kara looked at their faces. Four white, three black. All young—twenty to thirty-one. Some had kids. One was married. All but one were prostitutes and drug addicts. Of those found, they'd been murdered—one stabbed to death, four asphyxiated. All had drugs in their system.

The sad pictures of death and violence fueled Kara's anger. She felt the familiar rage bubbling up; only her experience and professionalism kept it at bay.

"Nearly three years ago Lettie Chaisson was murdered," Beau said, "her body found in the bayou. She was the first of five dead."

Lettie had been thirty-one. Next to her headshot was a smaller picture of a teenage Lettie where she looked happier and healthier. The black girl had once been pretty—exquisite bone structure and large brown eyes that dominated her face. But drug use had left her with a hollowed expression in the more recent photo. "What's this?" Kara asked, pointing to the smaller image.

"Lettie's senior picture. I cut it out of the yearbook. I wanted to remember that these girls had once had hope, had a future, before drugs started the slow march to death."

Kara appreciated seeing the victims as they had once been. She noticed that the larger picture was pinned with a magnet to the board, but underneath was another photo. She looked.

It was the crime scene image of Lettie's body, naked except for pink panties and a purple bra, tangled in vines on the edge of a river. She had been in an advanced stage of decomp even though she'd been found five days after her disappearance. That's what water and humidity did to the dead.

"I don't want to see them dead every time I come in, or have Mimi walk in and see something so disturbing," Beau admitted. "But knowing what happened to them—how they were left to the elements—keeps me going when I hit a brick wall. And I might see something I missed the first hundred times I looked at the photo.

"Lettie was single, left behind two boys who are now being raised by their grandmother in Lake Charles," Beau continued. "Nicki LeBlanc, the second victim, was killed six months later. She's a cousin to Jean Paul, who shot and killed the bartender Thursday night and allegedly killed himself in jail."

Michael asked, "Do you think Jean Paul targeted the bartender because he had something to do with the murders?"

Beau shook his head. "More than two years later? Probably not. Jake West was never a suspect. He might have had information, but I don't see Jean Paul killing him over it. And honestly, he and Nicki weren't close. Second cousins thrice removed, like damn near everyone in this town. Anyway, Nicki had a daughter who is pretty much being raised by her nineteen-year-old sister because their mother is wasted half the time. The kid wasn't even two when her mom was killed. She turned four early this year."

Nicki was white, had bleached blond hair in the picture and like Lettie, looked strung out, her eyes hollow, too skinny. Kara recognized the sad sign of addiction.

"Tanya was killed nearly a year after Nicki, Hannah six months after Tanya. Four dead prostitutes and few leads. Rumors were serial killer, truck drivers breezing through town, even a curse." He snorted. "There was a homeless veteran who lived in the bayou, minded his own business for the most part, but he came to town once a month for supplies when his check came in, sometimes caused trouble. Belligerent. Mostly because he didn't know how to deal with people. But he never did more than shout at people. Some thought he was the killer."

"Did you investigate him?" Michael asked.

"Of course—the chief thought he was the 'perfect' killer. To me, that meant perfect scapegoat. But there was no evidence that he was involved, and he had no connection to any of the women. He never went to the Magnolia Inn or The Fat Catfish—where the girls were last seen. He's dead now, drowned last year when the bayou flooded, destroyed his camp. Body washed clear down to Lake Pierre."

"Lily," Kara said, pointing to a pretty blonde with blue eyes. "She's still missing."

"Four months, almost to the day. No one thinks she's alive, including me. Jean Paul told me her body was dumped past Lantern Gate—"

"Where's that?" she asked.

"Just a spot in the river. The river narrows for about thirty feet, used to be a footbridge over it, but storms took it out every few years, and no one rebuilt it after the last hurricane. A good fishing spot for locals. Anyway, I went out there Friday and didn't see anything. I'd like to go down by boat because it's hard to get south of the gate on foot, the banks are too steep on the west, it's a mix of swampland and farmland on the east."

"You want company. I'll go," Michael said.

"Better you than me," Kara said, "with all those alligators I heard about."

Beau gave her a half smile. "They're mostly harmless."

"*Mostly*," she emphasized.

"A month after Lily disappeared," Beau said, "Ginny Chaisson was killed. That was early May. Around the same time, Ernestine approached me."

"That's her?" Kara pointed to the last picture—a light-skinned black girl with a big, bright, wide smile and golden brown eyes. It was clearly her senior photo. "She doesn't look like an addict."

"She's an outlier. She used on occasion, I suspect only when pushed to by friends. But she had friends in the business, hung out in sketchy places.

"Ernestine is developmentally disabled," Beau continued, "but can mostly take care of herself. If she had a better upbringing and parents who gave a shit, she probably would have done better for herself. Lives with her dad, a drunk who barely holds down a job as a mechanic. Gets a disability check that her dad drinks away, plus she works part-time under the table at The Fat Catfish cleaning up every morning—the place is a pit. Her aunt—Tammy Bergeron—is a piece of work. Can't get her on much of anything, but she's never met a con she couldn't hustle, and I suspect she moves some weight in narcotics, but nothing like the Cormiers."

Kara almost laughed. She knew con artists, and she would enjoy meeting Tammy Bergeron.

"But damn," Beau said, "that girl always had a smile for you, and I don't want her to be dead."

"You think she is," Michael said.

He nodded. "She'd been at the Magnolia when Jean Paul

shot Jake West. I told her to steer clear of the place and keep a low profile, but she called me late Friday night and said she'd made a mistake, admitted she went back there and also to The Fat Cat. I went to pick her up."

He walked over to a drawer, pulled out a map and unfolded it. He secured it with magnets to the bottom of the whiteboard. There were marks on the map—numbers and letters—and Beau explained they coincided with where the victims were last seen and where their bodies were found: 1A was where Lettie Chaisson was last seen; 1B was where Lettie was found dead; 2A where Nicki LeBlanc was last seen, and so on.

"Ernestine was supposed to be here, at the corner of Mills and Lake Pierre Road." Beau pointed on the map. "When I got there, she wasn't. This is too far for her to walk from her house or the bar—and the Magnolia is way up here." He pointed to a red dot just south of the interstate. "I don't know why she was there, what she said or to whom, or who picked her up. Someone must have. There are a few farms around there, but this isn't a stretch people walk."

"And then Jean Paul killed himself?" Michael said.

"When I was looking for Ernestine, the department called me, told me he was dead. Overdosed. That's when I called you."

"Someone brought him drugs in jail," Kara said flatly.

"They're calling it a suicide—but our coroner is a joke. Dr. Brown has been coroner for more than thirty years, he's in his seventies, and I suspect he'll never voluntarily leave office. He didn't even do an autopsy, just saw the body, the needle, ruled suicide."

"Not an accidental overdose?"

"He said suicide, making a lot of leaps that Jean Paul didn't want to go to prison and it was a solid case that he killed Jake as there were witnesses. He just pulled it all out of his ass, if you ask me."

"Accidental drug overdose or suicide still doesn't say murder," Michael pointed out.

"The security tapes had a 'malfunction,'" Beau said with sarcasm. "How did Jean Paul get the drugs? Why didn't anyone see him? If he was suicidal, did he say something, and if he did, why was he left alone? When I requested an autopsy, the coroner said his family doesn't want one, which means that Brown told them that if they wanted one they'd have to pay for it. I *know* someone killed him. Proving it?" He shook his head.

Beau removed the map from the board, laid it out on his cluttered desk. Kara and Michael stood on either side of him. "Tanya," he said, tapping on her photo. "Jean Paul told me he saw her getting into Officer Guidry's car the night she disappeared. And then the kicker—he also said Lily Baker was pregnant. If she was, no one knew—not even Ernestine. I'll talk to her family again, but they would have told me."

"But you can't prove it because her body hasn't been found," Michael said.

Kara examined a list of names on the desk. Preston Cormier, Gray Cormier, Johnny Baxter, others. "Who are these people?"

"Known drug dealers in town. All the dead women had associated with them at one point. Ginny Chaisson had been Preston's girlfriend for a time."

"Were Lettie and Ginny related?" Michael asked.

"Distant cousins," Beau said.

"You've investigated the Cormiers?" Michael said.

Beau nodded. "No one will talk—they're scared. And if the chief or Guidry is involved… I can't bring my suspicions to them. I felt out one of the deputies in the parish, and he set me straight. Sheriff Landry isn't involved, as he said, 'in the shit going down in St. Augustine,' but Landry isn't going to stick his neck out where he has no jurisdiction. Plus, the day manager of the Magnolia Inn is Landry's cousin and he knows damn well the place is a brothel. Ignores it."

"So you're thinking Sheriff Landry knows there's something rotten in the state of Denmark, but doesn't care," Kara said.

"I guess you could put it that way."

Michael was looking at the same list as Kara. "Who's Alston Gary? Also a dealer?"

"He's the district attorney. Virtually everyone I arrest walks because of him. Evidence disappears from the evidence locker. Witnesses change their story. I can't prove what Jean Paul told me, and now he's dead."

"He probably wouldn't have been a reliable witness," Kara said. "A drug addict arrested for murder pointing fingers at a cop. He didn't see Guidry kill Tanya."

"Exactly. And if I confront Guidry, he'll probably tell me sure, he saw her, he took her home, out of the kindness of his fucking heart. He was also seen with Nicki LeBlanc earlier the day she disappeared—not the last person to have seen her, but she was arguing with him. He stated, after she was found dead, that he was having a talk with her about public intoxication. And several witnesses came forward to confirm that Nicki was high that evening. You should have seen him make his statement—practically forced a tear from his eye when he claimed if he had only arrested her, she'd still be alive."

"When you called me," Michael said, "you didn't say serial killer. But these murders fit a pattern."

"It's not a serial killer," Beau said emphatically. "I suppose on the surface it looks good to blame an unknown serial predator, but too many things don't fit. First, Nicki LeBlanc was stabbed to death, not strangled like the others. Lily's body was never found, while the others were left in the open.

"My theory is that these girls knew something that got them killed," Beau continued. "Either about the Cormiers or Chief Dubois or Guidry. I don't know what they knew or who they knew it about, but this isn't a Ted Bundy or Jack the Ripper. This is someone who is killing with a purpose, not some psycho."

Kara said, "Devil's advocate. If they knew something, as you say, why nearly three years from the first murder to the last?"

"I can speculate, but nothing fits all the victims. I'm at my wits' end. That's why I called you, Michael. After Jean Paul's death and Ernestine's disappearance, it feels like everything is coming to a head." Beau paused, then said, "I got a call. A threat."

"What kind of threat?"

"That I needed to stop stirring the pot or people would die. Anonymous, I thought male but the voice was distorted. Could have been someone who was just scared and trying to get me to stop investigating. The chief has subtly threatened me—but nothing I can take to the bank, if you catch my drift."

"An in-custody death is cause for the FBI to come in and investigate."

"Like I said before, no one is going to talk to the FBI."

"That can be my boss's call," Michael said. "As far as I'm concerned, I'm your Navy buddy coming for a visit. I just happen to be a fed."

Beau looked at Kara. "I'm not a fed," she said.

"To be honest, I'm floundering here. Knowing my police chief is corrupt—and maybe half the cops on the force—is one thing. Proving it?" He stared at the board.

Beau walked over to the kitchen and opened the refrigerator. It was stocked with water and beer. He took a beer, offered one to Michael and Kara. Michael shook his head, Kara nodded. It wasn't like she was actually *working* right now.

Beau twisted off the cap and handed it to her.

"This could be a major federal investigation," Michael said. "Drugs, prostitution, corrupt government, cops. Public corruption, the FBI's bread and butter."

Kara snorted. "I'm all about the thin blue line, I'd die protecting 99 percent of my brothers and sisters in blue, but I'd rat out a murderous bastard in a heartbeat. Not everyone is me. If people down here aren't going to talk to the feds about the drug trade or murder, no one is going to turn on the cops, not when they have so much power. Not even fellow cops."

"That's the problem," Beau said. "Even if someone had solid evidence, everyone knows the wheels of justice move slow and they'd be dead before a case was built. If a witness dies or disappears? Case disappears along with them. I have informants and suspicions but nothing solid to build a case. Jean Paul was my best chance, but he wasn't exactly a good witness." He sat down on the couch and sighed. Kara felt for him. She had worked cases where she had nothing but her gut to go on.

"I get it," she said. "Better than you think. But there's always something to find. Having Michael and me here on the ground will help."

"This isn't going to be a walk in the park," Beau said. "And, Kara, you stand out like a fly on a wedding cake."

"I can blend."

"You're an attractive young woman, a stranger, who isn't a drug addict or prostitute. This is a dangerous situation. These people seem all friendly and apple pie on the surface, but some would drop you in the middle of the swamp without a second thought."

Kara was both amused and a bit suspicious. Beau seemed to be forthcoming, but there was a hint in his tone, or maybe his manner, that told her he had more. She said, "Beau, I can take care of myself."

"I know you're a cop, but—"

"I was an undercover cop for twelve years. I read people well. And right now, I'm reading you. What *aren't* you telling us?"

"About what? It's all here." He waved his hand toward the whiteboard. "Hard copies of police reports are in the desk. Four kids who no longer have their mother, three kids who are now orphans. I think a cop killed these girls—or knows who did and is actively covering up the crime. I don't think it's just one person."

It was the truth, but there was more. Kara was positive. Maybe he didn't trust her—he'd asked for Michael's help, not the FBI as a whole, and he didn't know her. "Beau. You can trust us."

"It's not about trust, it's that you're strangers." He ran both hands over his graying hair. "Shit, Michael, I don't know why I called you. You can't do anything. I was at my wits' end with Ernestine missing. It's my fault." His voice cracked. "I should never have talked to her. Never told her she could call me."

Michael said, "I'm glad you reached out. My boss will be down tomorrow."

"The chief isn't going to give him anything."

"You don't know Mathias Costa," Michael said. "He's going to talk to NOLA first, see what's what, then make the call on how to approach this situation."

"Remember, I still have to live here. There are more good people than bad."

"That's the way it always is," Kara said. "We don't want anyone else dead."

Michael said, "Let's go down to Lantern Gate. Where Jean Paul said Lily Baker's body might be? Is there any reason why you don't call in a search team?"

"The parish has a volunteer search and rescue, but I'd have to talk to the chief before he'd go to the sheriff. I don't trust Dubois, and the jury's still out on Landry. I need to be the one to find her. Then I'll call it in."

Michael glanced at Kara. "Do you have Jim's ETA?"

"I'll get it." She picked up her phone and stepped a few feet away to call Jim.

"Who's Jim?" Beau asked.

"Jim Esteban, our forensic guru," Michael said. "He's driving down in our mobile crime lab. He can run damn near any forensic test he needs without us having to go through a state or federal lab. He can investigate LeBlanc's death, analyze the drugs and body, and tell you whether it was murder or suicide or accidental. Maybe your informant did intentionally shoot up. Maybe he didn't know what was really in the vial. Mostly, though, if we find the remains of Lily Baker in the river, Jim needs to be part of the process from the beginning."

"The chief isn't going to turn over evidence to the FBI."

"If the FBI opens an investigation into the wrongful death of a suspect in police custody, they won't have a choice."

Kara put her finger up to signal that Jim had answered the phone.

"Hello, Jim, nice drive?"

"Relaxing," he said. "No traffic, I'm cruising along."

"We have an alleged suicide that might be murder—drug overdose—and we're looking for a dead body that may have been exposed for a couple months, probably not much left of her remains. When might you be here with the magic bus?"

"I made good time, so I'll be in Lafayette tonight. Matt and Ryder are flying in first thing in the morning."

"Great. Let me know when you're settled and we'll see about getting you the evidence."

"I'd like to maintain chain of custody, so I'll work with the local crime lab."

"It's a sticky situation. Don't come to St. Augustine until you talk to me or Michael."

"How sticky?"

"Well, you know all the stories over the years about corrupt politicians and whatnot in Louisiana?"

"So?"

"All true, and then some. Might be a cop or three involved."

"Now you have me concerned *and* intrigued."

"Just give us today to figure a few things out and we'll talk tonight. Drive safe."

"Be safe." He ended the call.

Kara and Jim had become friends over the last few months. Even went to a baseball game together, when the Nationals were playing his favorite team, the Texas Rangers. She wasn't much for baseball, but she had a lot of fun listening to Jim talk about the history of the sport, stats, team gossip while they drank cold beer and people watched. Honestly, she'd had more fun that day than in a long, long time.

Beau cut into her happy memory. "You're bringing in FBI forensics?"

"If we find Lily Baker's body, Jim is the best to process the scene," she said. "He was the head of the Dallas crime lab for a gazillion years, he knows what he's doing."

Beau looked panicked. "I'm already on thin ice here. I bring in the feds and Dubois will cut me loose."

"Buddy, you called me because you have five women dead, two missing, and a witness who died in custody under suspicious circumstances. You want justice for those women. I'm not ignorant of your situation, but now is not the time to get cold feet."

Beau didn't comment. He stared at his board, clearly torn. They were moving fast, Kara thought, maybe faster than he expected.

Michael continued. "You and I will go out to the bayou and look for Lily Baker's body. Let Kara go through your notes and evidence. She might see something you missed because you're too close to this. We'll regroup tonight and decide exactly how we can or should use Jim. My boss will be in Lafayette talking to the local FBI office tomorrow morning, and he gets things done. In for a penny, in for a pound."

Beau ran his hands through his curly hair. He let out his breath. "Okay. Let me tell Mimi we're going." He walked out.

Kara waited until Beau was out of earshot. "Keys."

Michael hesitated.

"You know," Kara said, "that I need to check things out at the Magnolia."

He tossed her the keys.

She caught them with one hand. "Your friend isn't telling us everything."

Michael frowned. "What makes you think that?"

"Tone? Something he said? More something he *didn't* say. Maybe it's a theory that he doesn't want to share, or maybe a secret he doesn't want us to know. I don't want to be blindsided."

"I'll see what I can find out."

"You don't have to push him," she said. "He's a good friend of yours, and you know I love to play bad cop."

"I'll get it out of him, if he's holding back anything."

Sometimes friendship clouded an investigation. Kara hoped that wasn't the case here.

Michael opened the cabin door and said before he walked out, "Be doubly careful."

"You know me."

"That's why I said it."

She winked at him. "Trust me."

7

As soon as Beau and Michael left, Kara pulled out the files from Beau's desk. It didn't take long before she realized that he had mostly theories and little evidence.

She sorted through the information: notes, autopsy reports, drug screenings, crime scene photos, witness statements. He'd tried to identify the last person or people who'd seen each of the women alive. Beau had done a decent job of re-creating each victim's last day.

She stared at the photos.

I know you.

She didn't actually *know* the women, but she knew what they faced. She understood their circumstances. She'd worked too long on the streets as an undercover cop to not understand how these girls were made.

Part circumstance. Where they were born, who their parents were, how they were raised, if they were abused.

Part personality. While anyone could fall down the rabbit hole, it was often those who couldn't see a way out who fell harder, faster. What was the difference between a poor kid like Michael who had pulled himself up and out of his rough, violent childhood...and the kids who didn't? That might be a question for the shrink of their team, Dr. Catherine Jones, but these questions were more philosophical than immediate. Kara would call her when she needed information to solve the case, not to shoot the breeze about psychology and human nature.

Besides, she didn't like the woman.

Drugs trapped far too many people. Those drawn to them had few defenses to say no. Peer pressure, the potential money windfall, the temporary relief of miserable living conditions, an addictive personality...many of the young didn't see that the drugs they used prolonged their circumstances. It was a cycle, one Kara had no idea how to fix or break.

But she could make life harder for the dealers.

She'd read a lot about St. Augustine while on the plane this morning, trying to get a feeling for the town and its people. St. Augustine was more than a stereotypical Southern town. She read about community fundraisers, parish fairs, church groups, the high school that graduated their first major league baseball draft pick three years ago and had businesses who'd donated money to bus the entire high school to the graduate's first major league game last spring in Texas. The kid, Lyle Aucoin, had donated money to put in a new baseball and football field at the high school and bought his mom and grandmother, who'd raised him, a new house in the nicest neighborhood of St. Augustine.

The town was divided by economy, not race. The wealthier residents lived north of I-10, or east of Lake Pierre Road, which divided the downtown. Looking at property records and Google Maps, most of these houses were over three thousand square feet. The homes in the well-maintained neighborhoods east of downtown were gated two-story brick houses, while the homes north of the interstate were rambling ranches on acreage or newer homes in a planned subdivision.

The poorer residents lived in small box houses or trailers or crumbling apartments—no gates, no fencing. They bled out of downtown south of the tracks or west of Lake Pierre Road. Farther south, both east to the river and west practically to Lake Charles, were farms—some with crops (corn grown for livestock feed was the largest commodity in Broussard Parish) and some that lay fallow, like the Hebert place. Cattle was another industry, but from what little Kara learned, no one here was getting rich off it. Last year's storms had wiped out the state's second largest pepper field south of the town limits, and she had no idea how that might have affected the people in town, but she couldn't imagine that it was positive.

Still, St. Augustine was on a major interstate, and there were several restaurants and motels along I-10, which helped with their tax base and jobs. The downtown area was quaint and had several businesses aimed at tourists. Antique shops. A bakery. Several gift and clothing shops. Even an art studio that sold the work of local artists (if you counted the entire state of Louisiana local).

There were definitely two groups. The middle class with white or blue collar jobs—including small business owners, retail staff, those working for the parish or city, mechanics, skilled labor—and the poor, who struggled to stay afloat and employed, many on public assistance.

Well, three groups. The last group preyed on both the poor and the middle-class. Corrupt cops, drug dealers like Preston and Gray Cormier, the people who kept the prostitution industry alive and well, along with many who traveled from Lake Charles or Lafayette in order to hide their perversions.

She couldn't solve the town problems. Maybe Beau and people like him, over time, would make a dent.

But she *could* solve these murders. And that meant she needed more than she could gather from newspapers and Beau's autopsy reports.

She needed to understand the players.

One thing stood out to her: there was no clear motive. No wonder so many people in town thought serial killer.

Kara went outside and grabbed her overnight bag from the rental car. She smiled and shook her head at the large suitcase and garment bag Michael had brought. She'd called him a girl when they met at the airport, but he just grinned.

She slammed the trunk shut and brought her duffel into the cabin's small bedroom. Unlike her partner, she traveled light: she didn't need a lot. She sorted through her belongings and pulled out a tank top that revealed her midriff and jean shorts that would show off her elaborate butterfly tattoo that was off-center on the lower right side of her back.

She had gotten the tattoo when she'd been planning an undercover op years ago and she loved it. She could have had a temporary tat, but decided to go all out. Colorful, neither too big nor too small. She also had a small red rose on her left ankle, with a long stem, complete with thorns. She'd gotten it shortly after she graduated from the police academy when her primary instructor, who had recruited her into undercover work, had called her beautiful and prickly.

Kara wasn't one to wear a lot of makeup unless she had to, and she didn't put any on now—it was too damn hot anyway. Her hair had curled in the humidity, making it look shorter than her shaggy shoulder-length bob, so that was good. She needed to blend in, not look like a cop, but not look like a prostitute, either. Just someone passing through… Visiting a family friend, if anyone asked. Less is more.

She surveyed herself in the small bathroom mirror. A couple

of her scars were visible. The knife wound on her back from early this year was fully healed, and the doctor who sewed her up had done an amazing job—the scar was narrow, faint, shouldn't attract attention. The gunshot she'd had in her upper right shoulder had actually been less serious, but it looked like the scar from a gunshot. She could only partly hide it with the strap from her shirt. Nothing she could do about it, so decided to ignore it. If anyone asked, she'd tell them to fuck off. That usually did the trick.

She put her knife in her front pocket and her gun under the driver's seat of the rental car. So they didn't stand out, Michael had asked for something older—the car was two years old with a serious dent on the back, but it was still relatively new. Fortunately, the drive from the airport had taken the shiny clean off the exterior. Kara removed the license plate frame advertising the dealership and tore off the stickers from the front and back window.

She texted Michael that she was leaving—it was three in the afternoon. She planned to be back by five, and would keep him informed if plans changed.

She set the Magnolia Inn into her phone GPS and had just started driving when *Mathias Costa* popped up on her caller ID.

She wanted to ignore Matt's call. They hadn't talked much in the last week, not since Catherine Jones almost caught them having sex last weekend. She was still angry about the whole thing. Angry about hiding in Matt's bedroom while Matt made small talk with Catherine and her family who had stopped by to drop off fresh vegetables they'd plucked from their garden. Mad at herself, mad at Matt, mad at Catherine. She didn't really know what to do about any of it.

She put all that on the back burner. Because? Five dead women. She picked up her phone.

"Hey, boss," she said, forcing casual and calm into her voice.

"Kara."

A little thrill washed over her when she heard his voice. She kept her reaction in check. Not only because she was still ticked off, but everything about her and Matt had become too fucking complicated. Until last weekend, she thought Matt might be getting too attached for her comfort. Now? She missed him. She didn't want to be on an emotional roller coaster. She missed what they had back when they first met—sex. Just sex. No emotional attachments. No stress over team members finding out that they were involved. No thought of the future. Just the moment. The way she preferred to live.

Maybe the big cooldown after last weekend was actually what they needed. So what, she missed sex with the hot Cuban cop. She'd get over it. There were other sexy men out there. Not that she had time to find one.

"Michael sent a message that you arrived safely and he and Beau were going out on the river to look for a possible body."

"Yep. I went through Beau's files and notes. There's a lot here."

"Tell me."

"Tonight. I'm going to check something out."

He was silent.

"Just to get the lay of the land. I got this. I'm not going to miss dinner. Beau said his grandma is making gumbo."

"Check in when you're done."

"And Michael knows where I'll be and my ETA. I know how to keep my partner informed." She'd reluctantly shared her GPS location with Michael, just in case.

"Good. I—"

He then stopped.

"Right back at you," she said and ended the call.

Neither of them needed to talk about last weekend or their future or sex. The next few days—or few weeks, depending on the length of the investigation—was about the dead.

Reminding herself of that fact kept her grounded.

8

Michael and Beau took a small motorboat out onto the bayou Sunday afternoon, the only way to effectively inspect the area south of Lantern Gate. They launched upstream, a full two miles from their destination, because it was the closest place to access the water, unless you had a small rowboat.

"I appreciate you coming down here so quickly," Beau told Michael as he maneuvered the motorized skiff through the bayou. The slow-moving river was between thirty and fifty feet wide, and Michael suspected six-to-eight feet deep at the center. Both sides of the river were covered with short trees and thick bushes, mostly yucca plants and tupelo trees this close to the farmland, plus a variety of bushes Michael couldn't identify.

No overhanging trees in this part of the river, and Michael was grateful. He hadn't been lying to Kara about the water moccasins, and he didn't want to encounter one dropping unexpectedly into their boat. While he was amused by Kara's fear of alligators, he shared her fear of snakes.

Michael didn't know much about Louisiana swampland, but he knew there were basically two kinds of swamp: the bayou like they were on now—lazy rivers of various sizes cutting through farm country and often ending in a lake, and the deep bayou— mostly south of here, plus some areas to the east, where you could easily get lost, with trees that covered the sky, hanging vines and Spanish moss that dropped snakes, and other critters that Michael didn't much want to encounter. The idea of getting lost in the middle of a swamp gave him pause. There was a large patch of those unfathomable thick trees growing to the east and he couldn't help but think what might be found there.

"You wouldn't have called if you didn't need help."

"It's unusual for the FBI to act so quickly."

"Matt's team is unique. We have a lot of autonomy." Michael liked what he was doing—the variety of cases, the flexibility, the team itself. Everyone was smart, well trained, dedicated. But he didn't like the travel. He preferred his house in Alexandria, the two-bedroom, two-bath, twelve hundred square feet of *his*. He enjoyed being there at night, going to work in the morning, returning and relaxing in his well-manicured backyard or in the Jacuzzi he recently put in. Which made the mobile response team a problem. Loved the cases, hated living out of hotel rooms. He would honor the two-year commitment he'd given to Matt, but wasn't certain he would stay beyond that.

Besides, he had no one to come home to. That bothered him as well, but this team made it difficult to start or maintain a relationship. Michael wanted a family—maybe because he lost his long ago. He was thirty-seven, a year younger than Matt. He didn't have the same biological clock considerations as women, but he wanted children before he was too old to play catch or teach them how to ride a bike.

"What's your partner's story? How'd an LAPD detective get on your FBI task force?"

"Short version? Kara helped on a case, had some problems in her own jurisdiction when her cover was blown, so Matt brought her onto the team. Don't know if she's staying for the duration, she's itching to go back to LA, but for now she's with us."

"She must have been effective."

"She was."

"I meant what I said, Michael. She sticks out. Young, pretty, sharp, but mostly, she's a stranger."

"We can't do anything about the stranger part, but if she doesn't want people to think she's a cop, they won't think she's a cop. We worked an undercover case together—she became a bartender, worked in the lion's den, no one suspected she wasn't exactly who she pretended to be."

"I don't think going to the Magnolia Inn alone is the smartest move."

Michael had told Beau Kara's plans during the drive to the river. He hadn't wanted her to go alone, either, but she'd be able to learn more than he could, simply because she could play the part better.

"We're not here undercover—didn't have time to set it up—but we might as well see what she can learn before the truth comes out." Michael glanced at Beau. "You don't think she's in danger, do you?"

"No." He paused. "I just don't know what's going on over there. My theories are half-assed, I'm the first to admit it. My gut says Preston Cormier had the women killed, but I can't prove it. My gut says the cops are helping him, but can't prove that, either. While four of the five victims had sex within hours of their deaths, they were prostitutes, so it's near impossible to determine if they were raped, had just come off the job or had consensual sex outside of work. Doesn't help that our coroner is a nothing burger."

"DNA?"

"Contaminated. They were dumped in or near the river. I mean, maybe if we had a stellar crime lab and competent coroner they could have found something, but I still think the physical evidence is weak. Water, animals, humidity, time—all destructive."

"Jim is as good as they get," Michael said. The still, wet air was getting to him and he unbuttoned his shirt.

"Buddy, take it off. You have an undershirt."

Michael grimaced. Yes, he was on a river in Louisiana, but he was always dressed for the job. Walking around in a white undershirt made him feel practically naked. He'd earned his nickname GQ. He took no offense when Kara teased him about his luggage.

"Come on," Beau laughed.

He reluctantly took off his formerly crisp, white shirt, folded it, put it under his seat. It would need to be cleaned and pressed. He'd realized as soon as he got off the plane in Baton Rouge that his standard attire wasn't going to cut it here. He might have to go casual this week: no suit, no button-downs, just khakis and polos. Even then, Kara would tell him he was overdressed.

"You okay?" Michael asked after Beau didn't speak for a spell.

"Can't get them out of my head. They all knew each other—some better than others. And I keep thinking, what was going on? What did I miss?"

Beau shook his head, obviously frustrated. "I've looked at the cases every which way," he continued, "but if the girls were all privy to something that someone—like Cormier or Guidry or the chief or, hell, anyone else—didn't want getting out, why kill these women over a period of three years? I've thought about rage—the girls said or did something to one of their regulars who then snapped—but I don't think anyone would be protecting a john. I would have heard rumors about it."

"Even if it's a cop?"

Beau shrugged.

"Kara thinks you're not being straight with us."

"I wouldn't lie to you."

When Michael didn't respond, Beau shook his head.

"Dammit, Michael, you think I'd keep you in the dark about something like this? I *asked* for your help."

"Lies of omission are still lies."

"I'm not lying to you about anything." Beau didn't say anything for a long minute. "Some of these girls—shit. Shit. It's my fault."

"Explain."

Beau whispered, "Ginny Chaisson."

When he didn't elaborate, Michael pushed. "Were you involved with her?"

"No, of course not! I wasn't involved with any of them."

"Okay."

"Why would you even say that?"

"Because you're not talking. Why was Ginny at risk because of you?"

"Ginny worked at The Fat Catfish, a cocktail waitress, I guess, though that's too fancy a term for the dive. Ginny was beautiful and sweet—I mean, stunning. No makeup, no glamour, but she could walk into the room and everyone would smile. She was the prettiest girl in town and caught the eye of Preston Cormier."

"The drug dealer."

Beau nodded. "She went to community college over in Lake Charles, bright girl, had a chance of making something of herself. Developed a drug habit, dropped out of college. Once she was working at The Fat Cat full-time, hooked on oxy, smoking weed day and night, she started trading sex for drugs. She would do anything for Cormier. She lost her glow." He shook his head.

"Anyway, I worked on her for months, trying to get her to talk to me, because I knew that she was close to Cormier. I wanted her to get me info. Used the fact that her great-aunt and Mimi were tight. Used her friendship with the victims. Then, when Tanya turned up dead, Ginny came out to the house one night and told me she was scared. She gave me information, but nothing I could build a case on."

"What information?"

"She saw Lettie—her cousin, the first victim—and Tanya—the third victim—at the Magnolia the night they disappeared. This wasn't new information, all the victims had a connection with the Inn. But the night they disappeared someone else was at the Inn—a lowlife called Buddy. Ginny said that Buddy gave her the creeps. It took me a few weeks—I had to be cautious in how I investigated him—but I learned Buddy's legal name was Robert Palfrey, a known drug dealer from Lake Pierre, town south of here. I thought this was a solid lead—that Buddy might be the killer. I investigated him quietly, caught him dealing drugs, arrested him. He was let go, no charges filed. I tried again—again, he was let go. Didn't say a word to me, but he sure gloated. The DA called me into his office and said that I was harassing Palfrey. Then, two weeks before Hannah was murdered, he was killed. The sheriff's department raided his house in a drug bust and he was killed when he went for a gun."

"So he wasn't responsible for the murders? Or was he?" Michael was confused.

"I don't know. But Hannah and Ginny were killed after he was six feet under. Still, he knew *something* and now he's dead, at the hands of a cop. It appears to be a justified shooting, but it was too damn convenient that he was killed. Maybe whoever he was working with—Cormier or the cops or both—thought he would crack if I got to him a third time, or maybe he mouthed off to someone. The DA himself called me the night of the raid, told me what happened, and said, 'You were right, but we saved the taxpayers money in a trial.'"

"This is the DA you believe is corrupt."

"Alston Gary is a lying piece of shit. I give him good cases, evidence goes missing, they walk. Even when I have evidence, he says it's not enough and cuts drug dealers loose. I can't get warrants to check finances or start an investigation—that's just not how it's done down here."

"Matt can open a federal case. Matt can get warrants."

"Like I told you before, you can be down here for a year and not be able to build a case. Talk to anyone in NOLA, they'll tell you the same thing."

"We get anything, at a minimum, Matt can get financial warrants. We have a whiz finance guy who can look at numbers and tell us what might be going on, give us a direction."

Beau considered. "It might be our only shot, but if you fail, I'm screwed. I'd have to go—but I can't leave Mimi here alone."

"Do you think someone would go after her?"

"No. If I left town no one would have reason to go after her. They'd just be happy I was gone. But she's eighty-four. She needs someone with her at the house. People in town will help, to a point. Her pastor suggested after Pop died that she sell the house and move to a smaller place in town. She nearly bit his head off. I can't leave her—and I can't force her to leave."

Michael understood Beau's commitment better than most. He would have done anything for his family. They were all dead now. His brother killed in a drive-by shooting. His mother killed by grief—grief prolonged by her drug addiction that started after his little brother was killed. Michael had been in and out of foster care since he was nine, both before and after his mother died. He never knew his father, and the only grandparent he knew—his great-grandmother—had died in a retirement home when Michael was in the Navy.

Maybe that's why he jumped at Matt's offer to be part of the

MRT. Because he needed people, especially after leaving the military, and this team was like family to him.

Beau continued. "People don't talk, because they're scared. I don't know why Palfrey was killed—maybe he was skimming from Cormier, or maybe they thought he was a weak link. I wouldn't have even looked at him if Ginny hadn't pointed me at him, and now Ginny's dead, too. One by a killer, and one by a cop. Which in this case may be one and the same."

Beau seemed skeptical that they were going to find justice for these women, but Michael had faith in his team—and their ability to find the truth. Fresh eyes were what they needed. By the time he and Beau returned this evening from the bayou, Kara might see the case from a different perspective.

"We're approaching the gate," Beau said after several minutes of silence.

Michael had assumed Beau meant a physical gate, but he was wrong. The murky river had no bridges, and he couldn't see a place where they could pull the boat up and get out without stepping in muck. He supposed some people might consider this peaceful, but Michael was on edge, as if someone could be lurking in the thick foliage that spread out from the water.

He saw a rotting dock—if you could even call it a dock—on the east side of the river. Above it, on the shore, was a shack that didn't look bigger than an outhouse.

"Is that the gate?" he asked Beau.

Beau laughed. "No. The gate is up ahead. It's not an actual gate. The river, as you can see, is pretty much the same width as it meanders all the way down to Lake Pierre, about twenty miles. But there's a narrow spot, maybe eight feet wide, that someone called a gate for whatever reason. They started calling it Lantern Gate because a hundred years ago, take or leave, there was a farm directly east of here and the only way to get to it was over a wood bridge that used to cross the river that the owner called his gateway. The farm went up in flames because of a lantern that got knocked over."

"Like the Great Chicago Fire," Michael said with a half smile.

"Pretty much. No cow involved, that we know about. And we don't get a lot of fires out here, because the land is wet year-round and water is certainly not a problem. But when you have fuel—hay, alfalfa, whatnot, and it's summer? Now, in hindsight, I might think it was deliberate, maybe someone wanted to burn down the farm. The owner died, the wife and kid escaped. But we'll never know."

Now Michael saw the gate, where the river went from more than thirty feet wide to eight. But it was a slight misnomer because the area to the east was a shallow swamp, into which the water could spread over the short levee during rainy season. The gate was about thirty feet long, and if Michael was standing in the boat, his head would be level with the ground. The remnants of an old footbridge were evident on the western shore. "I'm surprised the land hasn't given away in the floods."

"Me, too, but there's probably a reason. Maybe because it's so long? Too much earth to move? Reinforced long ago? Hell if I know. Geology isn't my area of expertise, but I heard the land was moved to create this, probably by that dead farmer."

"Stop," Michael suddenly said. Something had caught his eye. Where the river narrowed, just before the "gate," he thought he saw something bright—something that didn't fit.

Beau idled the motor. He looked where Michael looked.

"You were here Friday, right?"

Beau didn't answer as he slowly steered the small boat toward the shore.

The bright color was a yellow dress with white daisies. The yellow dress was stained with blood, on the body of a dead black girl, half-submerged in the water.

"Dear Lord," Beau said. "Ernestine."

9

After driving around to get a feel for the community, Kara sent Michael a text message when she arrived at the Magnolia Inn at quarter to four that afternoon. Best to keep him in the loop in case she needed backup.

The Inn was exactly as Beau had described it: a rambling, run-down former residence with what looked like a double-wide trailer tacked on to the south.

She was familiar with the type of establishment. There were many of them in California where she'd been a cop for twelve years. She could go into any city off an interstate, drive for five minutes and find the local no-tell motel, or a bar with a back room catering to the sex trade.

She didn't need Beau to tell her that the Magnolia Inn was that place.

Three men smoked cigarettes and drank what was likely bourbon at a shaded table in the corner of the raised porch. A few other chairs and tables were scattered around, worn and unused.

From the front, it was tired, dreary, but if she was at the end of a fourteen-hour drive she wouldn't care as long as the sheets were clean.

She didn't plan to sleep here.

Who are you right now?

Always important to immerse herself into the role.

She would be seen around town over the next few days or week or longer, so she couldn't pretend she was just driving through. It would make subsequent sightings suspicious. But she didn't want to drop names. Taking what she learned from Beau and read on the plane, she rolled her neck and stuck with her less-is-more strategy.

She parked, locked the car, walked inside. The three men on the porch watched her. She ignored them.

She'd been in worse, but not by much. No one was smoking inside, but memories of marijuana infused the dark room, from the heavy drapes to the stained carpet. She glanced around, putting a slight frown on her face.

"Lost?"

Asked by the fortysomething woman behind the bar, wearing a filmy blouse, unbuttoned, over a tank top. Short, bleached hair, full face of make-up, skinny. She'd been chatting with an old man drinking a pint at the end of the bar when Kara walk in.

"Not really." Kara walked over to the bar, sat down two stools from the old man. It made her twitch that her back was to the main door, but unless she sat at a table in the corner—which would be suspicious—she had no other choice. And at least from this angle, she had the bar mirror to watch anyone enter. A trick she'd learned long ago.

"Long drive," she said. "Do you have Coors Light in a bottle? I don't need a glass."

She never, under any circumstances, drank anything already opened, and that included draft beer.

She discreetly watched the bartender grab a bottle from a refrigerator under the bar and pop open the top with an opener attached to the wall.

"Happy hour, three bucks."

Kara always kept cash in her pockets. She pulled out a bunch of crumpled bills, counted out three, then added another on top of it. Folded the remaining bills and put them back in her pocket.

She much preferred tequila, but she needed a clear head, and beer was a good choice. It was her go-to drink when working undercover. Easy to fit in and not get drunk.

The old man looked over at her and she realized he wasn't as old as she'd initially thought. Telltale signs—teeth, wrinkles, sallow skin—told her he was a serious drug addict and not even forty. Her time working undercover had turned her off drugs forever. Not just because they fucked with your head, but they aged you, sometimes rapidly.

"Staying here?" he asked.

"Nope," she said.

"You'd fit right in." He winked at her.

She smiled as if she didn't know what he was talking about. Asshole.

A girl in her early twenties wearing a miniskirt and tight white T-shirt came in from a side door that Kara assumed led to the expansion. She was high, her eyes red, mascara smeared.

The girl sat down in the middle of the long bar. "Can I have a beer, Crystal?"

The bartender poured her a draft. She didn't ask for money. The girl drank half of it. "God, I still hate the taste."

At that moment, a short, skinny man of indeterminate age swaggered from the same door, walked over to the girl and nuzzled her neck while he grabbed her boobs. "See you tomorrow, sugar," he said. He was about to walk out when he saw Kara and paused, assessing her. Kara's skin crawled, but she drank her beer and ignored him.

"Hey, Crystal, can I get a beer? And another for my new friend here." He sat down next to Kara. Too close. He smelled of stale beer and body odor and had tats covering his arms. Not good tats, like her old partner Colton had that made up his one sleeve, but cheap tats in blue that bled into his skin until they were unrecognizable. He wore a necklace with what she assumed were alligator teeth.

"No, thank you," she said, making sure Crystal heard her. Must be Crystal Landry, the sheriff's cousin. Good to know.

"Manners and everything. Haven't seen y'all in here before."

She didn't comment.

"I just want to drink my beer in peace and get back on the road."

"Where you headed?"

"That's none of your business."

"Oh, feisty. I like feisty, don't I, Shari?" He glanced over to the girl who'd just given him a blow job.

Shari rolled her eyes and drained the rest of her beer. "I'm going to have a smoke." She walked out the front door.

"Leave the customers alone," Crystal told Kara's unwelcome seatmate.

There was something in her tone that caught Kara's ear. The jerk ran his hand over Kara's lower back, traced her tattoo with his thumb. "Hope to see ya again, sweet thing," he said, winked at Crystal and walked out. She glanced over her shoulder to make sure he'd left.

"Ignore him, he's harmless," Crystal told her. "You want another?"

"Sure," she said, put her empty on the edge of the bar in front of her.

"You okay?"

She put the beer down and Kara sipped.

"Yeah. I've dealt with assholes before." She dropped another four dollars on the bar.

"You look like you can take care of yourself."

Astute. Kara hadn't cringed when the stranger touched her. She could have easily brought him to his knees. Feigning fear had always been tough for her—even though she knew real fear. Real fear just made her angry, but at least she didn't have to fake it.

"I've lived alone for a long time, big cities and small towns." She shrugged. "Jerks are the same wherever."

"Where you headed?"

"Meeting up with a friend." *Less is more*, she reminded herself. It was so easy to fall back into her old undercover habits, come up with a story that everyone would believe. She was good at selling a backstory.

Crystal glanced over at the door when it opened, straightened almost imperceptibly. But noticing and analyzing body language made Kara a good cop.

Kara sipped her beer and looked in the mirror. Two men— one about five-ten, blond, clean-cut and the other, taller and rougher around the edges.

"Boys," Crystal said. "The usual?"

The shorter said, "Thanks, sugar. Jasper here?"

"Not yet."

The two men sat down in a small semiprivate room off the entrance that had a fireplace, unused, and had probably been the living room way back when. Kara could see the taller of the two reflected in the mirror behind the bar, but the other was out of view.

Crystal pulled a half bottle of whiskey from under the counter and two glasses from a shelf that looked marginally clean. She left the bar and walked over to the side room.

Jasper Steele owned and managed the Inn, but Beau had a note that someone must be backing him. That might be something for Zack to look into.

Zack Heller was the newest member of Matt's team and a white-collar crime expert. Matt didn't care much for him, but appreciated his skill set. Kara hadn't spent much time with him, but she had a different reason than Matt for distrusting him. Matt thought Zack was annoying. She thought he had secrets. But she couldn't put her finger on what bugged her, so put her reservations on the back burner. She would figure it out, eventually. For now, he provided much-needed financial expertise to the group.

Crystal came back a minute later. "Another?" she asked.

"Naw, I'm just going to finish this up and get going. But thanks."

She sipped again. She still had a half bottle left, figured she could park it here for ten minutes without raising suspicion.

She absorbed the atmosphere and people.

Kara liked dive bars, but the Magnolia had a darker undercurrent, and definitely felt more like a brothel than a hotel. She watched as, in the thirty minutes she sat on the stool, five people came in and disappeared behind the door that led to the sex rooms, for lack of a better description. Maybe not just for sex, but drugs. A place to get high and ride it out. With hard-core addicts came theft, violence and more drugs.

A girl came down the stairs. "Done," she said to Crystal. She didn't sit at the bar, but stood at the far end, opposite the old man, and seemed to be waiting for something.

The girl was underage. Eighteen or nineteen. Pretty with long dark blond hair pulled into a ponytail and hazel eyes that were too sharp to be attached to an addict. An outlier in this establishment.

Crystal went over to the cash register, pulled out what appeared to be two twenties, and walked over to the girl, handing her the bills. "See you Thursday, Winnie?"

"Yeah," Winnie said.

Kara noticed the kid saw everything. She'd assessed every person in the bar—the prostitutes laughing in the corner, the men in the semiprivate room. She said something to them as she headed toward the door. Kara thought Winnie asked if they'd seen Ernestine. Kara couldn't hear their response. Then Winnie said, "She was supposed to help me with the rooms today, didn't show. Just thought ya might've seen her at The Catfish. I can't go in there, ya know."

One of the men said something Kara couldn't hear, then they both laughed.

"Whatever," Winnie said and walked out.

But not before she looked over her shoulder at Kara's reflection in the bar mirror.

Winnie was subtle, but Kara didn't miss the once-over.

Kara's skin prickled. Winnie was different, and different could mean she had value for the investigation. But Kara wouldn't know unless she talked to her one-on-one.

She drained her beer, put it down and nodded to Crystal. "Thanks."

"See you around," Crystal said.

Kara headed for the door, glancing at the men in the side room as she was leaving, burning their appearances into her brain. Beau would know who they were.

She needed photos of all the players—not just the dead and missing women.

She reached to push for the door when it opened from the outside and a large man with a beer belly and beard almost ran into her. Late thirties, Caucasian, blue eyes, greasy brown hair.

"Well, how-do-you-do?" he said, looking her up and down.

"Hi," she said. "Excuse me."

He was packing—she could see the telltale sign of the butt of his gun through his sweaty shirt. He wore jeans with an unbut-toned faded denim shirt over an old Hard Rock T-shirt.

"Come, stay, have a drink on the house. I haven't seen you here before."

"Thank you," she said, "but I have to go."

"What's your name, sugar?"

She hesitated, half expecting Crystal to intervene. When she didn't, Kara realized that this must be Jasper Steele.

"Excuse me," she said quietly, trying to sound demure, but not quite pulling it off.

He didn't move, but she slid past him. He grinned down at her, intentionally looking down her shirt, his hand "inadver-tently" touching her ass.

If she wasn't on a case, she would have elbowed him hard in the chest. Instead, she walked away.

"Dammit, Jasper, she's just driving through and you have to be a prick?" Kara heard Crystal say.

Then Jasper said, "Hey, Gray, you're early..." and the door shut closed.

Were all the guys here horny bastards?

But at least she knew who those men were that Winnie was talking to. Gray Cormier and if she had to guess, the other was his half brother, Preston.

Kara didn't immediately spot the older teen when she left the bar, but when she started her car, she saw a lone figure walking down the road toward downtown.

Kara had to figure out how to convince the girl to talk. It couldn't be rushed, it couldn't be pushy. Just...

Wing it, Kara.

She slowed down when she reached Winnie and rolled down the passenger side window. "Hey, do you need a ride some-where?"

"Fuck off," the girl said.

Smart girl. Kara liked her already.

Kara pulled over in front of the girl and got out of the car. She walked over to Winnie. "I heard what you said to those two men."

"Snoop."

"Just someone who wants to know what happened to your friend."

"I don't have friends. You know, there's a couple girls back at the Magnolia who would be happy to take care of you, if the price is right."

Kara almost smiled. Winnie reminded her of herself way back when she had a chip on her shoulder so big it would take a hurricane to knock it off.

"I'm going to tell you something that could bite me in the ass, but I'm going to tell you anyway. My name is Kara Quinn, and I'm a *former* Los Angeles police detective." She emphasized *former*, because if Winnie found out she was working with the feds, she'd never earn her trust. But she didn't want to outright lie to her. "I know something's going on here, and I'm going to find out what. I get the feeling that you see everything."

"And keep my piehole shut. And you would, too, if you know what's good for you. Go away. And if y'all follow me? I'll call the cops. Don't think I won't. And cops in St. Augustine don't like strangers."

Kara let her walk away.

She would talk to Winnie again. Clearly, Ernestine was supposed to help Winnie clean at the Magnolia today, didn't show, and Winnie asked the men about her. Did they own the place? Were they silent partners? Or just known associates of Ernestine's?

Winnie knew what was going on, and Kara had to find a way to earn her trust. She got back in her car and left.

Winnie LeBlanc watched the girl cop, ex-cop, whoever the fuck she was, drive off. She'd known the woman was snoopy as soon as she saw her sitting at the bar watching everything in the mirror. Probably a narc. Or something. Maybe she wasn't even a cop. Maybe she was sent to town to keep an eye on things, maybe she worked for Jasper or Tammy or hell knew who, all because Jake got himself killed.

Winnie didn't give a shit about Jake. He was an asshole who had tried to get into her pants since she was fourteen. She told his mama about it because he was eighteen at the time, and his mama gave him a whipping. Jake kept pushing, but not hard, because he knew she'd go to his mama again, and the second time he might not have a dick to play with. And once she turned eighteen he didn't give her a second look, because she was too old for him.

He'd hurt one of her friends and she'd never forgive him for it, but Jean Paul wouldn't kill him for getting Penny pregnant— who willingly went to bed with the pervert—and he wouldn't kill Jake for taking Penny to have an abortion, even though Penny cried about it for weeks to Winnie. She couldn't exactly cry to her mama or daddy, since her daddy was a preacher.

But Winnie did give a shit about her cousin Jean Paul. He'd just gone in and shot Jake, bang-bang, and she was really, really worried she knew why. And if she was right, then she was up shit creek without a paddle, and she didn't know what to do.

But one thing she *wouldn't* do is talk to a maybe former cop who was probably lying through her teeth.

Jean Paul was the only person she'd trusted in town. She'd told him things maybe she shouldn't have, and maybe that's why he was dead. Not because he killed Jake, though that would be reason enough for some people. But because he might have said something he shouldn't have.

She mostly liked her cousin, because even though he was high more often than not, he wasn't mean. And he was helping her get the money to leave town before she ended up like the others. He said she wasn't a whore so she wouldn't end up dead, but he didn't know *everything* that she knew, and she was only alive because she knew how to keep her mouth shut. Mostly. Except for telling Jean Paul about what she and Jake did last month.

Winnie didn't know what to do, but not talking was the obvious answer. Let everything settle down.

She walked down the gravel road, turned left onto Main Street and through downtown. It was a long walk to The Fat Catfish, but she didn't have a car. Jean Paul used to let her take his truck when he wasn't using it. Maybe she could find it, if the police didn't have it. No one else would want the old piece of crap. Only Winnie knew where he hid the extra keys in the cab. If the police didn't have it, Nellie was probably using it just to spite Winnie. Winnie would take it when Nellie was sleeping.

She didn't like Nellie, and one-upping her would be fun.

Winnie wasn't supposed to be in The Catfish because she wasn't twenty-one, but Ernestine hadn't come in for two days to clean up like she did every morning, and Tammy promised to pay her double if Winnie took care of it. And it wasn't like she hadn't been here before when Ernestine was having a spell. Winnie came in, kept her head down and her mouth shut, and cleaned the disgusting place, then left. Tammy was a bitch who'd slap you into next week for any damn reason if she had a mind to, but she always paid in cash. Winnie *really* needed all the money she could get right now.

Tammy was drinking as usual, her large body crammed into the corner booth.

"You're late," she said. "You were supposed to come in this morning."

"I had to babysit."

Her mother had gotten wasted last night—like damn near every night—and didn't seem to remember when she was drunk that she had a four-year-old to care for, so Winnie stepped in. Bonnie Mae was her niece and her sister was dead, so if not her, who? Half the time Loretta LeBlanc dropped the kid off with a friend or relative and often didn't remember who she'd left her with.

Bonnie was the only thing keeping Winnie in St. Augustine. She wanted to take the kid with her, but panicked at the thought because what the fuck did she know about raising a kid? How could she make enough money to take care of herself, let alone Bonnie? Winnie could work, she'd do near anything but have sex for money—hell, if she could clean the bathrooms at this pigsty, she could clean any damn disgusting thing. But would it be enough? And what about all those things like school and clothes and finding a place to live and would she have to pay a babysitter to watch the kid? How was she going to get the money for that?

Except, she knew what *not* to do, and that was get wasted and pass out and ignore a hungry four-year-old who was crying her eyes out because she thought Memaw was dead.

The best thing about living here, in St. Augustine, was that Winnie knew everyone. If Loretta left Bonnie with someone, Winnie would hear about it, go get her and make sure she was fed and brushed her teeth and went to bed before midnight.

So it was hard, now, to think about leaving. But damn if she was going to get caught up in all the bullshit. She'd already done too many things that had her losing sleep at night, remembering that Nicki had started down the same path.

Except you're not doing drugs and you're not working on your back. You're not your sister.

Winnie did her work and really, really hoped that Ernestine wasn't dead. She liked the girl, but Ernestine was too sweet and too stupid and trusted everybody. Worse, she didn't know how to lie.

It was Sunday, so The Catfish wasn't all that busy. Maybe a half dozen heavy drinkers mostly sitting alone. Depressing. Winnie went to the storage room to gather up the cleaning supplies.

When she stepped out, she saw slimy Debra Martin saunter in and sidle up to Tammy in her booth.

Her heart skipped a beat and she went immediately down the short hall to the bathrooms.

Yeah, she knew a lot about a lot, and she wasn't going to talk. She didn't want to be dead. She just wanted to get the hell out of St. Augustine, and Jean Paul's death was going to delay her escape.

She might just have to find another way to get the money she needed.

10

Kara stopped by a small grocery store near the freeway to buy flowers for Beau's grandma Toni as a thank-you. She didn't know what else she might like, and she didn't want to insult her by buying food, though she stocked up on junk food and beer which was her midnight staple when she couldn't sleep.

She'd texted Michael when she left the Magnolia with her plans and ETA, but it wasn't until she walked out of the store that she had a response:

We found Ernestine's body. Throat slit. Don't know how late we'll be, more soon.

Dammit. Kara didn't know the girl, but had hoped the short window gave them the opportunity to find her alive.

She got into the car and hit Beau's address on the GPS. Fourteen minutes. Enough time to decompress so she could go back to Beau's war room and reassess the information with a clear head. She wanted to check if he had any surveillance photos to confirm the men she'd seen earlier were the Cormiers, plus learn more about Winnie.

Thinking through all of this, Kara wasn't really paying attention to the road. GPS was good like that—it directed you without you having to think much about it. She was on autopilot when the annoying computerized female voice said, "At the stop sign, turn left on North Memorial Boulevard."

She slowed, saw no cars on the two-lane road and turned left. The scenery changed from small houses and the occasional business to agricultural land. A pasture of cattle on the left, nothing on the right except barbed wire fencing.

Red and blue lights flared behind her. The cop hit his siren once.

Well, shit. How long had he been following her?

She pulled over immediately, hit Cancel on the dashboard GPS, then Cancel again to delete the address. She didn't want the cop to glance down and see her destination.

She hadn't been speeding—but had she missed a limit sign? Small towns often reduced speed along certain stretches as revenue enhancers. A way to make money on speeding tickets.

Well, maybe she was going a mile or two over the limit, but she had been cautious because of Beau's concerns about corrupt police.

She hadn't missed a stop sign, but had she made a rolling stop a mile back? Likely. She'd lived in California for the last twelve years; it was called a "California stop" for a reason.

Shit.

Just take the ticket and don't talk back.

He hadn't followed her from the Inn; she would have noticed, especially with her stop at the grocery. She didn't want to think that someone there called the cops on her. She wasn't drunk, but maybe they were suspicious. Which meant that they had given a description of her car to the cop.

She didn't want to reveal that she was a cop. That might blow Beau's investigation, since being incognito for as long as possible was an advantage.

Shit. Shit. Shit.

Wing it. What else could she do?

She rolled down her window as the officer approached, keeping her eyes on him and her hands visible. She'd worked plenty of traffic stops over the years, especially as a rookie, and she didn't want to give the cop any reason to get nervous.

"Good evening, ma'am. License and registration please."

"Of course. Can I ask what you pulled me over for?"

She looked at his nameplate. GUIDRY.

This was one of the cops Beau had flagged. Yeah, she didn't think this was a coincidence. Someone definitely called him from the Inn—possibly to find out who she was, where she came from, who she was visiting.

Stranger in town, have to check it out.

He didn't respond to her question. She said, "This is a rental car, not mine. The paperwork is in the glove box."

She reached over and opened the box, again debating whether to identify herself as law enforcement. She was *technically* still an LAPD detective and had an LAPD badge. That would go over better than the FBI.

She pulled out the rental agreement, then pulled her driver's license from her pocket. She still had her California license because she didn't have a permanent residence yet, and honestly, she didn't have the time or inclination to house hunt.

"California?"

"Yes, sir."

"And why are you in St. Augustine?"

"Vacation."

He looked at the rental agreement, turned the page. "This isn't your name on the agreement."

"No. I'm traveling with a friend."

"Michael Harris. Of Virginia?"

"Yes, sir."

"You're not authorized to drive this car."

"Well, technically, I didn't get put on the agreement, but that's really between me and the rental company." *Jerk.*

"Where are you staying?"

"A friend of Michael's."

"Can you please step out of the vehicle?"

"Why?"

"Just step out of the vehicle—" he looked at her license "—Ms. Quinn."

There was a sparkle in the cop's eyes, it was the only way she could describe it. He was enjoying his authority.

Asshole.

She stepped out.

Guidry was six feet tall, beefy and fit. He towered over her not-quite five-foot-four-inch frame, and by the way he crowded her, he was intentionally trying to intimidate her.

"Do you have any weapons on you?"

She almost asked, *Does it look like I have any weapons on me?* But didn't. She was wearing shorts and a tank top. Not a lot of places she could conceal anything. Except she had a knife.

"I have a knife in my pocket."

He raised an eyebrow. "Turn around."

She knew exactly what he was going to do.

"I can get it for you."

"You can turn around and comply with my lawful order."

She doubted there was anything lawful about this, but damn, she didn't know squat about Louisiana laws.

She turned around.

If she was any other scantily clad petite woman she would be terrified at this point. A truck passed them clearly speeding; Guidry didn't give it a second glance. But he said, "For your safety, please walk around to the passenger side of your vehicle and put your hands on the hood. Do not reach into your pockets or make any sudden movements."

She did what he ordered.

"Spread your legs."

She fumed, but complied. Yeah, she was pushing it, but she was going to nail him one way or the other, and the more she had, the better off she'd be when she had his ass fired. How far would he go? How much could she tolerate before she identified herself as a cop?

Would he even care?

He patted her down slowly. From this angle, if he had a dashboard camera it wouldn't capture his inappropriate manhandling, and he knew it. He ran his hands over her breasts—she wasn't wearing a bra, she didn't have big boobs so didn't really need a bra for support. She froze, ready to take him down, knowing she'd be in jail if she did. She was mindful of his weapons. He ran his hands over her hips, reached into her pockets, retrieved her knife with his right hand, pocketed it. Then he took his hands and ran them up and down her bare legs, all the way to her crotch.

"Tsk, tsk, a deadly weapon," he whispered into her ear. "I might just have to take you down to the station for a strip search." He ran his hand over her ass and squeezed, then laughed. "You'll like it, I promise."

"Take your hand off my ass or I will force you to eat your own dick."

She hadn't meant to sound so forceful, but when he put his hand between her legs, she flipped.

Fortunately, it worked and he stepped back.

She turned around, her cheeks red from anger, not embarrassment. She almost blurted out that she was a cop.

Almost.

He stared at her with narrowed, suspicious eyes.

Instead she crossed her arms over her chest and tried to look scared, or at least worried.

Nope, her anger was too deep. She forced herself to look down at his feet, hoping he'd think she was embarrassed, but her senses were attuned to any movement toward her. She didn't trust herself to say anything else, so remained silent.

He didn't seem to know what to do with her at that point. "Stay here. Don't move."

He took her license to his patrol vehicle and sat in the driver's seat. She didn't move.

She wasn't taking chances on walking around, but she didn't sit still well. Not in her makeup. So she bounced on her feet. She had to do something or she was going to blow.

Finally, ten minutes later he walked up to her, stood inches away. Stupid fool. If she was a bad guy, she could disarm him pretty damn easily. But he was focused on intimidating her, didn't see her as a threat.

"How long will you be in St. Augustine?" he asked.

She shrugged, averted her eyes. Damn, it was hard for her to pretend to be intimidated. Best just not look at him. She intentionally started nibbling at her thumbnail, then scratched behind her neck. A common habit among addicts. Let him think what he wanted.

"You don't know?"

"It ain't up to me."

She adopted a slight accent. Not Southern, but casual. Nothing that he would be able to pinpoint, but she didn't want him to look too closely at her, and keeping her dialect simple, clipped, would, she felt, speed this along.

"It's up to this…" he looked at the rental agreement "…*Michael Harris?*"

"Yep."

"Your boyfriend."

He wasn't asking a question, so she just shrugged, rubbed under her nose and sniffed.

He caught on real quick.

"Are you under the influence of any illegal substances?"

"No."

"How about we do a quick sobriety test, then, shall we?"

He hadn't asked if she'd been drinking, so that was interesting.

"I'm not drunk," she said clearly.

"I'll be the judge. See that white line on the side of the road? Walk it to my patrol car and then stop, turn around and face me."

That wasn't how you did a sobriety test, but she complied.

"Turn around twice."

She did.

"Now walk toward me."

Was he fucking kidding her? She couldn't wait to write this all out.

She complied.

"Stop," he commanded.

She stopped.

"Turn around, bend over and touch your toes."

"What the fuck?" It slipped out before she could stop herself.

"Do it," he said.

She did, now feeling humiliated, which was exactly what he wanted. She let the anger wash over her, then the calm.

Above all, be calm. Rational. Stay in control.

"Stand up, face me."

She did as instructed.

He handed back her license and the rental agreement. "Let's make this a short trip, Ms. Quinn. Here's your ticket. You ran the stop sign about a mile back, when you turned onto Memorial. Don't do it again."

She took the ticket, then held out her hand. "My knife."

He pulled it out of his pocket, looked at it. Opened it. "This is quite a nice-looking knife. Real nice." He held it right in her face. Her jaw clenched. "What's the magic word?"

She stared at him, didn't blink. "Please, Officer, may I have my knife?"

He snapped the knife closed inches from her face and smiled when she flinched. Then he reached around and put the knife into her back pocket. He let his hand linger inside her pocket for a second, then he pinched her so hard tears came to her eyes.

"Good girl," he said and stepped back. "Behave, Ms. Quinn. I will be watching you and Mr. Harris. I look forward to meeting him."

He walked back to his patrol and sped off.

She wanted to vomit. Instead, she got back in her car and drove straight to the Hebert property, plotting how she was going to take Officer Jerry Guidry down. She would enjoy every minute.

11

Kara offered to help with the dinner, but Toni waved her off. Beau had called to say he and Michael would be late, and Toni was putting aside a hearty portion for them. Beau told his grandmother that they'd found Ernestine's body, which left the woman melancholy. Kara chatted with her, trying to keep Toni's mind off the violence.

Michael texted her after she washed up.

A local team has been searching the area but haven't found any sign of Lily Baker's body. We found something interesting— more later.

Intriguing—and made her want to drive down to the river and help with the search. But if Michael needed her there, he would have asked her to come. Besides, it was getting dark and they wouldn't be able to search much longer.

She texted him back: Do they know you're FBI?

MICHAEL: Beau introduced me as his friend from the Navy. No one questioned.

Good, she thought.

She sat down at the kitchen table with Toni and ate the best soup—stew?—she'd ever had. She'd never had gumbo before, and Toni was pleased when she asked for seconds. They talked about a variety of things—Toni knew that Michael was an FBI agent, so Kara gave her some basic information about her own job. Toni shared stories that had Kara laughing.

She helped clean up the kitchen and then Toni said, "Now, Beau doesn't like when I have a little nightcap, but I think you might enjoy sharing a bourbon with me?"

"Yes I would," Kara said with a smile.

Toni smiled back. "Would you be a dear and get two high-ball glasses from the hutch in the dining room?"

The Hebert house was clean but cluttered. Toni had antiques and knickknacks all over the place, and the glass-enclosed hutch took up an entire wall. Old finished wood, filled with dishes and glasses. The piece was so huge that Kara suspected it had been built specifically for this wall.

All the cocktail glasses were on the far-right side, arranged tallest on the bottom to the shortest on the top shelf. Five shelves of drinking glasses, at least twelve of each, all different sizes, shapes and styles. She couldn't reach the top two shelves, and there was no stool for her to stand on. She considered pulling over one of the dining chairs, but that seemed rude.

She stood on her very tippy-toes and could just reach two

glasses on the third shelf. They were larger than what she'd consider a cocktail glass, but they'd have to do.

She brought them to the porch where Toni was sitting with a bowl of ice and a bottle of Southern Comfort.

Kara put the glasses down. "I couldn't reach the top two shelves," she said.

Toni chuckled. "These are just fine. They were given to me by my great-aunt in her will, along with a few other odds and ends. And her cat. I couldn't stand the cat and she knew it, but my Carl loved the fleabag. Used to feed it liver—fresh liver from the butcher!—on Sundays."

Toni dropped an ice cube in each glass and poured from the half-empty bottle, her hands shaking a bit. Kara resisted the urge to take over the chore. Toni seemed to be a woman who wanted to do things for herself, even when they became difficult with age. "I think Beau put my favorite glasses up high since he knows I can't climb my step stool anymore." She put the bottle down, leaned forward and whispered, though no one else was around. "For the future, the step stool is in the closet between the kitchen and the dining room."

"I look forward to our nightcaps."

Toni sipped the bourbon and leaned back. "Carl and I would sit out here near every evening after dinner, enjoy a drink and conversation. I feel him here, especially in the evenings when I get lonely. It helps."

Kara thought that was sweet, and she wondered what it might be like to spend her entire life with one person. She'd never expected to spend even a few years with someone, not with her lifestyle.

The sun was setting among the trees that lined the creek along the western boundary of the Hebert property. She tried to sip, but ended up drinking half in one long gulp. Bourbon wasn't her favorite, but this went down surprisingly smooth. "It's quiet. Beautiful." She paused as she heard crickets and frogs and another critter, she didn't care to know what it was. "Well, maybe not that quiet."

Toni laughed lightly. "I suppose it takes some getting used to for a city girl."

"I'm not really a city girl."

"You don't sit still."

"I get antsy." She sipped. "As a kid, we moved a lot. Now I have a place on the beach in Southern California. A tiny condo, but there's nothing like the sound of the ocean." Maybe that's why she hadn't been sleeping well. No ocean waves to lull her to sleep.

"Carl took me to Florida for our honeymoon. I didn't care to go on a honeymoon—all that money just to stay in a strange bed and eat out every night? But I fell in love with him even more when we walked on the beach and watched the sunrise in the mornings. He was a quiet man, and people thought him to be gruff, but there was no one more romantic than my Carl."

"You miss him."

She nodded, wistful. "I've known him my entire life. We went to school together. I was raised not two shakes of a lamb's tail from here. We married the day I turned eighteen—Carl was three months older. My pa would have approved of the marriage earlier, he thought Carl was a good man for his only daughter, but my ma was strict. Had to wait until we were eighteen." She smiled at the memory. "We had sixty-three years as man and wife. I'll see him again someday. Maybe this year, maybe next, maybe five. We have good genes in my family. My mother didn't pass until she was ninety-eight."

The woman sipped her drink. Kara had already finished hers and helped herself to another pour.

Toni had some similarities with her own grandmother—like the need to feed people—but Toni was more down-to-earth. Sharper. Kara's grandmother Em was an aging hippie who still smoked pot on a regular basis. She was sweet and kind and never watched the news because she didn't want to hear about anything sad or violent. While Beau was trying to protect Toni from the goings-on in St. Augustine, Kara suspected she knew everything there was to know about the murders and the missing women. Toni was smart. She might be a decade older than Kara's grandmother, but seemed to miss nothing.

"Beau said that you're staying out in the cabin, that Michael is staying in the house."

"I'm a night owl."

"Beau thinks I don't know what he's doing in there."

"Of course you do."

She nodded. "I let him do his thing, he's a good man. But these murders, poor girls, they're tearing him up."

"Did you know the victims?"

"Everyone knows Ernestine," Toni said. "Simple girl but sweet as pie. She used to work at Topp's, the grocery store, but a few years back she lost her job. I don't right know why. Her aunt—that woman—well, I can't say what I really think of her."

"I haven't heard anything positive."

"And you won't. I knew of the other girls, of course—knew their kin, at least. The Chaissons—two of the unfortunate girls were in the Chaisson family, and Helen is one of my closest friends, grandmother to Lettie, great-aunt to the other girl. We go to church together near every week. Helen can be a bit preachy, bless her heart, so she doesn't take to some of the antics of her kin. Her daughter did well, went to university, became a doctor and has been living in N'orlins near forty years now. But her son?" She shook her head. "Anyway, enough of that gossip. Nicki, I knew very well, bless her heart."

"Nicki LeBlanc?"

She nodded. "She was always looking for work. When she wasn't on those nasty drugs—I swear, Kara dear, drugs are the devil's doing, destroy so many good people."

Kara couldn't disagree with her. Might as well blame the devil.

"Nicki, though, she was always trying to stay clean and sober, and I wanted to help her. Her mother is a drunk, her father left when her little sister wasn't even out of diapers. And when Nicki came here to work around the house—I hired her a couple times a year to help me with some deep cleaning—she did a very good job. Hard worker, she was. She'd bring her sister with her, to keep her out of the path of her mother, I reckon. She'd give Winnie some chore, then give her a dollar for her help."

Winnie.

Winnie was related to one of the victims. Kara mulled that over in her head. She would have to think on how to approach her now that she had this information.

"Nicki had a kid, right?" Kara asked.

"I know it happens, but no father in the picture. Never did tell anyone who the daddy was to little Bonnie. She's four now, no mother, Loretta can't keep a job and has been on welfare for years. Claims disability—but I'm telling you, her disability would end if she stopped drinking." Toni cleared her throat, her lips pursed. "Now dear Winnie—only nineteen years old—supports the family, takes care of little Bonnie. I've hired Winnie from time to time, like I used to do with her sister, but the last few times I've called her, she's declined because of work. It hurts my heart to see her working two, three jobs in disreputable places because her mother is…" She cleared her throat and finished her bourbon, put the glass down.

Kara didn't know how—or if—she should ask Toni about how the town worked. Beau might get upset bringing his grandmother into the investigation, but she clearly knew a lot more than Beau thought she did. And she'd been here since the dawn of time, or close to it.

"Go ahead," Toni said. "I can see you have questions. Don't be shy."

"No one has ever accused me of being shy."

Toni laughed heartily. "Me, either."

Kara didn't want to overstep, and Toni, who might not truly understand the potential danger, could say something to someone. Tell her friend Helen who tells someone else and then the entire investigation gets blown out of the water.

"Let me tell you what I know, dear," Toni said. "I know my grandson believes that a police officer is involved in the murders of those poor girls."

She was surprised. "He told you that?"

"He thinks he's discreet, but he lives under my roof," she said with a chuckle. "I've picked up on things over the last few years. I may not know all the people involved, but I know what he's been doing. And I hear it in town—my friends think he'll solve these murders. Of course, they don't know who could do such a thing. They're divided between a serial killer like you see on the television, and one of the men who, well," she cleared her throat and whispered, "pays for sex."

"I really want to understand how St. Augustine works."

"I don't quite know what you mean."

"For example, how people fit into the community. Is there a mayor and how involved is he? Is there a nonelected town leader, like, a person or people everyone looks up to, respects? What they do and whether they would be likely to protect someone who commits a crime."

"Probably Philip Landry."

"Any relation to the sheriff?"

"Hmm—second cousin, no, third cousin, I believe."

"There are a lot of Landrys in town."

"Throw a stone, you'll hit a Landry. Philip was the mayor for a long time, thirty years—maybe longer." She looked up as if counting in her head. "I think he was first elected when that nice actor was president."

"And the mayor and council appoints the police chief."

"Yes. But Philip died a year before my Carl. When he died, I think our town was a little lost. He was…well, the glue, I guess you could say. A mediator. If two neighbors had a dispute, Philip Landry settled it, and all abided. Good man." She paused, then said, "His grandson, Peter Landry, was elected in a special election three years ago. He appointed the new police chief, the one my Beau doesn't care for."

"What does Peter do for a living?"

"I'm not right sure. Worked in the state capitol for a while, doing I don't know what, and then I believe he lived in N'orlins for a spell. He came back here, moved into his family home, one of the oldest in town, on the east side. Very stately. No wife or children." She cleared her throat as if she disapproved. "He might be a lawyer, but I could have that wrong. Insurance? Banking?" She shook her head. "I'm really not sure, but he seems to do well, because he bought a lot of property in town. Helen told me he bought every building on Canning Street."

"I don't know where that is."

"Old businesses, half of them were closed. Still are. We all thought he might renovate things, to bring in tourists and help the town. But they sit there. Oh, and he owns a restaurant in town, The Broiler, a very classy place. Too expensive—Carl took me there, bless his heart, for my birthday shortly after it opened eight years ago. Forty dollars—*forty!*—for a steak. I wanted to leave, but Carl said I was worth it. No one is worth a forty-dollar steak when I can cook us up a better steak dinner for ten bucks with all the fixin's. That's neither here nor there. I would have probably enjoyed the steak more if I didn't see the price. Fortunately, Carl agreed that we would split it, neither of us had the appetites as we did when we were young."

Kara loved this woman. She said what she thought.

"So he bought businesses and a restaurant. Anything else?"

"Not that I know of. He isn't as involved in town affairs as his grandfather had been. There wasn't a town event that dear

Philip missed, but Peter can't be bothered. He *occasionally* shows up but never stays long."

"You don't like him."

"I don't really know him, so I don't have an opinion."

That was untrue, but Kara didn't correct her.

Toni turned her head as lights glowed at the end of her long driveway.

"Be a dear and put this bottle in the cabinet next to the refrigerator?" Toni pushed the Southern Comfort over toward Kara.

"I'll do you one better," Kara said as she got up. "I'll wash the glasses and put them away."

Toni beamed. "I knew I liked you."

12

Toni insisted that Beau and Michael shower and eat before going across the yard to the cabin to work. An hour later it was completely dark, Toni had gone up to her room, and Beau told Kara what they'd found at Lantern Gate.

He was clearly upset. "She was in over her head," he said. "I have no idea what 'mistake' she made or who she talked to, but dammit!"

He slammed his fist on the kitchen counter then opened the refrigerator and grabbed a couple of beers. "Michael?" he said.

Michael shook his head and said, "I'll take a water."

Beau handed Michael water and Kara beer. She opened it, drank, then said, "Her throat was slit?"

"I'm pushing for an autopsy, but half the time Brown just looks and says, yep, slit throat is cause of death, no need to do more. He'll run tox screens and whatnot, but I doubt he does an actual autopsy. And the chief gave the case to a different detective!"

"Jim will be here tomorrow," Michael said. "He can assist."

"No way Brown is going to let an outsider in," Beau said.

"What about evidence?" Kara said. "Clothing, shoes, hair and fiber."

"Evidence has a funny way of disappearing in St. Augustine."

"More reason to have Jim review," Michael said.

"They're not going to let the FBI review anything!"

Kara watched Beau grow agitated and angry. She felt for him, but at the same time, complaining wouldn't get them anywhere. They needed an action plan.

"They aren't going to have a choice." Michael said what Kara was thinking. "Matt is on his way, and he's going to do whatever needs to be done."

"I don't think you understand, Michael," Beau snapped. "Your boss comes in, lays claim, it's just gonna be a couple calls and then wham, you'll be pulled off and I'll be stuck here with a killer who got away with murder."

"Trust us."

"I see what you're saying, Beau," Kara said. "The FBI doesn't usually investigate homicides. I pushed back and won more than half the time when the FBI wanted to take over one of my cases in LA."

"Louisiana is different. I don't know how to explain, but New Orleans FBI steers clear. They've had their hand bit too many times when they come into any of our communities and get next to nothing to show for it." Beau got up and grabbed a second beer. "I can't shake the feeling that the killer knew what Jean Paul said and killed Ernestine there to fuck with me. They must have known I'd inspect the area, and they *wanted* me to find her body."

It was a distinct possibility, Kara thought. She said, "Based on the other crime scene photos, none of the victims were hidden. Their bodies were found no more than five days after their deaths. This tells me that Lily's body was concealed, perhaps weighted down or left far from a road."

"If her body's in the river, there's nothing left," Beau said. "Bones scatter. The water is warm, there is a lot of fish activity, gators. We wouldn't find anything after four months."

"We could look for the skull, bones, run DNA on them," Michael said.

"Assuming that the killer intentionally weighed down Lily's body in the river," Kara said, "tells me that something about her death was different."

Michael nodded. "Evidence the killer wanted destroyed."

"What interesting thing did you find?" Kara prompted Michael, remembering his earlier text.

He glanced at his phone. "Matt's calling. He's going to want a debrief, and he needs to hear this, too."

He put Matt on speaker. "Matt, I also have Kara and Detective Beau Hebert here."

"Hello," Matt said. "Ryder and I are meeting with the SSA in the Lafayette Resident Agency at eight thirty in the morning—we're taking the earliest flight out. Jim's still driving, but should be down in a few hours. He'll stay in Lafayette tonight, then Ryder has a room for him—and you, if either of you need it—at a hotel in St. Augustine, north of the interstate."

"Did you read my memo on the body we recovered?" Michael asked.

"Yes. Anything new?"

"Autopsy tomorrow, though Beau thinks they might skip it because cause of death appears obvious. We're discussing the pros and cons of asking Jim to assist."

"They would be fools not to take our help," Matt said, "but I recognize that some places don't like federal assistance, and the FBI rarely comes in uninvited. However, I'm going to make the case to the local office that we need to look into the in-custody death of Jean Paul LeBlanc, and considering that the remains of a young woman were found today, I feel confident I can convince the police chief to at least let us help."

"With all due respect, Matt," Beau said, "no one in St. Augustine has to do anything for the FBI. You can be as sweet as honey and just as sweet they'll tell you to pound sand. Even if the town wasn't corrupt, they would still give you the cold shoulder."

"I'm aware that the situation is delicate, which is why I'm asking for a local agent to accompany our team. Smooth things over."

Beau seemed skeptical, but didn't argue.

Matt said, "You have six dead women, one missing, and an in-custody death of a man who may have known something about these crimes. We have cause."

"Sir," Beau said, "I didn't put in my report that Jean Paul talked to me about Tanya Ewing or Lily Baker. I didn't want anyone to know, because he feared for his life. And he's dead anyway."

"Once I talk to the local office, I'll have more insight and a clear plan. My boss is giving me a lot of autonomy on this, and I'm going to take it. If NOLA tries to shut me down, they're going to be in for a rude awakening."

"Michael, what else did you find?" Kara said, reminding Michael that he had been about to tell her something before Matt called.

"Before the authorities arrived at the river, Beau and I scoured the shore, looking for evidence. We found something, bagged it for Jim to analyze. It's a key attached to a rabbit's foot. Could have nothing to do with anything, but it wasn't far from the gate—the narrow part of the river where we found Ernestine's body—and it had been there for some time. Tangled in brush and sticks."

Beau said, "I'm going to talk to Lily's family, show them a photo of the key chain. It could belong to anyone, that place is a popular fishing hole, but considering what Jean Paul said, I have to wonder."

"Where's the evidence now?"

"Secured," Michael said. "I will personally deliver it to Jim tomorrow, to maintain chain of custody. Also, I'm going diving as soon as possible."

Kara's stomach rolled. "You can't go in the river, there are alligators!"

Beau shook his head at her, smiling. She was not humored. "It's not like they're fish swimming around. I examined the area, no sign of gators. But I'll check it all out again before I let my best buddy go down there."

"I don't know the terrain well, but I'd imagine the bones would be scattered and buried in the muck," Matt said,

"It's not going to be easy," Michael agreed, "and I won't be able to do it until Tuesday morning. I need your approval to have my equipment sent down from DC."

Matt asked, "Beau, how certain are you that your informant was telling the truth?"

"More certain than not," Beau said.

Michael said, "Even if we don't find her remains, there may be a rope or something that was used to hold her down. I know I'm grasping at straws, but I think this is important, and there has to be a reason that her body hasn't been found—possibly leading to evidence against the killer."

"Write it up, email it to Ryder, and he'll take care of it." Matt then said, "Kara, you said you were checking things out in town. Learn anything?"

Kara told them where she went and what she did, and how she

thought Winnie LeBlanc might have more information relative to the victims. "Is she a relative of Jean Paul?" she asked Beau.

"Cousin."

"Everyone is a cousin," she said.

"Yep," Beau said in all seriousness. "But they were closer kin than most. Winnie works at the Inn part-time, housekeeping. She's a good kid, sober, doesn't get in trouble. But her sister used to work there, and not as a housekeeper. I think Crystal feels sorry for Winnie—she's helping to raise her orphaned niece—so hires her for odd jobs that don't involve sex."

"Winnie didn't want to talk to me, but I'm going to work on her. I got the sense that she's observant. Plus, she was asking about Ernestine. I need time—she's prickly and distrustful."

"Tread carefully," Beau said. "Ginny and Ernestine—the last two victims—talked to me, and now they're both dead."

"It's not your fault," Michael said. They'd clearly talked about this before.

"Yeah, it is. I'll deal with it. What else, Kara?" he said, in an obvious shift to avoid talking about his misplaced guilt. "Did you check out The Fat Catfish?"

"I drove by, decided not to go in—if the two places are as connected as you think, I didn't want to be tagged as going to both the same afternoon. I'll check it out tomorrow. But I did get pulled over. Officer Guidry."

"So they know I brought in the feds. Shit."

"No," she corrected, "I didn't tell him I was a cop, and I'm *not* a fed. Plus, I didn't look like a cop, I was dressed for the Magnolia."

"If you were dressed that casual, he definitely wouldn't be thinking cop," Michael said.

She wrinkled her nose at him. "Hey, I have to blend in, right? And when do I get to show off my tattoo?"

"Kara," Matt said sternly over the phone, "report."

Matt had, of course, seen her tattoo. He liked it. She might have to remind him of that if she ever talked to him again about their personal life, because she was still angry about the Catherine situation.

"He gave me a ticket for running a stop sign," she said, "and he saw that the rental agreement on the car was made out to Michael. So word will probably get around pretty quick, just to give you a heads-up. And for the record, he's an asshole and I will nail him."

Her ass still hurt from where he'd pinched her.

"No one asked my name," Michael said, "so we're probably okay for a day or two."

"Did you run the stop sign, Kara?" Matt asked.

"I might have made a California stop, but…" She hesitated. She didn't quite know how to tell Matt about what happened, because there was nothing he or anyone could do about it. Yet she couldn't keep it to herself, because it might be relevant to their larger investigation.

"But what?" Michael said.

Clearly, she hadn't maintained her poker face, and Michael was eyeing her closely.

"I was going to write it up in my report tonight," she said lightly. "No big. In a nutshell? He was very handsy. I have a bruise on my ass from where he pinched me."

"He touched you?" Michael said, incredulous.

"He frisked me. We'll just say he made doubly sure I didn't have any contraband on me."

"God, I'm sorry," Beau said. "You should have told him you're a cop, there's no excuse."

"If he did that to me, he did it to others. Or worse. And no one has complained?"

"There've been complaints, but they don't go anywhere."

"They will go somewhere this time," Matt said over the speaker, his voice low and angry.

"I'll write it up, but let's hold off doing anything with it," Kara said. "We have more important things to focus on."

"We'll discuss this when I get there tomorrow," Matt said.

He wasn't going to let it go. "Whatever floats your boat, boss," she said. "One more thing. In my research today I was looking into how the police chief is appointed. He's nominated by the mayor and voted in by the town council. Unlike the sheriff of the parish, who's elected."

"Correct," Beau concurred.

"I want to dig into Peter Landry," she said. "He filled the mayor position after the sitting mayor—his grandfather—died. And he's the one who appointed Dubois. Dubois hired Guidry and half the force, getting rid of three cops who apparently had filed complaints against Dubois when he was an officer."

"How'd you learn that?" Beau asked.

"Your files. You have a shit ton of information here." She hadn't learned about Landry from the files, but decided not to mention that she'd talked to Toni. Beau might not be happy involving his grandmother, even just in conversation. "The girls weren't killed until after Peter Landry became mayor and appointed Dubois. So Dubois is a bad cop, gets promoted to police chief, fires the cops who complained about him and puts in his own people, including the asshole Guidry. Guidry came from Lake Pierre, which is barely a speck on the map."

Kara took a sip of beer, continued, "And then I was thinking, the guy you mentioned earlier, who'd been at the Magnolia the same day that two of the girls went missing—he was killed at his home in Lake Pierre for dealing drugs. And Guidry is from there...so maybe there's more to Palfrey than his drug-dealing lifestyle. Maybe there's a connection to Guidry."

"Was this Palfrey a suspect in the deaths of any of the girls?" Matt asked.

Beau said, "He was at the Magnolia on the nights that two of the first three victims disappeared, and was a regular john of the first victim. I had been looking at him for drug distribution, but couldn't build a case sufficient for the DA. I thought he was our guy, but he was killed in a drug raid before the fourth victim."

"Maybe," Michael said, "the recent murders are separate from the first three."

"Anything is possible," Beau said, though he didn't sound like he agreed.

"Beau has a lot of information in his files," Kara said, waving her arm toward the stack on the desk. "It's clear that these girls were killed by someone they knew. Prostitutes usually have solid instincts about potential dangers. They had the security of the Magnolia, the brothel, they didn't have to walk the streets. So why go off with a stranger? And four of them—if we include Ernestine's call to Beau the night she disappeared—expressed concern or fear that something was going to happen to them. Several witnesses told Beau that previous victims said something fatalistic in the weeks before their murders. That tells me that either someone threatened them, or they sensed someone following them, watching them. Angered the wrong person and knew that person had been responsible for other deaths. I don't know, but it's something to start with."

"If they all saw something specific, why three years between murders? Why not kill them all at the same time?" Matt questioned.

"That's the million-dollar question," she said. "Maybe it wasn't any *one* thing, but a series of events. Or they were all killed for different reasons. Ernestine was the only girl who wasn't an addict or a prostitute, and she knew all the victims. In fact, *all* the victims knew each other."

"Interesting point," Matt said. "It's getting late and I have an early flight. Kara, send me the names you need researched and as much information as you have, and I'll have Zack start looking at the finances and running background checks. Beau,

I know you are in a difficult position, but you called Michael, and you need help. Can we count on you?"

"Yes," Beau said. "When I first called Michael I expected to bounce ideas off him. I didn't realize how quickly y'all would jump. I'm afraid people are going to clam up."

"Like they were chatty before?" Kara said. She leaned over and put her hand on Beau's arm. "I get it, but if we don't find who's responsible for these murders, more women are going to die. You *know* that."

When Matt ended his call, Beau said to Kara, "I'm so sorry about Guidry and what he did—are you okay?"

"I'm fine. He was intentionally trying to humiliate me and when I told him if he touched me again I'd cut off his dick, he gave me a field sobriety test. But it taught me something. He's cocky and arrogant, and those are the men who make mistakes. He's going to learn I'm a cop in the next couple days, and I'm going to enjoy watching him squirm."

MONDAY

13

Kara fell asleep at two in the morning listening to crickets and frogs so loud she thought they were in the bedroom with her. She woke up at 6:10 to a rooster who sounded like he was cursing the sun for rising.

She didn't know whether to thank him for being her alarm clock, or shoot him for being so obnoxious.

She showered, drank a full water bottle with three aspirin—she knew better than to mix bourbon and beer—then toasted half-stale bread from Beau's meager supply of food. She made instant coffee in the microwave and grimaced at the taste. Toni was making breakfast in the main house, but she felt odd having the old woman wait on her. She needed to get over it—Beau said that his grandmother enjoyed company and loved feeding people. But Kara was a loner and sometimes small talk made her antsy.

She ate the toast with jam—homemade, by the looks of the mason jar and label with "Peach" written in shaky, but perfectly slanted cursive. The jam made the mediocre bread taste like heaven, so she toasted a second slice and walked around the living room, eyeing the work she'd done last night after the boys went back to the house.

She'd reorganized Beau's whiteboard so that instead of the photos of the dead going across the top, she put them in a far-left column. Across the top of the board she'd created columns so she could visualize each victim's last days.

After talking to Beau about the incompetent—or corrupt—coroner, she wasn't certain that time of death was accurate, but if it was close, all the women were killed within hours of last being seen.

She then put the map Beau had marked up on the far right of the board. He'd identified each key location, but she needed more. She stared at the marks, frowned, tilted her head.

No body was found more than ten miles from where they were last seen.

She wanted to see for herself where each of the victims had been found. She had crime scene photos of each body, but no scenery, no context.

Kara pushed aside her anger at what was done to these women—not just their deaths, not just how they'd been tossed away, but how they'd been treated in life. If she let the anger control her, she'd miss something.

There was time enough for rage later.

She turned to the next file—witness statements. The statements weren't thin, but they had little substance. Beau had done extensive work tracing the last weeks of each victim, but the picture that emerged was still fuzzy. A lot of *I heard* and very little *I saw*.

But one thing immediately emerged as she charted the witness sightings.

A half dozen people were identified as having seen Lettie Chaisson the night she disappeared, including Lily, Hannah and Ginny—all victims. Another witness was familiar—Bud Ewing. Bud and Buddy? She looked through notes—Bud Ewing was the third victim's brother. He died of a drug overdose four months after Tanya was killed.

Buddy Palfrey, the drug dealer who was killed in a police raid, died the same month as Bud Ewing. Were they friends? Enemies? She made a note to ask Beau about this because it seemed too coincidental. Both Bud and Buddy had seen the first victim the last day she was alive. Both died the same month.

Hannah Silar had not only seen Lettie the night she disappeared, but Nicki LeBlanc as well.

Tanya Ewing also saw Nicki.

Jean Paul LeBlanc had seen Tanya at The Catfish the night she disappeared.

And Ernestine had seen Nicki, Hannah and Lily the night *they* disappeared.

Witnesses became victims.

Had Beau noticed this? Had he thought it was odd? Yes, it was a small town, and yes the women all had reason to know each other because they ran in the same circles, but *damn* this was strange to Kara. Were there others who fell into the same pattern?

She continued putting names on the board.

Crystal Landry—she'd seen Hannah at the Magnolia, but didn't know when she left.

Jake West had seen all the girls at the Magnolia the last night they were alive. Now Jake was dead.

Jasper Steele, the night manager and part owner of the Magnolia, had seen three of the girls the night they disappeared.

She flipped through notes. Beau had written:

Why wasn't Johnny Baxter working the nights Tanya and Hannah disappeared?

She had no idea who Johnny Baxter was, but both those girls had been last seen at The Fat Catfish, and another note said that Elijah Morel was the bouncer and had covered the bar. What had he seen, if anything?

Lots of names. Lots of possibilities. But one thing was clear: all the victims knew each other; all the suspects knew the other suspects as well as the victims, and she was beginning to think there was more to learn about Bud Ewing's and Buddy Palfrey's deaths.

Michael walked in. He looked at the whiteboard Kara had reworked. "Did you even sleep?"

"Over four hours. Didn't think I could close my eyes with the damn crickets and frogs, but then went out cold."

Michael looked over her information. "Wow."

"Wow what?"

"Where'd you get all this?"

"Beau, but it wasn't organized. He probably has it all in his head."

She took a picture of the board in case Beau—or someone else—came in and messed up her organization. "I'm going to The Fat Catfish." She smiled. She loved the name but driving by yesterday it didn't look all that exciting.

"A dive bar at eight thirty in the morning? I don't care how good you are at blending, you'll stick out."

"First, I'm going to drive out to the body dumps, take pictures, look at the area. It's clear from the map that they were convenient to both the Magnolia and the bar—straight south out of town, turn right or left, but maybe I'll see something that's not evident in the crime scene photos. Which suck. There's only *one* from Tanya's murder. Just her body. If Beau hadn't written down the location I'd have no idea where it was. Join me?"

"I'm meeting with Jim later this morning, and Matt's heading to Lafayette FBI. He'll want to meet up—either before or after he talks to the police chief."

"Can I take the car?"

He nodded. "I'll get a ride downtown with Beau when he gets back."

"Where is Beau?" she asked.

"He went to question Lily's family about the rabbit's foot. Maybe it'll lead somewhere."

"We need all the luck we can get."

She took the keys from Michael.

He said, "Keep your location on, in case. If Guidry pulls you over again, tell him you're a cop. Show him your badge. Call me, call Matt, but don't put yourself in a potentially danger-ous position."

She frowned.

"Hey—it's coming from Matt. But I agree with him. We have no idea if Guidry is a killer or an accessory, but he *is* involved. Check in regularly, and I'll get Matt down here to look at your board. It's *really* good. I think we're going to solve this."

She was glad he liked her presentation, but she thought they were a long, long way from solving these murders.

14

Special Agent in Charge Mathias "Matt" Costa walked into the Lafayette Resident Agency of the New Orleans FBI at 8:20 that morning. The office was on the seventh floor of an eight-story building that housed a hodgepodge of white-collar businesses with a bank taking up the bottom two floors and a dental office on the top.

Matt had run a resident agency for several years in Tucson, Arizona. They were smaller than regional offices with anywhere from two to twelve agents and a couple civilian staff members or analysts. Under the umbrella of a larger agency—in Lafayette's case, New Orleans—they focused on a smaller jurisdiction with varying degrees of autonomy.

Matt had brought analyst Ryder Kim and Dr. Jim Esteban to the meeting with him. Jim was the former director of the Dallas PD crime lab and a sharp forensic scientist. He was thrilled that they finally had the mobile lab up and running. This was the first time they might have a chance to use it.

Danville didn't keep them waiting, even though Matt was early. "Coffee? Water?"

"No, thank you," Matt said after introducing himself, Ryder and Jim.

"You sure you don't want any coffee? It's early, and I know your flight must have left DC before dawn."

"Actually, coffee would be welcome," Jim said.

"Water for me, thank you," Ryder said.

Matt had already had so much coffee he was swimming in it, but accepted a water. He said, "I appreciate you making the time for us on such short notice."

"When headquarters calls..." Danville said with a half smile.

Curt Danville was in his late thirties, tall and skinny, with a baby face, thick head of prematurely gray hair, and clear blue eyes. He motioned for them to sit at a small table in his office, then stepped out for a minute before returning with a tray of coffee and water bottles. A tall, slender woman in a crisp, lightweight suit followed. Her long blond hair was pulled back into a tight ponytail that fell nearly to her waist.

"Gentlemen, I asked Agent Savannah Trahan to join us. She has the best insight for this situation. We don't have a large office here—six agents, one analyst and one admin. Other than me, Trahan has been here the longest, plus she's originally from Lake Charles, a city not too far from St. Augustine."

"Terrific," Matt said. He had wanted someone with local insight.

Danville said, "I know a bit about why you're here, Agent Costa, though surprised to learn that national headquarters was interested in a small-town case."

"I'm Matt, no formalities. I'm hoping we'll be able to establish a good working relationship."

Curt nodded. "NOLA said you were looking into an in-custody death in St. Augustine."

"Among other things." Matt opened his file, though he had memorized the details. "Jean Paul LeBlanc—arrested for the murder of Jake West, a bartender at Magnolia Inn. Are you familiar?"

"I pulled his file this morning," Curt said, sliding it over to Savannah.

"This is the third in-custody death in the last two years in Broussard Parish, and the second in St. Augustine," Matt continued.

Savannah said, "This is a suspected suicide, correct?"

"Unclear—without an autopsy, I don't know that they can determine suicide or accidental drug overdose. But one concern is how he obtained drugs while in the jail."

"How'd y'all hear about it so fast?"

Savannah had a slight Southern accent, but had either spent a lot of time outside the South, or had worked hard to soften it.

"We were contacted by a local officer who stated that Le-Blanc's death seemed suspicious to him, based on information he obtained from the suspect at the time of arrest."

"A St. Augustine officer? Who?"

"This has to stay in-house. He's willing to work with us, but if the chief knows he's talking, he could be suspended. We want him in play as long as possible."

"Of course," Curt agreed.

"Detective Beau Hebert."

"Hebert? I know him," Savannah said. "Not well, he's only been there a few years, if I recall."

Curt said, "Generally, in a case like this, we let the local jurisdiction handle it. To be honest, working in a federal office in Louisiana is very different than federal offices in other states."

"I'm aware," Matt said, "but Detective Hebert has made some serious accusations about possible corruption in the police force, including murder, and we're closely working with him to find evidence in order to open a full investigation."

"Why didn't he come to me?" Curt asked.

"Beau and one of my team members were in the Navy together. He reached out for advice, and I made the decision to come down. You're my first stop."

"I appreciate that," Curt said.

"Before we open a full investigation, we need to assess Hebert's information for ourselves, but I'm happy to share as much as I know with you."

"Thank you," Curt said, "but I don't think you really understand our precarious situation. I've run two major operations in the parish neighboring Broussard. We get no help from the local police. What makes this situation different?"

"Detective Hebert made a compelling case that he believes that Mr. LeBlanc may have been murdered because of information he knows about Lily Baker, who has been missing since April."

Matt laid out everything he knew—what LeBlanc said to Hebert, Ernestine Bergeron's status as confidential informant, her disappearance and subsequent murder.

"And you think that Ms. Bergeron's murder is connected?" Savannah asked. "But she's not a prostitute or addict, correct?" She glanced down at the notes she'd been taking while Matt spoke.

"Beau thinks she's connected because she knew the other victims," Matt said. "In fact, all the victims knew each other."

"Circumstantial," Curt said, "but I can see why Detective Hebert is running with the theory."

Matt was pleased that Curt sounded interested. "I need your assistance and expertise. I had hoped to simply go into town and ask for the records of Mr. LeBlanc's arrest and alleged suicide, but in light of the most recent victim, I'd like to offer more.

Jim ran the crime lab in Dallas for years. We have a mobile lab with more capabilities than most small towns. I feel we can at a minimum determine whether LeBlanc committed suicide as well as gather evidence from Bergeron's body. Hopefully that, when combined with evidence from the other victims, will lead to a suspect."

Savannah said, "The preliminary report states that Mr. Le-Blanc injected himself with heroin. A drug addict generally knows his limits, which is why the police believe it was an intentional overdose—suicide."

"Yet, someone gave him the drugs," Curt said. "A visitor, a cop?"

"If an employee of St. Augustine gave him the drugs, that person needs to be held accountable," Matt said. "If it was a lapse in protocol, we can offer security suggestions, without stepping on anyone's toes."

"I've been an agent for sixteen years and have never seen the FBI act so fast if there wasn't an immediate threat," Curt said.

"Like I said," Matt replied, "Detective Hebert made a compelling case. Bergeron had called him concerned about her safety and then went missing. The same night, LeBlanc died while in custody. Bergeron was a witness to the Jake West homicide, and it just seems to be too coincidental that she witnesses a murder, the alleged killer commits suicide, then Ernestine disappears and is found dead less than forty-eight hours later."

Matt let that sink in, then added, "My boss wants me to give him an assessment—do we need a larger investigation, should our team be involved, or should the national office direct NOLA to establish a task force."

"What do you need from us?" Curt asked.

"My ideal situation is to have active assistance from your office. A desk here, if you have the space, for Ryder and me to work for the duration of our investigation. An agent, like Savannah, who has deep knowledge of the community and can help us navigate what I recognize are difficult waters. If you don't have the resources, at a minimum, your backup should we need it once we gather more information."

"Savannah, do you think Tom can finish the Norwich case alone?"

"Sure, it's just a matter of paperwork at this point. You want me on this?"

"If you can. I don't want to take away from anything active, but I suppose a day or three to assist Matt's team would be possible?"

"I can do that," Savannah said. "I should tell you, Matt, they know me in Broussard Parish, so if you're wanting to go incognito, I'm not the right person."

"That's all right. I plan to state my case to the chief of police and ask for their cooperation."

"They don't like outsiders, and while I don't agree with their position, I understand. Whenever the federal government gets involved in local issues, they tend to cause more problems than they fix. There's a lot of bad blood between the FBI and other agencies and the local authorities, and not just in law enforcement. Hurricane relief and assistance has been a sore spot for decades, as one example."

"And that's exactly why I need someone like you with me. To help smooth things over."

"I'll do what I can, but I'm not sure even my Cajun roots are going to be enough to open the door."

He smiled. "We can try."

Curt settled Ryder into a vacant office and gave him a temporary key card. He also offered a guest room in his own home for the rookie analyst, which Matt appreciated and hoped bode well for the entire operation. But Ryder already had reserved rooms in a local hotel for the team, both in Lafayette and in St. Augustine. Matt wasn't certain how long Michael and Kara would be staying at Beau's house, but he agreed with Michael that they should remain in town.

While most of their decisions thus far were based on Michael Harris vouching for Beau Hebert, Matt trusted Michael's judgment. Michael's ethics were second to none. He had more commendations in his six years in the Detroit office than most agents had during their entire career. His reputation during his years in the FBI had him on the fast track to promotion, but Michael had indicated during his first assessment interview that he wasn't interested in leadership, he wanted to be in the field. His skill set was in high-demand, including munitions expertise, search and water rescue, and a number one ranking in firearms.

So Matt trusted Beau Hebert because Michael trusted Beau Hebert. Still, it was a potentially dicey situation that could cause problems for both the local FBI and national headquarters if their investigation yielded accusations without proof. The federal government couldn't imply, without evidence, that a local law enforcement agency was corrupt. If that got out in the press, the ripple effect would cause untold problems with future investigations all over the country, so Matt had to tread very carefully.

When they were done meeting, Jim left in the mobile crime lab to meet with Michael in St. Augustine while he waited for Matt's call that he had the green light to work with the local police.

Matt left the rental car with Ryder, and Savannah drove him to St. Augustine, which was thirty minutes west of Lafayette along Interstate 10. He had his bag with him because he hadn't decided whether to stay in St. Augustine or return to Lafayette.

He wanted to talk to Kara one-on-one, but she'd been prickly lately and he thought maybe he needed to give her a little space. He understood better than anyone that Kara was a private person and that she was still struggling with leaving Los Angeles. But they'd had a good thing going the last couple months. They'd come to an understanding after their last case on how they were going to manage their relationship, and it was working…then all of the sudden this last week she'd avoided him. She had a lot on her plate—finding a place to live, for example. He had wondered if she wasn't looking all that hard because she planned to return to LA after she testified. Unfortunately, he doubted that was an option—at least, not in the capacity she wanted.

He put that aside. In all honesty, he was more concerned that she'd caught the attention of a potential murder suspect…and if Officer Jerry Guidry wasn't a killer, he was definitely a bad cop.

"What else do you have?" Savannah asked. "Other than the word of a dead murder suspect and drug addict."

"This is Detective Hebert's investigation, I'd rather you get the details directly from him, so I don't get anything wrong."

Savannah was silent for a moment, then said, "Word of advice? Lose the formality. You're going to rub everyone the wrong way if you come in with airs and government authority. You want answers? Listen."

"I trust your judgment."

"So is this Michael Harris, friend of Beau's, here as well?"

"He flew down yesterday morning with a colleague." Kara had been excited about the assignment. It was only the four of them here in the field, plus Ryder in the office. Zack Heller and Catherine Jones were staying in DC. Matt was still looking for at least one more field agent for his team. He'd had three interviews scheduled this week, which were now postponed.

"So there's going to be what? Two, four—five including me—federal agents in St. Augustine, a town of less than ten thousand people?" She laughed. "No, we're not going to stick out."

Matt could see her point. "Michael and Kara aren't on-site officially. As far as the authorities are concerned, it's you, me and Jim."

"Hmm."

"You still don't think they'll cooperate."

"They'll be polite, then do everything possible to get you to leave quickly. Just remember—everything slows down in the South. Just because they don't operate at warp speed doesn't mean they're thwarting your investigation. And they won't take kindly to being rushed, especially since you're a Yankee."

"I'm from Miami, I'm hardly a Yankee."

She laughed. "You're one now. Remove the tie, loosen up a bit."

He immediately took off his tie. He didn't particularly like wearing them, anyway, but being in a suit commanded authority, something important in his position. He unbuttoned his top button.

She glanced over at him and smiled. "Better."

"Curt said you were local?"

"Lake Charles, about forty minutes west of St. Augustine. I left for college half my life ago—Texas. Didn't end up back in Louisiana until four years ago."

"What office were you in before?"

"Atlanta for two years, then Louisville, Kentucky, for four. But I asked to be assigned here. My dad had a heart attack, then my parents' house flooded, and I was going through a divorce—I wanted to be closer to family. Did a year in NOLA, then took the first opening they had in Lafayette."

"Are you aware of Detective Hebert's concerns about local law enforcement and corruption?"

She laughed, which Matt thought was an odd reaction to his question.

"I certainly wouldn't be surprised, though we don't have an open investigation into anyone in St. Augustine. Before I arrived, Curt was involved in an investigation in the neighboring parish. Corrupt sheriff. Over a year of interviews, reviewing records, coming up with a halfway decent case against him for bribery, ethics and campaign finance violations, among other things—and it went nowhere."

"Not enough evidence?"

"I don't know the details—talk to Curt. But the lawyers tossed the case and declined to prosecute and NOLA got slapped for harassment and running a fishing expedition. A couple people went to jail for minor infractions. Curt wasn't in charge then. His boss was promoted to be the ASAC of Houston. He would know details."

Matt made a note. It would definitely be worth talking to Curt and possibly to his former boss to find out what happened then and what they felt should have been done differently.

"We avoid the small towns unless we're specifically asked to assist," Savannah continued. "Most of my cases in the last two years have been related to the hurricane and flooding. I just wrapped up a yearlong investigation into a graft and corruption scheme involving an inspector in Lake Charles taking kickbacks and approving faulty construction. A lot of work done after Katrina wasn't to code and Ida revealed it. It was quite satisfying to arrest that bastard *and* shut down the construction company that paid him."

The FBI handled a wide range of cases, but a substantial number of them were white-collar and public corruption. Matt had never been drawn to that type of assignment—it was a lot of desk work and he preferred to be out in the field. But he could relate to being satisfied when you could prove that someone violated their duty for greed.

"Congratulations."

"Thank you," she said. "This situation in St. Augustine isn't the same thing."

"Beau is concerned about some of the cops the new police chief brought in."

"No one has filed a complaint, not even Beau. And even if he did, without evidence, are we supposed to go in and accuse a local cop of murder? See how fast you're run out of town. Even opening an investigation would be problematic."

"But it's possible."

"Anything's possible."

"It seems to me that this is a situation where the FBI *should* open an investigation."

"There have been no accusations about a specific cop suspected of killing a prostitute. No eyewitness on record. No physical evidence. No one willing to talk. Are you telling me that your team just goes into a town and starts investigating because of an unsubstantiated rumor?"

Matt understood where she was coming from, but he said, "The history of corruption in Louisiana—small towns all the way to the state house—is legendary."

"I'm not saying every parish is squeaky clean, but we pick our battles. We have made in-roads in gaining the trust of local law enforcement, but we don't interfere in their local affairs. If we did, we'd be completely ostracized and it would take decades to regain the small amount of trust we've built."

"I'd think six dead women and one still missing is a battle to pick."

Silence. He glanced over; her jaw was tense. He had angered her, he supposed, but someone needed to be angry about the dead.

"Do you have a plan?" Savannah asked after several minutes.

"Yes. I'm going to talk to the chief of police and be polite and cordial and like you suggested, not rush anything. I also have a carrot to dangle."

"What sort of carrot?"

"Money. Every local jurisdiction is strapped for cash. One of the reasons I was able to sell the concept of the mobile response team is through forensics. One of the primary reasons cases go unsolved is a lack of forensic capabilities. Small towns rely on state facilities to process evidence. Often by the time they get results back, the case is cold. Or the scene was compromised because of lack of training and tools. Our mobile lab—and my generous offer to take over the expense of any testing—is valuable. It's worth it to the FBI to spend money in local jurisdictions in exchange for good will as well as solving complex cases. It's a win-win."

"What if they say thanks but no thanks?"

"I would think—though I might not say out loud—why?"

"Control," Savannah said.

"Or because they don't want us to find out what they're doing. Even if a cop is not responsible for these murders, they have serious problems in St. Augustine, and are ill-equipped to solve these crimes. We can."

"I have a suggestion, Matt. If you're willing to take it."

"I have a half dozen very smart, very experienced agents who answer to me. I expect them to be honest, and I welcome advice and suggestions. In the end, I make the decision and if shit hits the fan, it's my responsibility."

"O-kay," she said. "This is my suggestion. Let me call Chief Dubois, tell him we're coming in. Give him the heads-up and why, make it sound casual. If we walk in there and surprise him? You're not going to get anything but a headache."

He weighed the option. He didn't really want to give them an early warning, but she was right—it might smooth things over.

"All right, but aren't we almost there?" He'd seen a sign a mile back that said "North Lake Pierre Road 7 miles."

She pulled off at the next exit, following signs for a chain diner, a gas station and fast-food restaurant. "I can always use more coffee."

15

Beau's first stop Monday morning was to the Baker house.

Rose Baker and her youngest daughter, Amelia, lived in a small farmhouse not far from Beau. They'd owned the land for generations, but didn't earn money from it. Rose's husband had been a trucker and was killed on the job, but he'd violated company policy and drove too many hours a week, resulting in his death benefit being cut in half. The money barely covered his funeral and the property taxes for the year. Rose was a housekeeper for several wealthy families in the parish to make ends meet. Lily's drug addiction had been hard on the struggling family, but her disappearance was worse. Rose had told her—and Amelia confirmed—that Lily had been trying hard to stay clean.

He caught Rose before she left for the day. Amelia was in the barn taking care of their animals—a flock of chickens and several sheep. She sold eggs at the local farmers market every Thursday afternoon and sheared wool twice a year.

Amelia was now fourteen; Lily would have been twenty-four this year.

"Beau," Rose said, letting him in the house. Her eyes asked questions she didn't voice.

"I have no news—or, not much news. Can we sit down?"

She led the way to the kitchen and poured him coffee without asking.

"Thank you," he said.

"Just tell me." She sat across from him, twisting a napkin in her hands. "Good, bad. You promised you wouldn't lie to me. I can handle the truth."

"I know, Rose. You're a strong woman. So I'll just come out and ask. I'm going to show you a photo—I need to know if you recognize it."

He took out the photo of the rabbit's foot and key.

"I've never seen it. Is it important?"

"I don't know," he said.

"Did you find—her? Was this—with—with her body?"

He shook his head.

"She's not alive," Rose insisted. "She would never leave without telling me. I thought for a while—a few weeks—that she might have left, to get away from those people pressuring her to go back, work for them—but not four months. She wouldn't do that to me, to her sister."

"I heard a rumor…" How did he say it? He shifted, uncomfortable.

"Just tell me, Beau, don't sugarcoat it."

"Was Lily pregnant?"

Silence, but surprise. "I don't honestly know. She didn't tell me—did a man—did he do this? Because of a baby?"

"I don't know, Rose, but I'm trying to figure that out. You said she was getting clean, Amelia said she was getting clean, hadn't fallen off the wagon in weeks. And I got to thinking, after I heard this rumor, that maybe she had a reason for that. Being pregnant would be a good reason, I reckon. You said she had gone cold turkey off drugs around Mardi Gras."

Mardi Gras this year was the end of February, seven weeks before Lily disappeared.

"That's right—she had come home that night—that next morning—worse than I've ever seen her. She was crying and said she didn't want to do it anymore and begged me to help her. She asked me to lock her in her room until she got over the withdrawals. She was so sick, but I didn't lock her in. I told her I couldn't do that, that she had to want it as much as I wanted it. She battled. Stayed in her room for days, crying, sweating, trying to eat what I made her, delirious one night with night terrors. Then she was better. Like she'd broken the demon inside her, the one making her hurt. I don't know if she stayed clean the whole time, but I never saw her like that again. I thought she gave up everything, then you told me she'd been at the Magnolia Inn and I thought I was wrong, that she was lost again." Her voice cracked and she stared at her hands.

Beau really hated to bring back the pain to this family who had suffered so much loss, but more, he wanted to find Lily, give her remains to her family for a proper burial. Find the person who killed her and punish them.

"Ernestine told me she wasn't using," Beau said.

"And now that poor girl is dead, too. What's going on in our quiet town, Beau? St. Augustine has always had problems, but we were a good little town with good people who looked out for one another, at least when I was growing up. And now…if I could afford it, I would take Amelia somewhere else. But this—" she waved her hand toward the window and the small farm beyond "—this is all I have. I own this land, my pa worked this land. I don't want to run away from my heritage."

The land—home, hearth, comfort—was what kept people rooted. And fear of the unknown, he supposed. Of not knowing if there was something better. Drugs and violence were everywhere, yet there was peace in having your own small slice of the world.

He pointed to the photo. "You don't recognize the rabbit's foot, but does the key look familiar?"

She shook her head. "It looks generic."

It was, and Beau had no idea how to find out what it opened. Or if it had even belonged to Lily.

Or her killer.

He said, "I want you to know that I'm going to be looking in the river for Lily's body."

"Why?"

"A hunch. Don't get your hopes up, and I'd prefer you didn't mention it to anyone, but if you hear about my search or anything I might find before I tell you, I don't want you to be blindsided."

"Thank you." She reached over, squeezed his hands tight. She might seem like a frail, grieving woman, but she had a steel core, and that would keep her going. "Be careful, Beau."

Tammy Bergeron didn't invite Beau into her house. That was a bad sign—Southern hospitality was real and even people who didn't like Beau would invite him in for sweet tea.

Instead, she motioned for him to sit on her front porch. She settled her hefty frame onto a sturdy bench. Her house was small, a two-room box that differed from its neighbors in that there was a detached garage. Most people didn't even have carports.

Tammy had her fingers in a host of illegal activities, from identity theft to growing pot in her garage, to running a few girls out of The Fat Cat. Her legitimate business was her ownership of three other small box houses on the street where she lived, and she managed the bar part-time with the owner, Billy Martin, an ornery seventy-year-old. The Fat Cat couldn't bring in much money, at least not legally.

"If you're here to tell me about Ernestine, Chief Dubois came out yesterday to tell me her body was found."

"You didn't report her missing."

"I'm not her mother. Did you talk to my no-good brother? She's his kid."

Beau had of course talked to Nels Bergeron yesterday. He and Michael had stopped on their way back from the river to notify him of his daughter's death. He hadn't reported her missing, said she was always out. His tears were real. He was a bastard, but he'd always had a soft spot for his daughter. When he was sober, at least, as he'd been when Beau spoke to him.

"I'm retracing her steps," Beau said to Tammy. "Ernestine worked for you part-time at the bar."

"Ain't no secret."

"When was the last time she was in?"

She didn't speak right away.

"Friday, I think. Can't be certain. It was payday, busy day. She didn't show up Saturday morning when she was supposed to clean the place, or Sunday. I called my brother, he started swearing at me so I hung up."

"Did you try Ernestine's phone?"

"She never answers her phone. Usually forgets to charge it. You know, Beau, she's not right in the head. Nice kid, don't get me wrong, she's my kin and I loved her, but she was stupid."

Beau tried not to bristle. He was having a difficult time with Ernestine's death. Two deaths now on his conscious. Ginny and Ernestine.

"Friday," he said. "What time was she at The Fat Catfish?"

Tammy shrugged, sighed. "She doesn't work Fridays, but she stopped by. Not too late, but we were busy."

"Who was working? Johnny or Elijah?"

"Both. It was *Friday*," she repeated as if she had to beat it over his head that the bar was busy.

Except he knew better. No one came in and out of The Fat Catfish without Tammy knowing about it. It's why he was concerned about Kara going there alone.

"I'm going to need to talk to Johnny and Elijah," he said.

"Go right ahead. Elijah is pretty broken up, I'll say."

Beau believed it. Elijah was a big black Cajun who likely had a half dozen concussions playing linebacker on the football team in high school. Word was he was sweet on Ernestine, and Beau used the word as his grandmother would. Beau needed to talk to him, but he wanted to talk to him alone—and that might be more difficult.

He didn't think that Tammy was involved in murder—especially her niece's murder. But because she had several illegal enterprises, she might not be inclined to help him solve this crime, if it shined a light on her operation. And he couldn't be certain she didn't know *something* about the dead women in town.

"Did Ernestine talk to you about anyone following her? Being worried about something?"

"You think it's the serial killer?"

Beau couldn't tell whether Tammy was saying it to mess with him, or actually believed there was a local serial killer.

"I think," he said cautiously, "that there are too many dead young women in St. Augustine and I want to find out who's responsible."

Tammy shifted on the bench, sighed. "Maybe you're just looking in all the wrong places."

Before he could ask her to expand on her comment, she hoisted herself up and said, "I have inventory. Johnny's opening today, Elijah comes in a bit later. I'll tell them you'll be coming by to talk to them."

Then she went into her house and shut the door.

Tammy Bergeron was hiding something, as sure as the sun would come up tomorrow.

★ ★ ★

The Magnolia Inn was quiet. The midmorning light exposed every inch of the tired interior.

Two of the regular girls, Shari and Terri, were relaxing in the corner watching a game show on the television and drinking what looked to be Bloody Marys with bacon, olives and celery. Probably the only food they'd eat this morning, if not all day. Crystal was sitting at a table next to the bar doing paperwork. She closed the ledger when she saw him.

"Detective. Can I offer you one of my special Bloody Marys? I just made fresh mix." She nodded toward the girls.

"Appreciate it, but I'm working."

He walked over to where Crystal sat. "May I?" He motioned to the chair.

"Sure. Coffee? It ain't bad." She nodded toward her cup. "I make the best Bloody Marys in the bayou but have to wait until after paperwork."

"Coffee would be great, thanks."

She gathered up her book and calculator and walked behind the bar. "Light, no sugar, right?" she called as she stowed her documents next to the cash register.

"Good memory."

She walked over with her own mug refreshed and his with a dab of cream. He sipped. "Good stuff."

"Chickory. Only way to go. What can I help you with?"

"You heard about Ernestine."

"Poor girl. I worried when she didn't show up Sunday afternoon to turn the rooms upstairs, she's always been reliable. But I thought it was her dad, you know how he gets."

Beau nodded, solemn.

"He okay?" she asked. "Nels has his troubles, but he took care of his girl."

"Took it hard."

"How can I help?"

"Ernestine was here late Thursday, the night Jake was killed."

She shrugged. "Maybe."

"I saw her when I arrived. She was sitting in the parlor." He motioned toward the semiprivate room off the main entrance. "Said she hadn't seen Jean Paul shoot Jake, but heard it and saw him with the gun."

Crystal said, "I guess I forgot she was here. She comes and goes. She was like a ghost sometimes."

"Do you remember if she was here Friday night?"

She frowned. "I didn't see her. I was here until about six. I don't usually work nights."

"Who was working?"

"Jasper. It's his place, so I told him he needed to cover Jake until we hire someone new. I don't need to be working 24/7."

"Is Jasper around?"

She shook her head, sipped her coffee. "Not until tonight."

"Did you see Ernestine anywhere after the shooting?"

"Can't say that I did," she said. "All I know is that she didn't show up Sunday noon, as she was supposed to, to clean rooms with Winnie."

Beau was undecided on how much Crystal knew about the murders. He appealed to her affection for the community and said, "Ernestine is the sixth dead woman in three years. And I suspect Lily Baker is also dead. All girls from our town."

"There's a lot more than six dead in town," she said. "More people have died of overdoses in the last three years than have been murdered."

"No argument from me, and you know I've made it a point to make life more difficult for the dealers. Look where that's got me—virtually every arrest I've made resulted in nothing."

"My point is that people die."

"Your people."

"Excuse me?"

"Don't play ignorant, Crystal."

She didn't comment. Leaned back in her seat and sipped her coffee.

"Four—maybe five—of these women were last seen here, at the Magnolia. All had been here within twenty-four hours of their deaths. That should give you pause."

"Don't put this at my doorstep, Beau Hebert. You should know better than that."

A threat? Maybe.

"I have work to do, so I suggest you come back and talk to Jasper when he comes in tonight." She got up, collected his coffee cup and walked through a swinging door, into the small kitchen.

He looked over at the two women in the corner; they'd been watching and listening to his conversation with Crystal. As soon as he caught their eyes, they turned away, back to the soundless television.

Beau left. He wouldn't be able to get either of them to talk within eyesight of the Magnolia; fear was a powerful deterrent.

Maybe he could get one of them alone. If he had a direction to pursue, even a rumor, he could work that angle.

Stop.

Wasn't that what happened with Ginny? He'd gotten her alone, pushed her to give him information, and she said she would find something because she, too, was suspicious. And now Ginny was dead. He wasn't going to put any of the other working girls in that same position. He could barely live with himself now; how could he live with himself if anyone else turned up dead?

Frustrated, with fewer answers than questions, he drove to the station.

Tammy's parting words came back at him.

Maybe you're just looking in all the wrong places.

Maybe he was. But if not Guidry and Cormier, then who?

16

By the time Matt and Savannah arrived at the St. Augustine police station at eleven that morning, he was antsy. Savannah had made an appointment with the chief, which meant that they had to wait at the diner for nearly a full hour.

He'd been productive during that time—talked to his boss Tony in DC, touched base with Michael and Jim, and texted Kara. He needed to get a lay of the land, and while he appreciated the assistance of a local agent, he trusted his team more.

Savannah pulled into the civic center parking lot and turned off the ignition. "Matt. You look angry and that's not going to get you what you want. Be casual."

"I took off my tie," he said. He was still thinking about the last text message he'd received from Kara. She internalized her cases and had deep empathy for the victims, hiding it behind a sarcastic exterior and false *c'est la vie* attitude.

I've been to every crime scene. They were dumped, like trash, close to roads where anyone might see but no one did for days. Lost and forgotten. Except Lily Baker: my gut says we haven't found her because the killer—killers?—fucked up. So they had to do something different. I'm off to check out the Fat Catfish incognito, then will join Michael and Jim at the hotel this afternoon.

He responded: Be cautious, check in regularly.

He'd wanted to say more. He'd wanted to talk to her about what she'd seen and felt at the crime scenes, be her sounding board. Give her the support Kara would never admit she needed. But now, they each had a separate job to do.

"Everything okay?" Savannah asked before getting out of the car.

"Good." He rolled his shoulders to relax. "Let's go."

The civic center was a square block on the south side of St. Augustine—City Hall, the district attorney office, another government building—maybe public works, Matt couldn't tell—and the St. Augustine Police Department. In the center of the block were pathways that connected the buildings, with benches, a fountain and a statue of someone Matt didn't recognize featured in the center.

They entered the police station and Matt took off his sunglasses, put them in his pocket. The lobby was a small, functional room with linoleum and plastic chairs and a wall with framed photos of former police chiefs, the current police chief enlarged in the middle. Dubois had dark hair and a mustache with broad shoulders. Late thirties, which was younger than Matt had expected. A desk sergeant slid open the window. "You must be Special Agent Trahan," he said.

"Yes." Savannah showed her badge and ID. "This is Special Agent Matt Costa. The police chief is expecting us."

Savannah had told Matt that she was going to introduce him as simply an agent because his title might raise the hackles of local cops.

"I'll take you to his office," the desk sergeant said. He pressed a button and when the door on the right buzzed, Matt grabbed it and held it open for Savannah.

The sergeant led them around the outside of the surprisingly quiet bullpen and then down a short, wide hall. Two doors on either side, all closed, and an open door at the end that led into a large, windowed office.

"Agent Trahan," Dubois said with a smile as he rose from his seat and walked around to shake her hand. He was several inches shorter than Matt. "Nice to see you again." He turned to Matt. "I'm Chief Richard Dubois, call me Rich."

Matt introduced himself, thanked Rich for his time. The chief motioned for them to sit at a small four-chair table under the window that looked out at the park they'd just walked through.

The functional office was modest in appearance. A wall of bookshelves was filled with legal tomes that looked untouched. The desk neither cluttered nor clear, suggesting he didn't let work back up. A dozen photos of Rich and a boy through the years, one prominent photo of Rich with the now young man in a graduation gown. Clearly related, though the child was a few inches taller.

Rich followed Matt's gaze, smiled. "My son, Ricky. He's in college now. Near full scholarship, in the Navy ROTC program at Tulane. Smart kid. Smarter than I was at his age."

"Congratulations," Matt said.

"You have kids?" He looked from Savannah to Matt.

Savannah shook her head, and Matt said, "Two nieces and a nephew I spoil when I can."

"I wish I had more, to be honest, but Ricky was my one and only." He smiled wistfully, leaned back in his chair. Matt saw no photos of a wife, even in Ricky's younger pictures.

Rich said, "I hear your office is interested in the death of Jean Paul LeBlanc." He slid a file over to Matt. "I took the liberty of pulling his file for you."

"Thank you," Matt said. He didn't open it. "We appreciate your diligence."

"It surprised me that NOLA even called about it."

"I'm not from the New Orleans office," Matt said. "I'm from DC."

He could feel Savannah tense next to him.

"Oh?" Rich said casually.

If Matt attempted to deceive the chief, it would be worse for them when Dubois undoubtedly learned the truth. He would play the humble card as best he could, but he wasn't going to lie. Just a little misdirection. "My boss," he began, "has been tracking in-custody deaths for quite some time. It's one of his pet projects."

"I suppose I understand, but it seems he could have called, rather than send an agent all the way down here. And so quickly. Mr. LeBlanc only died Friday night."

Matt left the implied question unanswered. "I'm not here to ring up you or your staff. We're assessing procedures in multiple towns to see how we can better assist small communities."

"As y'all know, we're strapped for resources these days, but generally, in my experience, help from the feds comes with some mighty thick strings."

"That's definitely something for us to assess—whether strings are even warranted. Because we're a pilot program, my team and I are here on Uncle Sam's dime. I'd like to show you and your officers our mobile crime lab."

Rich leaned back, looked skeptical. "Mobile crime lab?"

"It's run by the former director of the Dallas crime lab and we are capable of running a multitude of tests. In fact, when I came in this morning, Agent Trahan said that there was a body found in your jurisdiction that may tie into a series of deaths over the last few years. That's exactly the type of situation that the mobile lab is perfect for."

The chief didn't comment.

Matt continued, "Perhaps my team can assist with the autopsy, use the crime lab capabilities, all without your department having to spend a penny. No strings, but it gives us a case study to show other communities how we can help them with their unique—and costly—cases."

"I don't know about having St. Augustine be a guinea pig for some highfalutin federal program," Rich said.

"I took the liberty of looking into the deaths of the five prostitutes—and the missing person, Lily Baker, who fits the same profile," Matt said.

Rich narrowed his eyes at Savannah. "You're from Lafayette. Is your office investigating these murders without talking to me first?"

"No, sir," she said. "As far as Lafayette and NOLA are concerned, this is a local matter. However, we have been tracking all violent crime in our jurisdiction, so when Agent Costa arrived this morning, we shared what we knew."

Rich shook his head, turned to Matt. "So both Lafayette and DC have been tracking us?"

The chief was defensive, and defensive cops usually shut things down. Matt couldn't have that. "If by 'tracking' you mean following the case from the beginning, no, sir, we haven't. We've only become aware today." Slight fib. "As I discussed with Lafayette this morning, the details have the hallmarks of a serial killer. I'm not saying that's what you have here—you know the town better than we do—"

"I do," Rich said. "I've lived here my entire life."

"And since I'm here with my team, I think we can help—no strings."

"You do know that all the victims were prostitutes," Rich said. "Prostitutes and drug addicts. Their lifestyle invites violence."

They didn't deserve to be murdered.

"True," Matt said, "but it's my understanding that the latest victim wasn't a prostitute or an addict."

"Yes, and I don't believe it's connected to the others."

Beau hadn't told his boss that Ernestine had called him, but it would come out when the investigator pulled her phone records. He wondered why it hadn't yet been done. Matt didn't say anything; he didn't want the chief to know that he was working with the detective at this point.

"Let us help," Matt said. "We have resources and equipment. Again, no strings. Jim Esteban is one of the best in the country. He might be able to see something with fresh eyes." He had to be careful implying that the chief or his people missed anything.

"I'll think about it," Rich said. "If it's okay with you, I'll send some of my people over to meet your forensics expert, look at your mobile crime lab. Make an assessment."

"Great, we'll be ready for you," Matt said.

Rich stood, clearly signaling that the meeting was over. "I'll walk you out."

He remembered Savannah talking about the slower pace of the South, and he had to suppress his natural inclination to push. This was likely the best they were going to get right now. Take a day to see what the chief did, assess what Beau and Kara learned today in the field, decide how to proceed. Maybe the chief would surprise him.

Rich walked them down the hall and around the bullpen.

"Jerry." Rich gestured to a large officer whose chest strained his buttons. Jerry approached the group. "Agents, this is Jerry

Guidry, one of my top officers. I brought him on because of his experience with drug-related crimes, and he's local, from the next parish over, not too far from here. You're from Lake Charles, Agent Trahan?"

"Yes, sir. Call me Savannah, please."

Guidry. Matt kept his face blank, resisting the urge to confront the man. This was the cop who pulled Kara over and sexually assaulted her. She didn't call it that, but Matt knew exactly what it was and Guidry should be fired. He glanced at the man's hands, pictured them manhandling Kara, and forced himself to remain calm.

It was a he said/she said situation. Matt believed Kara one hundred percent—she wasn't prone to exaggeration and, if anything, she likely downplayed what happened. But Guidry wasn't a federal employee and Matt had no jurisdiction over him.

But by the end of this investigation, he would have the man's badge, one way or the other.

"I'll have Jerry check out your crime lab," Rich was saying. "And Detective Armand." He turned to Jerry. "Is Andre around?"

"He went to talk to the doc a few minutes ago."

Savannah said, "Is that the coroner?"

Rich nodded. "Dr. Judson Brown. He's examining the victim now."

"I'm happy to send over Dr. Esteban," Matt said. "He's in town, has experience—"

Rich waved his hand. "No need, Dr. Brown knows what he's doing. Cause of death is clear—her throat was slit. Blood loss. He'll verify, of course, run a rape kit and whatever else he does, and then give his report to Armand."

"We can bring the crime lab to you," Matt offered.

Guidry looked at his watch. "I'm going out on patrol in a few, but I'll touch bases with Armand and we can head over there around two, two thirty?" He glanced at Rich.

"That's fine."

Matt made a note in his phone. "We're at the North Lake Hotel."

"You're staying in town?" Rich looked displeased.

"For a few days." He held up the LeBlanc file. "Thanks for this, I'll let you know if I have any questions."

They left and Savannah said, "Well, he didn't kick you out on your ass."

"He will. He doesn't want our help, but he's being polite. He'll answer my questions about LeBlanc, pretend he's helping, but then he'll just say thanks, no thanks. I hope we find Lily Baker's body before then."

"Excuse me? Did I miss something?"

He glanced at her. "One of my people is trained in underwater search and rescue. He's going to dive tomorrow in the area where LeBlanc indicated Lily's body was dumped in the river."

"If her body has been in the river for the last four months, there's nothing left."

"Probably not, but even a skull would be enough to give her family closure. We might get lucky. If there's anything to find, Michael will find it."

Savannah didn't say anything for a moment. "If Dubois finds out…"

"He will, if we find anything. And then I won't be playing nice."

17

Kara spent all morning checking each location where the victims were found. With each stop, her anger grew.

The women were tossed by the side of the road, garbage, inhuman and worthless to the killer. Drugged, used, beaten, strangled. Nicki brutally stabbed to death—according to the autopsy report, she'd been stabbed where she died, blood soaking into the earth, cast-off staining shrubs and trees. Violent anger, a rage not seen with the other victims. Which told Kara that the killer hated Nicki, or she'd done something to fuel his rage.

Other than Nicki and Ernestine, the women could have been strangled in a car and dragged no more than thirty feet to be unceremoniously dumped on the edge of a canal or the river.

Discarded without thought because the killer had neither remorse nor fear of being caught.

That's what stuck out most to Kara—the boldness. All women last seen in town. The killer didn't care if there were witnesses; he was confident no one would talk. And if they did? No one could prove anything. The women were societal throwaways, drug addicts, prostitutes, barely scraping by.

All the women were killed and dumped within a ten-mile radius of St. Augustine. No fear of evidence, no fear of exposure, no fear...

Except for Lily.

Lily was the anomaly. No one, including Kara, believed she was alive. She supposed...maybe...if Lily had someone to help she could have just disappeared. Yet, Lily was a small-town girl who had rarely left the parish. According to Beau, she wouldn't have run away without letting her mother know she was okay.

Lily *was* dead, but her family had no closure.

Kara's hands tightened around the steering wheel so hard her knuckles hurt.

She pulled over near the last crime scene on her list—that of the third victim Tanya Ewing. Outside the town limits, along a swampy river that rolled slowly through farmland. She wouldn't even call this a river—it was practically standing water that crawled south, narrower than the main river to the east, with lots of trees growing out of the water, making Kara think of the water moccasins Michael told her about.

She looked at her map, trying to get a feeling for where this was in relation to every other crime scene. Southwest. This swampy area eventually bled into the river where Ernestine's body had been found, about three miles downstream. But here, everything was mush.

She was glad she wore her boots. She hadn't expected the ground to be so soft, especially in summer. She was on Lake Pierre Road because there were no roads nearby that went east or west. The killer had to have been driving south, away from town…then pulled over and dumped Tanya only feet from the road. She'd rolled down into the water.

She remembered the crime scene photos—Tanya's body had been covered in sludge, a muddy mess that had nearly swallowed her. A fisherman had found her while he was out in the swamp—based on the photos, the water had been higher in the spring.

A wood cross with artificial flowers, now faded and muddy, lay in the muck. Kara stared at it for a long minute, then squatted and righted the cross. She couldn't get it straight, but at least it was upright. She wasn't a religious person, but whoever put this here had mourned the dead woman, and Kara respected that.

She stood a moment later, looked around. She could see her car on the side of the road, but nothing else. Just swamp and thick trees to the east, and fields to the west. The river where Ernestine had been found went at a diagonal, toward the town of Lake Pierre southeast of St. Augustine.

Buddy Palfrey had been arrested for Tanya's murder, but released for lack of evidence. The circumstantial evidence was thin. And therein lay the primary problem: there was no evidence. In all the cases, the lack of physical evidence tying *anyone* to the murders made their job next to impossible.

Kara took one last, long look around. She was already sweating. It wasn't that it was hot—yet—but the humidity was off the charts. She felt like she'd just stepped out of the shower.

While she hadn't learned anything new, she had connected with the dead. The victims deserved justice. Kara needed to solve this case. If the FBI walked away, she knew in her heart that others would befall the same tragic fate.

She walked back to her car and decided now was the time to check out The Fat Catfish. She'd change in the car, adopt a new persona to blend in. She texted Michael her plans.

He responded: Watch your back.

18

Beau walked into The Fat Catfish just after noon. The place opened at eleven. He'd first driven by Tammy's place—her car was still there, so either Johnny or Elijah was working.

A couple people were already drinking. A guy who Beau knew lost his job a few months ago sat by himself at a table staring at his near-empty draft. Three old veterans were sitting in a corner booth arguing good-naturedly while watching a silent television that played sports 24/7. A young woman with short messy blond hair that obscured her face, wearing clothes just a little too small, sat alone at the bar drinking a bottle of Coors Light. He thought he recognized her, but wasn't certain in the dim lighting. Maybe he'd seen her working the Magnolia, but she wasn't local—he'd remember if she were.

Johnny was behind the bar changing out a keg. He glanced up at Beau, then went back to his work. He was a short, wiry man in his forties who was stronger than he looked. His arms were filled with tattoos, likely the rest of his body was similarly covered. One side of his neck had a tattoo bleeding out from under the gray T-shirt. Most of the art was mediocre, leaving his skin looking blue rather than decorative.

"Off duty?" Johnny said. "Draft?"

"Working," Beau said. "Ernestine."

Johnny wrangled the keg into place, then picked up the empty and walked to the back. Beau waited, glanced over at the woman again. Did a double take.

She winked at him.

Kara Quinn. She'd done something to her appearance…she had on heavy eye makeup, mascara smeared under her eyes. And she'd put something in her hair to make it curlier, then pulled it forward, as if she'd just rolled out of bed and hadn't touched it.

He'd seen her briefly this morning. Then, she'd been dressed in jeans and a T-shirt, her hair brushed back into a stubby ponytail, no makeup. She'd replaced her jeans for short-shorts and tied her white T-shirt under her breasts, revealing a butterfly tattoo on the right side of her back. He could even see her thong underwear peeking out.

He looked away, embarrassed to be staring. He was surprised. He'd known she was going to check out The Fat Cat, but he hadn't expected the transformation. He hadn't recognized her. What was she up to?

When Johnny came back, Kara said to him, "Sugar?" She tilted her empty bottle back and forth. "Would ya mind?" She smiled both sexy and sweet and Johnny grinned, retrieved a bottle, opened it and put it in front of her. She'd adopted a subtle

Southern accent, nothing overt, but just enough that even Beau would have thought she was from the South.

She reached into her tiny pockets and pulled out a couple crumpled dollar bills, left them on the bar, sipped her drink and rubbed her nose with the back of her hand.

Now Beau understood what Michael had meant when he said if Kara didn't want anyone to think she was a cop they wouldn't. She intentionally made herself up to look like a hooker who'd just gotten off work, or a girl who'd partied all night. Though Beau had figured she was around thirty, she looked much younger now.

"I need a minute, Johnny," Beau said.

"Don't know what to say."

"Did you see Ernestine on Friday night?"

"Yep."

"What time was she here?"

He shrugged. "She comes and goes. It was busy."

"Who did she talk to?"

"Ernestine talks to everybody."

"Tammy didn't have her working, did she?"

"Ernestine cleans in the mornings."

"You know what I mean," Beau said.

Johnny didn't say anything, but shook his head. Then, almost as an afterthought, Johnny said, "Elijah told Tammy no more of that, not with Ernestine."

"What time does Elijah come in?"

"Not today," Johnny said.

He'd have to track him down at his house.

"Was anyone giving Ernestine trouble?" Beau asked. "A regular? A stranger?"

"I'm not going to jam people up," Johnny said.

"She's dead," Beau said bluntly. "Her throat was slit and she was dumped at Lantern Gate. Her body just out in the open for the critters. You good with that? A girl you've known her entire life?"

Johnny didn't say anything. He served the three veterans another round, though Beau hadn't heard them ask.

He came back, looked at Kara and motioned to her half-empty bottle.

She shook her head. "Still nursing it, sugar." She put the bottle to her lips and Johnny watched as she drank. She licked her lips and gave him a tired smile, then looked up at the silent television as if she was bored and just counting the minutes.

"Johnny," Beau said, slapping his hand on the bar.

"I don't know what to tell you, Beau. She was here, left when it was still busy. It was Friday, you know how it is."

Checks came on Fridays. Paychecks, welfare checks.

"Who was giving her a bad time?"

"It was teasing. You know Ernestine. They laugh, she doesn't understand they laugh at her so she laughs with them."

"And Elijah just let it happen?"

Silence.

"Johnny, I want to find who killed her."

"Talk to Elijah," Johnny said after a minute.

"Thanks for nothing." Beau walked out. He waited in his car a minute, half expecting Kara to come out, but she didn't.

He left for Elijah's house.

Kara watched Johnny pull out his cell phone after Beau left. Was he calling this Elijah? Someone else?

"When you coming up?" Johnny mumbled. He listened, said something that Kara couldn't hear, then listened again. "No, it's just all fucked."

He ended the call and went into the back room.

When you coming up.

That implied someone not in town. There wasn't much south

163

of here. Lots of land and swamp, a few towns, and sixty miles away the Gulf of Mexico.

Kara waited until Johnny came back out before she drained her beer and put it down. She waved her fingers at him as she slid off the stool. She purposefully bent over to slip on the sandals she'd intentionally kicked off. She felt his eyes on her.

"You new in town?"

She stretched, shrugged. "Just kinda passing through. Don't really have a place these days."

"Magnolia's always hiring."

She shrugged.

"Where you from?"

"Well, that's a story. My daddy moved us around a lot."

"If you need a place, aren't afraid of a little work, the Magnolia'll take care of you. Just up Lake Pierre Road, turn right just before the interstate. Tell them Johnny sent you."

She shrugged. "I kinda like working for myself."

"Can be dangerous."

"What isn't these days?" She grabbed the worn, oversize purse she had on the stool next to her. She'd borrowed it from Toni. It was stuffed with things—change of clothes, her gun, odds and ends so that it would appear that she was a nomad.

And it had worked.

She almost wished she could have gone undercover. This town was so predictable, she thought as she stood.

Predictable except she had no idea who was killing these women.

She really wanted to see who might come in, though. She had a feeling Johnny's call was important. She asked, "Little girls' room?" She pointed down the hall toward the storage room.

"Yes, ma'am," he said.

She smiled and went into the bathroom. Did her business—two beers went right through her. She drained a water bottle and ate half an energy bar since she'd only had the toast for breakfast.

She wasn't about to get drunk, though honestly after looking at the crime scenes this morning, she wanted a bottle of tequila and a day to brood about the bullshit people did to each other.

That could wait until she caught this killer.

She checked her appearance—damn, she was good. Her raccoon eyes might be a bit much—she washed her hands, then rubbed wet fingers under her eyes to try to get rid of some of the mascara. Didn't do much good. Oh, well.

She walked back out and saw Gray Cormier at the bar talking to Johnny. As she walked by, Cormier was saying, "It's still on, I just need another driver."

"When's Debra going to be here?"

"When she feels like it, the bitch."

And then she was at the door, out of the place and didn't know what they were talking about.

Maybe Beau knew who Debra was.

She walked a block to where she'd left the rental, because she didn't think a hooker would have a decent car. Maybe if she was a high-priced call girl out of LA, but not a streetwalker in the bayou. She slipped behind the driver's seat and turned the ignition. The air blasted at her and it felt so damn good.

She'd planned to go back to Beau's place and shower, but Matt called as she pulled away from the curb. "Can you meet at the hotel for a debrief? Jim has a suite, so we have plenty of room."

"Can I use his shower?"

"Did something happen?"

"Just did a little recon, don't look too professional now."

"We're in room 110, which has a living area. Jim has 108 and Ryder reserved 112 for you or Michael if you need it. They're connected."

"Be there in a few."

She ended the call. The Catfish wasn't far from the interstate—a couple minutes south. She passed the road that led to the Magnolia, drove under the freeway, and the North Lake

Hotel was only half a mile up. She considered what she had learned. Not much, except that Johnny definitely knew something more than he told Beau. Killer? Maybe, maybe not. Who did he call? Elijah? This Debra? Or Cormier, who got there in minutes? Maybe the owner of the dive, Martin. Billy Martin. According to Beau's records, he was an ex-con who'd inherited The Fat Catfish from his uncle and didn't live in town.

She was still depressed about her morning drive to the crime scenes, and sitting in the sad dive bar for an hour had only further depressed her. The only fun part of the day was when Beau finally recognized her.

But then his words were cutting.

Her body just out in the open for the critters. You good with that? A girl you've known her entire life?

It had made her think a lot about the victims. Whether they could find enough evidence to put their killer behind bars. To give these women justice.

A girl you've known her entire life…

The girls knew their killer. The evidence was clear—no struggle, minimal defensive wounds. They left with someone who didn't arouse suspicion—like a cop. A friend. What motive? Why them? Why now? Why Ernestine? What had she known that made her a threat to the killer?

Kara walked into the hotel and the older woman at the reception gave her a once-over and pursed her lips, but didn't say anything or stop Kara from walking down the hall.

Room 110 had double doors, signifying a suite. She knocked and a few seconds later Matt opened the door. He stared at her for just a second too long, as if he didn't recognize her, then he frowned.

She said, "Short version? I wanted to check out The Fat Catfish. Had to blend in. Long version? Wait until after my shower."

She looked around the room. It was a living room with couches, a desk and an actual bar—without alcohol. Through the window she could see the mobile crime lab, which was probably why Jim wanted the ground floor. Doors to the right and left led to the adjoining bedrooms.

Michael was there, Jim—who had a grin on his face when he saw her and made her at least not feel totally stupid—and a tall, very attractive, impeccably dressed blonde woman standing next to Matt. Matt, in his suit, but without his jacket and tie, wearing his shoulder holster that Kara always found a turn-on.

Kara felt distinctly out of place. She never felt out of place. She never felt uncomfortable. Self-confidence was her middle name. Why was she nervous now? Because of how Matt looked at her? Surprised...*embarrassed?*

Screw that.

She extended her hand to the woman. "Detective Kara Quinn," she said.

The woman hesitated just a second, then shook her hand. "Special Agent Savannah Trahan." The fed touched her as if Kara had cooties, dropping her hand immediately.

Kara said to Jim, "Which room can I use?"

He pointed to the door on the left. "Do you need anything?"

"A fifth of tequila, but I'll wait until tonight," she said with a big smile and went into the bedroom, firmly shutting the door behind her.

Dammit, not quite the way she wanted to make her entrance.

19

Matt didn't know why Kara was dressed like a prostitute. It wasn't just her clothes—there was nothing overtly wrong with the shorts and crop top, though she was on duty. He'd also rarely seen her wear anything where she couldn't conceal her weapon. But it was the whole package—the clothing along with thick, smudged makeup, the excessive costume jewelry, the oversize bag, the messy, sexy hair. It was the image she had wanted to project, and she did it well—it's why she had made a good under-cover cop. He knew that she'd planned on checking out The Fat Catfish, but he didn't expect her to work that hard to blend in.

Why not? That's what Kara does. That's why she's a great cop. And it's why you worry about her.

He glanced at Michael, but Michael didn't seem to have a re-action to Kara, and Matt wondered if he was overreacting because another federal agent was in the room.

Or because Matt was in a relationship with her.

Jim said, "Can't wait to hear the story, should be a good one."

Jim and Michael liked Kara's stories, and at the beginning Matt thought she exaggerated, but learned pretty quick that Kara usually downplayed her adventures—which was why he was certain that Guidry had behaved worse than Kara told them.

But he was concerned in part because he knew how Kara internalized these cases. Especially cases like this, where the victims were vulnerable and often ignored by society and law enforcement. He remembered how they'd ended up working together in the first place. She'd been put on administrative leave after a fatal shooting in a Chinese human-trafficking case where children, women and the elderly had been forced to work in a major Los Angeles sweatshop. She'd lost her informant and blamed herself. As Beau Hebert seemed to be doing with this case.

Matt admired Kara's steadfast determination and loyalty, but he also saw the dark underside of her calling, that she could be single-minded in her focus, to her personal detriment. He would have to protect her from herself, which meant keeping an eye on her.

Matt shook his head to clear his thoughts. "Michael, what's Beau's ETA?"

"Any minute."

Jim said, "I want to talk to the coroner, look at the evidence they have on both the LeBlanc death and the six women. They probably have a bare bones operation here. I could very well see something we can help with."

"The police chief is thinking about it," Matt said. "He's sending a detective and cop here to look at your lab. You'll sell them."

"If you couldn't convince them, Matt, I don't know if I can," Jim said.

"You know more about the capabilities of that RV than anyone. The chief seemed interested, but he may have been humoring me." He glanced at Savannah. "Agree?"

Savannah said, "More or less. It's highly unusual for the FBI to come in and offer services." She sat down on the corner of a couch, stretched out her long legs. "They're weighing their options. It's difficult for a small town to give up so much control to an outside agency, even if the town is aboveboard. And if they're dirty? They're not going to budge."

"And," Michael added, "when they find out that Beau called us in, they'll slam the door. No one asked who I was yesterday, so Beau introduced me as his friend from the Navy. We were out fishing, found the body. But it's only a matter of time." He glanced at his phone. "Good—I got the confirmation that my dive gear has shipped. It'll be here tomorrow before 10 a.m." Michael grinned, his smile bright against his skin. He was in his element here. He loved when he could use his unique skill set in the field. "I'm looking forward to it. I've never worked in these conditions before."

"I heard you spent a week in Chesapeake Bay in June," Jim said. "Was that training or recovery?"

"Both," Michael said. "An old freighter had sunk more than a hundred years ago. We used the hull for training, but also had a dive team from a university join us to collect artifacts. It was pretty damn cool."

"The river is cloudy, visibility is next to nothing," Savannah said. "Do you really think you'll be able to find anything?"

"Modern technology," Michael said. "I have lights, equipment, all the tools I need. And I've been refreshing myself on river techniques. After Katrina there was a major recovery case, and my instructor Lee was one of the divers involved. He surpasses me—and there aren't many better than I am. I'm talking to him tonight for his advice. If Lily was down there at any point, even if her body has been consumed by fish, I'll find something. A rock that doesn't belong in the river. Rope. Plastic, clothing, shoes—a skull or bones. Lee's going to help me prepare, know what to look for."

Matt answered a knock on the door as Michael was speaking. Beau walked in, closed the door immediately. "I came in through the side entrance, didn't want the desk to see me. By the end of the day, everyone will know the FBI is in town." Beau grabbed a water bottle that was on the counter, opened and drank half of it. "So, Elijah Morel wasn't at The Fat Cat or home," Beau said. "His neighbors don't know where he is, or aren't talking." He glanced at Savannah. "Agent Trahan?"

"Good to see you again, Detective."

"So Lafayette is on board?"

He sounded surprised.

"Curt asked me to assist y'all for a couple of days. Don't know if I was any help." She glanced at Matt.

"You were," he assured her.

"I talked to the chief," Beau said. "He didn't say a word about you talking to him. I pushed again to get Ernestine's homicide, he wouldn't budge. Told me to stop asking questions, it's not my case."

"Who called him?" Michael asked.

"Could have been anyone, but my money's on Crystal."

"Who's the detective working the recent homicide?" Jim asked. "Is he any good?"

"Andre Armand. Only been here two years, he doesn't know the town or the people. The only plus is that he hasn't shut me out. I think he'll keep me in the loop." Beau paused. "I had to tell him that Ernestine called me Friday, my number is going to be in her phone records. I made up a story, but it's close enough to the truth he wouldn't question it. I didn't give him details, except that she was a witness to the Jake West murder, which was already in my report."

"As my great-grandma always said," Michael offered, "don't borrow trouble. We'll see what happens, if anything, and go from there. We're here, Beau. We're not walking away."

Michael, like Kara, seemed to have become invested even after only twenty-four hours. Michael had reason—he and Beau were brothers-in-arms. Kara—well, Matt thought, because she was Kara.

"After reading Kara's report last night," Matt said, "I reached out to Catherine. Sent her what we have so far."

"Who's Catherine?" Savannah asked.

"Profiler. She has questions for you, Beau. I think we need to set a conference call for late this afternoon."

"She's not coming down?" Michael asked.

"Neither of us think it's necessary for her to be on-site," Matt said. Catherine was still adjusting to her new role in the MRT unit and working hard to balance her work and family life after what had been a really rough year. If he needed her in the field, she would come, but unless it was critical, he was fine with her being on-call for the team.

"Does she have my cases?" Beau asked, skeptical. "I didn't write everything up, it's a mess."

"Kara put together a detailed report about each of the victims and crime scenes—I assume she got all that from you. She sent it to Catherine and me this morning."

"You were right," Beau said to Michael. "She's good. I walked into The Fat Cat, didn't even recognize her. Didn't know who she was until she winked at me."

Kara walked in through the adjoining door. "Told you I was good," she said with a smile.

Kara had completely transformed. She wore jeans and a tank top, wet hair brushed away from her freshly scrubbed face. She dropped her bag on the floor and pulled out a half-eaten energy bar, then walked over to the small kitchenette and started making a pot of coffee. "Jim, you should see if the hotel can give us an unlimited supply of coffee." While the coffee brewed, she sat on the bar next to it, waiting. Part of the group, but off to the side. She always seemed to do that, preferring to observe.

Matt wished she took better care of herself. She practically lived on energy bars.

"I miss Ryder," Jim said. "He had our war room stocked in Friday Harbor, I didn't even have to think about food."

"Pizza's on its way," Michael said, glancing at his watch. "ETA fifteen minutes."

"Where'd you leave Ryder?" Kara asked Matt.

"He's working out of the Lafayette office running backgrounds and doing research."

"And coordinating," Michael said. "Without him, my dive gear would probably be on its way to Hawaii. Though if it were, I wouldn't mind joining it."

"Count me in," Kara said with a grin.

Matt felt like he was missing something, but ignored them. Michael and Kara worked well together after a rocky start, largely because of the last case they were on. Michael had saved Kara's life, but more than that, they'd developed a symbiotic relationship and adjusted to their different approaches to investigating. It seemed to work for them.

Michael and Kara were his field agents—the two who did most of the investigatory work. They had to work well together or the team would fall apart.

Michael was a strict rules follower: diligent, loyal, straightforward and the most trustworthy person Matt had ever worked with. Because of his background in the SEALs and on the FBI SWAT team in Detroit, Matt relied on Michael for security and tactical intelligence. If Michael had a flaw, it was his inability to see nuance in cases, to work subtle angles. For Michael, cases were black-and-white. When he had to go undercover three months ago, lying even for the case was so hard on him that Matt promised he wouldn't have to do it again.

Kara was the opposite. She thrived in undercover work. She could see a lie a mile away, worked interviews with suspects and victims so smoothly that Matt had already written two commendations for her file. She could read between all lines in an investigation and see things no one else seemed to notice—until she pointed it out. She could blend in anywhere and her street smarts were as good—maybe better—than Matt's. Her flaws? She took personal risks, more than Matt was comfortable with for anyone on his team. She was a loner and disconnected from the people around her, yet developed a deep empathy with the victims which pained her. Mostly? She was a rule breaker, which had gotten her in trouble with LAPD, and it would get her in trouble with the FBI. Matt would do everything in his power to protect her: she was effective and one of the best cops he'd ever worked with. But he kept waiting for her to overstep so far that he wouldn't be able to save her career.

Honestly, if he could blend Michael's tactical brains and disposition to follow the rules with Kara's stellar instincts and deep empathy, he'd have the perfect agent. Yet, together they found a balance and made a good team.

When the coffee was done, Kara poured a cup. Jim and Beau followed her lead.

The pizza arrived and Matt grabbed a slice, then sat with his phone scrolling through messages, most of which didn't need his immediate attention. He was pleased that his team worked well together and genuinely liked each other.

Jim had taken Kara under his wing, and Kara seemed to enjoy it. Right now he was showing her pictures of his grandkids on his phone, talking about how his granddaughter was playing T-ball and his grandsons were playing soccer and how he couldn't wait to go back to Dallas for a weekend of games. And Kara, who hated small talk, seemed to be enjoying the conversation, asking questions and laughing at something Matt couldn't hear.

Ten minutes later, Matt said, "Okay, break time's over." He told them what happened at the police station and that he wasn't optimistic for cooperation. "However, Detective Armand and Officer Guidry will be coming over shortly to view the mobile crime lab, and Jim will make his pitch to assist. At that point, we'll determine our next move."

Kara rolled her eyes. "I'll disappear."

"Eventually, he's going to know you're a cop," Matt said.

"Not today."

Savannah looked lost at the exchange, so Matt explained. "Guidry pulled Kara over yesterday. He was unprofessional, to the point of criminal conduct. We'll be taking his badge when this is over."

"I doubt that will happen," Savannah said. "They're going to protect their own, especially against outsiders."

"Drop it for now, Matt," Kara said.

He looked her in the eye. "I'm not letting it go."

"Killer first, pervert second."

She took another bite of her pizza.

She was right. He didn't have to like it, however.

Beau gave them the rundown on tracking Ernestine's last day. "Johnny claims he doesn't remember when she was there on Friday, it was so busy." Clearly, Beau didn't believe him. "Kara was just telling me Johnny called someone as soon as I left."

"Yep," she said, grabbing a second slice of pizza. "I couldn't hear the entire conversation, but he asked when the individual was coming *up* and at the end said and I quote, 'It's all fucked.'"

Beau said, "It could be the owner, Billy Martin. Usually comes up a couple times a month. Lives down in Lake Pierre."

"I'd have stayed," Kara said, "but it would have attracted too much attention, and I'd reached my two beer undercover limit. When I was coming out of the ladies' room, about fifteen minutes after you left, Beau, Johnny and Gray Cormier had their heads together. Johnny wanted to know when Debra would be there, and Gray didn't know, called her a bitch. Do you know who they were talking about?"

"Debra?" He shook his head. "I might be able to find out."

"I could go back. It's dead during the day, but I suspect busier after five."

Beau nodded. "Lots of regulars, so strangers stand out."

"But you didn't?" Savannah asked, skeptical.

"I'm whatever I want people to see," Kara said. "I did a stint on Vice when we were trying to nab a perv—long story. But I can walk the walk."

Matt hadn't heard that story. He hadn't heard a lot of Kara's stories.

She continued. "I might be able to sidle back in there tonight, see what's up. We'll play it by ear."

"Only with backup," Matt said.

"Of course, boss." She drained a water bottle, then went back to her coffee. "Jim, I went out to the crime scenes today, read through all the reports. You should read them. Maybe you'll see something everyone missed, since you speak that language."

"I read what you sent, Detective, but you have more at your house, right?" Jim asked Beau. "Photos, toxicology, evidence reports?"

"I suppose we can move everything here," Beau said. "But—"

"We'll copy everything you have," Matt said. "If it's safe at your place, we'll keep it there. And for the next day or so, you shouldn't be seen here at the hotel."

Savannah said, "You keep evidence at your house? How is that not violating a half dozen laws and regulations?"

"Only copies and my personal notes," Beau said. "Physical evidence is stored in the evidence locker. I don't trust Dubois. He's either directly or indirectly involved in these murders, and if he sees how I'm connecting dots, he's going to destroy evidence or remove me completely from this case. So I copied everything, took my own photos."

"We may not be able to pull the cases from St. Augustine, but if we open a public corruption case, we'll have more leeway."

"You need to tread carefully," Savannah said. "NOLA seems to be fine with you quietly looking around, but they're not going to be happy if an FBI squad—especially one they don't control—starts investigating a local police department."

"My boss will smooth that over," Matt said. He'd learned a long time ago that the best way to instill loyalty in his unit was to respect their personal commitment and drive. If he pulled Michael and Kara now, they would lose respect for him, and the next time he needed them to go above and beyond, they might balk.

"I recognize this is a delicate situation," he continued. "I don't know if you're going to find Lily Baker's body, Michael, but that's our best chance right now. Jim is in charge of any evidence you uncover. How many people do you need on the river?"

"I should be there," Jim said. "I'm aware of the problems with water retrieval, and I can quickly preserve anything you find."

"I also need Beau," Michael said. "He needs to keep an eye on potential dangers as well as steer the boat."

"Dangers—oh," Matt said.

"I still think this is a dumb idea," Kara muttered. "You're more than dinner for a gator, Michael. You'd make a nice family meal, satisfy those nasty reptiles for a week."

Michael laughed. "It's just a precaution and Beau knows what to look for."

"When we went out yesterday I saw no signs of gators in that section of the river. They're going to be further south, my guess, and they don't like open areas. But I'll keep watch because the weather is warm, and they're more active the hotter it gets."

"I didn't need to hear that," Michael muttered.

"I've always had your back, buddy."

"I want to track down that girl I spoke to yesterday," Kara said. "Now that we know Ernestine is dead, I might be able to convince her to talk."

"What girl?" Savannah asked.

Kara didn't answer, but instead said, "And be a part of the conference call between Beau and Catherine. I have a few questions for our pet shrink."

Matt was glad Catherine wasn't around to hear Kara call her their "pet shrink." His phone vibrated and he glanced at the message. "Guidry and Armand are on their way. ETA ten minutes."

"And I'm outta here," Kara said.

"Michael," Matt said, "go with Kara, talk to Catherine, arrange a good time for the conference with Beau. Let me know when and I'll be there if I can."

"I should disappear as well," Beau said. "Don't need the chief to know I've jumped ten feet over his head."

Detective Andre Armand was a quiet man, tall, and on the skinny side of lean. He listened to Jim as he explained the crime lab and how it worked. Guidry had comments and questions, some of them snide and irritating, cementing him on Matt's blacklist.

They were standing outside the RV. While it was a large vehicle, because it had been retrofitted and decked out with extensive equipment, more than two people inside at any one time was tight. So Jim ran through his capabilities, what tests they could perform, and how they were connected to the FBI lab at Quantico to turn around results quickly.

"Must be nearly a million bucks in equipment," Guidry said.

"Just about," Jim said.

Matt knew that all told, the mobile crime lab had a price tag that far exceeded a million dollars, but he didn't say anything.

"It's worth every penny," Jim said. "I used it locally a week ago, just to give it a run-through. A triple murder in DC. We were able to process blood and fiber almost as soon as we obtained the samples, ran prints, computer simulations and more. Uploaded everything to both the DC crime lab and Quantico. Found the killer within twenty-four hours because we could handle the evidence promptly. We streamlined chain of custody, have a secure safe for evidence, a drying closet, a refrigerator for blood and fluid samples, and even a cold storage drawer."

Armand asked his first question. "You have the power for cold storage?"

"Yes, Detective—an on-board generator with seventy-two hours of juice. I'm hooked up to the hotel's power, but if I had to, for example, transport a body to a state lab, I would be able to do so. But that's not our primary purpose. The mobile response team travels to remote areas of the country, so having a lab to process 99 percent of the evidence that we might encounter is going to save lives and solve cases."

"We aim to develop a good relationship with the local authorities we assist," Matt interjected. "So far, our team has been welcome everywhere we've been."

Jim nodded. "I've assisted local forensic investigators, before we had the mobile lab. Also, I can perform an autopsy here if necessary."

"You have the room for an autopsy?" Armand asked. "Can I see?"

"Of course. Officer, would you like to join us?"

"Andre's the geek, I'll stay put," Guidry said. He looked at Matt and Savannah. "Seems like y'all are here to stay."

"As I told your chief this morning, we want to help."

"And if he says no?"

"I would find out why, see if we can come to a mutually satisfactory agreement. We want the same thing, after all."

Guidry looked around the parking lot, did a once over of the RV again, rocked back on his feet. "Seems that every time the feds stick their nose down here in the bayou we're the ones who get screwed."

"It wasn't me that screwed over anyone," Matt said, not backing down. "My team doesn't need the credit."

"You think that's what this is about? A pissing contest?"

"No, I think your chief has valid concerns about external law enforcement agencies coming into his jurisdiction. I also think he cares about his community and will take all the help he can get in solving six murders and finding Lily Baker."

Matt was watching Guidry closely, but he didn't react to Matt's comment.

A moment later, Armand and Jim exited the mobile lab. "Want to take a peek, Jerry?" Armand said.

Guidry shook his head. "You like?"

"It's state-of-the-art. Pretty damn cool."

"Think they can help with your case?"

"Possibly."

"Then write it up for the chief." Guidry said to Matt, "We'll get back to you in the morning."

Then he walked away.

Armand thanked Jim, then followed.

"Well?" Jim said.

"They're not going to let us in," Matt said.

"Andre asked good questions, paid attention," Jim said. "He sounded like he'd welcome the help."

"Guidry doesn't want us here and my gut tells me he has the ear of the chief, not Detective Armand. They're going to try to send us packing."

"But we're not going," Jim said.

"No, we're not."

20

Kara asked Beau if she could ride with him.

"Sure, why?"

"I have questions."

She climbed into his car and he started driving. "I'm just going to drive around, see if I can spot Elijah's truck." He first drove by The Fat Catfish, then Elijah's house. His place was at the end of a long road. Beau turned around and parked under a tree, kept the engine and AC running so they wouldn't sweat a gallon in the humidity. "I'm just going to wait a few, see if he shows." He glanced at her. "I didn't recognize you at The Fat Cat. Not at first."

"I know."

"You were really an undercover cop?"

"Twelve years, mostly undercover. Recruited out of the academy for an undercover gig at a high school because I was young and could blend. Did good, liked it. You? Navy first or college?"

"LSU. Naval ROTC, so went into the Navy as an officer. Lived on campus even though my dad lived nearby because I couldn't wait to get away from him. He's not a bad guy, but we didn't have a lot in common, and I didn't really care for his wife. My mom died when I was seven." He paused. "St. Augustine isn't a bad place to live. Most of the folk here are good people. Kind. God-fearing. Love their neighbors, take care of each other."

"I'm not judging."

"Maybe I am."

She glanced at him. He was quiet, contemplative, so she didn't comment.

A moment later, he said, "I came here for my grandparents and because I wanted some peace after some shit went down in the Navy and I retired. I saw problems—they predate the chief, to be honest. But the problems before the chief were drugs, prostitution, overdose deaths. The Cormiers had their fingers in everything and I wanted to take them down, but Dubois was an officer at the time and he protected them. I don't know why. I think it has to do with his son, but could never figure it out."

Kara's instincts twitched. What her former partner Colton used to tell her was her secret weapon.

I don't know how you do it, Kara, but you have this criminal radar, like this invisible antenna comes out of your head when you sense trouble. It's your secret weapon. It helps keep you alive.

But her secret weapon couldn't keep Colton alive. She pushed her partner's murder back down in the box, firmly shut it. She still missed him.

She asked innocuously, "Dubois's son?"

"Ricky. He's in college now, nineteen or twenty. Dubois got

his high school sweetheart pregnant—star athlete, high school cheerleader, a little Jack and Diane action, then three months after graduation, Ricky was born. When I first heard Dubois's story I admired him for five minutes—his girlfriend had Ricky, then left town to go to college, decided she didn't want any part of his life. Even her family moved away. Dubois raised the kid on his own. By every account he was a good dad and his world revolved around his kid. Went to community college, became a cop, provided for Ricky. There were rumors when I first moved here…that Ricky was selling drugs at the high school. Nothing solid, and Ricky was a good student, a nice kid—I met him a few times. Didn't have the look of a dealer. 'Course, looks can be deceiving. After Dubois was appointed chief, Ricky's best friend overdosed, and I started looking more closely at him and his activities. Dubois shut me out. And then I had Nicki Le-Blanc's murder on my plate—at first I didn't connect it to Lettie because Nicki was stabbed to death—then Ricky was off to college."

"So what you're saying is Dubois's son was possibly involved with the Cormiers during the time that two prostitutes were murdered and his best friend died of a drug overdose."

Beau was silent.

"Who was the kid?"

"The OD? Ethan Davis. He was raised by his grandmother. His parents aren't in the picture." He paused, glanced at her. "Miriam Davis."

She smiled. "I didn't ask."

"You were going to."

This was just way too coincidental for her to ignore.

"What are you thinking?"

She didn't have her thoughts in order, not yet—too many facts and theories were swimming around, she couldn't grasp any thread and have it make sense in the fabric of the evidence they had. Instead, she said, "Can you drive by Winnie LeBlanc's house?"

Something clicked… Winnie was nineteen. Ricky Dubois was near the same age. She probably went to school with him, knew him—and Ethan.

He hesitated then pulled away from the tree, and back down the long country road. "You're not going to tell me what's in that head of yours?"

"Isn't college out for the summer?"

"Ricky didn't come home, if that's where you're going with that," Beau said. "I heard he was working in NOLA—he goes to Tulane. Probably has a summer job there, more opportunities to work than here."

Or maybe he didn't want to be around his father.

Winnie LeBlanc lived closer to town than Elijah Morel. The LeBlanc house was two blocks west and over a narrow canal from The Fat Cat. Kara peered into the canal with narrowed eyes, expecting to see an alligator or three soaking up the sun. No alligators, the canal was a mostly dry cement gully that she supposed was used for flood control. Not that the region had a lot of control over floods. It went under the road and then she lost sight of it.

"So, if I got this right," Kara said, "Loretta LeBlanc is an addict on welfare, her oldest daughter was an addict and prostitute who had a kid, and nineteen-year-old Winnie is clean and sober, not selling sex and practically raising her four-year-old niece, no dad in the picture."

"Yep. I think Nicki was trying to get clean, for what it's worth. She was trying to be a good mom. Just couldn't quite break the habit, and was killed before she could get everything together."

"Whoever killed these women didn't care what they wanted, what they were doing, if they had kids, if they were trying to clean up their lives, if they had people who loved them. None of that mattered to the killer."

Kara would find the truth. She had to—for people like Winnie LeBlanc who would be trapped in this cycle unless someone helped her shatter it.

Beau drove by the LeBlanc house slowly, but didn't stop.

The house was different from its boxy neighbors. Built on an oversize corner lot, raised foundation, a porch on two sides and curtains in the windows. Children's toys littered the porch, and several flowerpots framed the front door. It was tired and badly in need of paint. The roof had been patched with odd sizes of lumber, and one corner had green plastic stapled to keep out the elements. But for all the physical problems, someone was trying to make the house a home.

Winnie, maybe. For her niece? Or for herself?

If anyone was home, they didn't have a car. There was no garage or carport, no car parked on the weed-infested gravel that encircled the house. A metal swing set was attached to the ground—rusting, but with new seats on the two swings, the shiny red rubber standing out against the old metal. The slide even looked functional.

Beau drove on. "What are you thinking?"

"Do you know anything about Winnie's schedule?"

"She cleans rooms at the Magnolia on Sundays and Wednesdays. Works odd jobs here and there."

"Where does she hang out? School hasn't started yet, has it? She's graduated, right?"

"Probably did, she's nineteen. School starts next Monday. There's a few places teens and young adults hang out, but I wouldn't know about Winnie. She's usually home nights, though—because of her niece."

Kara had an idea, but decided not to mention it to Beau. It involved his grandmother, and she wasn't certain how agreeable he'd be. He and Michael would be at the river tomorrow morning, and that would be the perfect time for her to talk to Winnie.

The more she thought about it, the more she liked her idea. She'd come clean with Winnie, as much as she could, and hope that Winnie talked.

Winnie knew the town's secrets.

"Beau, let's talk to Miriam Davis."

He continued driving. "You're going to have to spill your theory, Kara. I can't start stirring the pot here. Ethan's overdose was over two years ago. And if Dubois hears about it, he's going to call me to the carpet."

"And I need contact information for Ricky Dubois at Tulane," she said as if he didn't speak.

"If I'm fired, there's no one here who cares about what happened to those women."

"Now is the time to be bold. Pussyfooting around for the last three years has resulted in six dead women and no suspects."

"That's not fucking fair, Quinn."

Maybe, maybe not. But six dead women in three years—and a sprinkling of drug-related deaths? "It's not on you," she said. "It's the system. But we can fix it. Now is the time."

"I'm doing everything I can without being pulled from the investigation."

Kara was glad Beau was frustrated. That frustration needed to turn into controlled anger so he would push harder to find the truth.

"You might *think* the Cormiers are involved," she said, "and Dubois is covering it up, and you might *think* Guidry is a killer and we know he's a pervert, but you don't *know*. You have no evidence of any *specific* crime that Dubois or Guidry or the Cormiers committed. You said yourself that the girls asking questions are putting themselves in danger. Who are they in danger *from*? Who's this Debra that Johnny mentioned? Is the new mayor who appointed Dubois involved and if so, how? We need answers, so we ask the questions. Ricky Dubois has answers."

"You have no proof that Ricky knows anything, and it'll get back to his dad."

"We need to shake things up." She paused. "Put this on Matt. He'll take the heat, keep you out of it."

"I don't know."

"I do."

Beau drove by The Fat Catfish again. "Elijah's truck isn't here. Dammit." He turned south again.

She wasn't going to drop this. "Think about it, because I'm putting this all on Matt's plate. He's the boss, he'll make the call." She was pretty confident he'd make the right call.

Beau didn't say anything.

"Miriam Davis," she said. "Now is as good a time as any."

"So much for keeping a low profile."

"Like I said, I'm not going to advertise I'm a cop, but I'm not lying about it, either."

"So I say you're FBI?"

"No, I'm a detective. That's what my badge says. We can make up some bullshit about how I'm investigating a case that may tie into a drug case here in Louisiana. We're friends, I came out to see what's what. One thing I'm real good at is weaving a story on my feet. Get me in the door, I'll find out what she knows, if anything, about her grandson's death."

"Be gentle. She cared about him."

"All the better."

Miriam Davis lived in a classy brick house on the northeast side of town, on a tree-lined street along with other attractive, well-maintained brick homes. Hers had a large plate glass window in the front, a side porch and inviting cushioned chairs. Beau explained that Miriam was a retired schoolteacher and well loved in town. Her husband died of a heart attack more than a decade ago; he'd worked for the Broussard Parish Public Works Department as a civil engineer.

Beau was still uneasy about this, but Kara told him to trust her. "Maybe there's nothing to be learned. But don't you think that it's a bit suspicious that Dubois's son was suspected of dealing drugs, then his best friend dies only months after your first victim turns up dead? And then Nicki LeBlanc is killed a few weeks later? I've investigated drug cases before. I hate them. They're nasty, the people are nasty and violent, and usually the cases are a mess. But this is a murder investigation that has collided with a drug investigation, and they've gotten away with it for too long."

"But how could Ethan's OD be connected to these murders?"

"I don't know, but it's a good place to start. Can you get the police reports? Autopsy? Witness statements? Was this your case?"

He shook his head. "The detective who handled it retired— Andre Armand took over for him two years ago."

"Is the old guy still around?"

He shook his head. "Moved to…hell, I don't know. We weren't really friends. New Mexico or Arizona, someplace where it's hot and dry."

Beau turned off the ignition. Almost immediately, Kara began to sweat. "I'll never get used to the humidity," she said.

He glanced at her outfit but didn't say anything.

"What's wrong with the clothes?"

"The tank top doesn't scream professional. I mean, it's fine, we're casual here, but…" He shrugged.

Beau was dressed in khakis and a short-sleeved button-down shirt, badge and gun on his belt.

"I got just the thing." She opened her backpack and pulled out a loose-fitting, buttonless jacket. It was long-sleeved, but lightweight, and best, it was some sort of synthetic material that didn't wrinkle. She shook it out and put it over her tank top. She then retrieved her badge and clipped it to her waistband. She hadn't blow-dried her hair, so it was a wavy bob. She fluffed it with her fingers, it fell, not quite touching her shoulders. *Thank you, humidity.* Pulled out a mascara wand from the front pocket and whipped her lashes into length. Found a lightly colored lip gloss, smoothed it on.

She looked at him and smiled. "I don't do makeup, so this is going to have to be enough."

"You clean up well."

She smiled broadly. "I do, don't I? Now, just introduce me, be friendly, I'll take it from there. I'm real good at lying and half-truths."

Beau clearly wasn't a wing-it kind of investigator, and she appreciated that he agreed, albeit reluctantly, to go along with her plan.

Beau knocked. Two little dogs started barking and a woman called for them to settle down. They continued to bark.

The door opened. Through the screen Kara saw a woman shorter than her with tall, fluffy white hair and rosy cheeks. She wore a housedress and a red-and-white-checked apron. If she weighed more than a stick, she would have looked like Mrs. Claus. Waves of cinnamon and spices and other good things hit Kara in the nose and her stomach growled.

Mrs. Davis smiled. "Beau? Is that you?" She put on glasses that were hanging on a chain around her neck. "Beau Hebert! It is so good to see you. I hope there's nothing wrong with Toni." Her smile wavered.

"No, Mrs. Davis, my grandmother is doing great, thank you. This is a colleague of mine from Los Angeles, Detective Kara Quinn, and we've been talking about a case of hers. I know this is a very sad subject, but we'd like to ask you a few questions about your grandson's death. If you don't mind."

"Oh, my. Did another young man die?"

Kara said, "It's complicated. Would you mind if we come in?"

"Goodness, where are my manners! Skippy, Mitsy, out of the way. Shoo!"

The little Yorkies were cute, but yappy.

Mrs. Davis opened the door and the dogs twirled in circles at her feet. They yapped until Beau squatted and let the dogs lick his hands. They immediately started jumping and practically smiled at the attention, but they stopped yelping.

"They remember you, Beau! Even after all these years." Mrs. Davis was pleased.

"Dogs know dog lovers."

Mrs. Davis motioned for them to join her in the kitchen. "I just need to take my bread out of the oven in a few minutes, so let's sit in the kitchen, shall we?"

"You make your own bread?" Kara was impressed.

"Banana bread today. Four loaves. Beau, I'll send one home with you. Toni loves my banana bread."

"Everyone loves your banana bread," Beau said. "I'm certainly not going to turn it down."

Mrs. Davis beamed. She went to the refrigerator, took out a pitcher of what Kara suspected was sweet tea, and put it on the table. She retrieved three glasses from a cabinet, and then sat down. The two dogs ran over to dog beds near the back door, circled a few times, then lay down, heads up, tongues out, watching the people in the room.

The kitchen was larger than Kara's entire condo and had a welcoming country table in the middle. In fact, compared to the house that they'd walked through, this seemed to be the largest room.

As Beau poured three glasses of tea, he said, "Mrs. Davis is St. Augustine's best cook."

"Now, shush," she said. "No one can beat Toni's gumbo."

"Maybe not, but your baking is heavenly."

"I love baking. Keeps me moving. My husband, God rest his soul, bought this house because of the kitchen, and I will never move. I know it's too big for just me, but my daughter and her family come for a visit from Houston several times a year. Now, tell me about why you've come all the way from Los Angeles to little St. Augustine?"

Mrs. Davis pulled a large strainer over to her. It was filled with green pods. She started popping them and out rolled several peas into another bowl. Interesting, Kara thought. Her hands worked quickly shelling the peas.

"I'm sure you're aware that drug overdoses have unfortunately increased over the last few years," Kara began. She drained half the refreshing tea in her glass. "Beau said it hit you personally."

She nodded solemnly. "Ethan was a good boy, and I miss him. But I had caught him twice with drugs in the house, told him no more. He told me he would obey the rules—he wanted to, bless his heart. But drugs are from the devil, and the devil is always whispering in your ear. If you don't have the strength to ignore him, then he gets you."

"I asked Beau for the records of Ethan's death because I've been tracking drug suppliers and one of my informants is from Lake Charles, which isn't far from here. He had some information going back a few years, so when Beau and I were talking we thought there might be a connection between Ethan's supplier and the suppliers I'm now tracking."

"I can't say that I completely understand, but whatever you need, I'm happy to help. I just don't know what I can tell you."

"Drugs move around through networks all over the country—through Mexico and up north to Canada, overseas. I recognize this criminal activity is nearly impossible to stop. I want you to know, I don't blame the users like your grandson—I blame the people who get them hooked. Those are the people I'm going after."

Mrs. Davis nodded. "I see. And yes, there always seems to be more dangerous drugs out there and more families get hurt."

"How were Ethan's grades?" Kara asked. "He was a junior or senior when he died?"

"Near the end of his senior year," Mrs. Davis said. "He'd just turned eighteen. And his grades never went down. I was a teacher for thirty-two years, fourth and fifth grades. A wonderful age. When kids are still curious and full of hope and can see their possibilities. Ethan always had As and a few Bs. He struggled a bit in English—he was dyslexic, so reading was hard for him, but I worked with him and he was doing so well. I was proud of him."

"You said you found drugs here, in the house?" Kara prompted.

"In his backpack. The first time, he denied they were his, but finally he admitted it. Asked my forgiveness, which I gave as long as he didn't bring them back in the house. I watched him closely, and I didn't see any changes. I might be old and retired—that was my last year teaching—but I know what to look for."

Odd, Kara thought. Unless she didn't want to see—many parents, or grandparents, were in denial of their children's drug use.

"Did he have any friends that you felt were contributing to his problem?"

"Goodness no. I knew all his friends, they were all good kids, good families."

That didn't mean squat when it came to drugs, Kara thought.

Mrs. Davis continued. "His best friend was Ricky Dubois. They were two peas. Ethan's girlfriend—well, she was a good girl, but her family, I was worried when he went over there. I was afraid that's where he might have picked up his bad habit."

Kara knew, deep down, who Ethan's girlfriend was. "You're talking about Winnie LeBlanc?" She stated this as if she knew it as a fact, as if she was privy to case information.

Mrs. Davis nodded. "Her father was a—well, I can't say it in polite company. And her mother? Loretta LeBlanc never did a day's work. No wonder poor Nicki got caught up in trouble.

I remember her when she was nine, bless her heart. Sweetest little thing. Then…well, I will not speak ill of the dead. And I don't blame her. Not with her mother, and the rumors about her father—"

"Excuse me," Kara said, "what rumors?"

"I can't."

Beau said, "There was a rumor of, um—" he cleared his throat "—abuse in the house."

Kara knew exactly what he meant, though she didn't know why these people couldn't come out and say the LeBlanc patriarch was a child molester. "Nicki, not Winnie?"

"That man left when Winnie was just starting school," Mrs. Davis said. "Loretta finally had the backbone to kick him out, but that was the only backbone she ever showed."

Mrs. Davis paused when her timer went off. She walked to the stove and pulled out four loaves of banana bread. The smell was amazing, and Kara realized she was still hungry.

"Ten minutes to cool," she said to Beau. "Then I'll wrap up a loaf for Toni."

"Much obliged," Beau said.

She turned off her oven and sat back down, went back to shelling the peas. "Anyway, that's neither here nor there. Winnie has a good head on her shoulders. She planned to go to college. She's a smart girl, could have gotten a scholarship, state and federal grants, and she's a hard worker."

"But she decided to stay and take care of her niece," Kara concluded when Mrs. Davis didn't finish the thought.

"She's very responsible. I had hoped that Loretta would get her act together, do the right thing."

Clearly, she hadn't.

Winnie was hanging around the same people her sister had been. Winnie was friends with Ernestine, at least insofar as they had worked together cleaning the Magnolia Inn. And Ernestine was dead. Had she talked to Winnie about what she might know? Was the teen in danger?

"As I said, I'm trying to trace drugs that landed in Los Angeles and came from Louisiana." Kara knew enough about the drug trade to lie smoothly. "As you might know, some drugs are more dangerous than others. Some drugs are mixed with dangerous chemicals which helps us track them." A simple explanation, but Mrs. Davis didn't need to know more.

The old woman put the peas aside and looked at her wrinkled hands. She still wore her wedding ring, a simple gold band. "I don't want to know things like that. I don't know how I can help you—as I told the police when they came here after—after finding Ethan—I didn't know how he got the drugs."

Kara reached out and touched her hand. She wasn't a touchy person, but after only twenty-four hours in the Deep South, she realized that people here expected it. They hugged, they touched your arm, they wanted—needed, maybe—a personal connection.

"I know this is difficult for you, Mrs. Davis. And I'm sorry to bring up what was an awful time for you."

Mrs. Davis patted her hand, looked her in the eye with a small smile. "You're a good girl, Detective Quinn. I hope you find what you're looking for."

"I will. In the report, there was an accusation that Ricky Dubois may have had more information about how Ethan obtained the drugs that killed him. Ricky was his best friend."

"Ricky is a good boy. He and Ethan—they did everything together. Ricky did not approve of Ethan's drug use. I heard them arguing—" She stopped herself.

"About?" Kara prompted.

Beau spoke up. "Miriam, I know this is hard for you, and I know you don't like to think ill of people. We're not asking for you to tarnish anyone's good name. We're just looking for the truth, before more young people like Ethan die."

The old woman's pale blue eyes watered. "Ricky told Ethan that if he continued down this path that the drugs would kill him. I thought that, more than my rules, had changed Ethan. He seemed to go back to his old, happy self. But then he...he died."

"How long after that conversation?" Kara asked.

"The boys were taking down Christmas decorations outside. I was in my room, didn't mean to eavesdrop."

So end of December or early January. Ethan died only a few months later, before his high school graduation.

"Did Ethan have other friends, outside of Ricky and Winnie?"

"Everyone loved Ethan, but he didn't go out much because of his job."

"Where did he work?"

Beau said, "The grocery store, on East Main."

Mrs. Davis nodded. "He'd worked there part-time since he was fourteen. Stocking shelves. Then when he was sixteen he started near full-time. Weekends and some nights and every holiday they were open. I had a small college savings account for him, but he wanted to contribute, and he knew college was expensive. He and Ricky planned on being roommates. Winnie, dear girl, was a grade younger, but she talked about following them. And now—I'm glad Ricky is at Tulane. That he was able to put all these sad things behind him and make something of himself."

As soon as they got into the car, Kara said, "I need all the reports about Ethan Davis's death. Especially forensics. And a list of every OD in the parish from the year before Ethan's death to now. I'm going to ask Jim to go over them with a fine-toothed comb."

"I don't know that I can get all that. It could raise flags if I pull Ethan's files."

"If you don't, we're never going to solve this case."

Beau pulled away from the curb. "I'll pull them after hours

when no one is around. I doubt anyone will notice since the case is so old. But there's nothing to suggest that Ethan's overdose is connected in any way with my homicides."

"I don't know what, but there's something here." She was mulling everything over in her head. "I need to talk to Ricky, to Winnie, look at the files—I need a primer on the local drug trade."

"Slow down—"

"When exactly was Ethan killed? Mrs. Davis said before his graduation?"

"Last day of March."

"Nicki was killed less than two months after Ethan died. She knew him through Winnie. He worked at the local grocery store, everyone in town probably knew him. Maybe Nicki knew more about his death and the killer couldn't risk her talking. Ricky knows *something*. Maybe he and Ethan were both dealing drugs. Maybe they had a change of heart. Why leave Ricky alive? Father is a cop...don't kill the golden goose."

"You're not making any sense."

She was talking to herself, as she often did when she was working through a complex problem with only some of the puzzle pieces in hand. She could almost see the picture. It was fuzzy, there were missing pieces, but she knew something was here, in the overdose death of a high school senior and the suspicions surrounding the police chief's son.

Beau was obviously skeptical, but she couldn't put her thoughts into exact words. If she tried, they'd remain elusive. All she knew was that she needed to talk to Ricky and Winnie—but she would have to be cautious with both. Ricky, because he may be dangerous. Winnie, because she may be *in* danger.

Maybe she had it wrong. While there were an unusual number of overdose deaths in this small town, ODs nationwide had increased over the last several years from a longtime plateau. So it wasn't unusual to find a cluster of ODs in one small region.

But a town with less than ten thousand people? What about the parish? What about comparable small towns in other parishes?

She called Ryder before Beau could ask her any more questions.

"Hey, Ryder, it's Kara."

"Good afternoon, Detective."

"Lose the formality. I need a favor."

"A favor is asking me to pick you up at a bar after you drink too much to drive."

"Ouch. You're never going to let me live that down, are you?"

"Probably not."

Ryder had loosened up just a bit over the six months she'd known him. He had a dry sense of humor, was quiet and supersmart, and picked up on everything—even if he chose not to comment. She appreciated his discretion. She hadn't wanted to call Matt the night she'd gotten wasted after hearing bad news from her boss in LA about the pending trial of David Chen, the human trafficker and sweatshop owner she'd arrested at the beginning of the year. Mostly because Matt would want to discuss it, and she just wanted to hit something. Plus, it had been a work night and she and Matt had agreed that they wouldn't see each other off-duty during the week to avoid rumors and all that nonsense. Matt had told his boss—required because she was his subordinate, and because he was concerned if someone else told Greer that it would be worse—but they hadn't announced anything to the world, and that was fine with her. How much Ryder knew about her relationship with Matt she didn't know, but the analyst wasn't stupid.

"It's work-related."

"So you want me to do my job."

"You're getting kind of testy these days. I think I liked it better when you were more robot and less human."

"What can I do for you, Kara?" he asked, humor in his voice.

"Overdose deaths in St. Augustine, Broussard Parish. Going

back four years. Trends. A comparison with neighboring parishes."

She could hear Ryder typing. "Okay, I can do that, but most databases are going to be behind twelve to eighteen months."

"That's okay. I'm really interested in the two, three, four years ago. Also, very, very, very quietly look into Ricky Dubois. His name might be Richard Dubois, Jr."

"It is," Beau said.

"Legal name," she told Ryder. "Goes by Ricky, twenty, attends Tulane University. But he's the son of the police chief and I don't want the chief to know I'm looking at him."

"I can get some things without raising flags. Anything else?"

"I assume Matt already asked for financials on the Magnolia, Fat Catfish, things like that?"

"Yes, Agent Heller is working on that."

"Can you throw some more on his plate?"

"I live to give Agent Heller more work."

She almost laughed. She turned to Beau. "What's the name of that grocery store?"

He looked at her skeptically, then said, "Topp's Grocery."

She said to Ryder, "Topp's Grocery, on East Main Street in St. Augustine." She asked Beau, "Who's the owner?"

"Joseph Kelly."

She relayed the name to Ryder.

"Got it," he said.

"And finally, Peter Landry."

"You already put him on the list."

"Right, but he bought up a bunch of property—when, Beau?" she asked him.

"Before he was mayor. Five, six, seven years?"

"Did you hear that?" she asked Ryder.

"Got it." She heard him clicking on the keyboard. "I assume you haven't talked to Costa yet."

"Don't tell me I have to go through him first. I hate bureaucracy."

"You don't have to go through him. Put it in your daily report. We need to have documentation when and if something goes to trial. And though you detest writing reports, yours are very good."

"They are? I'm flattered."

"I'll let you know when I have something."

"Thanks, buddy." She ended the call with a smile. Matt always gave her shit about her reports, but Ryder processed everything for the team, the central repository, the Father of All Things MRT, and he said they were good. She was going to enjoy rubbing *that* under Matt's nose.

If she and Matt ever had another private conversation. Because at this point, she wasn't sure where they stood anymore.

Then she sent Ryder a text message. Did Matt ask you to run Agent Savannah Trahan?

A moment later she got his response.

Yes.

She smiled. Matt was a good cop.

21

Matt followed his GPS to Beau Hebert's house. Savannah was in the passenger seat, sending her boss a report, and Jim was in the back sulking. He hadn't wanted to leave the hotel—or the RV.

Matt wanted to move everything—documentation, meetings, Michael and Kara—to the hotel. He didn't think it was a good idea, or appropriate, to have their primary war room at a personal residence. But technically he wasn't here: this wasn't an official FBI case yet. They were in the exploratory stage.

He glanced in his rearview mirror. "You're fidgeting, Jim."

"I don't like leaving the crime lab unattended."

"Separation anxiety?" Matt teased.

"That's a million-dollar RV, Matt. If anything happens to it, Tony will have my ass—and yours, too."

"They installed state-of-the-art security and we'll be alerted if anyone so much as breathes too hard on the door. It's the middle of the day. I think it'll be fine."

"It is so sweet, Matt. I don't think you appreciate the capabilities we have."

"I do."

"I should have asked for a tour," Savannah said.

"I'll be happy to show you around," Jim said.

"I'd enjoy that."

Matt glanced at his phone and read a cryptic message from Ryder.

Call me when you can talk.

Ryder may have found something on Savannah Trahan or Curt Danville—he'd asked Ryder to pull both files, make sure everything was kosher. Matt didn't want to look a gift horse in the mouth, but he'd expected more pushback when he talked to the Lafayette office. Maybe there was nothing to find.

Matt wished they had more time to prepare. There were a lot of files to catch up on. He'd agreed to move quickly because of the missing girl—now dead—who had been Beau's informant. That meant juggling a lot of things in a town that didn't know the meaning of the word *rush*.

Beau lived out in the middle of farmland. It was a bit run-down, but had a quaint and homey feel. As soon as Matt drove up, Michael came out of the larger of the two houses, flanked by a tiny old woman.

Michael introduced the three federal agents to Toni Hebert, who looked a bit overwhelmed, but hospitable. "If I'd have known I was having this many people, I would have saved my gumbo for today."

"Mimi," Michael said, "you do not have to feed anybody. Except for me, of course. They'll all be gone before dinner."

He kissed the top of her head and she beamed.

Michael was a charmer with all the ladies.

"Now, dear boy, I'm not letting anyone leave here hungry. I'll put something together. Just a little something."

"Beau is going to be mad at me if I let you do that."

"Pshaw. No one *lets* me do anything. I'll do what I damn well please. I'll call you when I have a tray for you to bring down. Y'all, go ahead, do what you do."

"You'd better tell Beau this was your idea."

"My grandson knows I have a mind of my own. Where'd you think he got his?"

She shuffled inside the house.

Michael said, "I love her. Wish she was my kin."

"She treats you as if she is," Matt said.

Michael grinned. "Beau's a lucky guy. Everything is set up at the other house." He led the way across the packed gravel drive.

"That's where Beau lives?" Savannah asked.

"No, he's in the main house. Uses this smaller place as his office."

They walked inside. Matt looked around, recognized Kara's handwriting on the whiteboard.

"Where's Kara?" Matt asked.

"She and Beau are still out," Michael said. "She checked in thirty minutes ago, said they were interviewing someone about her grandson's overdose."

Matt studied the whiteboard. Kara had unique shorthand, but he had grown to recognize it. "This—" He gestured to a box of names. "She identified six people who had last see Lettie Chaisson alive at the Magnolia Inn and are now all dead. That's a damn coincidence." Many of those names overlapped sightings of other victims, but Matt couldn't help but focus on the fact that many of these witnesses were dead—either drug overdose or murder.

Savannah said, "The victims all worked there. I wouldn't say coincidence. But why are Lily and Ernestine marked as 'outliers'?"

Michael said, "Because Ernestine wasn't a prostitute or addict, and Lily Baker's body hasn't been found."

"That doesn't mean anything," Savannah said, "especially if she was dumped in the river."

"That's what we're thinking happened," Michael said, "but the other victims were found within days. Kara thinks, and I agree, that the killer didn't want authorities to find Lily's body."

"Hmm, maybe…" Savannah said.

Matt excused himself and stepped outside to return Ryder's call.

"What's going on?" Matt said.

"So far, after a basic review, Trahan and Danville are clean. Trahan's divorce was final seven years ago, her ex-husband is remarried, no criminal record. Danville has been married fifteen years, no children, wife is a teacher. I put a call into ASAC Logan Sheffield in Houston for his assessment of the investigation six years ago, as you suggested, and asked him to contact you directly."

"Thank you."

"Kara asked for a background check. She's writing it up, but you should know that it's the son of the police chief."

"Did she say why?"

"I didn't ask." Ryder gave Matt the basics about Chief Dubois's son. College, NROTC, summer job.

"Who else?" Matt asked.

"No one, but she added another business to Zack's list, plus the mayor's properties, and wanted to make sure we were investigating Trahan."

What about Savannah had raised Kara's hackles? He hadn't noticed anything at the hotel, but Kara had a good poker face.

"The primary reason I wanted to talk to you was I found some interesting information about Peter Landry, the new mayor."

"I didn't put him on the list."

"Kara sent me his name and a few others last night. Do you want me to wait for your approval?"

Clearly, Matt needed to talk to Kara.

"No. Kara isn't going to have you running in circles. If she wanted information on Landry, she has a good reason."

Matt vaguely remembered her mentioning him, but he'd then been sidetracked by Officer Guidry's sexual assault.

"Her instincts were right. He was investigated by NOLA FBI for an insurance fraud scheme seven years ago."

"Indicted?"

"No. This is where it gets murky. He was in a partnership with three other men. One of the men, Derek O'Neill, ended up confessing and claimed his partners didn't know about it, that he had written up the bad policies on his own. He was arraigned, pled guilty, but wouldn't accept a plea agreement which would have required him to provide additional information that may have implicated his partners. Maximum sentence and he died in prison six months later. I'm still trying to find out what happened to him. Landry and his partner, Jasper Steele, walked free."

"Steele. That's the guy who runs the Magnolia Inn."

"Yes, sir."

"You said there were three partners."

"The last one I am having trouble identifying. His name isn't in the database, or on any of the records. I need to contact the agent who worked the case."

"Do that. We need all the players. You said seven years ago?"

"Yes. Landry stayed in NOLA, but Jasper Steele moved to St.

Augustine and bought the Magnolia Inn. Landry didn't move to St. Augustine until after his grandfather died."

"When did he start buying up property?"

"I'm still going through property records—it's more difficult than you think, because they're not all online. The only one I can find in his name is for a restaurant called The Broiler. That was before everything went down in NOLA—he bought it eight years ago. Zack is also researching LLCs, including the LLC that owns the Magnolia. According to Kara, Landry bought up a bunch of property in the business district, but I can't find anything in his name."

Shell corporations could conceal the identity of the property owner, but the information was there if you knew where to look. "Good. I need a report from Zack by tomorrow morning—everything he's found, what he's still working on. In writing."

"I'll let him know."

Matt saw a car coming down the drive—Beau and Kara.

"Thank you, Ryder. This is good. Make sure you listen in to the conference call with Catherine. You need to be kept in the loop."

"Yes, sir."

He ended the call as Kara and Beau got out of the car.

First thing he noticed—Kara was wearing makeup. She rarely wore makeup, which told him that she went to interview a professional or someone who expected her to be professional. She was playing a part. Twice in a day—went from prostitute to senior detective in a blink and wardrobe change.

She appeared to be irritated at Beau.

Beau said to Matt, "Either Kara is the smartest cop on the planet or she's going to get us all fired."

"Smartest cop," Kara said.

"This is about the background on Chief Dubois's son," Matt guessed.

"He's going to find out, and he's going to run you out of town," Beau said. "Then my investigation will be shut down."

"We're not leaving until we're ready to leave," Matt said.

Kara snapped her fingers, pointed at Matt. "Exactly what I said. Beau—I understand where you're coming from. You're hyperfocused on six dead women. I've been where you are. I know it's hard to let go. All I'm asking is for you to look at the case from a different angle. At the beginning you thought this was about drugs—and I think you're right. But maybe not for the reasons we initially thought." She turned to Matt. "You talked to Ryder."

"Yes."

"I need to go to NOLA and interview Ricky Dubois."

"No," Beau said.

"Not up to you," Kara said.

Matt needed to fix this. Earlier, Beau and Kara were working well together, but something happened when they were in town and now they weren't on the same page.

"If anyone interviews Ricky," Matt said, "it'll be Michael."

Kara didn't look angry, just surprised.

"Okay, why?"

"Because Ricky's NROTC, right up Michael's alley. He'll respond better to someone who's been in his shoes."

"That makes sense. Good."

"Richard will find out," Beau said.

Kara shrugged. "Maybe, maybe not."

"Of course he's going to call his father!"

"If he's guilty, he will. If he's innocent? I don't know."

"Guilty of what?" Matt asked.

"Drug dealing and accidentally killing his best friend. I need Winnie LeBlanc to talk. I have an in now—her boyfriend died of an overdose and she knows a lot about it. Her boyfriend was Ricky's best friend."

"You're going to put her in danger," Beau said. "Didn't I just explain to you that I put Ginny and Ernestine in the morgue? Because they were talking to me."

"And I told *you* that's not your doing. Shit, Beau! If you worry that everyone you talk to is going to turn up dead we'll never solve these murders. We're up to what, ten now? Eleven if we include Lily? Probably more, whenever Ryder gets me the OD reports."

"Whoa, where did we get eleven homicides?" Matt asked.

Kara smiled slyly. "They're all there on the board. And I think Catherine will agree with me. I'll explain everything when we get inside, okay?"

The door of the main house opened. "Beau! I have some food for your friends!"

Kara said, "I'll get it. Just…have an open mind, okay?"

She headed toward the main house.

Beau said, "My head is spinning."

"Let's hear what she has to say. Kara has a sharp head on her shoulders. Do you know what she meant about the eleven homicides?"

"She's pooling the dead women with related deaths—the dealer in Lake Pierre who was killed in a police action, one of the victim's brothers who died of an OD, Ricky Dubois's best friend, and—get this—she started mumbling about Jake West. What does West have to do with anything?"

"I don't know," Matt admitted. "But if Kara sees a connection, there's probably a connection."

22

Matt wished he had sent Savannah Trahan back to Lafayette.

It wasn't that he didn't trust her. She was a vetted agent and had been particularly helpful today. She had a lot of knowledge and insight about St. Augustine and the greater community.

But she wasn't one of his. She wasn't part of his team.

Kara hadn't been on your team in March when you brought her in to catch the Triple Killer.

That was different, he told himself, though it wasn't. If anything, Savannah had a better background and profile than Kara. She was an FBI agent, for one, not a local cop. She was college educated with the same type of training Matt had.

But his team had developed their own rhythm, and Savannah changed it. He felt Kara especially holding back, and he didn't want that—he needed his team to be completely forthright and honest at all times, to share theories and ideas freely. It's why they worked well together, and something Matt had tried to cultivate in all his previous leadership roles. While he was confident and could make hard decisions, a leader was only as good as his team.

He set up his laptop so they could Skype with Catherine. Jim had already started going through the forensic documentation, muttering, "This is bullshit!" and "They didn't run a screening!" and "Why didn't he do an autopsy?"

Once his laptop was set up, Matt called Ryder from his computer. The young Korean American analyst popped up onscreen. It was close to five—six in DC—and they'd already had a long day. But Ryder didn't look tired.

"Ryder, we're all here," he said.

"One moment, I'll bring Dr. Jones in," Ryder said and his screen went black.

Kara was eating a sandwich. Beau's grandmother had made a large plate of food that rivaled any caterer.

"You're a lucky man, Beau," Michael said as he picked up his second sandwich.

"I hope she's not working too hard."

Kara said, "I told her to sit down and relax."

"She won't, not if the kitchen is a mess."

"I cleaned up. I left her eating a sandwich with some fresh lemonade." She sipped her own lemonade. "Can you believe Toni made this from actual fruit? It's better than any I've had."

Dr. Catherine Jones came on-screen with Ryder in the upper left-hand corner. Catherine was a professional in all things, her dark hair up and off her face, her makeup subtle but perfect, her jewelry expensive and classy. She was sitting at her desk at Quantico, her bookshelf of legal and medical tomes behind her. They'd been friends a long time—her husband, Chris, was

Matt's closest friend. He'd been an usher in their wedding and was godfather to their daughter.

"Catherine, good to see you." Matt introduced Beau and Savannah. "So, who's the killer?" he joked.

She shook her head good-naturedly. "I read everyone's reports, and reviewed additional information that Kara sent over this morning. But I have questions first for Detective Hebert because he's been investigating these murders for three years. Probably the most important at this point—do you know why the coroner didn't perform complete autopsies on any of the victims?"

"Dr. Brown has been coroner for over thirty years," Beau said. "He visually inspects the bodies. Nicki LeBlanc was stabbed twenty-seven times. He told me, and I quote, 'I don't need to cut her open to know she was stabbed to death.' He draws blood and runs standard toxicology screens, sends them to the state lab—that's how we know that all the victims had high levels of opioids and alcohol in their systems. You should have those reports."

"I do. So there was no physical autopsy, just a visual exam, on the victims. That clarifies things."

"Not for me," Jim interjected. "I've been reading through these reports—I wouldn't even call them reports. This guy should be fired."

"The coroner is elected," Beau said. "Only requirement is that he be a medical doctor who has a practice in the parish. Judson Brown qualified." Beau glanced at Savannah. "You know how these towns are, Agent Trahan."

"Yes," she said. "Small towns like their own. Once a person or family rises to a position of power, it's almost impossible to remove them. There are no term limits in most of these parishes, so you find a mayor you like, who knows everyone and jumps through whatever hoops the community puts up, and they'll be mayor until the day they die."

"Like Landry," Kara said. "Peter Landry took over from his

grandfather a little over three years ago. Everyone loved the grandpa. Peter won because of nepotism."

"It's not nepotism," Beau said, "not in the way you think about it. It's community. The Landrys have been in the parish since before Louisiana was a state. They have roots. Roots are important here. Family, community, a cultural understanding that no one who wasn't born and raised in a similar parish can really understand."

"Small-town politics on steroids," Kara said.

"Hell, forget the Mason-Dixon Line, most people here think everyone who lives north of I-10 is a Yankee," Beau said.

"True," Savannah concurred.

"I studied the demographics of the region," Catherine said. "Between post-pandemic economic troubles and three major floods over the last twenty years, the community is struggling. The parish has one of the highest incidents per capita of overdose deaths of any parish in the state. It's difficult to compare because the parish is so small. Any tiny increase in overdose deaths would seem unusually large, but the numbers are rather staggering."

Kara said, "I asked Ryder to run a list of all overdoses in the last four to five years—to compare the year or two before Landry was elected and the three years since. But I also want names and circumstances."

Interesting, Matt thought. Kara had essentially restructured the case around the election of the new mayor—which was, in fact, a beginning of sorts: the new chief of police, the dead women, the possibly related overdose deaths. Now he finally saw what she had seen.

"He can get statistics," Beau said, "but I don't think he'll be able to pull reports. Broussard does the bare minimum in reporting to the state and federal authorities, and they're probably behind."

"Can you get files?"

"The coroner's office would have the data," Beau said. "I don't know how good it is."

"I'll get it," Jim said. "I need to go in there and talk to this doctor."

Matt thought that was a good idea, but before he could comment, Beau said, "Jim, with all due respect, he's not going to give you shit."

"I'm used to dealing with stubborn coroners. We had our fair share of them in Texas."

Before the conversation derailed, Matt steered it back to Catherine. "Let's talk about our next steps after Catherine finishes her profile of the killer."

"Or killers," Kara interjected.

"Excluding Ernestine Bergeron for the moment," Catherine said, "all the other victims, including the missing Lily Baker, were known sex workers and drug addicts. Lily Baker's family stated that she'd been clean for approximately two months. If the statement about Ms. Baker's pregnancy is accurate, this could be true. Pregnancy is often a motivating factor to seek help. But with no body, we can prove neither."

"But if we find her body intact? We can get DNA on the baby, right?" Beau asked.

Jim spoke. "Best guess is she was between three and four months pregnant. If the body had been found immediately, a competent autopsy would be able to extract DNA from the fetus. But if the body has been destroyed, there wouldn't be any fetal tissue to work with. Extracting DNA from bones is already a difficult process, fetal bones at that young gestation would be near impossible and extremely expensive."

"Even if the body has severely decomposed," Catherine said, "you should be able to obtain DNA to identify Ms. Baker, correct?"

"Yes," Jim said. "A skull, femur, pelvis—those are the most likely to be intact after four months. No major storms since she disappeared helps keep any remains near the dump site as well, since the river is slow-moving and the riverbed soft."

"Don't underestimate the destructive nature of alligators," Beau said. "They can scatter bones far and wide."

Matt noted that Kara visibly shivered. She had an aversion to all things wild. If it wasn't a house cat or pet dog, she avoided it. When they encountered a rattlesnake on a morning hike they took back in June when they had a weekend alone together in Tucson, she froze. A human threat she handled with confidence; an animal threat not so much.

"Going back to the cases in hand," Catherine said, "we have limited evidence. Because the women were sex workers, it's difficult to determine whether these crimes were sexual in nature. With the shoddy forensics, I'm skeptical that the samples were properly collected. The autopsy reports are incomplete. The coroner didn't indicate whether there had been any tearing in the vagina or the anus. It could be that he didn't see any, thus didn't write it down."

"Lazy bastard," Jim muttered.

Catherine continued, "A forensic sex crimes expert may be able to analyze the crime scene and autopsy photos."

"One of the preeminent sex crimes experts works out of Quantico," Matt said. "If you need her to consult, I'll pave the way."

"As Kara determined this morning," Catherine said, "and I concur from the reports and crime scene photos, most of the women were disposed of without ceremony."

"Like trash," Kara muttered.

"No attempt to conceal the crime," Catherine continued. "All near roads, except for Ernestine, correct?"

"That's right," Beau said. "It would take a four-wheel drive to cross the muddy field to the river's edge."

"My educated guess is that the killer strangled their victims in a vehicle or near a vehicle, and dragged or carried them to their final resting place, no more than thirty feet. There was bruising on the arms, neck and face of the victims who were strangled, but no sexual bruising—no bruising on the breasts, buttocks or stomach. I am confident that these weren't sexual crimes."

Savannah Trahan spoke up. "If I may ask a question?"

"Go ahead, Agent Trahan," Matt said.

"What if we are dealing with a serial killer targeting prostitutes? As you undoubtedly know, ma'am, prostitutes are common targets of psychopaths. Easy to find, easy to get alone."

"True," Catherine said. "I can't rule it out, but because Nicki LeBlanc was stabbed to death—brutally—I don't think we're dealing with a traditional serial murderer, and I don't think their sex work was the primary factor."

"Yet," Savannah continued, "she could be an anomaly, she may have been killed by someone completely different for a different reason."

Catherine nodded. "I considered that, and this is a good segue into why I dismissed that theory. First—Nicki may have been killed by a different person than the man who strangled four other victims, but the information we know suggests that she was killed for the same or similar reason as her peers. All six deaths—including Ms. Bergeron—are connected. By connected, I mean the same person killed them or *had them killed*. Not because they were driven to kill, as with a serial killer. These murders seem to be about business."

Bingo, Kara mouthed. Matt thought he was the only one who saw her lips move. Though Catherine and Kara did not personally like each other and had butted heads more than once, they were often on the same page when it came to psychological analysis. While Catherine had the education and FBI experience as a profiler, Kara had an unusually firm grasp on human nature, especially when it related to crime.

Catherine said, "While the method is personal—the motive is not, with the exception of Nicki LeBlanc. The victims knew their killer. The victims didn't fear for their lives until the killer's hands were around their neck. They may have been high and unable to fight back, or not realized they were in danger until it was too late. The more I look at what we know and where we can make an educated guess, I believe that the individual who strangled four women is not the same person who stabbed LeBlanc to death."

"What?" Beau said, surprised. "But you just said they were connected."

"Connected, yes. But the methods are distinctly different. Nicki's murder was particularly brutal. Remember," Catherine continued, "a profile is simply an educated analysis of available information. If you uncover new information, I will adjust my profile if warranted. The murders themselves are rash—the killer didn't care about evidence. They're bold, careless and aren't concerned about being caught. My sense is that a law enforcement officer would take far greater care in disposing of the bodies and ensure that there was no physical evidence linking him to their deaths—even if he could control the investigation. So while an officer may have been privy to the murders, I don't think he is the killer."

Catherine continued. "Ernestine's murder is unique. It was quick. She was killed where you found her. Someone drove her there, walked her across a marshy field to the river and sliced her throat from behind."

"You can tell that from the pictures?" Beau asked.

"I don't have the forensics report—and I would revise my opinion if the report contradicts my theory—but the photos showed no bruising on her body. Her throat was deeply cut and she bled out immediately. The killer didn't want to look her in the eyes when she died, which is why she was face down. That is distinctly different than the previous victims."

"Different killer?" Matt asked, leaning forward. He could picture it. A man walking with Ernestine, talking to her, taking her to the river, standing behind her, maybe holding her, then slicing her throat fast.

"I can't say," Catherine said. "What I'm comfortable saying is that the killer genuinely liked Ernestine and felt guilty killing her. She was the only victim fully clothed. The others were in varying degrees of undress. Ernestine died quickly, faster than manual strangulation. If he killed the other women, he doesn't feel remorse. But for Ernestine, he has intense guilt. If you find a suspect, he will confess. Highlight anything personal about his relationship with her, then show photos of her dead body. His guilt will compel him to respond."

A guilty conscience made mistakes, Matt thought. If they identified and interviewed a suspect, Matt would be able to break him.

"Now," Catherine said, "this doesn't mean he's guilty of all the murders. Kara laid out a theory that the women were pieces of a larger canvas. That may be true. There is a cluster of drug-related deaths between the murders of the first and fourth victim. But based on the very limited evidence we have, I can't agree or disagree with the theory. We simply don't have enough information."

"Because my witnesses all get killed!" Beau started to pace.

Matt felt for the detective, but hoped he would regain control. Matt had no authority over him and didn't want him to go off half-cocked.

Kara walked over to the computer and sat down to take center stage in the conversation with Catherine. "Let me add to my theory," she said. "I've been thinking about this all day. Jean Paul LeBlanc killed Jake West. Then he told Beau that Lily was pregnant and he saw Tanya get into a police car the night she was killed."

"Yes, that's in the reports," Catherine said, sounding impatient.

"Why did he kill Jake West?" Kara asked.

"I don't understand the relevance."

"It doesn't fit. It doesn't fit any of these murders."

"Because it's likely not connected," Catherine said. "He could have had a personal beef with the man."

"Yet, Jean Paul's in the middle of all of this. He had been one of the last people to see two of the previous victims the nights they disappeared. He had knowledge of Lily's pregnancy—"

"If she was pregnant," Catherine interrupted.

"And he told Beau that if he went to jail he'd be dead," Kara continued as if Catherine hadn't spoken. "He implied he knew more, and I don't know that he did. I think he told Beau everything he knew because he was in danger. Why keep the secret? He killed Jake West for a *reason*. No one is trying to figure that out because Jean Paul is dead. Both cases, closed."

Beau stopped pacing and said, "I don't understand your point."

"No one is asking what his motive was," Kara said. "He had to have one. You said he wasn't drunk or high when you arrested him."

"So?"

"So he probably wasn't drunk when he shot Jake West. He's drinking at the bar, gets up, they have words, then he kills him, walks out and *no one* stops him. There's a shotgun and a handgun under the bar, yet Jake didn't go for them. Neither did the others who work there after Jean Paul killed the bartender. They just let him walk away. We need to find out why Jean Paul killed Jake."

Everyone was silent. Then Savannah asked, "What does that have to do with these murders?"

Matt bristled a bit at Savannah's tone—borderline dismissive, exasperated as if she thought Kara's theory was a waste of time.

"They all worked out of the Magnolia Inn," Kara said. "Jake was the bartender. Ernestine worked there, as a housekeeper. Jean Paul is related to one of the victims." She shrugged and leaned back in her chair. "Maybe they have nothing to do with each other, what do I know?"

Matt knew Kara well enough to know that she thought she was on to something.

"Kara," Matt said, "you and Beau interviewed a woman today about the overdose death of her grandson. You think that's important."

"Yes." She cleared her throat, drained half a bottle of water. But she was thinking, always thinking. Matt could see her wheels turning. Was she holding back because of Savannah's comment? "Beau said there was a rumor that Ricky Dubois was dealing drugs to high school kids. He's the son of the police chief, off-limits, protected, whatever. His best friend dies of an overdose, and he goes off to college six months later, doesn't come home. Beau can't remember if Ricky has been home in the two years since he left for Tulane. Guilt? Or is he innocent and just leaving behind sad memories? I don't know. That's why I want to talk to him. But I agree with Matt—Michael is best."

"Why?" Catherine asked.

Matt said, "Ricky is in the Naval ROTC program. Michael is a veteran. I would ask Beau to do it, but Beau works for the police department, making that a lot more complicated than it needs to be."

"I'm diving tomorrow," Michael said.

"Tomorrow night or Wednesday," Matt said.

Savannah asked, "What's the rush? What could a kid who hasn't lived here in two years possibly know about these murders?"

"If he was involved, he'll know about the drug trade," Kara said. "If he wasn't, he might know who Ethan Davis bought from, some of the players. Information."

Catherine said, "We don't have enough evidence to point to any specific type of killer or even if there is more than one killer, though I am leaning to Nicki LeBlanc being an outlier. While generally, we should look to the first victim to uncover more information, in this case you need to look at Nicki Le-

Blanc. Her murder was more violent than the others'. The killer was enraged. Twenty-seven stab wounds—he couldn't stop himself. If she *was* killed by the same person, then her murder was brutal for a reason."

"Twenty-seven stab wounds and no physical evidence on the body?" Matt said. "Stabbings yield solid evidence—the killer often cuts himself, or leaves hair, skin, other trace on the victim."

"Well, shit," Jim said. "This is—dammit, Matt, can we just take over already?"

Matt turned to his forensic expert and frowned. He had never seen Jim so agitated. "What are you looking at?"

Jim held up a thin file. "Nicki LeBlanc! They didn't collect any trace evidence. Nothing. They *washed her body* to prepare for the visual examination. *Washed her before collecting trace!* On a brutal murder like this you need hours to go over the body, head to toe, clipping, taking samples, extracting hair, fiber from *every single wound*. They didn't do that. They washed her body then did a visual exam and said, yep, she was stabbed to death, on to the next."

Kara walked over to Jim and looked at the folder he held tightly. He pointed things out to her, and Matt noted Kara's presence immediately calmed the crime scene expert.

Catherine continued. "It's possible, with the exception of Nicki, that the women were killed to serve the larger business."

Matt let that settle in. "Hired, as in a hit man?"

"Hired, as in someone who is told to 'take care of' a situation. Beau," Catherine said, "can you elaborate more on the Cormier brothers and how you view the hierarchy?"

"Preston Cormier is in his late thirties, charming, clean-cut. Smooth and pretends he's completely legitimate. His half brother Gray is nearly a decade younger. Loses his temper easily. Defers to Preston when they're together, but by himself gets in trouble. He's been arrested multiple times for drug possession—charges always dismissed, thanks to the DA. Alston is a big part of the problem." Beau hesitated.

Kara pushed. "And?"

"I—" He stopped himself.

Matt said, "Beau, you need to be up-front with us. We came here because Michael vouched for you. *Solely* because Michael trusts you."

Michael turned to his longtime friend. "You have another informant, don't you?"

"I'm not going to out this person, not right now. This person is risking not only their career but their life if Alston Gary finds out I have someone in his office."

"We'll table this discussion for now," Matt said. "But you and I will discuss it privately."

"Other players? Or just the Cormiers?" Catherine asked.

Beau nodded. "If it's drugs, it goes through the Cormiers. Jasper Steele is involved through them. He owns the Magnolia Inn. I doubt Tammy Bergeron, who runs The Fat Catfish, is running hard drugs, but I could be wrong. She generally works cons, identity theft, has a couple of girls working out of the bar, sells pot she grows herself in small quantities."

"There was a discrepancy in two statements," Kara said. "Jean Paul said he saw Tanya getting into a cop car, and two witnesses claim that they saw Tanya driving away with Buddy Palfrey."

"Based on the timeline, they both could be true," Beau said, "but I can't follow up on any of them because they're all dead."

That sunk in. Matt knew this case was different from the beginning, but now it hit him that every potential witness had been killed.

Beau continued, "At the time, Buddy told me that he dropped Tanya at her house. Her brother—Buddy's best friend—backed him up. But Tanya's brother said she got mad at him and walked out sometime in the wee hours of the morning. She didn't have a car, but she lived near downtown so could walk most anywhere, including the Magnolia. So at two in the morning, how did Jean Paul know she got in a police car?" Beau shook his head.

Catherine asked, "Do you have an idea of how the drugs are moved in and around town? Do they distribute the end product or are they middlemen or suppliers?"

"Based on what I've observed and a few people who have given me pieces of information," Beau said, "the Cormiers are distributors—not just in St. Augustine, but the region. Mostly pills—started with oxy, has been shifting to fentanyl last few years. Pills are easier to transport, store, sell. Don't need to be cut, repackaging is easy. I don't know where they're getting them from."

"Virtually all fentanyl in the country comes up through Mexico," Kara said.

"Two years ago," Beau said, "I spoke to a DEA agent and he made it clear that he was only interested if I could get their suppliers. If I could flip them, then he'd bring the case to his boss. But I can't even get them on a lesser charge."

"Do you know how they're getting the product?" Matt asked.

"They likely get their shipments by boat—from the Gulf—but distribute through the back roads," Beau said. "That's my educated guess. When you talk about suppliers and transportation routes, that's way over my head—that's why I reached out to the DEA."

He sounded extremely frustrated, and Matt didn't blame him. Beau was practically a one-man cop shop and no one person can solve every crime.

"The Magnolia Inn is the Cormiers' hub," Beau continued. "I think—can't prove—that the girls are go-betweens. If one of the johns is an undercover cop and a girl gives them their package of pills, it's only that girl who is wrung up—she doesn't even know who's in charge, and even if she says, 'Gray Cormier told me to give John Doe the package,' she's still a drug addicted prostitute, which makes the case shaky from the get-go."

"I'll reach out to some people who know how this works," Matt said. "See what I can learn about the drug network in this area."

"I'm pretty sure I understand the basics," Kara said. "They get pills from Mexico. There are so many waterways here it's easy. A ship comes in, anchors out in the gulf—different places each time to avoid DEA and Coast Guard detection. Smaller motorboats meet the ship, collect product, disburse in different directions heading to coastal cities. NOLA, Galveston, Pensacola, smaller towns, wherever they have a connection. If one boat gets picked up by the Coast Guard, they still have ten other boats delivering product. They build in a 50 percent loss from law enforcement and theft, so if six of ten boats get through, they profit. My guess is that Cormier is working with a group like that. Meets them once or twice a month for his supply, then repackages and distributes to his territory. Once the pills leave the boat, it's completely Cormier's business."

"And the DEA won't touch it unless we can get the big ship," Beau said. "Which is fucked because a small town like St. Augustine doesn't have the resources to tackle that magnitude of an investigation."

"They're counting on that," Matt said.

"And if Cormier is caught and turns on the organization, at most they'll get the small boat that delivers to him. Those boats are a dime a dozen. Someone will step in to fill the void." Kara shook her head. "This is why I avoided drug cases, for the most part. I had my fair share, but if I could take down a sweatshop or a corrupt politician or a meth lab, I was much happier. International drug distribution is a beast of its own."

"This is good to know," Matt said. "Ryder, can you follow up with the FBI-DEA liaison and find out what they know about this distribution method, and if anyone in southern Louisiana is on their radar?"

"Yes, sir," Ryder said.

"I wish I could give you a clearer profile," Catherine said, "that the killer is thirty, balding and lives with his mother. I can't. This is a difficult case for a multitude of reasons, and if someone in law enforcement is involved, it makes it much more difficult."

"I'll work on whatever physical evidence there is," Jim said. "I'll find something the coroner didn't because he didn't even look."

"I leave those decisions to Matt," Catherine said. "But yes, there could be something that was overlooked, intentionally or not. If you continue to feed me information, I may be able to shape the profile into something more useful."

Matt said, "This is very helpful, Catherine." It was getting late, and they now had new investigatory leads. His head was filled with a long to-do list he itched to jump on, but before he could end the conference call, Kara spoke.

"What if," she said, "this is an organized group. Like—like maybe an outlaw biker gang. They have several people who are capable of doing violence—maybe on orders, maybe on their own—but there is one leader."

Catherine considered, then said carefully, "I don't think we have enough information to make that determination."

"But," Kara continued, "just play a little *what-if* game. *If* the deaths of Bud Ewing and Buddy Palfrey and Ethan Davis and Jake West and Jean Paul LeBlanc are directly related to the murders of five prostitutes and Ernestine—what kind of person can control that? Meaning, how can they keep people from bolting or walking or talking?"

"They threaten them," Catherine said simply. "Fear is a powerful deterrent."

"And, if they weren't sufficiently scared or did something not in the best interest of the organization, killing them would send a message to the others to stay in line."

"Possibly," Catherine said, sounding skeptical yet interested.

"And who has that kind of power?" Kara asked.

"Someone in a position of authority."

"Like a cop," she said. "Or a crime lord who has proven they can and will kill."

"Theoretically, in your what-if scenario, there would be one primary person in the criminal organization making decisions—who lives, who dies, who kills. Like your example of an outlaw biker gang—a close group of individuals all capable of violence—there is always a leader. The leader is almost always a man. In this fictional case, the individual would be of above average intelligence, is charismatic, and above all, ruthless. Quietly so. More Bernie Madoff than Ted Bundy."

Beau looked down at his phone, then stepped out. Matt was too interested in Kara and Catherine's conversation to find out what was so important to the detective that he would walk out of this conference.

Catherine continued, "To reiterate, you need to focus on Ernestine's killer—and Nicki LeBlanc's murder. If you find Lily Baker's body, see what you can learn from it."

Matt said, "I can't help but note that the women were treated far more brutally than the men. Men were shot or overdosed—perhaps tainted drugs—while the women would have known they were dying."

"True," Catherine said. "The critical question we're facing here is how deep is the corruption? The only way these women could be killed with such impunity is because someone in the police department or the coroner's office is involved, as Beau believes."

No one wanted a corrupt cop. They did exponentially more damage to the profession than anything else. The more Matt learned about how the St. Augustine Police Department was structured the more he believed Beau was right.

Beau walked back in. "Elijah Morel was found dead in his

truck off Canal Road, not far from where we found Ernestine's body. And according to witnesses, he was one of the people who talked to her Friday night at The Fat Cat before she disappeared."

TUESDAY

23

Michael's dive equipment arrived at 8 a.m. and he and Beau left immediately for the river; Jim was going to the morgue to glad-hand the coroner and access any evidence that he could—then would meet them at Lantern Gate, as close as he could get without getting the RV stuck in the muck.

Kara was relieved when they finally left—she had arranged to talk to Winnie this morning, and she didn't think Beau would be happy that she'd roped in his grandmother to get her here.

Last night when Kara helped Toni with the sandwiches, she'd asked if Toni would mind calling Winnie over to clean the house for an hour or two. Kara would pay her for her time—the kid needed the money, and Kara didn't want her coming all the way out here and leave empty-handed. Winnie had jumped at the opportunity and told Toni she'd be there at nine.

After their meeting the night before, Kara had pulled Matt aside privately as he was about to leave with Savannah to go back to Lafayette.

"I'm talking to Winnie tomorrow," she said.

They were standing outside the small house, alone. It wasn't that she didn't want to tell her team, but she wasn't sold on the new agent. Trust came slow to her. It took months before she trusted Matt's team. And she still didn't fully trust Catherine or Zack, but for different reasons.

"What if she won't talk?"

"I have the Ethan Davis card. I think she was his girlfriend—and I know that she was friends with Ethan and Ricky Dubois. It's an angle, and right now one of the few that we have. Nicki was her sister. It might be a slow process to turn her, but I think she'll help."

"Tread carefully."

"I understand kids like Winnie. She's smart with a healthy dose of fear, and she's looking for an escape. I can get through to her."

She frowned as bugs flew around them. They were glowing. "What the hell are those?"

Matt grinned. "Fireflies."

"Those are real?"

"Yes."

"Do they bite? Like mosquitos?"

"No."

"I don't think bug butts should double as light bulbs."

"Kara," he said, his voice growing serious, and Kara knew she didn't want to continue this conversation.

"I said I'd be careful."

She knew that wasn't what he was going to say.

"We haven't talked in over a week. Did I do something to make you mad?"

By "talked" he meant "had sex." Clearly they talked—they worked together.

"Do I look mad?"

"You don't do mad like other people. I just want to make sure we're okay."

"We're fine."

"You don't sound like you believe that."

"Matt—drop it. Now's not the time or place. We agreed to be strictly professional when we were working. We'll talk when this is all over, okay?"

He stared at her, an odd look on his face. Did he look hurt? She couldn't stroke his ego now.

She walked back into the house and left him standing in the driveway, surrounded by fireflies.

She didn't know how to talk to Matt. She realized what happened the other weekend had really thrown her for a loop. They'd agreed to keep their relationship discreet, but hiding in his bedroom hadn't been her idea of fun. Especially since Catherine already knew they were sleeping together, and she'd come over to Matt's house uninvited. So discretion, sure—she wasn't going to screw Matt on his desk, no matter how fun that might be. But they had a rare day off and she had been enjoying herself.

She didn't even know how to describe how she felt. Humiliated? No. Maybe. Embarrassed? Yeah. Stupid. Uncertain. Nervous. Confused.

She rarely felt any of those emotions, and it had tightened her up into a hot mess.

She didn't like that. She suppressed all those foreign feelings and that made her tense and crabby.

And then she got angry. Anger was an emotion she could handle.

Kara was always confident, always in control, so losing that confidence in herself and her ability to manage this relationship with Matt threw her for a loop. She didn't want to be in this position, *ever.*

Because all those conflicting and confusing emotions told her she had gotten far too close to Matt, that she was depending on him to provide her with...with what? Well, more than sexual satisfaction, apparently. Any other man, any other time, and she wouldn't have given a fuck. She might have even laughed about it.

Ha, ha, I'm naked in your bed while you get rid of your guests, let's get down and dirty when they're gone.

Not with Matt.

Kara was pacing Toni's kitchen thinking about Matt, about how to approach Winnie, about Jim—she was a bit worried about him talking to the coroner alone—and running through their debriefing with Catherine last night. So many things to think about and keep track of, in a town where everything ran at half-time. Toni, dressed in slacks and a pale pink blouse, came into the kitchen.

She looked happy and had applied a bit more makeup than usual, plus additional jewelry. Toni was adorable and Kara was falling in love with the old woman. She had a soft spot for grandma types, and made a mental note to send her own grand-mother—the only family member she cared about—a postcard before she left. Em would love it.

"Are you sure I shouldn't be here when you talk to Winnie?" Toni asked.

"It's better if you're not," Kara said. "And you had plans this morning, right?"

"I always shop Tuesday mornings. Senior discount at the grocery until noon. But I've known Winnie since she was knee-high to a grasshopper. I think she'll talk to me."

"Maybe, but that might be a problem. She might have seen things that she wouldn't be comfortable sharing with someone who knows her, that she'd only be comfortable sharing with a stranger. I'm used to working with kids like Winnie."

"All right, I'll go, then. I'll be home by eleven. Help yourself to more coffee, sweetie. I made a fresh pot after the boys left."

"If I can stay to help with the groceries, I will."

"I've been taking in my own groceries just fine for my entire adult life. Beau coddles me. If I need help, I'll ask, I promise you that."

Kara watched Toni drive off, then poured a cup of Toni's very strong, very good coffee.

Thirty minutes and counting.

Jim Esteban drove the RV to the coroner's office, located across the street from the police station. Earlier, he'd had a nice chat with his son-in-law. That always put him in a good mood. He couldn't have picked a better man for his only daughter if he'd tried.

He'd done what Matt suggested and contacted the detective in charge of the Ernestine Bergeron murder investigation, Andre Armand, who seemed fine with meeting Jim, said he was happy to walk him through the procedures.

He arrived at eight thirty. Detective Armand was waiting for him outside. "Dr. Esteban," he said. "Good to see you again." He opened the door and Jim walked through.

"Like I said yesterday, call me Jim."

The tall, slender black detective nodded. "Jim. We might have a small problem—Dr. Brown doesn't like anyone stepping into his business."

Jim bit back a snippy comment. "I understand, the morgue is his domain. But you still have six dead young women and little evidence, so anything we do can help."

"Well, we figure we know what happened to Ernestine Bergeron," Andre said.

"That was fast."

"Elijah Morel was smitten with her, according to people who knew him. The night she went missing, she was flirting with someone else, and he became enraged. Killed her. Then killed himself. The knife that killed her was found in his truck."

"When did you process the evidence?"

"First thing this morning. Brought everything in last night."

"Prints? Blood?"

"I turned the knife over to the lab, and Dr. Brown said it's her blood. He's been here since six this morning. We're a small parish, but we have a basic lab."

Jim wondered if the lab was staffed, or if Dr. Brown did everything himself.

His unspoken question was answered when Andre walked him into a small room with minimal equipment—a couple microscopes, computer, a dryer, a refrigerator, a fume chamber for processing fingerprints, and a bio-hazard workstation likely for working with blood and tissue. The equipment was old, but the lab was clean.

A young man was sitting at a metal desk. He glanced up. "Oh. Hey, Andre."

"Donny, this is Dr. Jim Esteban, he runs that mobile lab I told you about, with the FBI. Jim, Donny Daigle manages our lab and assists Dr. Brown."

"Good to meet you," Jim said. The kid didn't look old enough to drink.

"Maybe you can give Donny a tour of the lab as well."

"I'd love it," Donny said. "I'm such a geek."

"Sure, we can do it whenever you want. Are you the only one here?"

"Full-time, it's me and Cheryl, who is Dr. Brown's pathologist. We have four or five officers certified for evidence collection."

Jim wasn't used to such a small operation—he had run the Dallas crime lab and had more than fifty employees just in his division, and that didn't include the medical examiner's office, who they worked closely with. He'd run the criminal division, and that included CSI and laboratory services.

"Jim has some questions. He wanted to meet Dr. Brown."

"Did, um, Chief Dubois clear it?"

Andre shrugged. "He told me to be hospitable."

"Well. Okay. What do you wanna know?" Donny asked.

Jim had a lot of questions, but he was now concerned about the too-quick resolution of Ernestine's murder. "Andre here said you processed the knife that may have killed Ms. Bergeron."

"Yes. First thing this morning."

"May I take a look at the report?" Jim asked.

Donny looked at Andre, who shrugged and said, "I don't have a problem with it."

"Doc Brown hasn't signed off on it yet. It's not much." He tapped on his computer and a moment later the printer spit out a piece of paper. He handed it to Jim.

Blood: A+

Jim assumed Ernestine was A+, but so was 40 percent of the population.

Double-edged blade, six inches long. Wood handle.

No prints.

"No prints?"

"No, sir. The killer wiped them off. I mean, there were signs of the handle being cleaned."

Andre said, "He probably planned to get rid of it, but the guilt ate him up."

Catherine said whoever killed Ernestine liked her, would feel guilty. But would he then have the wherewithal to wipe down the knife…then shoot himself?

"Where's the comparison with the blade to the wounds on Ms. Bergeron's neck?" Jim asked.

"Um, well, it's the same blood type and the knife was found with the killer."

That was a big leap. Just because a bloody knife was found in Morel's truck didn't mean he killed her. Yes, solid circumstantial evidence, but Jim wouldn't take it to court, not without more.

Jim said, "For your records I can match it up, confirm what you suspect."

"Well, we don't need to because her killer is dead, so it's not like there'll be a trial." Donny glanced at Andre.

Jim couldn't believe this was how they ran the crime lab. He wasn't used to this, and he was trying to control the overwhelming need to tell everyone here they were grossly incompetent.

Instead he said, "Your lab, your rules. I'm also looking for the autopsy and toxicology reports for Mr. Jean Paul LeBlanc."

"We don't have those back yet. We sent them to the state lab. It takes four to six weeks before we get anything."

"That's typical," Jim said. "I can run them today. You can join me and I'll show you the capabilities of my mobile unit."

"Really?" At first he sounded excited, then he hesitated. "Well—I don't know."

Andre said, "Chief Dubois is helping the FBI in their investigation into LeBlanc's death. He obtained drugs while in custody, so the chief wants to know how that happened."

"So we can do this?"

"I don't see why not," Andre said.

"Well, I have to ask Doc Brown."

"I'd like to meet him," Jim said. He had other things he wanted to look at, but he'd take it one step at a time.

Donny got on the phone. "Cheryl," he said. "There's an FBI agent here to talk to Doc Brown. Andre's here, said the chief okayed it." He listened. "Okay."

He hung up and said, "He'll be here in a few minutes."

"Why don't you show me around? Where do you store evidence? I'm particularly interested in the physical evidence from your murder victims."

"We have an evidence room."

"But what about biological evidence? Clothing, shoes, hair and tissue samples, things like that."

"If it has to be refrigerated, we have a refrigerator in the evidence room. Everything is labeled."

Donny sounded defensive, but showed Jim around the lab. Like most small-town labs, they had minimal capabilities. As long as they could process evidence and prepare it for the state lab, that was what mattered—collect evidence, protect the integrity of same, and maintain chain-of-custody were the three minimums that small labs had to be able to do.

Jim wasn't sold that they were doing any of that.

A round, bespectacled man with a thick gray mustache walked in. He was nearly bald and wore medical scrubs that strained over his stomach. "Donny, Cheryl said we had a visitor?"

Jim introduced himself. "I was hoping to talk to you about your procedures, but also discuss the Jean Paul LeBlanc death investigation."

"Yes, Rich said your office was interested in that case. I'm happy to give you our reports. It was a clear case of overdose. We sent blood samples to the state lab to determine what exactly he injected himself with, but those won't be back for a time. We know it was an opiate, but for a detailed analysis, we have to wait for the state lab."

"My mobile lab is equipped for complete drug testing. I would be happy to show you how it works. Perhaps we can take a sample from Mr. LeBlanc and I can run it through, show you how we get our results so quickly."

The doctor frowned. "To what end?"

"To find out what killed him."

"I know what killed him. He injected himself with heroin, which resulted in an overdose death. His heart stopped."

"Did you complete the autopsy?"

"There was no need for an invasive autopsy when the investigation indicated that he had injected himself with illegal drugs. I don't understand why you're questioning our procedures. We may not be Dallas, but we handle our own."

"I wasn't implying you didn't, but I think it would be beneficial to know if the heroin was tainted, to get that information out to the community so that no one else needlessly dies."

"And we'll have that information shortly. I asked the state lab to expedite."

"Great, but I can give you the answer in hours, not weeks."

"To be honest, I'm skeptical that your offered assistance is without strings."

"My boss, Agent Costa, has offered my services without any strings or cost. You can trust him, he's a man of his word. We just want to help because your town has been recently overwhelmed. For example, I can download software for your lab tech to run comparisons between the knife found in Mr. Morel's vehicle with the wound on Ms. Bergeron's neck. He can keep the software, it comes in very handy for a multitude of injuries."

The doctor frowned. "See, this is the problem with bringing your big-city ideas into a small town. If it looks like a duck and quacks like a duck, it's a duck. Andre learned that Elijah Morel was jealous of Ernestine's flirting. In a rage, he slit her throat. His guilt then compelled him to kill himself, proven by the fact that a knife with her blood was found in his truck, which was found near where he'd killed her. That's good detective work. Now you may have the money and resources and staff, to run through multiple blood tests and computer simulations, perform unnecessary autopsies when cause of death is more than clear, and 99 percent of the time confirm the original investigator's conclusion. But it's a waste of time and resources here."

There was so much wrong with what Brown said, Jim didn't

know how to start. Including that there was no rage in Ernestine's murder. It was simple, efficient.

"But what about the one percent?" Jim said, trying hard not to sound judgmental. Cutting corners to save time and money. Jim couldn't fathom how anyone could run a forensics lab with such an attitude; it went against everything he believed in.

"In this case, the evidence is clear. And regarding Mr. LeBlanc? If there's anything unusual about the drugs, then we'll find out shortly. You're not going to be here with your highfalutin mobile crime lab indefinitely. We're going to have to run our lab the old-fashioned way. Now, Donny will be happy to show you our facilities and walk you through our procedures. Other than that, I respectfully ask you to let us do our job."

Dr. Brown looked at his watch, said, "I have to return to my practice. You have my directive, Donny. If you have additional questions, Dr. Esteban, you can make an appointment with me for Thursday morning."

He walked out. Andre seemed sheepish, but Donny looked relieved that Brown was gone. "Do you still want the tour?"

Jim looked at the time—9:15. Michael wouldn't be diving until after ten, so he had a few minutes. He would document everything he could.

He didn't know if Dr. Judson Brown was corrupt, but he was clearly an arrogant and incompetent know-it-all.

Jim listened, wrote down multiple violations of basic protocols—particularly how they stored biological matter. He noted that virtually every box with victims' clothing was moldy and improperly stored. It was a challenge in moist, humid environments like Louisiana, which meant that proper drying of bloody clothes was critical.

Basically, every piece of physical evidence from the six murders was contaminated. No way any of it could be used to learn anything, let alone used for trial.

At ten, Andre walked him to his RV. "Thank you for at least

getting me in there," Jim said to Andre. "I'm sorry if I sounded irritated. I do appreciate your time."

Andre handed him a brown paper bag. "I thought you might want this." Then he turned, whistling, and walked back to the police station.

Jim frowned, looked in the bag. Enclosed was a thick plastic biological evidence pouch. Inside the pouch was a syringe.

24

When he saw the Houston area code on his phone, Matt stepped into the office that Ryder was using in the Lafayette field office and closed the door.

Ryder motioned if he should leave, and Matt shook his head. He sat in the visitor chair across from Ryder and answered the call. "Costa."

"This is Assistant Special Agent in Charge Logan Sheffield," the caller said. "Is this SAC Mathias Costa?"

"Call me Matt."

"Sorry it took me so long to return your call. I understand you're investigating a possible serial murderer in Broussard Parish."

"Yes, though our profiler doesn't believe we have a serial killer." He gave a very brief rundown on why his team was here and that they hadn't opened an official investigation. "Are you familiar with the mobile response team?"

"Your analyst—Ryder Kim—explained when he spoke to my admin. What can I help you with?"

"When you were in charge of the Lafayette office, your team was involved in a major investigation in the parish adjacent to Broussard. It lasted nearly two years and yielded three federal indictments."

"If you can call them that. Three people went to federal prison for public corruption, but I never felt right about any of it."

"Do you doubt their guilt?"

"They deserved to do some time, but they were minor players. They didn't orchestrate the operation."

"What can you tell me?"

"The elected sheriff directed his deputies to pull over any car with out-of-state plates. On the surface, nothing overtly illegal, but it smelled like a revenue scam—pulling in money from out-of-staters who didn't want to fight a ticket. Then we learned that the office was not only charging more for the out-of-state tickets, but several individuals stated they hadn't broken the law they were written up for. Two people came forward to tell us that they'd paid cash to a deputy when he pulled them over and he let them go. He was one of the three indictments. He plead guilty and served a year. He's the only one I wanted in prison because there's nothing I dislike more than corrupt cops."

"And the other two indictments?"

"This is where it gets trickier. After the complaints against the sheriff and several deputies, we asked for records from the parish clerk and the sheriff's department. We got next to nothing. We got a warrant for records, and they weren't there or they were incomplete. Every time we interviewed someone, they answered 'I don't know' to most questions. No one cooperated.

It was like the whole parish just shut us out. Our agents were treated like crap. One agent tried to fill his car up at the gas station—the clerk shut off the pump, then pretended he didn't know what happened. Two other agents—one of them Curt Danville, who you've met—went to retrieve computers to send to Quantico for analysis. When they returned to their vehicle, all four tires were flat. Security cameras had been turned off. Constant friction and huge frustration for my staff. I wanted so badly to indict the sheriff, but I couldn't get anyone on record. Then he retired with full pension."

"What were the other two indictments?"

"We'd caught the sheriff's civilian assistant in a sting. Planned to convince her to turn state's evidence. Full immunity. She wouldn't budge. Scared. She had two young kids, had lived in the parish her entire life. I didn't want to indict her, but she gave us no choice—she'd been caught falsifying legal documents. She served two years and has since moved away. I felt bad about that. She committed a crime, sure, but she wasn't in charge, and we could have protected her. The second was a lowlife we nailed for obstruction of justice. Just a thug who we knew—couldn't prove—worked at the behest of the sheriff. He didn't flip, but I didn't think he would. He got six months and is probably back doing the same shit for the new sheriff."

"Did you work on any cases in Broussard Parish?" Matt asked.

"A few—a tax fraud case with a rancher, an EPA case, a major multi-jurisdictional poaching case, though that was more than ten years ago."

"We've been looking at Peter Landry, the new mayor. He took over for his grandfather Philip Landry after the latter died three years ago. The younger Landry was investigated in NOLA for an insurance fraud scheme. One of his partners went to prison, he didn't. His other former partner owns a seedy bar here in St. Augustine. And there's a fourth partner, but the name wasn't in the records. We're researching that."

"Landry. Yeah, I remember that case, though it wasn't mine. I didn't do a lot of insurance fraud, but post-Katrina fraud investigations exploded. People bought too-good-to-be-true policies after the big hurricane, and then when they had damage in the next storm, the policies didn't pay. That was maybe six, seven years ago, right?"

"Yes."

"And he's on your radar, why?"

Matt gave him the brief rundown on why Kara was suspicious of Landry.

"Landry was an insurance broker and a lawyer," Sheffield said, "though I don't think he practices law anymore. When he did, it was insurance related, maybe some real estate law. I don't remember much about it, but NOLA would have the records."

"We reached out to them," Matt said. "Regarding our current investigation, we were called in by a detective whose informant died of a drug overdose while in custody, and another of his informants had her throat slit."

Silence on Sheffield's end.

Matt continued, "I have six dead women and one missing." He gave Sheffield the bare bones about the case, how he offered help and resources, and his frustration that the police chief wasn't cooperating.

"They won't," Sheffield said. "What do you think I can help you with?"

"Two things. First, I mostly wanted to see if your investigation had anything to do with drugs. We have a working theory that these deaths stem from the drug trade."

"Well, we weren't looking at drugs six years ago—we were looking at public corruption. If there was a drug angle, it was outside of our purview. Do you have anything solid?"

"Not yet." He told Sheffield what he knew, then said, "Everyone who's talked to the detective about the murders is dead.

I think something's here. I'm looking for advice on how to solve it."

"You won't."

"I don't accept that."

"You've talked to Curt, right?"

"Of course. He's lent me an agent, someone local."

"I loved working out of Lafayette. I love Louisiana, and I may end up retiring there when the time comes, though Houston is growing on me. The people in the bayou are good people. But they don't trust government in general—there's a lot of reasons, some legitimate, some not so much. They don't forget anything, so if a hundred years ago during prohibition some federal agent came in and killed their great-great-granddad over his moonshine still, they're going to remember exactly what happened, a story passed down through the generations.

"Then you have economic hardship and the floods and the fuckups from all levels of government, but mostly the federal response. Resentment. Most people just want to be left alone to raise their families and work and go to church. Especially in the bayou—once you get to Baton Rouge or NOLA you have different considerations. But out in Broussard? It's one of the smallest parishes and they're not going to help any federal agency."

"Six dead women," Matt repeated.

"I don't think anyone who is law-abiding would intentionally withhold information. But it's like there are two societies. Not black and white, not even rich and poor. It's really criminal and noncriminal—and the criminal are white, black, rich and poor. They keep their business to themselves, handle their problems internally and only face serious problems when their criminal enterprise bleeds into the noncriminal class."

"And when that happens?"

"You hope the local police do the right thing."

"And if the police are part of the problem?"

He didn't say anything.

"So we're screwed," Matt said.

"The local detective has the best chance to convince someone to turn state's evidence. But if they know others have been killed because they talked? You're going to have to find something to give the state attorney general a reason to create a task force. And then wait years for resolution."

"What about going after them the old-fashioned way?"

"What way is that?"

"Eliot Ness style."

"Tax evasion?"

"Where there are drugs there is money laundering. One of my team members is an expert on white-collar crime, so we're looking into the businesses we believe are hubs for illegal activity—a dive bar and a bar that is cover for a brothel are only two of them."

"Magnolia Inn."

"You've heard of it."

"It's been a house of ill repute for, well, as long as I remember."

"Still is. Peter Landry's former business partner bought it."

"That's an angle. I hadn't thought of that."

"Do you know Sheriff Landry?"

"I remember him."

"What's he like? Can I approach him about the problems in St. Augustine?"

"I had no evidence that he was corrupt, but he'll only work with the feds if it's in his best interest. I have a meeting, Matt, but you said there were two things?"

"You told your superiors six years ago that you felt one of your agents was compromised."

Silence.

"Logan?"

"That was a classified internal document."

"I work directly for Assistant Director Tony Greer."

"I don't want anyone knowing my suspicions. Not even Curt, who I trust and never suspected. After an internal investigation into my entire team, the office didn't find anything, and I don't want rumors to start flying."

"This is between you and me."

It took a moment, then Logan said, "The Lafayette office is small, you know."

"I'm aware. I was the SSA of the Tucson Resident Agency, eight agents and an analyst."

"We're smaller, but you understand. Everyone worked on everything. That nearly two-year investigation took hundreds of hours. Early on in the investigation, we had a deputy in the sheriff's department who was willing to talk to us off the record. I personally went down to meet with him because he was skittish. He never showed. I reached out to him later, and he went off on me. Said he couldn't trust me or anyone in the FBI and he'd be lucky if he had a job anymore. I learned that he had been fired for false arrest and perjury. He left, I tracked him down. Told me to go to hell, that I burned him. I didn't. The only people who knew his name and that he wanted to talk with us were in my office. With me, that was only seven people. Curt's the only one who is still there."

"You vouch for Curt."

"Yeah—I do. I've known him almost since he was a rookie, and he's always done the right thing. Sometimes a little too slow, cautious, meticulous, but in this day and age, meticulous is a virtue."

"And NOLA investigated and didn't find that anyone had ratted this guy out."

"Correct. But if I were going to rat someone out? I wouldn't use computers or phones or anything that could be traced. I would do it face-to-face, drop a physical note, something like that. And while the ASAC in NOLA took me seriously, I don't know if anyone else did. I didn't have any facts, and the former cop wasn't talking."

"I'd like those names."

Logan didn't say anything.

"I'm not going to ring anybody up, I promise. I can get the names of the agents and staff assigned to Lafayette during that time. You can do it faster."

"Other than Curt, no one is still there. I don't feel good about putting agents out there, agents who have been cleared of wrongdoing."

"But you still think that one of them told the sheriff that your informant was talking to the FBI."

Silence. Then, "Yes."

"I need the names. Someone may still have a local connection, and they wouldn't have to be local to obtain confidential information"

"To cover my ass, have your boss request the file from OPR. You request that, it'll save you time—names, interviews, investigation, the whole nine yards."

"Thank you."

"I wish you luck, Matt. I don't envy your team. But be careful. We were dealing with public corruption—no one got violent, and the vandalism was more annoying than serious. But drugs in the bayou? Those people will kill. And they don't care if you're a federal agent."

Matt remembered that Beau had been threatened after Jean Paul died in jail. He would have to remind everyone to watch their backs. He wasn't going to lose one of his agents.

"They've already killed," Matt said, "and my team is going to stop them."

25

Kara sat on the porch where she could see anyone approach, but where they wouldn't be able to clearly see her. She heard a truck—an old, loud truck that was in need of a new muffler—long before she saw it. It bounced along the gravel drive toward the Hebert house.

Winnie got out of the driver's seat. She wore cutoff jean shorts and a dark green T-shirt. She walked around to the passenger side and wrenched open the door. A little girl climbed out with curly brown hair and big golden eyes. She was talking, but Kara couldn't hear what the kid was saying.

Damn. She'd brought her niece. Kara was going to have to shift gears—she'd planned on being blunt and showing Winnie the crime scene photos, but no way was she letting a little kid see that shit.

When Winnie reached the porch stairs, the kid ran up calling, "Mimi! Mimi! Mimi!"

"Bonnie Mae! No running!" Winnie called after her.

Then Winnie saw Kara. "Well, fuck," Winnie said.

"Fuck," Bonnie repeated.

"Is Mrs. Hebert even here?" Winnie said.

Kara shook her head.

"I can't believe this." She turned around to leave.

"Don't go, Winnie. You need my help."

Slowly, Winnie turned to look at her, arms across her chest. "Give me one good reason."

"I'll give you two. You, Bonnie."

Winnie looked perplexed. "I don't have to talk to you."

"Give me ten minutes."

She stared at Kara, chin up, defiant.

Bonnie said, "Can I color? Can I get the crayons? Can I play with the dishes? Can I? Winnie? Can I? Please?"

"What does she usually do when you're helping Toni?" Kara asked.

"There's a box of toys in the living room."

"Let's go."

Kara moved to the door. Winnie didn't budge.

Kara, hand on the door, said to the teenager, "You have a decision to make, Winnie. You can make a choice to have a future for yourself and your niece. Or you can leave and pray you don't end up like Ethan and Bonnie doesn't end up like Nicki. Because if you walk away from me, all you'll have are your prayers."

Kara walked inside, letting the screen door close behind her.

Kara went directly to the kitchen because it was the most comfortable room in the house.

She pulled out lemonade and cookies—she ate a cookie because Toni really was an amazing cook—and waited. She poured more coffee. And waited. Feared she'd miscalculated.

Then she heard Bonnie exclaim, "Can I play?"

"Do not touch anything that's not in the toy box, okay, Bonnie Mae?"

"I promise, I promise!"

Little feet scampered into the living room. Winnie saw Kara standing in the kitchen. She'd put three cookies on a plate and poured juice in a glass. "Can I give these to Bonnie?"

Winnie frowned. She walked to the kitchen cabinet and retrieved a plastic cup, poured the juice from the glass to the cup, and took it with the plate into the living room. Then she came back.

"Ten minutes," Winnie said.

"Sit."

"No."

Kara sat at the table, sipped her coffee. "Help yourself."

Winnie didn't move.

"I've never been in your shoes, Winnie, but I've been in similar. I know what it's like to have shitty parents and learn to do everything yourself. I know what it's like to be alone even when surrounded by people. I know what it's like to feel trapped and not see any way out."

"You're a cop. You'll say anything to get me to trust you."

"I won't lie to you. The truth is ugly, Winnie, but you know that. You learned it a lot earlier than I did."

"Are you really a *former* cop from Los Angeles?"

"Yes and no."

"Oh, fuck, you think I'm stupid?"

"I think you're a survivor. And I think you would have bolted from St. Augustine after Nicki was killed if it wasn't for your niece and the fact that your mother is a drug addict and can't take care of herself, let alone a kid."

"So who are you? No lies."

"Detective Kara Quinn. I get paid by the Los Angeles Police Department, but I don't work for them. I'm on loan to the FBI."

Winnie rolled her eyes. "Fuck."

"Yeah, that's what I thought when I first started working with them," she said with a slight grin. "The team I'm on is based out of DC and we travel. Last case was in the San Juan Islands, off the Washington State coast. Gorgeous place. I'd move there in a heartbeat if I wouldn't be bored shitless."

"What kind of case?"

Kara couldn't tell if she was interested or just making small talk while she figured out how to get out of here.

"Someone set off a bomb and killed nine people."

"Did you find out who did it?"

"Yep."

"They in prison?"

"Dead."

"You killed 'em?"

"Nope."

"Then how'd they die? Did they blow themselves up?"

Kara would never forget. It still gave her nightmares on occasion, but she didn't want to talk about it, not even to a kid who had probably seen just as bad. So she said simply, "They blew their brains out when they realized they weren't getting away with murder."

Winnie stared at her. Bonnie ran in with her empty cup. "Can I have more, Winnie? *Pul-eeze?*"

Winnie took the cup, walked to the counter, poured more lemonade and handed it to Bonnie. The kid carefully walked back to the living room so she didn't spill.

"Sit," Kara said. "Please."

She waited. Thirty seconds later, Winnie sat across from her, but she didn't relax. Still looked ready to bolt, defiance oozing from every pore.

"Ask me anything," Kara said.

"Why are you here? In St. Augustine?"

Kara had cleared it with Matt already. It was taking a risk, sharing information with Winnie. But Matt trusted Kara, and Kara trusted her gut, and her gut said that even if Winnie didn't help, she wouldn't talk.

"Beau Hebert asked my partner for help," Kara said. "They were in the Navy together. Said one of his witnesses was dead of an apparent suicide, and one of his informants was missing."

Kara watched Winnie. The kid had a great poker face, but her eyes narrowed. "Ernestine."

Kara nodded curtly. "Now she's dead. Do you know how she died?"

Winnie shook her head.

"Her throat was slit. Our profiler said whoever killed her liked her and had her turn around so he couldn't see her eyes when he killed her. My partner and I went through everything Beau has. I snooped around some before everyone here finds out that I'm a cop, and it's pretty clear that something rotten is going on. I think you know the what and the who."

Winnie didn't say anything.

"I'm being straight with you, Winnie. Your sister was brutally stabbed to death. Your cousin allegedly killed himself in prison after shooting Jake West for no *apparent* reason. You know a lot more than you've told anyone. In fact, I think you were smart keeping your mouth shut."

"And now you want me to talk. That would be stupid."

"Maybe. Maybe you remain silent and we hang around here for the next couple of weeks trying to find the person—or people—who killed six women, and probably killed Lily Baker. Try to figure out how Jake West's murder fits into everything, hope to find the truth about Jean Paul's death and if he killed himself or..." she paused a second, stared at Winnie to get her point across "...if he was murdered.

"And," Kara continued, "if we don't have answers and are

called to another case in another state, we'll have to leave and everything continues the way it is now. With the Cormier brothers running drugs and the cops turning a blind eye and more of your friends dying."

Winnie didn't say anything.

"Ethan Davis allegedly died of a drug overdose. I know that you, Ethan and Ricky Dubois were three peas in a pod, as Mrs. Davis said."

She'd actually said that Ethan and Ricky were peas in a pod, but Kara's gut told her that Winnie was part of it. And by Winnie's expression, Kara was right.

"What happened to Ethan?" Kara asked.

Winnie shook her head. When she didn't talk, Kara said, "You realize that eventually you're going to be dragged into the same mess as your sister." She paused. "Unless you're already there."

Winnie's head shot up and her eyes narrowed. "Fuck you. I'm not making money on my back. And I would have had enough money to leave if—"

She stopped.

"Go on."

"It doesn't matter anymore. He's dead."

"Your cousin. Jean Paul." It was a guess. Kara figured she was right.

"I don't do drugs. I've never done anything more than smoke a little pot, and I don't even like it. I keep my head down and don't get on *anyone's* radar."

"And how long is that going to last? You try to dress down and not stand out, but you're a pretty girl. Working at The Catfish and the Magnolia Inn, you think they're not going to ask you to do more? Maybe not prostitute yourself, but make deliveries? Be a lookout? Drive down to the coast to pick up the next shipment of drugs coming in from the Gulf?"

Kara stared at the girl and knew the truth. Well, shit.

"What are you doing, Winnie?"

"Like I'm going to tell a cop."

"I'm the only person who can help you."

Winnie snorted. "You know nothing. You want me to end up like Nicki? You think my mom can take care of the kid?"

Winnie was agitated and scared.

Kara was losing her. She had to push, but if she pushed too hard the girl would leave.

"Jean Paul knew that whatever Nicki had found herself in the middle of was bad, and he was trying to help you—protect you. I'm not surprised he was helping you get the money to leave town." Was that why Jean Paul killed Jake West? To protect Winnie? Why?

"Why do you fucking care?" Winnie asked. "You're here now, but you won't give a shit what happens to anyone when you're gone."

"Why did your cousin kill Jake?"

Winnie shrugged, crossed her arms over her small chest, glared at Kara.

Okay, this kid had a bigger chip on her shoulder than Kara ever had, and that was saying something.

"I will find out."

Winnie snorted.

Kara gave her a half smile. "Do not underestimate me, Winnie, and I won't underestimate you. I know this business. It's the same everywhere, just different people, different roads. I'm going to tell you what I think. Ethan died and something happened. I don't know if it was an accident or not. I don't know how involved Ricky Dubois is in this business. He left for college—and according to my sources he hasn't returned in two years. That makes me think he *escaped.* He escaped St. Augustine and is never coming back. So either, the rumors about him dealing are true and he just moved to dealing in college, or they're true, but his best friend's death was a major wake-up call for him, and he separated himself from the business."

Winnie shook her head, chin up.

"I'm wrong?"

"*Maybe* he never dealt at all."

Kara stared at her. For the first time she sensed that while Winnie wanted to talk, between fear and distrust, she wasn't going to. But desire was the first step.

Kara was really going out on a limb, but she said, "My team is going to talk to him."

Winnie jumped up. "No! God, you want him dead like Ethan?"

"He knows what happened. Three years ago, Lettie Chaisson was strangled. A few months later, Ethan died. Something changed in town. Overdoses increased. More women died. Police killed a dealer in Lake Pierre. Lily Baker went missing. I don't know if it was the election of Peter Landry, or the appointment of Ricky's father as police chief, or the hiring of Officer Jerry Guidry, or all of the above, but everything started after Peter Landry came to power. Lettie. Ethan. Your sister. The Cormiers—they're tools, aren't they? A means to an end."

Winnie would never be able to play poker. It *was* all about Peter Landry.

"I can help you, Winnie. I can protect you. But you have to tell the truth—and tell me how deep you're in this mess. I'll get you out—"

Winnie ran out of the kitchen. "Bonnie! We have to go!"

"I don't wanna—"

"Do not back-talk me, Bonnie Mae!"

Kara let her go.

She had a lot to think about.

26

By the time Matt arrived at the river, it was just after ten in the morning and already hotter than Hades and twice as humid.

Michael was ready to dive. He and Beau had taken a boat down the river because Beau wanted to be close to the surface to watch for any predators and be ready to immediately jump in to help Michael. Matt and Savannah drove as far as he dared into the field, then he asked Savannah to stay at the car to wait for Jim and hiked the rest of the way to the river by himself. He had a sniper rifle and would be looking along the shore for alligators, while Beau would focus on the water. Beau thought they were clear, but better safe.

Matt wore khakis and an olive green T-shirt. His shoulder holster with his primary weapon and a backup strapped to his thigh reminded him of the years he'd served as part of FBI SWAT. It had taken him months to get used to the weight of a gun against his thigh, but now it was like an extension of himself.

Jim's ETA from the coroner's office was twenty minutes. Matt told him to park behind his car, rather than trying to bring the RV closer to the riverbank.

Jim had told him that Detective Armand had given him the syringe that Jean Paul allegedly used to inject himself. That was both interesting and potentially a key piece of evidence, depending on what Jim learned. Unfortunately, they might not be able to use it in a future trial because Armand's actions destroyed the chain of custody. Jim would write up the circumstances, there might be a legal precedent that the AUSA could exploit, but it was problematic.

Matt positioned himself on the bank at the edge of Lantern Gate, rifle ready. The spot gave him a good view of the river both up- and downstream as well as a prime view of both shores on either side of the boat. Michael looked at Matt from the boat. "Ready?" he called.

Matt checked his weapon and gave Michael a thumbs-up.

Michael pulled down his face mask, turned on his oxygen and adjusted the light on his headgear. He had a bag with tools he might need strapped over his shoulders. Leaning back, he fell into the river, disappearing in the murky water.

Matt didn't see any giant reptiles, but he kept his eyes out for them. He'd run into crocodiles in Florida—he'd been to the Everglades many times, especially while growing up. He kept his distance and had never been bothered by them, but he knew they could do damage and they were of particular threat to small pets. One of his girlfriends in high school had lost her poodle to a crocodile.

He didn't know if Louisiana alligators behaved the same as

Florida crocodiles, and he didn't want one taking a bite out of Michael, so he watched for any signs of movement along the shore or near the surface of the water. Beau was doing the same thing.

Matt had asked Michael to surface every five minutes just to make sure that he was safe, since he was under water alone. The river was only ten to fifteen feet deep, so this wasn't cumbersome on Michael. The third time he surfaced he was a good fifty yards downstream from the boat. He waved to Beau, who gently motored toward him, but before Beau reached him, Michael went under again.

Matt looked at his watch and waited. Kara texted him.

Call me when you're done.

He pocketed his phone and looked along the shore again. No gators, nothing out of the ordinary.

He heard a vehicle and glanced to the west. Jim was parking the crime lab RV behind Matt's sedan on the side of the road, a good hundred yards away. His radio beeped.

"Costa, it's Beau."

Matt pulled out his radio. "Find something?"

"A plastic barrel."

Matt looked out to where Beau was standing in the boat. They were fifty yards south of the Gate. Michael was going under again. "What's Michael doing?"

"He's taking pictures and measurements. Wants to know if Jim is here yet."

"Yes."

"We'll bring it up onto the boat if we can, then decide how to get it to shore."

"Don't move it until Michael talks to Jim."

"Roger that."

Jim approached Matt, Savannah walking next to him. "Any luck?"

"Michael found a barrel."

"Wood? Plastic?"

"Plastic." Matt handed Jim his radio.

Jim said to Beau, "What size is the barrel?"

"Michael says it looks to be fifty to fifty-five gallons, appears sealed, no obvious label, settled on its side."

"I hope the seal is intact," Jim muttered. To Beau he said, "Don't move it yet. Ask Michael to take pictures of the lid—I need to see what kind of seal is on it first, figure how best to extract it."

"Roger. One minute."

When Michael came up, Matt could see Beau talking to him, and Michael took the radio from him. "I'm going to send you the photos. It'll just take a second."

It took several minutes before the photos came through to Jim's phone. He scrolled through them.

Matt looked over his shoulder. The barrel might have been blue, but it was hard to tell with the algae growing on the outside. It was half-buried in the muddy riverbed. There were no visible labels. Michael had taken close-ups of the lid. It appeared to be plastic but with a metal rim.

"Good, good," Jim muttered. "I don't see any dents on the rim, but because it's partly submerged, we have to be careful." He got back on the radio. "Michael, if there is a body in the barrel, it's going to be fully decomposed. Basically, liquid and bones. Carefully, turn the barrel upright. Make sure the seal is intact. We don't have any equipment to pull it up, so you'll have to be careful getting it onto the boat. Because the water isn't deep, there won't be a major pressure change, but be mindful. Once in the boat, keep it upright."

"Roger that. I'm going down again."

There was no good place to safely bring up the barrel here,

so Matt said, "We'll have to go back to the launch in town."
He didn't like that idea. Someone might see them. Then again,
maybe he *wanted* a confrontation with the chief of police. This
pussyfooting around wasn't his style.

He and Jim waited until Michael and Beau navigated the
barrel onto the boat using a combination of ropes, Michael's
strength and a sturdy net. As soon as they were done, Michael
called Matt. "The seal is intact. We'll meet you at the dock."

There was no guarantee that human remains were inside the
barrel. Could be toxic waste, could be agricultural supplies.

But Matt believed they had found what was left of Lily Baker.

27

Toni Hebert didn't go out every day like she used to. For eighty-four, she was healthy as a horse, but slower, more fragile, tired more easily. The only medication she took daily was half a pill of the lowest dose blood pressure medicine and a daily vitamin. She ate well—though her appetite had diminished some as she aged—and had a nighttime drink, that her dear grandson frowned upon. But her nightcap with Carl had been a staple in their relationship for over sixty years, and that nightly shot of bourbon gave her fifteen minutes to remember she'd lived a good life.

If God wanted her to join her dear husband, she would be fine with that. Not that she would do anything to speed things along. She enjoyed her life. She had friends, had Beau, and still believed she had a thing or two to do before she left God's green earth. And her mama and memaw had both lived to be in their nineties, so she figured she had a few years left.

Toni felt as if she should have stayed and helped Kara talk to young Winnie. Beau thought she was an old woman who needed to be sheltered, as if she didn't know the troubles that went on in town. She wasn't senile. She talked to people, she read the news. One of the ladies at church had lost her granddaughter to that evil man who killed women. Toni prayed for them daily and was proud that her grandson was a police officer and he would solve these horrific crimes.

Not that she didn't worry about Beau a smidge.

Toni walked slowly in her sensible shoes, selected a cart with wheels that all went in the same direction—nothing was more annoying than a stubborn shopping cart—then entered the market. One of the two cashiers looked up and smiled. "Good morning, Mrs. Hebert."

"Good morning, Jane," Toni said with a smile as she turned right, toward the produce, so she could select some greens to feed her guests. A pot of jambalaya would be in order. It would last them a couple days. She had most of the ingredients at home, except for the shrimp and sausage she would need. And of course the holy trinity: celery, onions and bell pepper.

She ran into Violet Daigle at the fish counter. They chatted about the guest minister who was in town for the month while Pastor Ken was on his yearly sabbatical. Then while she was selecting some canned goods she ran into Melanie O'Brien. She attended St. Bartholomew's, the Catholic church. Melanie had been a teacher for forty years, had taught Toni's two children, and they'd become friends. In the dairy section, Toni put milk, butter and cream in her cart. She had picked a bucket of apples yesterday from her four apple trees and thought a cobbler would go well with the jambalaya. She'd told Beau to invite all of those nice FBI agents to supper tonight. He'd looked surprised.

Do you honestly think I didn't know that your friend was an FBI agent? Did you think I was senile and forgot you told me about him many times? I'm not an idiot, Beauregard Jefferson Hebert.

Her grandson told her to not trouble herself with cooking. She ignored him, of course. Cooking was *not* trouble. She enjoyed it more than anything else she did these days, and she loved having people to cook for.

She went to Jane's register because she liked the girl. Speedy wasn't her middle name, but she was friendlier than Eloise Kelly, the daughter of the Topp's Grocery owner, who was as sour and unpleasant as her father.

While waiting for Violet to finish with Jane, Toni talked to the widower John Thibodeaux, who had been friendly with Carl over the years. His wife had passed thirty years ago, and he had plenty of women who took care of him—not that he needed it. She'd been to his house several times with Carl for dinner and John could feed himself just fine.

"There's an RV at the hotel north of the interstate," he said. "Nice one, too. Jill said it belongs to the F. B. I." He drew out the letters as if to punctuate the point.

"Really?" Jill was John's daughter and worked as the head housekeeper for the hotel.

"They have a suite of rooms. I thought maybe Beau might know what's all goin' on there."

"If he does, he doesn't talk to me about it." She snorted, said in a stage whisper, "He thinks crime would damage my delicate sensibilities."

John laughed. "Well, I suppose it's to be expected," he said. "They found the poor Bergeron girl dead in the river Sunday. Such a sweet thing. Walked by my house darn near every day, waved if I was on the porch. 'Good morning, Mr. Thibodeaux!' she'd say as if she was genuinely happy to see me."

"She was a ray of sunshine," Toni agreed. "Didn't deserve such a fate."

"So is that why they're here?"

"I can't right say, John. Like I told you, Beau doesn't talk to me about his work." Which was true, even if Toni knew more than she said to her longtime friend.

Violet left, waving to Toni, and Jane started ringing up the items Toni placed on the conveyor belt. "I heard about the FBI, too," Jane said. "My cousin works at the clerk's office. Two FBI agents came in to talk to the chief yesterday. A man and a woman."

"Maybe the chief asked for help," John said. "He's out of his element, that's for sure, with five dead girls."

"Six," Toni said. "Six with Ernestine."

"And Lily Baker's still missing," Jane said quietly. "I went to school with Lily. She was a year younger than me, but she was always really nice. In high school we had PE together and even though she could run fast, she would run with me, even if Mrs. Duncan told her to leave me behind." Jane was a bit on the chunky side. Nothing had changed since high school.

"You have an awful lot of shrimp there," John said as Jane rang up three pounds of fresh shrimp. "Feeding an army?"

Toni didn't particularly like people prying into her business. She found it rude, though gossip was somewhat of a Southern tradition, she supposed. "Beau has one of his Navy friends visiting for a few days. A hearty young man who likes to eat. I'm making cobbler. I'll make you a tray, if you'd like. I'll have plenty."

"I love your cobbler, Toni dear. But don't go to extra trouble for me."

She waved her hand. "No trouble. You know me, idle hands and all that."

Jane took off 10 percent for Toni's senior discount, and Toni paid for her groceries. Jane bagged them up. "Do you need help? I can get Timmy from the back."

"No, you didn't fill the bags too heavy for me, I appreciate that. I'll be fine. I'll bring you by a cobbler, John, on my way to Thursday lunch at church, leave it on your porch if you're not home."

"Mighty obliged," he said as Jane started ringing up his much smaller order.

Toni pushed her cart outside and used the button on her key ring to pop open the trunk. Carl had bought this car ten years ago and it had all these amazing bells and whistles. Everything was automatic. The air-conditioning worked, unlike the temperamental AC in the old truck she drove for near thirty years. Toni didn't like spending such money to buy a car, but Carl said they needed it, and it would last them until they couldn't drive anymore. She took it in regularly for all those things you did to make sure cars lasted—checkups and oil changes and every thirty thousand miles a big workup. She budgeted for it. But even after ten years, the car only had forty-one thousand miles on it.

She pushed the cart to her trunk and started putting the bags inside. Yes, Jane was sweet to give her many, many bags each with only a few items.

"Let me help you, Mrs. Hebert."

She looked up, startled, her heart racing. She hadn't heard anyone approach her, and she was concerned that her hearing might be slipping.

"Officer, I swear, you shouldn't sneak up on an old lady like that." Officer Guidry, his tag said. She'd met him, she believed, once or twice. He wasn't from St. Augustine, that much she knew. She also knew that Beau didn't like him, and she trusted her grandson's judgment.

"Sorry, ma'am."

The officer quickly unloaded her cart, then closed the trunk. "Thank you, Officer," she said.

He didn't move, blocking her path to the driver's door. "There seems to be a lot of activity at your house, Mrs. Hebert."

"Is there now?"

"We're doing more patrols in the rural parts of town, what with all the trouble. And you're so remote out there, alone most of the time."

Toni didn't feel comfortable with this conversation. "I've lived in my house for sixty-six years, Officer Guidry."

"Your grandson works long hours."

"I'm sure you do, too. I need to get my produce in the icebox, if you don't mind?" She made a move toward her door. He didn't budge.

"You know, Mrs. Hebert, Beau's on mighty thin ice these days. I would be very careful. He might just anger the wrong people."

John Thibodeaux walked out of the store with two bags, one in each hand, and looked over at them. He hesitated as he watched them. Toni, overwhelmed with relief at the friendly face, called out, "John dear, I have that recipe for you." She turned to the officer. "Excuse me, young man."

Now Officer Guidry stepped aside as John approached the car. "Toni?" he questioned, concern on his face.

"It's right here in my purse," she said. She reached inside and her hand was shaking.

Guidry didn't move for a long minute. She handed John a piece of paper, then the officer left. She was still shaking.

"What happened, Toni?" John asked.

She shook her head. "I don't like that man, and he wouldn't let me pass."

"You need to tell Beau."

"No. No—it's nothing. He and Beau, I think, may have a disagreement."

John's lips tightened. "Toni, a good man does not scare an elderly woman."

"Are you calling me old, John?" she said lightly.

"Only in years, not in spirit." But his face was still filled with concern. "All that FBI stuff I mentioned is true, and it's because of Beau, isn't it?"

"I don't know," she fibbed. "I don't know what's going on, except that Beau is going to find out who killed those women. He will, and their killer will be brought to justice. Because that's what honorable men do."

She looked toward Guidry as he climbed back into his patrol car and drove away. She breathed easier.

"It's fine, John. Thank you for helping."

"Please be careful." He took her hand, squeezed. "If you need anything, call me. I'll be at your place in two shakes of a lamb's tail."

Kara sat in the middle of Beau's small house rereading the files on each of the murders in case she missed something the first time around.

She wanted to throttle Winnie, force her to talk, but that wasn't going to get her anywhere. She hoped that if the teen *really* thought on it, that she'd come clean.

It worried Kara that Winnie was already involved with the Cormiers. Maybe nothing serious—yet. But the longer she was involved, the deeper she got, the more danger she was in. How did Kara get through to her? How could she help her? This town was all Winnie knew. It wasn't like she could easily disappear, leave her niece in the hands of her drug-addicted mother. Kara had seen how Winnie looked at the kid—she loved her. That's why she stayed.

Except... Winnie was looking for a way out. Her cousin Jean Paul had been helping her—and then he killed Jake West.

Why? Motive, motive, motive...that's what she was missing. Greed? Jealousy? Anger? Those she understood. Even psychopaths she sort of understood. There were nutjobs out there who liked to hurt people for fun.

But there didn't seem to be any specific *reason* for these murders.

She wanted to do some more research in town, but Matt didn't want her going without backup, so she'd have to wait until Michael returned. She was about to call him for his ETA when she heard a car coming down the gravel drive then stop in front of the house. She glanced out. Toni was back from the store. Kara got up to help her with the groceries. When she stepped outside, Toni was still sitting in the car.

Kara walked over to the car but came at her from the front so that she wouldn't startle the woman. Toni looked upset, her hands still gripping the wheel. Was she having a heart attack or something? Kara rushed over to her and opened her driver's door.

"Toni? What's wrong?"

Toni looked at her. "I—I—um—"

"Let me help you."

Kara leaned over her little body and unclasped the seat belt, then helped Toni out of the car.

"I'm fine," Toni said. "Fine—I'm sorry, I don't know where my mind was."

"Something is wrong."

"Would you be a dear and get the groceries from the trunk? I think I need something to take the edge off."

She shuffled slowly up the porch steps into the house. Kara knew the woman was elderly, but she'd never acted *this* old.

Kara unloaded the car as quickly as possible—she managed to bring everything inside in two trips. When she came back the second time, Toni was sitting at the kitchen table with a glass of bourbon. At eleven in the morning.

Kara sat down across from her.

Toni smiled, but it didn't reach her eyes. "I just had a little scare, it was nothing."

"What kind of scare?" Kara watched her closely.

Toni obviously didn't want to tell her.

"Toni, talk to me. What happened?" She paused. "Do I need to call a doctor? Beau?"

"No—do not tell him." Now she sounded like herself.

"I can't promise that."

Toni took a small sip of her bourbon. "One of the officers made a comment. It was innocuous, but there was…well…he meant something he didn't say."

"He threatened you."

She shook her head. "He threatened Beau. Commented about there being a lot of people at my house, and Beau had better make sure he doesn't anger the wrong people."

Toni closed her eyes.

Kara wanted to beat up someone.

"Who said this to you?"

"One of the new officers. I don't know him well. Guidry. You can't tell Beau, Kara dear. He'll be worried. And he might stop looking for who killed those poor women. I could never live with myself if his worry over me had him ending his investigation. We need to find out what happened to them, to sweet Ernestine."

"He has to know," Kara said. "I can't keep this information from him. Neither can you."

Toni didn't say anything. Then, "Would you be a dear and put my perishables away? I think I need to take a little rest."

"Should I call a doctor or something?"

"No. Don't be silly. I'm fine. Drinking before noon—what was I thinking!"

She'd barely had two sips.

Toni got up, squeezed Kara's hand and exited the room.

Kara called Matt.

"Where are you?" she asked.

"At the river. We found a barrel."

"Did you say *barrel*?"

"Yes. Fifty-five gallon plastic barrel with a metal seal. Definitely big enough for a body. We just got it into the mobile lab. Jim is going to head back to the hotel and open it in a controlled environment."

"Officer Guidry threatened Beau's grandmother. Not in so many words, but it was clear. He fucking confronted her at the grocery store during senior discount day! She doesn't want anyone to know, but I can't keep that secret."

"Dammit," Matt muttered. "I'll talk to Beau when he gets here. Find a way to keep him from going off on the guy."

"Winnie is the key," Kara said. "She's scared, didn't say much, but enough where I'm certain they're running drugs up from the Gulf. I need to go to the Magnolia and The Catfish again."

"Not alone."

"Yeah, yeah, I need someone to watch my ass. We don't have enough people. I'm not leaving Toni alone right now."

"What's your plan at the bars?"

"Watch, listen. I know what to look for."

"Do you think you're going to find anything? Is this the best use of our time?"

"I don't know," she admitted. "But where are we? What are our options? I need something to leverage with Winnie."

"Michael and Ryder are going to New Orleans tomorrow morning to talk to Ricky Dubois. If he has answers, Michael will get them. Then maybe you'll have something specific to approach the girl with."

"That's good. But I still need to figure out who the players are. What I really want is to meet Peter Landry."

"So far, he's clean. But the records of the Magnolia Inn are murky. Zack is tracing the LLC, but even if we do find something there, it's not going to help us catch the killer."

She was getting a headache, and money trails weren't her strength. She said, "I'm staying with Toni until someone relieves me. Let me think on Landry. Maybe you should do an official meet and greet and I can watch, incognito. Or I can follow him." Now that was an idea.

"Don't do anything without talking to me first. I gotta go."

Matt ended the call. Kara went up to check on Toni; she was lying on her bed, fully clothed, staring at a photo of her dead husband. Kara decided to leave her be. She went to the small house, gathered up the files she'd been looking through and brought them into the main house to continue her review. She sat in the living room where she had the best view of the road leading to the house. She wanted Guidry's head on a platter. No way was she going to let him get away with threatening an old woman.

No way in hell.

28

Jim was in his element in the RV, Matt thought.

They were back at the hotel and Matt was the lone observer while Jim processed the barrel. There were several steps he needed to do before he opened the seal, including an X-ray. Matt hadn't even been aware that there was an X-ray onboard, but he shouldn't be surprised. The RV seemed to have everything a crime lab needed.

The barrel was generic—thick blue plastic, now faded, and stained with what he assumed was algae. Once they removed the remains Quantico might be able to trace it and find the supplier, match it with lots sold locally.

The first thing Jim did was photograph the barrel from all

sides as it rested in a shallow stainless steel tub on the table in the center of the RV. Then he collected and labeled samples from several spots on the barrel. He had weighed it when he first loaded the barrel onto the RV—there was a lift on the back, which made the process much easier than Matt had expected.

The sealed barrel weighed 134 pounds.

Lily Baker had weighed between 110 and 115 when she disappeared. A 55-gallon plastic barrel would weigh between 20 and 25 pounds.

After Jim collected trace evidence from the barrel's exterior, he unlocked a cabinet and extracted a handheld digital X-ray machine. "Matt, stand behind the curtain." Jim absently motioned to a thin, lead curtain that was pulled back and attached to the wall.

Matt did as instructed and waited until Jim called him back. He resecured the curtain and watched as Jim plugged the X-ray into the computer and uploaded the images.

Immediately, it was clear that there was a body inside. They could see the skeleton in a contorted position, dark matter all around.

"Is that her body?"

"It's liquefied," Jim said grimly. He scrolled through the images. "There's nothing left, other than her bones." He zoomed in on a section. Matt couldn't tell what he was seeing—it looked like ribs and the vertebrae all twisted to him.

Jim frowned, scrolled to another picture. "Well," he said. "I won't be certain until I drain the barrel and put the skeleton back together, but I'm almost positive that she was in fact pregnant. Hard to tell with these images, but between three and four months. If the fetal femur is intact, I can give you a decent estimate of gestation."

He scrolled several images over until he found one of the victim's head. Brighter white oblong shapes were visible. "Here, here—these appear to be bullets in her skull."

"She was shot twice, stuffed in the barrel and dumped in the river."

"My guess, but I'm not putting it down until I do a thorough exam. The good news—if there is any—this barrel is solid. No leakage."

"Can you do the autopsy here?"

"Yes, this table is reversible. I can turn it around and it gives me a six-inch tub. I'll drain the bones, collect any evidence, clean the bones, drain again for trace and put the bones in order. It'll take time, and I'll need help."

"Anything you need."

"Not you or Michael, you have too much on your plate right now and Michael, though a good investigator, is not experienced with this level of detail work. And while Kara is willing to do almost anything, she doesn't have the patience for this work, and she doesn't like forensics. She doesn't need any more reasons to keep her up at night."

Matt didn't realize that Jim and Kara had gotten that friendly.

"Ryder was an Army medic, he can—"

"He would be competent, yes, but I'd like to hire a private pathologist who specializes in bones, or ask Tony to send someone down from Quantico. One day—might be expensive. But we need to do this sooner rather than later, and we can't ship the barrel back to Quantico. I suppose I could drive it back…"

"We need you here. We're still trying to get the toxicology and trace on the other victims. How long will the autopsy take?"

"Several hours. Not more than a day. DNA will take longer."

"Can you establish paternity?"

"Possibly. They can extract DNA from the femur if intact and determine paternity if there's someone to compare with. It's not easy, it might be expensive, but it can be done. I would send the fetal bones to Quantico to handle."

"After you talk to Tony, put together a basic report—include a couple of photos. Nothing about the bullets or the baby, just confirm that there's a body inside, likely a 110–115 pound female, if you can comfortably say that. I want to give it to Dubois."

"Why withhold information?"

"Because if he's involved in her murder, or protecting someone who is, I don't want them to know that we might have forensics…or that she was pregnant. Let's keep that to ourselves until we have more information."

"All right, I can do that, then I'm going to run the syringe that Armand gave me."

"How long for results?"

Jim smiled. "Faster than you've ever gotten lab results before."

Beau ended the call with John Thibodeaux and almost punched his fist into his car. At the last minute he extended his fingers and slammed his flat palm on the hood, leaving a dent.

Guidry had threatened his grandmother.

Beau saw red.

He opened the driver's door when Matt Costa stepped out of the RV. For a minute he wanted to ignore him, find Guidry and pummel him.

"What's wrong?" Matt immediately said.

He didn't want to tell him, but he knew he should. "Guidry," he spat out as he slammed the door shut and leaned back against it. "He threatened my grandmother at the grocery this morning."

Matt said, "I planned to tell you."

"You knew?" Beau pushed.

"Your grandmother told Kara, and I said I would talk to you when you arrived. Kara is staying with her until you return."

"That's good. Dammit. Dammit! John said that Guidry intimidated her, wouldn't let her get into her car. I need to go home."

"I understand your anger, but steer clear of Guidry. You're going to jeopardize this case if you go off half-cocked."

"What case? We have shit. That bastard will pay for threaten-

ing Mimi." Beau knew Matt was right, but Guidry intentionally intimidated his grandma who had never hurt a living soul.

"There's a body in the barrel we found, and a fetus. Evidence
of two bullets."

Beau was stunned. "How do you know so fast?"

"X-rays. We're calling in a bone expert to assist Jim with the
autopsy. But I need a safer place for the RV, not here. I'm going
to send him to Lafayette."

"Why not take it to a lab?"

"Even if I rush this through Quantico, it could take weeks
for results. Jim can get results tomorrow. And I can't spare Jim
driving the RV to Quantico yet, we need him local."

"Is this now your investigation? Officially?" Beau wanted the
FBI to take over everything, but also recognized there would
be huge problems with that. Dubois would stymie Matt. Use
the delay to intimidate witnesses, destroy evidence, or worse.

"The body in the barrel is now a federal investigation. Once
we have more information from the autopsy, we'll see what we
can do for the rest. I know if I tell Dubois to move over, I'll get
even less cooperation. I had a long conversation with the former SSA of Lafayette, and I think our best recourse is to keep
the other murders separate from Lily Baker until we can connect them through evidence."

"Dubois will still put up roadblocks."

"Which is why I'm not telling him everything we know.
I'm going to tell him about the barrel and that there is a female
body inside, that's it."

"He's going to ask how you found it."

"I could say that you and Michael were fishing and something caught on the line."

"They'll know Michael's a fed. So far they haven't made the
connection."

"I'm going to tell him my office had a tip. I don't have to give him details. But he's going to know real quick about Michael, if he hasn't already put it together."

Matt was right, of course, but Beau still wished he had more time before it came out. "I'm concerned about my grandmother. I know her, Matt, she's never going to leave town, not even to stay with my dad for a week or two."

"We'll have someone with her at all times. Between Kara, Michael, Savannah and you. Is that good? I can ask Curt Danville in the Lafayette office for another agent."

"Maybe. I need to see her, find out what he said, how she's doing. Do you need me here?"

Matt shook his head. "Go home. Talk to Toni, you'll feel better. But, Beau—do not confront Guidry. We will get him—if for nothing else, what he did to Kara the other day. Understand? But if you go after him, we're screwed."

"I won't seek him out, Matt, but if he comes for me or mine? I will put him to the ground."

Beau got in his car and sped out of the parking lot.

Matt watched Beau drive off, not certain he had convinced him to back down. He texted Kara and told her Beau was heated and on his way home, gave her the heads-up that he knew about Guidry's threats to Toni. Then he went into the hotel room to talk to Michael.

Savannah was sitting at the desk on the phone, and Michael had showered and changed and was drinking a cold water bottle. Matt helped himself to one from the minifridge and told Michael what Jim had said. "He's putting together a report. We're not telling them everything, but we have to tell them something."

"Do we?"

"It's going to get out, and this way, we control how much they know and when they know it."

"I trust you, boss."

"I don't know about this one," Matt admitted. "Kara is antsy. She's been sitting on Beau's grandmother all morning." He told

Michael about the threat from Guidry. "Beau's heading home. I suspect he's going to stay for a while. Kara has a plan—if you can call it that. I'm going to let her run with it, but I need you to be prepared if she calls for backup."

"What plan?"

Matt didn't know how to describe it. "Surveillance, tracking, she wants to see who talks to who, where they go."

"You think she can do it? In the rental? Guidry knows what she was driving."

"Ryder got her a rent-a-wreck or something. He's bringing it out and then driving back to Lafayette in the RV with Jim tonight. With what we've found, and the fact that he's exposed here—even if I moved you and Kara to the hotel to keep an eye on things, I can't risk the evidence. So I'll have Ryder go back with him. I'll stay here."

Savannah got off the phone. "I might have something for you."

"We can use a break."

She stood, stretched, crossed over to where Matt and Michael were talking. "I talked to my former boss in NOLA. He knew about the Landry fraud investigation, and more. He thinks the partner who confessed and went to prison didn't talk because he was protecting his wife and kid—that's why he testified that he acted alone. The wife got a windfall—when her husband was killed in prison, she collected a cool two million in life insurance."

"When was the policy taken out?" Matt asked.

She looked at her notes. "More than a year before the indictment, so nearly two years before he was killed."

"Hard to prove premeditation."

"My boss said that he wanted to nail Landry and Steele, but couldn't prove anything. They said all the right things, were shocked that O'Neill had committed such blatant fraud. He's emailing me everything he has."

"What about the fourth partner?"

"I mentioned that, he didn't remember a fourth partner, but he's checking the files. It's in archives, might take a day or two. Not all older closed cases have been digitized yet."

"This still doesn't put us any closer to learning whether he's involved with murder," Michael said. "Someone going from insurance fraud to drugs? What's the path?"

Maybe they were wrong about Landry. But Beau wasn't wrong about the timeline: People started dying after Landry was elected and then appointed Dubois the chief of police.

"We look into everyone connected to these women until we rule them out," Matt said. "Michael, as soon as you're done in New Orleans tomorrow, get back here. We need to reexamine Lily Baker's life. Beau is a competent detective, but he has no support. We need to look at everything with fresh eyes, beginning to end." And hope to find the smoking gun.

29

Kara had convinced Toni to save the jambalaya for tomorrow. Not only were they working all night, she'd had a scare this morning and needed to take it easy. The fact that the old woman didn't argue with her told Kara she really had been shaken.

She had word from Matt that there was a body in the barrel, likely Lily Baker but they would be doing a full autopsy tomorrow. She appeared to have been shot—two bullets in her skull—and there was also a fetal skeleton.

Kara was reminded how much she hated people.

Ryder was on his way, and she couldn't wait to get out of here. She adored Toni, and the downtime had given her the chance to again review Beau's notes and files, but now she was restless. She compiled a list of people she wanted to track and was ready to go.

Beau drove up and jumped out of his car. He ran up the steps then stopped when he saw Kara sitting on the porch typing up her report on her phone. She was trying to be good, but the FBI had more paperwork than the LAPD and it drove her crazy.

He strode over to her. "You should have called me. Told me about Guidry."

"I told Matt, he said he'd tell you, and Toni didn't want me to say anything. I told her I couldn't do that, but I didn't want you distracted from watching Michael's ass. I didn't want him to become gator chum."

"You have a huge misconception of the bayou."

"So there are no gators here?"

He sat down. "John Thibodeaux called me. Told me he had witnessed Guidry blocking Mimi's path. Said she looked scared. That's not like her."

"I'm not going to lie, she was shaken," Kara said. "I sat with her, talked to her and haven't left the property. I don't think she should be alone."

"Thank you. What did he say?"

"He threatened you. That there are a lot of people here and you'd better not anger the wrong people."

"Fuck."

"You said it. Would these people really go after an eighty-some-year-old woman?"

"If you asked me last week, I'd say no. But now? I don't know. They would go after me. I've gotten veiled threats, and I've been careful, but clearly Matt's presence has stirred the pot. Scaring my grandmother is the first attack."

"What are you going to do?"

"I want to knock him on his ass."

"Get in line."

"But your boss told me to cool off."

282

"He's smart about these things."

"Maybe, but the longer he's here, the more repercussions there'll be. I don't know what's going to happen, who might get hurt." He glanced toward the front door, his expression both angry and worried.

"Nor do I. But we're going to get to the bottom of this, Beau." She looked at her phone. "Ryder's going to be here in fifteen minutes with my incognito vehicle. I need to dress the part. Talk to Toni, you'll feel better."

Kara went into the small house and sorted through her things. Earlier, she'd borrowed a man's plaid shirt from Toni—it had belonged to her husband, Carl. She hadn't gotten rid of all his things, and told Kara she could keep the shirt.

Carl hadn't been a large man, but the shirt hung loosely on Kara, which was what she wanted. She put the thin, dark plaid over an army green tank top, rolled the sleeves up to her elbows. It was faded, a hint of bayrum infused in the old fabric. She wore it with jeans. Too fucking hot for jeans, but if she wanted to be a farm girl, this was the attire.

She pulled out her fake hair from its protective box. There were several ways to change your appearance so someone didn't immediately recognize you. Changing hair and makeup was the single best way, which was why her messy hair and heavy makeup yesterday had confused Beau. This time, she brushed her hair tightly back and secured it to her left side with a rubber band. Some of her shorter hair on the right escaped, but that was okay. She then attached the fake braid—which almost perfectly matched her own hair color—and secured it with two additional bands. If someone looked closely, they might be able to tell it was an extension, but when she put on a baseball hat she'd found in Beau's closet—a purple cap with LSU stitched in yellow—it looked natural.

No makeup—not necessary. Scuffed, low-heeled boots which

were her favorite shoes. And then she holstered her gun, adjusted it to the small of her back so it was concealed under the loose shirt, pocketed her knife, and she was good to go.

By the time she stepped out, Ryder was talking to Beau in the war room.

"I never know what you're going to look like next," Beau said.

"That's how I keep men on their toes," she teased. "Hope you don't mind I borrowed your hat."

"Go right ahead. Looks good on you."

Ryder tossed her keys. "I got you a truck like you asked. It's beat-up, definitely looks the part, but the engine is solid."

"Thanks. I knew you'd come through. I'll drop you off near the hotel. I don't want anyone seeing me there dressed like this in case someone's watching."

"I emailed you the list of businesses owned by the LLC in question," he said. "Zack has been putting in extra hours."

"I saw. The Broiler—the restaurant—seems legit, but are the others suspicious?"

"The restaurant is owned by Peter Landry, LLC. It appears to be completely aboveboard, his legitimate business. His other properties are owned by Apex Gulf LLC, and his name isn't clearly on the records. It took Zack a while to drill down and find the trail. Landry's the attorney of record—he created both LLCs as well as the LLC that owns the Magnolia Inn. But the difference is that Landry doesn't appear to have control over the Magnolia LLC, Steele does. He could be a silent partner, but that's harder to prove."

"Okay," she said slowly, "Landry is involved in some way with Apex—but is there a figurehead?"

"No. And there's nothing illegal about the way it's established, because he's the designated contact. They file on time, no red flags."

"Even though he was under investigation by the FBI."

"Just because someone is under investigation doesn't mean they're guilty," Ryder said.

"Do we know the fourth partner yet?"

"No. Matt is working on it. Agent Trahan has been working her contacts in NOLA, but so far no one seems to remember, and it's not in any of the records. Zack is digging around as well, but it was a local business, and that means getting someone in the local registrar's office to pull original paperwork more than a decade old. I'll text you if I learn anything new."

"Thanks, Ryder," she said, then turned to Beau. "Did you talk to Toni? She okay?"

"She's mad."

"She should be."

"I'm gonna stay with her, but there's so much to do on this case."

"I went through everything again, wrote out a bunch of questions I had—most of them you probably can't answer. But maybe one of my questions will spark a memory or give you a different direction. Look at the victims from a different angle, recheck key dates, witnesses. And I'm really curious about Debra."

It took Beau a moment. "You mean the woman Johnny Baxter was talking about to Cormier?"

"Yeah. It was the *way* he was talking. I can't put my finger on it. But it's someone I don't know, can't put a face to. She doesn't live here, and I don't know how she fits into the puzzle."

"I'll look at what you put together. And, um, thanks for being here for my grandmother. She really likes you."

"I like her, too."

Kara had a list of vehicles she was looking for. The old truck that Winnie was driving, registered to her cousin. Gray Cormier's Dodge Ram or Preston Cormier's sports car. Jasper Steele drove a year-old red Ford F-250. Peter Landry drove a Cadillac Escalade—pricey car for a small-town mayor, she thought.

Maybe his lawyering and insurance businesses paid super well? Did he still work in either capacity? More questions to answer.

None of the vehicles were at the Magnolia, so she decided not to go in. Instead, she wrote down the license plates of the four vehicles in the lot.

She drove by The Fat Catfish, did the same. She wanted to go in, check things out, but wasn't certain that Johnny Baxter wouldn't recognize her. Probably not but she didn't want to take the risk, two days in a row.

Then she drove by every property Peter Landry owned through his LLCs.

She'd mapped them, but looking at them from a year-old Google image wasn't the same as in person.

The Broiler was owned by a separate entity, and it was open only for dinner, from four in the afternoon until 10 p.m.—midnight on Fridays and Saturdays, closed on Mondays. Two vehicles were there now, neither of which were on her list.

She drove by Landry's house—not too far from Mrs. Davis, only a block over and farther east, toward the river. A much larger spread. Open acres filled with trees, lush green landscaping, a swimming pool in the back (per Google satellite images). Far too big for one person.

Landry was unmarried, no children.

She then headed toward what she was calling "Landry Row," where he owned every property on one street. West Canal was on the opposite side of town from the Magnolia, parallel to the interstate. According to Zack, half the properties were unused and half were leased to local businesses—auto repair, a dismantler, a nursery (for plants, not infants), a self-storage facility. At the very end was a warehouse—no signage, locked fencing and security cameras. She couldn't risk someone watching real time—there were two vehicles inside the fence (not on her list)—so she did a U-turn, discreetly snapping photos of the facility and the cars as she did so, hoping Ryder could enhance them.

The last property owned by Landry was just south of the St. Augustine town line, fifty acres with no nearby neighbors. On Google Maps it looked like a farm—growing pot was her first thought, but that would be too obvious. It bordered the river— well south of where Ernestine's body was found. Unfenced, but it wouldn't be easy to drive up to the house without being seen.

There were five structures she saw from the maps—a small house, an outbuilding, a barn and a larger barn that looked more like a warehouse. The last structure was a boathouse on the river. Could have boats there—looked like it could fit two. Landry had bought the property shortly after moving to St. Augustine. Did someone live here? It wasn't his public residence.

If she was right about how the drugs were being shipped into town, having a place adjacent to the river would be perfect. It was in the parish, outside St. Augustine town limits, and maybe—if Matt decided he wanted to rope in the sheriff—it might be easier to raid the place.

Still, she had no evidence that there was anything illegal going on here and they had no evidence that Peter Landry was a criminal.

The best way to check out the farm would be from the river, but Kara knew next to nothing about boats. While she could pilot a basic motorboat, she didn't know anything about the waterways here and would probably end up in the middle of the gulf if she tried to navigate them.

She and Beau should come down here tonight with the cover of darkness. See what was going on.

She headed past the farm, turned around just as she reached the Lake Pierre town limits, then drove north to pass it again. A quarter mile after she passed the driveway heading back into town, she spotted Winnie LeBlanc driving south in her beat-up truck, coming toward Kara.

Kara slowed down, averted her head slightly as Winnie passed her on the left, then in her rearview mirror watched Winnie turn into Landry's driveway.

What are you up to, Winnie?

She was worried about the kid. Worse, she feared she was already in too deep for Kara to save her.

A horn blared and she refocused her eyes in front of her. She'd drifted over the line and nearly hit an oncoming truck—Gray Cormier's Dodge Ram. She immediately corrected, and he flipped her off as he drove past.

He, too, turned into Landry's driveway.

Fuck.

Kara headed back to town and called Michael.

"Winnie and Gray Cormier are at Landry's farm south of town," she said. "I want to look at the place tonight from the river."

He didn't say anything.

"Not alone," she said. "I wouldn't know where the hell I was going. But something is going on there and the only way we can get close is on the water, however much I hate the idea."

"You'll be happy to know that alligators get sluggish at night, just like all reptiles."

"You made my day," she said.

"I'll talk to Matt and Beau. Aren't you running a stakeout tonight at The Broiler?"

"Yeah—at seven. I want to check out The Fat Catfish again, now that it's closer to five and busier. Can you park yourself outside in case I run into some trouble?"

"I'll do that. I'm still at the hotel, give me fifteen minutes."

"Text me when you're in position."

30

Matt decided to wait until Jim and Ryder were safely back in Lafayette before he took Jim's report to Chief Dubois. He didn't want to risk Dubois doing something like putting a boot on the RV. Though Matt didn't think there would be a violent confrontation, he was worried about the evidence.

Before Jim left, he'd run the syringe. As soon as Matt read the report—separate from the report on the body—he knew Jean Paul LeBlanc's death was no accident or suicide.

First, there were no prints on the syringe. Not a cop or a paramedic or Jean Paul. It had been wiped clean.

And second, the heroin was cut with strychnine. The poor man was dead in minutes.

"A real autopsy would have showed this," Jim had said. "The toxicology should show it as well, but had that damn coroner just done his job, we would have known before now."

"He was murdered."

"Unless he decided to shoot himself up with rat poison, yeah, I'd say homicide."

A surefire, but painful, way to die.

After Ryder sent him the message that he and Jim had arrived at the Lafayette office, Matt and Savannah went to the police station. He had been tracking Kara's progress all over town; she'd gotten a lot better at keeping him and Michael informed of her movements. Ryder had said her disguise was good and at first glance no one would recognize her, and Kara said she was just doing surveillance and promised to call if she changed her plans.

He had to trust her. He just wished she didn't take so many risks.

If she didn't, she wouldn't be Kara.

Savannah had been quiet this afternoon after she got off the phone with her contact in NOLA. She was on her laptop, said she had to respond to messages she'd been neglecting, and he reminded her that he and his team appreciated that she'd given so much time to them. "And sorry about the late night tonight—if you can't join me, I can do it alone."

"It's fine. I don't have any place to be, no one expecting me. Divorced, remember?"

Now they were at the station and she was refocused on the case.

Dubois made them wait, even though he knew they were coming. When they were finally led back to his office, it was after five. Guidry was in the office with him.

"You remember Officer Jerry Guidry?" the chief said.

"Yes." This was the cop who had intentionally intimidated an octogenarian. Had felt up Kara in the line of duty. Keeping his temper in check was becoming increasingly hard to do.

"I'll get right to the point. My team had a tip that the body of Lily Baker may have been dropped in the river south of Lantern Gate, near where the body of Ernestine Bergeron was found. I sent a diver—"

Dubois cut him off. "Hold up right there, Agent Costa. You had a tip and didn't inform me?"

"I asked that we work together. You declined. The tip came into the FBI. I was under no obligation to inform you."

"That is unacceptable."

Matt handed him the report that Jim had prepared. "I sent a certified forensic diver to inspect the area. He found a fifty-five gallon plastic barrel, sealed, fifty-eight yards from the southern edge of the land known as Lantern Gate. With the assistance of Dr. Esteban, we extracted the barrel cleanly and began to process the evidence."

"That is within St. Augustine city limits," he said. "I expect you to turn over all evidence to our coroner to investigate."

"If you look at the report, you'll see that we X-rayed and weighed the barrel. Inside are the skeletal remains of a female, approximately five foot three and 110 pounds. That would match the description of Lily Baker. Algae and matter on the outside of the barrel suggests that it has been under water for a minimum of two months. Those samples will be analyzed to give us a more specific time frame. We're bringing in a forensic anthropologist to assist in the autopsy, and will of course provide you with a detailed report as to our findings, including DNA confirmation, cause of death and any other evidence we uncover."

"This is unacceptable, Agent Costa. The FBI has no right to come down to St. Augustine and investigate anything, then cut us out."

"I came in yesterday morning explaining why we were here and that we wanted to work with you. You declined—your coroner told Dr. Esteban that his services weren't needed or wanted, and you didn't provide me with any of the files related to the six murders my office is interested in, and only a basic report on Mr. LeBlanc's in-custody death. I'm not going to apologize for following a tip about a missing woman."

"Who called in the tip?" Guidry asked.

"It was anonymous," Matt lied smoothly.

"I don't believe you," Guidry said.

"I don't care."

Dubois put up his hand. "Stop. Do you think I don't know what's going on? You've been working with one of my detectives and going behind my back on an investigation in my jurisdiction. I want you out of town, and I will deal with Detective Hebert accordingly."

Savannah interjected, "Rich, I'm sure we can come to a satisfactory agreement. The resources we can offer—"

He cut her off. "You should be more concerned about the damage your office has done to relations here and in the parish. It's not done this way, and you know it, Agent Trahan."

"You have seven dead women in your parish, a bar shooting, and a man who died while in your custody," Matt reminded him. "You should have been asking for our help long ago."

"Do not tell me how to run my department. Unless you turn over the evidence you uncovered, you're no longer welcome here and will be getting no access to my department or my coroner."

"I'm sorry you feel that way," Matt said. This conversation had devolved quickly, but he couldn't back down now. "If we find any connection between the six women who have been murdered, and the body we recovered today, my office will be seeking jurisdiction over all seven murders. We should want the same thing here, Chief. Justice for those women. Putting a killer in prison. I don't want to do this without your help, without your blessing. But if you leave me no choice, I will."

"You have no rights here, Agent Costa."

He tossed his card on top of the report that Dubois hadn't

picked up. "That's Special Agent in Charge Mathias Costa," he said.

He and Savannah left.

"Fucking prick," Matt said.

"Matt, there had to be a better way."

"This is out of control and we're going to put an end to it now. One thread that Lily Baker's murder is connected to the others, these cases are all ours."

"Maybe we shouldn't go to The Broiler tonight."

"Now's the time to do it. I want to see what Peter Landry does."

"If he knows about Beau's involvement, then he might know about your team—Kara and Michael."

He'd been thinking about that, too. He sent a message to both of them to watch their backs, the meeting with Dubois went worse than expected. Then he called Beau, told him what happened.

"I just got the call," he said. "I'm suspended."

That was fast. "Beau, I'm sorry. I had to push when he wouldn't back down."

"I can weather the storm. Take him down, Matt."

"It's going to be dicey for the next few days, Beau—but we're not going to hang you out to dry."

"I called Lily's mother and told her we may have found her remains, that I wanted her to be the first to know and I would tell her once we confirm. She won't say anything—I just felt she has the right to know."

Not ideal, but Matt would have done the same thing. "I understand."

When he arrived back at the hotel, Matt told Savannah, "Why don't you go in and relax, I have to call my boss."

"I need to call Curt as well—he's going to hear about this sooner rather than later."

Savannah took the key that Matt offered her and left. Matt

needed to be able to talk freely, and Tony might have a few choice words at how Matt handled this.

Matt called his boss. "Tony, I put the St. Augustine police chief on notice that we may be taking jurisdiction over the seven murders."

"*May* take jurisdiction? I read Jim's report about the body in the barrel. What happened?"

"I gave a version of the report to Dubois. He barely looked at it. Told him if there was a connection between this body and the other dead women, that I would be seeking jurisdiction. I offered to work it together, but made it clear if he wasn't willing, this case is mine."

"Okay."

"Okay?"

"Honestly, it should have been ours four women ago. I'll handle the fallout. But here on out, do everything right. We'll be under a microscope."

31

Kara swaggered into The Fat Catfish as if she had been working outside all day and was bone-tired. At five o'clock the place was far more crowded than it had been yesterday at noon. It catered mostly to blue-collar types at this hour—the working class that Kara had always felt most at home with. She didn't think the bar was as bad as Beau had made it out to be. Silent sports on the televisions, a jukebox playing country. She preferred rock, but didn't mind country.

A waitress came over to her—tired, weary, with a thin T-shirt that tightly outlined her ample breasts and jean shorts not unlike what Kara had been wearing when Guidry pulled her over. In the two minutes that Kara had been sitting at the small table, she'd watched three men touch the waitress's ass and one pinch her nipple.

Kara would tip her well. She'd gotten the message from Matt about how fabulous his meeting with Dubois went. She figured after tonight she wouldn't be having this kind of fun, running around incognito. Which was fine by her. She'd learned most everything she could at this point.

"Whatcha drinkin'?" the waitress asked.

"Tequila, straight up."

She scribbled out something on a napkin and walked away.

Kara generally didn't drink hard alcohol while working undercover, but she'd only have one, and because she was here yesterday drinking a bottle of Coors Light, she didn't want Johnny behind the bar to remember the order and give her undue attention. Though she'd changed her appearance—and he'd been mostly looking at her breasts and ass yesterday—she was still the same person, and bartenders tended to be more observant than the average person.

Tammy Bergeron was in her booth—Beau had given Kara the lay of the land, described the large, light-skinned black aunt of Ernestine perfectly. She was holding court, it seemed. Men and a couple women milling about. One would sit down, they'd talk, get up a few minutes later, another would sit down.

Interesting.

Was she giving orders? Passing something under the table? Probably not—while Kara couldn't see under the table, she'd have been able to tell if these people were stuffing something into their pockets, or leaving something with Tammy.

But it was odd, and it intrigued her. It was like they were giving her reports.

Doubly interesting.

Johnny Baxter was behind the bar, keeping pace with the orders but not rushing.

Unlike yesterday, she wouldn't be able to hear any conversations over the music and chatter. She discreetly took pictures of everyone in the bar.

When the waitress came back with her tequila and said, "Five bucks," Kara gave her ten and waved her off. The girl gave her a double look—probably not a good thing, but Kara wasn't going to be here long. "Thanks, sugar," the girl said.

She deserved a hell of a lot more after all the handsy bastards she had to put up with.

She drained the tequila in one gulp. It burned going down. Definitely cheap stuff.

A woman came out of the back. She hadn't been in the bar when Kara came in twelve minutes ago, so she must have come in through the back door—which Kara knew to be accessible only to exit in an emergency or with a key—or she'd been in the back office.

She had dark hair cut short, dark eyes, pale skin and a long, narrow nose. She was no blue-collar worker—she wore cream slacks, a loose-fitting blouse and jewelry. Kara didn't know anything about jewelry, but this stuff glittered like diamonds. Two large men walked in behind her, one black and one white, clearly bodyguards, both packing heat under their loose-fitting jackets.

Kara took pictures as the woman strode toward Tammy.

The people around Tammy's table scattered, going back to their own seats. The woman paid them no attention.

Tammy's face was unreadable, then she smiled.

"Debra, you're late."

Kara couldn't hear what Debra said, but she sat down and a waitress brought over a drink—a Manhattan. Kara didn't know jewelry, but she knew her alcohol.

The men were watching the crowd.

Who was Debra? This was super interesting and Kara knew if she got up now, it would be suspicious. When her waitress came over again, she asked if she wanted another.

Consciously avoiding looking at Tammy's booth, Kara said,

"Yeah, sure." She slipped the waitress a twenty and a five and asked quietly, "Who's talking to Tammy?"

She didn't need to look. "Debra Martin," she whispered. "Owner's daughter. She fucking scares me."

Then the waitress scurried off. Kara noted that the twenty went into a different pocket than the five.

Smart girl.

A short, broad-shouldered thug with a skinny friend came over and sat across from her. "Hey, sweetheart, what's your name?"

She stared at him, silent.

"Don't be that way. Let us buy you a drink."

"Go away," she said.

"That's not what you mean."

"It's what I said."

He laughed. "Girls say a lot of things they don't mean."

His wiry friend sat next to her, effectively cutting off her exit.

She let them make the jokes and talk as if they thought they could get her into bed, because they weren't touching her. She had one eye on them and one eye on Tammy and Debra.

Debra got up to leave and Kara wished she had been a fly on the wall of that conversation. Debra left the same way she came in, her bodyguards following her.

Lots and lots of questions…

The waitress came back with her tequila. The girl frowned at the two men. "You want something else, boys?"

"Just Little Miss Tight-Ass to loosen up some."

"Don't be jerks," the waitress said.

"Don't be a wet blanket, Ella."

"Don't make me call Johnny over," Ella snapped.

Yeah, let's not have that, Kara thought.

She sent Michael a quick text: Come to the door, stay outside.

She stood. The short guy didn't move. "My boyfriend just texted me that he's outside. You'll want to get out of my way."

"Boyfriend? Does he make you feel *goooood*." He put his hand on her thigh and rubbed.

Ella walked toward the bar and Kara didn't want Johnny to intervene. She took her tequila and tossed it in the man's face then kicked his chair over and he went sprawling on the ground, but at least he got out of her way.

She didn't wait to see what happened. His burly friend called her a bitch. She strode out the door and Michael was standing right there, as she'd asked.

The two men came out the door and Kara put her arms around Michael, and said loudly, "Honey, he touched me."

Michael looked at the men and growled. Literally *growled*. Kara would have laughed if she wasn't trying to play a part.

"Hey, sorry, man, we didn't know she was taken. No hard feelings?"

Michael didn't say a word.

They went back inside without comment, and Kara grinned. "Damn, that was fun."

"You have an odd definition of *fun*."

"Let's go, I have to change for dinner."

"We have a lot to discuss."

She stood on her tippy-toes and kissed him on the cheek. "Then drive slow."

32

The Broiler was the upscale restaurant in St. Augustine. Landry didn't operate it, but word was he ate there several nights a week, and after some digging, Ryder learned that Tuesday was his standing working dinner with his small mayoral staff—chief of staff, administrative assistant and constituent liaison.

Made of stone and on a corner lot with a discreet entrance covered by some sort of flowering vine weaving through a lattice that attached to the roof, The Broiler had a quaint yet exclusive facade. They served steak and fish, and boasted a dark decor and pricey menus. There was a bar—what one might call a gentleman's lounge—and when Matt walked into the restaurant with Savannah, he saw that Kara was already there. He wouldn't have immediately recognized her if she hadn't told him what she was wearing—dark jeans, cowboy boots and a silky burgundy spaghetti-strap tank top.

As always he had that jolt when he laid eyes on her. A complex blend of lust and love, of frustration and respect, of desire and worry. Worry because there had been something going on with her for the last week but she wouldn't talk to him about it. He could practically feel her slipping away from him. A blink later and he'd buried his emotions.

Kara was in the bar to keep an eye on the room, to assess Landry and his group after Matt and Savannah left. Michael was situated outside to follow anyone Matt flagged. For now, this was reconnaissance. He wasn't certain it was going to work after his confrontation with Chief Dubois this afternoon, but he was willing to take the risk and he had both Michael and Kara as backup.

Kara had made several interesting observations today, and the added player of Debra Martin made for a twist. Matt had begun to wonder if maybe the recent events—starting with the murder of Jake West—might have to do with a power play. That maybe Debra and Tammy were making a move on the Cormier operation. He'd broached the subject with Beau, and the detective was speechless. He had been so hyperfocused on Preston Cormier that he hadn't even considered someone was weaseling in on their operation.

Still, it might be unrelated. Matt had sent the name up the chain of command, now all he could do was wait, observe, and work his damnedest to prevent anyone else from dying.

Savannah didn't think this ploy to create tension between Landry and Dubois would work, and frankly, neither did Matt. Matt and Michael had talked at length about their options, and they agreed that if they put enough pressure on the players, something would give. It was clear that for three years, whoever was running the drug operation in St. Augustine had been working freely and without fear of arrest. They were brazen and bold and Matt wanted to take them down.

But he needed solid evidence.

Five minutes after Matt and Savannah were seated, Landry walked in with his assistant, a lanky brunette with a curvy body. His other two staffers were already there—sitting in a booth across from Matt. It was after seven—Landry was a few minutes late. He looked directly at Matt, said something to his table that Matt couldn't hear, and then turned and crossed the small restaurant to where Matt was sitting. "Agent Costa, correct?" Landry said.

"Yes. We haven't met."

"No." Landry extended his hand. "I'm Peter Landry, the mayor of St. Augustine."

"Matt Costa, FBI. This is Special Agent Savannah Trahan, from the Lafayette office."

Landry took Savannah's hand. "Ma'am, good to meet you." He then said to Matt, "Rich—Chief Dubois—is a bit ruffled that the FBI is here without being invited. I told him it wasn't a slight on our department, but I should have reached out earlier, especially in light of the fact that your people apparently found a body in the river this morning."

"Yes. I'm happy to sit down and meet anytime you'd like."

"Richard said you were leaving."

"He wants me to leave. He, in fact, ordered me to leave."

"I'm sure that's not right. He'd told me that you had offered resources to help us solve these awful murders. I told him that was a good thing. But it is a small town. Perhaps he felt it was a demand, not a request? I'll talk to him. We all want the same thing."

"That would be helpful, thank you," Matt said.

"He showed me the report you gave him this afternoon, about the body stuffed in a barrel? I'm so sad about this tragic turn of events. Do you think your lab can identify the remains?"

"Yes," Matt said without hesitation.

"And you'll let us know," Landry said.

"Of course. That's why I gave the chief the preliminary report—I want to keep him in the loop."

"But isn't that the role of the St. Augustine Police Department? I don't mean to be rude, I appreciate anything the FBI can do to help, but it's our jurisdiction, we should be investigating these crimes."

He was trying to play both sides, which was typical of politicians whether they were corrupt or not.

"We have better facilities and more resources. And to be perfectly honest, Mr. Landry—"

"Please call me Peter. Throw a rock, you're going to hit a Landry." He smiled widely.

"We've been following this case for a while and the lack of progress after the murders of seven young women is cause for concern," Matt said. "My boss wants me to make sure that your department is capable of handling the investigation. At this point, I can't give him that reassurance. Sometimes, people need help and don't want to ask."

"Rich will ask if he needs the help."

"On the contrary, there have been many inconsistencies in the forensics—" Matt stopped himself. He had said what he wanted to, and now he needed to make Peter Landry sweat. "Anyway, not appropriate conversation for dinner. Would you like to meet tomorrow?"

"I can free my schedule."

Matt handed him his card. "The printed number goes to my assistant, and I wrote my cell number on the back. Either one works to reach me. Pick the hour, I'll make the time."

"I appreciate that. You may not know, but I own this restaurant. Your meal's on the house."

"I appreciate the offer, Peter, but we're not allowed to accept gifts—including meals."

"I did not know that. Well, enjoy, the food is the best this side of the Mississippi. The best food east of the Mississippi is my sister restaurant in N'orlins." He smiled, nodded at Savannah, and went back to his table.

"You were right," Savannah said quietly.

"I usually am."

"I can't believe he glad-handed you like that. You're going to meet with him? Do you think he'll force Dubois to work with us?"

"Fifty-fifty that he calls." Matt glanced over at the table. Landry was looking at him; when he caught Matt's eye he smiled and tipped his glass of wine in a toast. "He really wants to know what we know. And yes, he'll want Dubois to work with us as long as everything is contained in town. If he's involved—and I think he is—he'll want to maintain control."

"Maybe he's what he appears to be," Savannah said. "A mayor just trying to smooth things over between his police department and federal law enforcement."

"That's what he wants us to think. But Kara thinks he's in charge, and I trust her instincts." *More than anyone.*

Kara was enjoying her martini. She didn't drink them often, but when they were made right—and this one was perfect—they were liquid pleasure.

Matt had handled Landry perfectly. She couldn't hear the conversation, but she'd watched the back-and-forth, the body language, the smiles, the way Landry kept glancing over at Matt and Savannah after he'd returned to his table.

There had been nothing interesting going on in the bar half of the restaurant. The Broiler catered to the wealthier members of the greater St. Augustine community. Well, duh, she thought—forty-dollar steaks. Her martini was *fifteen* dollars. She could buy a whole bottle of not-dirt-cheap vodka for that.

"Hello, gorgeous."

Preston Cormier took the seat next to her. With a charming smile he said, "Please don't tell me your boyfriend is coming right back."

She tilted her head to him. "Seat's all yours."

He obviously didn't recognize her from the Magnolia—and she made sure her tattoo was hidden because the butterfly might be recognizable. The other day, she had dressed like a working girl for the Magnolia, and tonight she was classy and hot, if she did say so herself.

"You're not local. I don't quite place your accent. It sounds a bit Southern, but not Louisiana. You've been away from home for a long time."

"You're close."

"Is this twenty questions?"

She sipped her martini. "I don't know you."

"My manners." He extended his hand. "Preston Cormier."

"Kara Quinn." She avoided fake names if she could because they were harder to remember.

She shook his hand and he kissed hers. She refrained from bursting out in laughter. It was such a sleazy pickup move, especially in a place like this. She also couldn't help but notice that Matt was keeping his eye on her.

"So, how close was I?"

"I was born in Birmingham, my parents divorced and my mom moved me to California when I was fifteen. Now you."

"St. Augustine born and raised."

The bartender approached. "Mr. Cormier, your usual?"

"Thanks, Tuck."

"You've never lived anywhere else?" Kara asked him.

"Sure, I lived in N'orlins for a few years, still go there often—I have a little place right in the French Quarter."

That was news. When they'd run Preston Cormier, they didn't find any property outside of St. Augustine. It could be under another name, an LLC, or he was lying through his teeth to impress her.

"I love the Quarter, I've only been a couple of times. There's this amazing breakfast place right on Chartres a couple blocks from the cathedral. I can't remember the name."

The bartender put a double Scotch over ice in front of Preston. "Fleur De Lis?" Preston suggested.

"Maybe?" She smiled and shrugged. "I'd know it if I saw it. It's been a while."

She'd done some research on NOLA but no way was she going to be specific. She knew there was a cathedral, and she knew the major streets, and figured because they were known for their food, there was probably a great breakfast place somewhere. Being vague was always smart. "Another place I had the best gumbo I've ever eaten. I couldn't even *guess* what the name is."

"With your body I'm surprised you eat anything." He put his hand on her hip. Lightly, testing the waters.

"I believe in taking care of my temple," she said in a low voice. "I love food."

"Have you had dinner?"

"Yes."

"Too bad."

Landry got up from his table and walked through the bar. He caught Preston's eye, then went down the hall, behind the bar.

"If you could give me one minute and not let anyone else take this seat?"

"Sure," she said. "You have until I'm done with my martini." She sipped again.

He drained half his drink, put it down and followed Landry. That was very interesting.

Her phone vibrated. Then again. Then again. Damn.

She glanced into her purse. Her phone was next to her gun. The texts were from Matt.

Did they leave?

What's your plan?

We're leaving, I have your back.

She looked over at Matt and gave him just a subtle shake of her head. She closed her purse and drained her martini.

Four minutes after Cormier left, he returned. "I'm glad you waited. Meet me here tomorrow night for a drink? Same time?"

"You're leaving already?"

"Duty calls."

"I may not be in town tomorrow."

"Where are you staying?"

"My cousin's place in Evangeline."

"Who's your cousin?"

She raised an eyebrow. "I don't *really* know you. My kin are wary. Were even wary of *me* when I showed up yesterday on my way to Miami, since I haven't been visiting in a couple of years. Sort of the shoot-first-ask-questions-later type, but they're good people." She smiled slyly, leaned forward. "You sure you have to leave? Just one more drink?"

He looked at her lips as she licked them, then down her tank top to the top of her breasts.

"Damn," he said, "sometimes I hate my job." He reached out and put a hand on her waist, harder this time, his thumb rubbing discreetly under her breast. "If I kiss you, maybe you'll come back tomorrow."

"Maybe I will," she said.

He kissed her, tasting of the Scotch he was drinking. Then he stepped back and smiled. "I really wish I could stay."

"Bye, Preston," she said and turned back to the bartender. She pointed to her empty glass. "One more, sugar."

307

"Put it on my tab, Tuck," Preston said, winked at her and walked out.

Matt was paying his check, and Kara didn't want to leave too quickly after Matt and Savannah so she waited. She only took a couple small sips of her martini—she wouldn't finish it, they had too much work to do tonight—and counted the minutes.

Kara sat in the beat-up truck with Matt. They were parked down the street from The Broiler. Michael had followed Landry; Savannah had followed Cormier. They were waiting for reports.

"You let him kiss you."

"Just part of the act." She glanced at him. "Jealous?"

She didn't know why she said that. She didn't care. Matt didn't answer.

Michael called. Matt put him on speaker. "You were right, Kara. He went to the Magnolia Inn. How'd you know?"

"Cormier was here. When Landry went to the bar, ostensibly to check on something, they had a conversation. I couldn't hear what it was, but Cormier was hitting on me and then left. I had a feeling they would be meeting up there. Is he also there?"

"No."

"Damn. I hope Savannah doesn't lose him. Something's going on, but I can't follow him. He'd recognize me."

"Savannah knows what she's doing," Matt said.

Kara didn't comment.

"How long do you want me to sit out here, boss?" Michael asked.

"Twenty minutes unless you hear from me. Then we regroup at Beau's before we go out to the river. Take photos of every license plate—without being seen. Maybe it's a meeting, or maybe he just wants to get laid. Savannah's calling. Let me know if you need us. We'll stay here until you're back on the road."

Matt clicked over to Savannah. "Costa."

"Cormier is heading south on Lake Pierre Road. We're the only cars on the road."

"I'll bet he's going to the farm," Kara said.

Matt told Savannah, "If he turns off, keep going down several miles, don't slow. Stay far back."

"I know how to tail someone," she said, irritated.

"Meet at Beau's house. Check in regularly."

"I will." She ended the call.

"That was fun," Kara said.

"Why don't you like Savannah?"

"I don't know her. If I don't know her, I don't trust her. I'm sure she's fine."

"Her contacts have been useful. And we need the extra body. She's going to stay with Beau's grandmother tonight while we check out the farm."

"Four of us on the boat?"

"Michael's driving to Lafayette so he and Ryder can leave early in the morning for NOLA. It's a two-hour drive from there."

Again, silence. This was getting damn awkward.

Matt's phone rang.

It was Michael. "The girl just drove up."

"Winnie?" Kara said.

"She's going inside."

"I need to—"

"No," Matt said. "You gave her an opportunity to come clean. You go in now, it puts you and her in danger. We can't protect her if she doesn't want our help."

"We *will* protect her," Kara said. "She doesn't want this, but she doesn't see a way out."

"Michael," Matt said, "keep your eye on the place. Let us know when and if she leaves and if she's with anyone."

"Roger."

Matt ended the call and said to Kara, "You did everything you could. Now it's up to her."

Kara didn't say anything. How could she explain? They *had* to find a way to protect Winnie, even if she didn't say she wanted it. Kara understood the kid. She wanted an escape, but every door had been slammed in her face.

After a full minute of silence, Matt said, "If she leaves alone, you can approach her. Last chance, Kara. I'm not putting you or anyone else on my team at risk."

Winnie stood to the side at the meeting in the Magnolia, not wanting to draw anyone's attention. She just wanted to do this thing and go home.

She hated this place because she knew exactly what people did here. Nicki always came home high, with bruises and worse. She didn't even know who Bonnie's dad was. Some loser in town? Some stranger from the road? Winnie wanted to run away because why was that kid her responsibility?

But she couldn't let Bonnie suffer. None of this was the kid's fault. If Winnie didn't find a way out for her niece, no one else would do it. She felt hopeless.

"With Jake gone, Gray's going to handle the pickup," Jasper said. "Winn, you do the same thing you did with Jake and all will be good."

She nodded. What else was she going to do?

You should never have told Jean Paul that you were riding with Jake down the bayou. He thought he was helping you by killing him. He just made everything ten times worse.

"I should bring Shari," Gray said, frowning at Winnie.

"No," Jasper said. "Winn's clean, Shari can't get her head outta her ass half the time. And they know Winnie. We send in two new people? You'll both be dead and we'll lose our connection to the product."

Jasper, Gray and one of Gray's idiots, Kenny Duncan, were

sitting around a table drinking. She hated them. She just wanted her money so she could disappear.

And leave Bonnie Mae with Loretta? Yeah, right.

Everyone else gets dead and she really didn't want to die. She didn't know why most of Nicki's friends were killed. She had ideas, but she didn't know for a fact. But Ernestine? That girl knew *nothing* and they still killed her.

"What's going on with the fucking feds hanging around town? If they're still here Thursday, we're fucked," Kenny said.

"They don't know shit," Gray said. "Just shut up about them. It's fucking Tammy we have to watch out for, don't forget it."

It wasn't Tammy, Winnie thought—but damn well didn't say. If they knew she knew what she knew, they'd probably kill her on general principle.

She turned and started for the door.

"Winnie!" Jasper snapped. "Where you going?"

"I gotta pick up Bonnie Mae from Crystal. It's near ten, you know how Crystal gets if I'm late."

"You ready?"

"Yes. Can I go?"

He waved her off.

She couldn't get out of there fast enough. This was the last time.

Last time. Last time.

Maybe if she repeated it enough she'd believe it.

Kara was waiting for Winnie when she arrived at her house just after ten that evening. She stayed in the shadows, not wanting to put the teen in danger, if someone was watching the house.

Bonnie was asleep in the back of the truck. Before Winnie could get the kid out, Kara said, "Winnie."

The girl whirled around, looking ready to fight.

Fight, to protect her niece. When it had just been her, she wanted to run.

Good instincts.

"This is your last chance," Kara said quietly. "We can help you."

"This is the worst time for you to be here," Winnie hissed.

"At your house or in town?"

She didn't say anything.

"Your mother's passed out on the couch."

"Always is," Winnie muttered.

"My boss is the most trustworthy person I know. He will move heaven and earth to get you and Bonnie into WITSEC. Do you know what that is?"

She didn't say anything, but Kara suspected she knew.

"You'd have to leave everyone behind, but you and Bonnie would be free. Safe."

Winnie didn't say anything. Kara hoped she was listening. Really listening.

"I think," Kara said quietly, "that the Cormiers were working for Tammy until Peter Landry came to town. Now they're working for him, and Tammy is pissed. I don't know who Debra Martin is, but I know she and Tammy are in it together—and I think all the dead are casualties of this war between Landry and Martin."

It had been something Kara was mulling over all day, but especially after what happened at The Catfish this evening.

Winnie said, "There will always be someone else."

She wasn't wrong.

"But you don't have to be part of it. Give me one thing. Something I can parlay into more information, into action. And then stay away from everyone until this is over."

"I can't. I got myself into this mess."

"I can get you out."

Winnie didn't say anything, but she didn't make a move to

grab Bonnie and go inside. They were standing in the shadows of the house, and if anyone was watching, they wouldn't see Kara, who'd put on a black hoodie over her tank top.

"Thursday night. I can't back out."

"Where?"

She didn't answer. "You asked me why my cousin killed Jake. He did it to save me, but it ended up condemning me. The devil you know and all that. Now go." She didn't yell, she didn't cry, she just said it simply.

Kara left.

33

They were on the river, and Kara felt an unusual sense of peace.

Odd, she thought. Maybe because there was a new moon, casting little light, only shades of dark and darker. Maybe because Beau assured her that the alligators would be sleeping, if they were around here at all.

Savannah Trahan had reported that there were lights and activity at the farm, but couldn't get close enough to see what was going on so returned to Beau's house. It was nearly midnight now, and they hoped to be able to observe from the rear of the farm, near the boathouse. If they could get close, they'd take photos with the night camera Matt had procured.

Matt said they didn't have enough details from Winnie, but

he would fight to get a warrant to put a tracker on the truck she was using.

"You did everything you could," he whispered to Kara as Beau navigated.

"She feels stuck," Kara said. "No options. No way out. I should have found better words."

"Your theory is solid. The timeline matches up. They are in the middle of a turf war, The Catfish versus the Magnolia. Two groups competing for a limited client base."

"The timeline doesn't match up perfectly. Landry started buying land years before he moved here, starting with the Magnolia. So what happened three years ago? Did it all just change or step into high gear because his grandpa died and he ran for office?"

"Possibly. They expanded, or Landry realized he could undermine Tammy and expand his base. She wouldn't play."

Kara wasn't certain. They had a lot of pieces, but she couldn't put them together to see a clear picture.

A bump under the boat and a splash had Kara gripping Matt's thigh with one hand and reaching for her gun with the other. "What the fuck?"

"A fish," Beau said, his voice full of humor.

"Are you sure? It sounded big for a fish." Her heart was racing, pounding so hard she could feel it pulse behind her ears. "You swore to me the alligators were sleeping. You said they wouldn't be in the water."

Matt put his hand over hers, pried her fingers out of his muscle and squeezed.

"Kara, alligators are reptiles. They're lethargic at night. If they're around here, they're sleeping on the banks."

"What if they smell us?"

"They won't. And they wouldn't care if they did."

Kara mostly believed him, and besides, what choice did she have? She'd climbed into this damn boat and now was stuck halfway between the dock and the farm.

Matt didn't release her hand. Normally, she'd pull away—they were working. But it was dark, they were on the river and there *might* be alligators watching them from the banks. And, if she was honest with herself, she had missed their personal connection the past ten days.

A moment later, Matt said, "If there's a rivalry—a war—why is Gray Cormier consorting with the enemy?"

"A cold war?" she offered. She had to figure it out but now she had a headache.

Beau said, "Maybe I was wrong."

"About?"

"The Cormiers."

"They're deep in it," Kara said.

"Not about that—about their relationship. They're half brothers. Preston, the older brother, always in charge. Gray in his shadow. What if Gray is tired of taking orders from his brother and is working for Tammy and the Martins behind his back?"

Kara mulled that over. "To what end?"

"Power. To one-up his brother. I don't know." He paused. "Ernestine was Tammy's niece. I don't think she had anything to do with killing her. She loved her, in her own way. But Ernestine went back and forth between the two places. Like Gray. What if she said something to the wrong person? Or she saw something she shouldn't have. Not about talking to me, but about Gray. If he's playing both sides, he couldn't risk her telling anyone."

"So, did Elijah Morel kill her or is he being framed?" Kara asked.

"Million-dollar question," Beau muttered.

"Catherine said Ernestine's killer would feel remorse," Matt pointed out. "We have to consider the manner of her death, and while the killer seems capable of near anything, I don't think he would have changed his MO just to throw us off."

"Elijah was sweet on her," Beau said. "But everyone liked

Ernestine. Even Gray Cormier. He might have felt guilty. Anyone would. She was trusting, walked right out with someone to the river, no defensive wounds on her arms. She knew her killer very well."

They grew silent as they neared the farm.

They rounded a bend and the lights from the farm illuminated the entire area—including the river. Beau quickly cut the motor.

"What are they doing?" Kara asked.

"Shh."

Then she heard it, a motor, coming from the south.

"We're too close," Matt whispered.

They didn't dare move. They were still in the shadows, but their momentum was pushing them toward the light.

A boat with faint lights came around the curve ahead. It slowed, then pulled up to the dock next to the farm. Two men got out. They were barely visible from the distance, and Beau said he didn't recognize them.

"We have to turn around," Matt said through clenched teeth. He was tense, and he slowly reached for his gun. "If someone sees us, we're dead in the water. Literally. They have the high ground."

"They have to go inside or they'll hear the motor," Beau whispered.

"We don't have time."

Suddenly, Beau slid out of the boat and into the water. He pushed the boat hard against the easy current to buy them more time, then said, "I'll meet up with you at Lantern Gate." Then he waded to the shore.

"Fuck," Matt said through clenched teeth. "Kara, watch his stupid ass."

She had her gun out and was looking at the shoreline for threats. Beau climbed up the slope, agile as a monkey, then lay flat on the ground.

No one had spotted him.

Though Beau had bought them a little time, they started drifting again toward the circle of light.

Matt took the lone paddle from the bottom of the boat and as quietly as possible rowed them back the way they'd come. Kara kept her eyes on the shore; she saw Beau run low toward the warehouse. She'd done some stupid-ass things in her life, but nothing like this.

They went around the bend and Kara couldn't see Landry's property anymore.

"How far to Lantern Gate?" she asked.

"A half mile."

He took the paddle out of the water, started the motor, and turned the boat around.

Twenty minutes later, they saw Beau emerge along the river's edge. He climbed down into the water, then onto the boat.

"You stink," Kara said, trying to lighten the mood.

"You fucking idiot," Matt said. "You put us all at risk!"

"It's a major repackaging center."

"You searched without a warrant!"

As if Matt hadn't yelled at him, Beau said, "It doesn't look like they have any product right now, they're prepping—unloading boxes of prescription bottles. Probably for fentanyl or oxy. It's what the Cormiers are good at moving. This is bigger than I've ever seen it. Preston's there right now. If we can get a team—"

"Beau, you're on thin ice," Matt said. He started up the motor again and was moving fast in the water—angry, and Kara didn't blame him. "We need a warrant. We don't have one. We don't have probable cause. We don't have shit!"

"These people killed seven women. I'm not going to—"

"Stop. We're here because of you, but if you fuck this up by going off half-cocked, they will all walk, and we'll never get them. Not on drugs, not on murder. Seven women are dead, Beau! Do you understand?"

No one said anything for a long time. "What's your plan?" Beau finally said. He was angry, but at least he deferred to Matt.

Kara would have been willing to do recon, but she agreed with Matt on this one—they needed a warrant. She didn't want any of these bastards slipping away because they cut corners.

Even if they had less than two days to build a solid case.

"I'm working on it," Matt said. "But it starts with what Michael can get out of Ricky Dubois. Kara thinks he has information. If he does, Michael will move heaven and earth to get him to talk."

Kara couldn't sleep after her shower, so she grabbed a beer from Beau's fridge and stared at the faces of the dead. Faces that looked right back at her from the whiteboard.

Beau was up at the house with his grandmother, and Matt had left with Savannah as soon as they returned from the river. She didn't know if he was staying at the hotel or going back to Lafayette. She told herself she didn't care.

But she did.

She was exhausted, but hoped the orchestra of crickets and frogs lulled her to sleep like it had every other night she'd been here. She was surprised at how the sounds of nature calmed her.

A knock on the door had her jumping to her feet. Visitors after two in the morning were never good news. She grabbed her gun and opened the door.

Matt stood there. "I saw the light on."

She looked at the main house behind him. Only the porch light on.

Matt walked in. "We didn't talk after the river."

She closed the door behind him. "What happened to discretion?"

"Kara—we haven't had five minutes alone together."

"We're working."

She really didn't want this conversation now. She was tired,

Matt was frustrated with Beau, she just wanted to go to bed. Alone.

"I wanted to make sure that you're okay."

"You could have called."

"You kissed him."

"He kissed me."

"Dammit, I didn't mean for it to go that far."

"I went with the moment."

She walked over to the couch and sat down. She hadn't been sleeping even though it was nearly two in the morning; she didn't know if sleep would come, no matter how tired she was. She had too many things on her mind—worry about Toni, Winnie, Beau. Trying to put together pieces that were just starting to look like they fit. There were too many players, too many moving parts, too many things that could go wrong in the next two days before Winnie put herself in danger because she felt she had no other choice.

Matt sat down next to her. "I've missed you."

She didn't say anything.

"What did I do? Tell me, because I know something has shifted and I need to fix it."

She couldn't explain. It would sound stupid. She was just so weary right now and she didn't want to talk about *them* when she was worried about other people.

It was easier to worry about others than it was to think about her relationship with Matt.

"I'm tired, Matt."

He looked hurt.

"I'll go," he said quietly. "You're right, I shouldn't have come. I just wanted to see you." He took her hand, ran his fingers along her palm. She couldn't help but warm at his touch. It was always like that, even when she didn't want it. "It's been a rough couple of days and after tonight…well, sometimes, just looking at you gives me peace."

She wasn't expecting Matt to say anything like that.

"I'm not a peaceful person," she said.

He gave her a half smile. Sort of cocky, sort of sad. "No, you're not. But… I don't know. I just…" His voice trailed off, then, "I really want to kiss you."

"I'm not stopping you."

She should. She should tell Matt to leave, that they would deal with everything when this case was over, but the one thing she and Matt did well was *this*. Sex. He wanted to think it was more, but she couldn't—the closer she got to him, the more she had to lose. So it had to be sex, just sex. She had to show him it was just sex.

He leaned over and kissed her. Soft, romantic. It was too quiet, too sweet, too intimate. How could one kiss twist her emotions into such a knot of desire and questions, doubts and needs?

She couldn't do sweet, not now when she was still angry with him, when she was half in love, when she didn't *want* to love.

So she leaned into him hard, focused on their lust. Lust she understood. It was the common language for her and Matt, no matter how hard he tried to maintain control. She knew how to set him off. She knew every inch of his body; she knew how to make him let go. To give her what she needed, to take what he wanted.

"Kara," he breathed when she pulled her mouth away from his. His hands were under her shirt, on her breasts, squeezing, touching. "Bed."

He tried to get up. She didn't let him. She straddled him, pulled off her shirt and his mouth claimed her breasts. She arched her back and let herself enjoy the sensations that rushed through her. The heat, the need, the desire that filled her every time Matt's mouth was on her body. His day's growth of beard was rough on her soft skin, a complete turn-on. She held his head to her chest and he sucked until she felt the heat pool between her legs. Dear God she could lose it all right now if he just kept his mouth right there, if he reached down and touched her…

She didn't want to need him. She had told herself from the beginning that the need was about sex, orgasm, release. She was always happier after sex, as if the orgasm purged her of her demons just for a while—keeping them at bay so she could function.

The longer she was with Matt, the more she craved *him*…not just the intense pleasure they shared.

It has to be just sex.

She didn't want to give more. She didn't want to take more. It might break her into a million pieces.

But you want it. You want it all, the whole package.

They'd agreed to no pressure. No planning for a future. Just to live in the present. Maybe a bit more than friends with benefits, but not a *Relationship*, with a capital *R*, with all that entailed. Her life was too unsettled. She didn't even know where she would be in two months or six months or a year. She had never done relationships, because they complicated everything.

Yet with Matt…she didn't crave other men. She didn't want to be with anyone else. But…her privacy was everything to her. Her place, her home, her mind and body, protecting all that, her space, her heart.

And maybe that was the problem. She had no home, no foundation. She'd been forced to leave Los Angeles and her tiny, perfect beach condo behind. She was living in a weekly rental in DC when they weren't on a case. She lived out of two suitcases and felt…lost.

She didn't want to be lost.

"Kara, babe," Matt whispered. "What's wrong?"

"Nothing."

"You're shaking."

She pushed the conflicting thoughts aside, violently, because they would cloud her judgment. Instead, she put everything into

Matt, into the now, into this moment where she was going to take what she wanted.

"For you."

She needed hard and fast, no soft kisses, no murmurs of affection, because that wasn't them, it shouldn't be them. It couldn't be them.

They were unsustainable.

So she devoured him until he stopped talking, stopped asking questions. She felt him ready for her, as she was for him. As she always was for him, and only him.

She reached down to his pants, unzipped him. He gasped.

"Oh, Kara," Matt moaned. "Slow. Down."

She leaned over and breathed heavily into his ear. "No." She bit his lobe, just a little too hard, and his body jerked as he clutched her, squeezed her, rubbed her back, brought her close to him. They'd played enough games in bed that she knew every single forbidden touch, nip, bite Matt desired.

Kara squirmed out of her jeans and the brief movement away from him had Matt trying to put her on her back. He wanted to regain control. As if there was ever any control between them when they were naked.

She had her pants off fast and was straddling him again.

"Give me a minute. I'm so close, Kara, I want you to enjoy…"

"You think I'm not enjoying this?" She kissed him lightly on his jaw, then licked him. He wasn't expecting the tenderness and he gasped.

Then she slid onto him and he was very ready, very hard, so she sank all the way down and his head fell back and he groaned. She gave him five seconds where she sat on him, adjusting to him, feeling him…mostly because she, too, needed to catch her breath. She, too, was close to the edge. She stared at his handsome face, his tan skin glistening with sweat, with the heat of the humidity and their passion. She stared at his closed eyes, his exposed neck, his sweat-soaked T-shirt.

She couldn't think about Matt, the man, or herself, the woman, or anything about what they were together, what they could or couldn't be. Everything was a mess, her life, her confusion, frustration, love.

Not love.

Lust.

She rode him, to prove that it was just lust, not giving him an opportunity to slow things down, not letting him take control. Prove to herself that it was sex, it was orgasm, it was the much-needed release after a fucked-up day.

"God Kara, God Kara, God Kara..." His hands dug into her bare ass as he arched up and she pushed down and they came together fast, explosive, take no prisoners.

He wrapped his arms around her and pulled her to him, kissed her face, her neck, her chest, her face again. She let him. She relaxed into him for this one moment in time where she let herself feel his love.

Love.

She didn't know what she was doing. She was making a fucking mess of her life and she was going to be burned.

Her heart rate slowed. She wanted him to stay. She needed him to go. Because she knew when this *relationship* ended— and it would end, it had to—that she was going to hurt. It was going to hurt bad. She didn't want that pain. She'd spent her entire life avoiding emotional attachments so she would never feel that pain.

She slid off his lap and he reached for her. "It's late, Matt."

"Let's go to bed."

"Good night." She slipped away before he could pull her back into his arms. Because she didn't know if she could tell him to leave if he kissed her again.

Kara walked into the bathroom and felt as if she would cry. But she didn't. She washed her face and leaned against the counter until she felt she could face Matt if he were still there.

She came out ten minutes later and Matt was gone. She hadn't expected him to be there, even though a small part of her heart wanted him to stay.

She also didn't expect the note he left on the kitchen counter.

K ~
We are going to talk about this. I know you're angry with me and struggling with something. You can't keep it bottled up. I fucked up? Tell me. I love you and I'm not giving up.
~ M

Damn him.

Damn, damn, damn!

I love you.

She didn't want to hear it, and she certainly didn't want to see it in writing, which somehow made it more real. He'd underlined words for emphasis, but double underlined *I love you.*

She grabbed the paper, intending to throw it away, but when she heard the sound of the paper crinkling as she balled it in her fist, she stopped.

Her life just got a helluva lot more complicated.

WEDNESDAY

34

Ricky Dubois worked at a coffee shop from four thirty to eight thirty, four mornings a week. The rest of his time was spent in summer classes and his NROTC commitments.

Michael and Ryder arrived outside the coffee shop at five thirty. They made good time because there was no traffic, and Michael was driving.

Ryder said, "He has a 4.0 GPA, high marks in ROTC, and is on a full academic scholarship. He lives in ROTC housing for free. He has a car—a ten-year-old Ford Ranger—and while he has a small social media footprint, he rarely posts anything. The last post he was tagged in was with friends when they were doing drills and his team won a flag competition."

"Hard to do."

"I barely made it through basic training," Ryder said.

"You're in good shape."

"I was scrawny then. I've tried to keep the little muscle I gained."

Michael knew that Ryder had spent four years as an Army medic after going through his college's ROTC program and studying premed, and he currently served in the reserves. Michael had enlisted in the Navy right out of high school, and while Matt had thought he would be the better candidate to talk to Ricky, Michael had wanted Ryder with him because he was closer in age and experience to the young man.

Being a medic in the military wasn't an easy career path, especially when deployed. Ryder didn't talk much about his time in the Army, but then again, he didn't talk much about himself at all.

"I'll start," Michael said, "but feel free to ask questions or comment. You know the goal."

Ryder almost smiled. "I do?"

"Find out if he knows what's going on in St. Augustine."

"According to Kara, he knows and we're supposed to get him to talk."

"Kara only has a theory," Michael said. "We need to ask the right questions to prove or disprove. But if she's right, I don't think he's going to turn on his father. Family loyalty, even in a broken home, is hard to break."

"Maybe."

"Why do you say that?"

"He doesn't go home," Ryder said. "He doesn't have to work because he has a full scholarship between NROTC and academics. He receives a small stipend. He could easily go home for the summer—but he chooses to stay here and work. He has no credit cards, no debt, lives frugally and is currently getting paid to live on campus as an RA for a summer program while the ROTC dorms are closed. This suggests that he's putting all his money in the bank. His car isn't new, if he has a girlfriend he doesn't post anything about her on social media and she doesn't tag him, and he's taking summer classes that he doesn't have to take."

"Overachiever?"

"Diligent, hardworking, disciplined, distanced himself from his hometown. He might not want to talk about his father, as I told Kara when she called me last night, but he will likely talk about what happened to his friend Ethan."

Because Ryder wasn't generally chatty, Michael sometimes forgot how damn smart the kid was. Over and above book smart—which he was—but people smart.

They went into the coffee shop. There was a short line of customers; Ricky was working with a girl ringing up orders, while two other staffers were preparing the drinks. Ricky was average height with a close-cropped military haircut and perfect posture. He wore the coffee shop's blue apron over a black T-shirt and jeans. He smiled at the customers and seemed friendly, calling them by name if he knew them.

Michael and Ryder got in Ricky's line and when they reached the cash register, Michael ordered coffee and a pastry and Ryder picked up an apple from the bowl on the counter. Michael paid, then showed his federal identification and badge. "Ricky, we need to talk. Can you take a short break?"

Ricky looked at the badge. "Yes, sir. Give me a minute."

Well trained. Military recruits naturally deferred to authority.

Michael and Ryder took their purchases to the most private table, in the far corner.

Ricky didn't appear to be suspicious or worried. He finished his line of customers, talked to his coworker, then took off his apron and walked over to where Michael and Ryder sat. He didn't sit until Michael motioned for him to do so.

"What can I help you with, sir?" Ricky asked.

"You're in Navy ROTC?"

331

"Yes, sir. Is this about the program?"

"No, but I was in the Navy for ten years, enlisted out of high school. My partner Ryder was Army ROTC. You chose it?"

"Yes, sir. Tulane is a good school, I wanted to come here, but it's expensive. I made sure I had the grades and I applied into the program. I am honored they chose me for a scholarship. I plan to stay in the Navy for a career."

"What do you want to do?"

"I'm in the engineering program, with an emphasis on mechanical engineering. I want to work on engines, or wherever the Navy feels I'll serve them best, sir."

Definitely a smart kid.

"We're investigating a homicide in St. Augustine."

He didn't show a reaction, except for a slight frown. "I haven't been home in two years. I don't know how I can help you."

"I need to be blunt with you, and I hope you'll feel like you can speak freely with us," Michael said.

"I will do what I can, but like I said, I don't go home."

"Why is that?" Michael asked.

"It's complicated." Which was shorthand for he didn't want to talk about it.

"Are you aware that seven young women have been murdered over the last three years?"

"Seven?" He frowned. "I knew there were several. One of my friends, her sister was killed."

"The latest victim is a young woman named Ernestine Bergeron," Ryder said, speaking up for the first time. "She worked with your friend Winnie LeBlanc."

"Ernestine?" He sounded surprised. "She's dead? That's why you're here?" His voice rose, then he cleared his throat and regained calm. "I knew her. But I wouldn't know why she was killed or—you don't think Winnie had anything to do with it! Winnie would never, not in a million years. Do you need a character reference? I'll stand up for her."

"That's helpful," Michael said. "Like I said, we need to be blunt. Time is not our friend. Yesterday, we found the body of a woman in a barrel dumped in the river near Lantern Gate. We have reason to believe she's Lily Baker, who has been missing for four months."

"Why aren't you talking to my father?" Ricky asked quietly. "He *is* the chief of police."

Michael hadn't expected Ricky's hint of sarcasm.

"We have been working with him, or trying to. The police in St. Augustine aren't being cooperative. There have also been witness statements that a law enforcement officer was the last person seen with two of the victims. This makes us extremely wary of sharing too much information with the local police department, until we can rule out corruption or worse."

Ricky didn't say anything. He stared at his hands, which were clasped firmly in front of him.

Ryder said, "We're not asking you to turn against your father. We have no evidence that he is involved in any of the homicides. Our evidence, though limited, is that he has turned a blind eye to the actions of one of his deputies and may, in fact, be covering for him. What we really need from you is to understand how the town works."

"Hell if I know," he said quietly.

"Your best friend died of a drug overdose," Ryder said. "We believe these murders are connected to the drug trade going in and out of St. Augustine. And that, in fact, Ethan Davis's death may be connected to our current investigation."

Ricky sucked in his breath and closed his eyes. Michael let him compose himself. When he did, he sat rigid. "What exactly do you want to know?"

"Was Ethan's overdose an accident? Or could there have been a chance that he was murdered?"

"Ethan was my best friend." Ricky paused, then continued, looking Michael in the eye. Yes, a strong kid. "He started using drugs. I told him to knock it off. I've never used. Never will. Winnie and I tried to…what is it? Like an intervention? And we thought it worked, but he just got sneakier. So I got sneaky. I tried to find out who he was buying from, how he was getting the money—I mean, he made money working at the grocery store, but not enough to pay for all of it. I learned he was working for them."

"For who?" Michael asked.

"Preston Cormier. To the best of my knowledge, he runs most or all of the drugs through St. Augustine. I followed them, had pictures, had evidence. I just wanted Ethan to wake up, to see what this was doing to him, what it was doing to Winnie. Her sister was already a lost cause." He took a deep breath. "I shouldn't say that. No one is a lost cause, not until they're dead. But Nicki had a kid and she still couldn't stop using, so I just wanted to show Ethan that he had a future only if he could fight this addiction. I know it's not easy, I know there's a lot that goes into addiction. I took a psychology class last year just so I could understand, and I still don't, not completely."

"There are as many factors as there are people," Michael said.

"Yeah, well, maybe. But anyway, I followed Ethan and found out he was working with Cormier to bring drugs up from the Gulf. I had photos, pictures of them with the drugs. I knew Ethan, being under eighteen, would get a slap on the wrist— I'd hoped he would then wake up, go to rehab. But Cormier? This would nail him. Or so I thought."

Michael suspected the answer, but asked anyway. "Who did you talk to?"

"My dad." He said it as if he wanted to be angry, but instead a small sob escaped. He composed himself, then said, "He destroyed everything. He yelled at me—he had never raised his voice to me my entire life, not even when I broke a window playing baseball too close to the house. Not even when I skipped school to compete in a fishing tournament down in Lake Pierre, driving his old truck even though I didn't have my license. But he was angry. And scared. That's what did it for me—he was scared and I had never seen my dad scared. A week later, Ethan died of an overdose. I have no reason to believe it wasn't because of his own addiction that he died, but it was an eye-opener. I couldn't look at my dad. I blamed him for not stopping it. I'd given him proof! Then he said something to me, the day I graduated from high school. He said, 'You're a better man than me, Ricky. Leave St. Augustine and never come back.'"

Ricky looked down for a moment, then met Michael's eyes again. "The only person I've talked to since I left home is Winnie. She's been saving money to leave, but she won't leave without her niece, and she's only nineteen. I wouldn't know what to do with a little kid, either. I told Winnie I'd marry her as soon as I graduated, and she and Bonnie will be taken care of. Military housing, benefits, everything."

"Do you love Winnie?"

"Not like that, but I couldn't save Ethan. I can save Winnie."

"What did she say?"

"What do you think? She has pride, more than me, I suppose. And a spine of steel. She said her cousin Jean Paul was helping her, and that she'd come to NOLA when she had enough money, asked if I could help her find a job. Of course, I said yes. I know enough people, I could get her a cheap place to live, help her get Bonnie into school, whatever she needed. I tried to send her money but she sent it back. If she was here, I could do things for her she wouldn't know I was doing."

Ricky Dubois was a good man, Michael thought. He would make a fine officer in the Navy.

"Jean Paul killed a man named Jake West, then he died in custody. The police department said he committed suicide. My team has evidence that he was murdered."

"Jean Paul? Murdered? Oh, God."

"One of our agents is trying to convince Winnie to cooperate with us. She's scared, and she's on the fence. We can get her into WITSEC if that's what we need to do, or at a minimum put her and Bonnie into protective custody, but she has to help us. We don't have the smoking gun, so to speak. We know a lot of the players, but we don't know how all the pieces fit together."

"Can you protect her? Really? You're not just saying that."

"She has to want it," Michael reiterated.

Ryder said, "One of our colleagues has developed a theory that there is a cold war in St. Augustine. That two factions are working against each other, and that the dead are collateral damage in this cold war. One faction is run by the new mayor, Peter Landry, who appointed your father as chief of police. He co-opted the Cormiers' operation and they now work for him. The other faction is run either by Tammy Bergeron, Ernestine's aunt, or a woman named Debra Martin, whose father owns The Fat Catfish. Or both, together."

Ryder left out the information that Gray Cormier may be playing both sides, or undermining his brother. That was probably wise. Michael didn't think that Ricky was lying to them, but the situation was still delicate.

"I can't speak to that," Ricky said. "I can tell you that Ethan worked for Preston Cormier bringing drugs up from the Gulf. Ethan sold drugs at the school for Cormier until I found out. Maybe he just got better at keeping it from me. That's what I knew, that's what I could prove."

"Mrs. Davis thought you and Ethan were best friends up until he died."

"We were—but that didn't mean it was easy. I was trying to save him the whole time. Maybe that was foolish, but…anyway, we were on the verge of graduating and I had saved up enough money to send him to a thirty-day rehab center I found in Lafayette. And then we could go to college together and everything would be the way we planned it when we were kids."

"And what happened?"

"He didn't want to go. Said he could quit anytime. And Winnie said he had to want it or it wouldn't stick. She was right. And then he was dead and my dad wasn't the hero I thought he was."

"Do you know how Peter Landry fits in?"

Ricky shook his head. "I barely knew him. He was only mayor a year or so before I left."

Ryder said, "Are you still in contact with Winnie?"

"Yes."

"We know she's working for the Cormiers."

"She wouldn't."

"She may not have had a choice. If she turns state's evidence, we can protect her. She doesn't believe us."

"Of course not. She doesn't know you, she only knows that people die if they step out of line."

Michael said, "Do you know anything about the murders of Lettie Chaisson or Nicki LeBlanc? Those were the two women who were killed before you left St. Augustine."

"If I knew anything about their murders, I would have said something. I may have turned my back on the drug situation after my father destroyed the evidence I collected, but murder? I would tell you."

"You knew Nicki?"

"Yes. She's seven years older than Winnie, but they're nothing alike." He paused. "Their father was a pervert. He did things to Nicki—and I think that twisted her all up. Winnie was too young to remember him when he left, so that's good."

"Do you know who her closest friend was? Who she might have confided in?"

"No one. Nicki wasn't a nice person. Mean and angry and just...you know she was a prostitute, right?"

"All the victims were, except for Ernestine."

"Yeah. Well, she lived a certain lifestyle that pretty much meant she trusted no one. If anyone was close to her, it was Winnie. But if Winnie knew who killed Nicki, I think she would have done something about it. So you know what? I'm glad she didn't know, because I don't want her to end up dead, too." Ricky looked from Michael to Ryder, then said, "I'll call her. I don't know if it'll help, but I will talk to her."

"Thank you," Ryder said. He slid over his card. "Anything we can do for you, let us know."

Michael drove over to the FBI office so Ryder could pick up a copy of the archived file from the investigation into Landry and his partners. While they were driving, he called Matt and filled him in on the conversation with Ricky Dubois. Matt was quiet, which meant he was either thinking or angry.

"Do you think he has any information that would assist us in getting a warrant?"

"No. Nothing but his word, which I believe. He's an upstanding kid, forthcoming, and I don't think he lied about anything. If anyone has information to get a warrant, it'll come from Winnie LeBlanc, unless you can find a way to flip Chief Dubois. I suspect the chief pushed Ricky out of town to protect him."

Matt said, "You're sure Ricky will call her?"

"He said he would. I believe he will."

"Okay, I'll let Kara know so she's prepared. I'll talk to the chief. Good work."

"Ryder gets at least half the credit."

Michael ended the call as he pulled in front of FBI headquarters. He parked in a loading zone, but waited outside the car while Ryder went in to pick up the files that were waiting for him. It was humid, even at seven thirty in the morning, but there was a breeze, which felt good. The drive back was going to take longer than the drive here because of traffic, and he needed to stretch his long legs. But Ryder took much longer than Michael expected. Finally, he emerged from the building and walked down the sidewalk to where Michael waited.

"I had to flash my badge to two cops who were dying to

give me a ticket for parking here," Michael said, partly in jest. Then he noted a disturbed expression on Ryder's face. "What happened?"

Ryder got into the car, so Michael followed suit. "I have the name of the fourth partner," he said.

"Isn't that why we came here in the first place?"

"His name is Robert Abbott. He's the district chief of staff for Congressman Jordan Emerson."

"Oh, shit."

"It gets worse," Ryder said. "The ASAC told me he gave this information to Agent Trahan yesterday afternoon, on the phone, when the file came in. She told Matt the office didn't have the name of the fourth partner. While I was standing there, he looked at the computer and the reason we didn't have it at the beginning is because his name was deleted in the system. It's only in the physical file."

"Deleted on purpose?"

"It was deleted with an admin code, so he can't tell me who authorized it, but he told me when—five years ago."

"Let me guess—Trahan was in the NOLA office five years ago."

"Yes, and it was right after Emerson was elected to office, when Abbott had just started working for him."

"Why?" Michael wondered out loud. He didn't expect Ryder to answer.

"Abbott is her ex-husband."

Jim was looking forward to meeting Dr. Justin Lind with Louisiana State University. He'd heard of the forensic anthropologist—had even read some of his research on working with bones recovered from floods—but he'd never had the opportunity to meet him.

Lind was coming from Baton Rouge and estimated he'd arrive by eight in the morning. Jim was antsy to get started, so he walked from the hotel two blocks away to where the RV was parked in the lot next to FBI headquarters. They had been able to pull an industrial power cord out to the RV so Jim didn't need the generator.

He unlocked the RV, then turned off the alarm and turned on the lights. Medical grade lighting had been installed, making the room bright, but not too hard on the eyes. He turned on his equipment, and flipped the table to give them the basin they'd need to work with the liquefied remains. He attached hoses to the underside and secured the collection bins so that the remains and potential evidence could be safely stored. He checked the HEPA system: operating at 100 percent.

A knock on the door had Jim thinking Dr. Lind made good time; he was fifteen minutes early. He opened the door, heard footsteps, but didn't see anyone.

"I'm here," Jim said as he stepped out. "Do you need help with…"

Blinding pain in the back of his head had him on the ground; his wrist snapped, then the second blow left him unconscious.

35

Matt and Kara arrived at the hospital at 8:45 that morning; they had practically flown down I-10 from St. Augustine as soon as SSA Curt Danville called Matt about Jim.

Danville met them in the emergency room. "Dr. Esteban is still unconscious, but he's breathing on his own," he said. "I'm waiting for the doctor to give me an update."

"I need a guard on Jim 24/7," Matt said.

"I'll make it happen."

"What more have you learned?"

Curt had already told Matt that Dr. Lind found the RV un-locked and Jim unconscious when he arrived at five minutes to eight. He immediately called an ambulance, then Curt, and Curt called Matt.

"Dr. Lind stayed with the RV because the evidence was compromised—the barrel with the victim's remains was opened and some sort of chemical was causing a reaction. He's going to try to preserve as much as possible. We don't believe the attacker completed whatever he set out to do, but we don't know what he was after—other than destroying any evidence of Lily Baker's homicide. Perhaps you have someone who can analyze the security system and know what happened?"

"We have cameras in and around the RV," Matt said. "Ryder is almost back from NOLA. He knows the system, so he'll work with Dr. Lind. I need your team to pull all security feeds in the area, from this lot and nearby businesses."

"Already in process."

Matt said, "Did you ask Agent Trahan to come into the office?"

"Yes, but I wish I knew why. You were vague."

"I have questions for her, and depending on her answers, I may ask for her to be suspended pending a full investigation."

Curt bristled. "Savannah is a good agent who has done exemplary work for me. She's been at your beck and call for three days."

Matt told him what Ryder uncovered. Kara stood there, unreadable. She hadn't said much on the drive out here, either. Matt had spent most of the drive talking to Ryder, Tony in DC, Curt Danville and the hospital.

"I want to say there must be a logical explanation," Curt began.

"There isn't. I will listen to what she says to determine how deep her deception goes."

The doctor came out and Matt introduced himself as Jim's boss. "Status?"

"He's still unconscious. His X-ray shows a hairline fracture on his skull, minimal swelling on his brain—this is a good thing. We're going to do an MRI shortly. He's breathing on his own, but we're giving him an oxygen supplement."

"He's been unconscious for over an hour," Kara said. "That can't be good."

"It's not necessarily bad. We're closely monitoring him, and the MRI will give us more information."

"Can I sit with him?" she asked.

"Of course. Sometimes talking to a patient can help. He's not in a coma, his body is responsive to external stimuli and, as I said, all his bodily functions are working as they should. That is all good. Of course, as with any serious head injury, sometimes we have to wait and see."

She looked at Matt. "You don't need me in the interrogation, do you? I mean, I'll be there if you want me, but I won't be nice. So you probably don't want me."

"Stay with Jim. I'll come back as soon as I'm done."

Kara held Jim's hand while he lay in the hospital bed unconscious.

"Okay, Jim, you need to wake up. I can't sit here forever, I have a stack of murders to solve. But no way in hell am I going to let you die."

Of course he didn't wake up. He had a traumatic head injury—a hairline fracture on his skull. That was bad, no matter what the doctor said. She wanted to kill the person who did this to him.

She hated hospitals. She didn't know why, maybe it was the smell, maybe it was the death, maybe it was the fear and pain and sorrow that seemed to permeate the walls. It was probably all in her head.

Maybe her fear stemmed from all the emergency rooms she had paced over the last twelve years waiting for word about a fellow cop who'd been shot in the line of duty.

But for now, she wasn't leaving Jim's side. He *had* to pull through.

Jim Esteban was everything she had wanted her father to be. Smart, funny, dedicated, caring, noble, kind, devoted to his family. When he wasn't talking about the job—which he loved talking about—he talked about his daughter and her kids and his son-in-law. Jim was a bit overweight and he had the Columbo vibe going—a bit on the sloppy side, a bit absentminded when it came to anything outside of his job—but she was comfortable around him like she was with few other people.

She had never considered that he might be in danger. He had started as a cop—in his old jurisdiction, crime scene investigators were sworn officers—then moved into forensics, then went for advanced schooling and his doctorate, then ran the Dallas crime lab. He was supersmart but never acted smarter than the rest of the team. He once told her that she had street smarts in spades and not everyone needed college to be educated. She loved him for that, especially since she often felt out of her element when Catherine and Matt started talking—Catherine intentionally talking over her head at times.

They'd become friends. She didn't quite know how it happened—they'd worked a few cases together, known each other for only six months—but he was living part-time in DC with his sister and when he was in town he always asked Kara over for beers. Jim's sister, a veterinarian, had his same easygoing personality. Jim took Kara to a baseball game just three weeks ago, shortly after they returned from the San Juan Islands. His sister got the tickets but had to work and Jim invited Kara. She had never been to a baseball game before, but she'd had fun and Jim seemed to enjoy explaining the game to her, talking about the history and old-time players.

"Jim, we need to go to another baseball game. I still don't get it, it's kind of boring and the beer costs a fucking lot of money, but the hot dogs were probably the best I ever had, and the company was pretty good." She let out a half-hearted laugh.

In fact, Jim had been the only team member who reached out to her outside of work, just to socialize.

She didn't count Matt. She probably should—they saw each other quite a bit outside of work, nearly every weekend they weren't working in the field. But they couldn't go out and do fun things because they were keeping their relationship on the QT.

"K."

She looked up from where she'd been staring at her hand holding Jim's. Relief washed through her, and she blinked back tears. Where had those come from?

"Jim." She wanted to make a joke, say something light, but her heart was still too heavy.

"No sad looks. I'm okay."

"I need to get the doctor. You were unconscious for a long time." She got up to leave, but he held on to her hand, so she sat back down.

"How long?"

"Two hours. You have a concussion and broke your wrist when you fell."

"I was stupid."

"You couldn't have known."

"Someone knocked on the door. I thought it was Dr. Lind. I didn't ask, just opened the door. Didn't see him, stepped out and wham."

"Did you recognize who hit you?"

"No. It's a blur. I used to be a good cop, I don't know why I didn't have my gun with me, why I let someone lure me out. I'm so stupid."

"No. You're not. Dammit, they could have killed you."

"They didn't. They wanted to destroy the evidence." He moaned.

"Are you okay? Let me get—"

"I'm going to be fine. I'm upset, angry—the evidence is gone, right?"

"They opened the barrel. Curt says it was contaminated, but your doctor friend is seeing if he can salvage anything."

"Damn. Damn!"

"You are more important," she said forcefully. "Fuck it, Jim, you're making me emotional and weepy, and I'm not going to let you do that. Don't scare me ever again."

Jim's smile relieved her, but she was still all twisted up from what happened. "I already uploaded the photos and lab tests to Quantico. There will be something we can use. How bad is the damage to the RV?"

"I don't know. It wasn't destroyed or anything, and Michael and Ryder should be back from New Orleans by now. I'm going to get the doctor and call Matt, okay? And Matt hired private security to sit on your door. They'll be here soon."

"There's no need—"

"Yes, there is. Someone tried to kill you. Maybe they didn't *want* to kill you, but they could have, and I for one am glad that Matt's taking precautions."

She got up and, again, he reached out and squeezed her hand. "K—"

She turned and looked at him.

"Be careful. I don't want anything to happen to you."

"Careful is my middle name."

He chuckled, then closed his eyes.

36

Matt had Curt put Savannah in an interview room. He wanted her to feel the full weight of her actions. He wanted her to know that this wasn't something she could talk her way out of.

Mostly, he wanted her to know that he needed answers right now.

As Savannah's supervisor, Curt joined Matt, but on Matt's side of the table. By the look on Savannah's face when they walked in together, she knew exactly why they wanted to talk to her.

Matt sat down. "This interview is being recorded and will be sent to the Office of Professional Responsibility for further investigation and disciplinary action. Agent Trahan, yesterday afternoon you spoke to the ASAC of the New Orleans FBI office. He identified Robert Abbott as the fourth partner who'd worked with Peter Landry, currently a person of interest, when they were under investigation for insurance fraud, correct?"

"Yes." Her voice was a squeak.

"You told me at that time that the ASAC did not have the name of the fourth man, is that also correct?"

"Yes."

"Is Robert Abbott your ex-husband?"

She nodded.

"Answer verbally, please."

"Yes, he is my ex-husband."

"How long were you married and when did you divorce?"

"We were married for eight years, divorced seven years ago."

"Was your divorce because you knew that your husband was involved in a criminal investigation?"

"No. I didn't know anything."

"You didn't know about his business dealings?"

"We were living apart that year. I was working from the Louisville FBI office, and Robert was in New Orleans. I didn't know he was the subject of an investigation at the time."

"Did you redact his name five years ago when you were in the NOLA office?"

She hesitated.

Matt said, "I will remind you that as a sworn law enforcement agent and employee of the Federal Bureau of Investigation that you need to be truthful at all times. Did you redact his name in the computer file?"

"Yes."

"Why?"

"He was hired to work as the district chief of staff of a newly elected congressman and didn't want it coming out that he had been investigated by the FBI—even though there was no evidence of wrongdoing and he was cleared," she added quickly.

"Did you ask him anything about that case?"

"He told me his partner Derek O'Neill had confessed and that Robert had nothing to do with the crime. But, it would look bad and he didn't want the congressman's political enemies or the media to exploit it. Robert had just remarried, his wife was pregnant with twins, and I—I had a moment of weakness. I should have told you yesterday when I found out."

She hesitated, and Matt saw that she now realized where her lies had taken her.

"Yesterday."

"I mean—"

Matt didn't sugarcoat it. "You knew from the very beginning that your ex-husband had been working with Landry and Steele, and that those men were under my scrutiny. You not only lied to me yesterday, you've been lying to me from the very beginning."

She didn't say anything, but to her credit she didn't look away.

Curt said, his voice softer than Matt's, "You understand, Savannah, that this act puts all your cases in jeopardy."

Now tears formed in her eyes but she blinked them back. "I'm a good agent. I've done great work."

"I always thought you had. But now I have to thoroughly review every single case. Even the fraud case in Lake Charles."

"It's airtight!"

"Maybe it is. But if the media or the defense gets wind of the fact that an FBI agent falsified a report—even five years ago—they're going to be all over us. So we're going to have get ahead of it, review every detail. Hundreds of hours of manpower."

"I'm sorry," her voice cracked.

Matt said, "Have you called, emailed, texted, spoken to your ex-husband in any way since you were assigned to assist my team on Monday?"

She hesitated just a fraction of a second too long.

"What did you do, Agent Trahan? I remind you that I am

349

in the process of getting a warrant for all your personal phone and email records."

"I didn't tell him anything about the case. Nothing about your team, I swear. All I did was tell him that the FBI was looking into his old partners and that I hoped he'd broken ties with them as I advised five years ago when he asked me to—to redact his name."

Matt slammed his hand on the table and Savannah jumped. "And you didn't *think* that he could have *called Landry*? Put our entire investigation in jeopardy? Put *my team* in danger?"

"Robert is not—"

"You don't know! What we *know* is that O'Neill confessed and was killed in prison. Jasper Steele owns a brothel and runs prostitutes. Peter Landry is suspected of running drugs, and may be conspiring with a murderer. And you think your ex-husband is clean? That he's the only one of those four men who were in business together for years who never did a dirty deed?"

She looked down at the table.

"When did you tell him? What day, what time?"

With shaking hands, Savannah pulled her personal phone out of her pocket and slid it over to Matt.

He looked through her messages.

On Tuesday, just after noon, Savannah had texted her ex.

SAVANNAH: We need to talk. Call me.

ROBERT: I'm in a meeting.

S: It's important.

R: About?

S: I hope you really cut ties with your old partners because the

FBI is looking at them again. I don't want you getting caught in the cross fire.

R: I'll call you in ten.

Matt looked at her calls—the incoming call from Abbott lasted three minutes shortly after the texts. There were no other recent texts or calls to that number, though that didn't mean she didn't have another phone or called from home or Abbott used another number.

Prior to this text exchange, Savannah and Robert texted only periodically, and mostly about mutual friends and family: Robert asking if he could help after Savannah's parents' house flooded; Savannah wishing Robert happy birthday; Robert sending a family portrait of him, his wife, his twin girls.

His wife looked familiar. He sent the image to himself so he could think on it. Maybe he knew her? No. He didn't think he knew her. Maybe she was famous? A model? She was pretty enough for it, with classic girl-next-door good looks.

"Who's his wife?"

"Elizabeth. Elizabeth, um, Anderson, I think. Now Abbott."

"What does she do?"

"She was a wedding planner before they got married."

"And you get along with your ex, his new wife?"

She shrugged. "More or less. I didn't want kids, Robert did, end of story. It was an amicable split. I don't think he did anything illegal. It's not him. I mean—maybe he knew what his partners were doing, but he ended it with them. He cut all ties. That says something."

"That's not up to you to investigate," Matt said.

"I'll give you everything I have. I'm not holding back."

"The problem? You had a three-minute-long conversation with your ex-husband and I don't know what you said."

Curt said, "Savannah, I need your badge, your gun, your credentials. I'm asking you to make yourself available if we have additional questions, do not leave our jurisdiction until you hear from me, and you'll want to be prepared for the OPR investigation."

Matt walked out of the room. She would be fired. But if her actions resulted in anyone dying—if her actions put anyone on his team in danger, or the girl Winnie—he would make sure she was prosecuted.

Michael had watched and listened to the entire interview through the two-way glass. "I'm sorry, Matt," he said.

"It's my fault." He wanted to hit something. He should have dug further back, deeper, harder, *something!*

Michael said, "How about it's no one's fault except the woman sitting in that room." He gestured to Trahan, who wiped tears from the corners of her eyes while Curt spoke to her.

Matt looked at his phone. "Kara says Jim is conscious. She wants to go back to St. Augustine and talk to Winnie, and I need to talk to Chief Dubois alone. Can you make sure Ryder has everything he needs in the RV? I need you in St. Augustine as soon as possible, but I don't want you to leave Ryder until you are confident that he is protected."

Michael nodded. "I'll let you know when I'm on my way."

Curt came out of the room. "Agent Costa, I didn't know."

"There's enough blame to go around, but not on you. You can take care of this, right? I'm going back to St. Augustine."

"Yes. And anything you need—backup, research, anything—call me directly."

Matt told Kara what he learned from Agent Trahan as they drove together from Lafayette to St. Augustine. She didn't say anything.

"Kara, I'm sorry, I shouldn't have put so much trust in her when I didn't know her."

"Landry knew."

"About?"

"If Robert Abbott was his business partner in a scam, he had to have known that Abbott was married to a federal agent."

She was right. Matt hadn't thought of that.

"So when you and Savannah were at dinner yesterday at The Broiler, I'll bet he called Abbott, asked him what was going on. What would he say?"

"He would know we were looking at him. But Abbott could have called Landry earlier, so Landry may have known before The Broiler."

"I have to get Winnie out of this. If they're running scared or tightening the ship they're going to cut loose anyone they don't a hundred percent trust. And by 'cut loose' I mean kill. And I swear, Matt, if Savannah told them about me working on Winnie? If that puts her in danger? I will kill her."

While Matt was just as angry, he hoped Kara didn't threaten her to anyone else. It never went well when someone with a badge and gun verbally threatened murder, even if they didn't follow through.

A minute later, Matt said, "I'm going to work Chief Dubois."

"You think you can flip him?"

"I'll exploit his love for his son."

She didn't say anything. He didn't know what she was thinking about. He glanced at her. She was staring out the window, an angry frown on her lips, concern etched in her forehead.

"Jim's going to be okay," he told her.

"I know. The doctor said he'll call you later today, but doesn't expect Jim to be released before tomorrow, maybe Friday."

She was still sullen.

"You're mad about Trahan."

"Mad? Yeah, but who the fuck cares? I've run into fucking corrupt FBI agents before." She glanced over at him, but he couldn't read her expression. "*I'm fine.* Stop trying to dissect me."

"I'm not."

She ignored him.

"Is this about last night?"

"What about last night? Sex?"

"Are you upset about the note?" He had thought long and hard before leaving the note, but felt like he had to—because he didn't understand what was going through her head. They had been so good, and then a brick wall.

"Just stop."

"What's going on, Kara?" He could feel her tension in the seat next to him.

"Other than seven murdered women, one of my favorite people hospitalized with a concussion and broken wrist, a couple corrupt cops, a drug dealer who seems to own the town, and an eighty-four-year-old woman who was threatened in the fucking grocery store? What else should I be angry about?"

Matt knew it got to her—it got to all of them—but for Kara, these young women were personal. He thought he understood her—but the more he got to know her, the more he wondered if he really did.

"Talk to me."

"I am."

"We're alone in this car, you can say anything. You have been short-tempered and irritable and it's not just about this case. Like on Friday when I suggested I cook for you and you said you made plans."

"What, I'm not allowed to have friends outside of you?"

"That's not what I meant—"

"Then what?"

"Since you moved to DC we've been together every weekend we weren't working. You were in training all last week and I didn't get to see you. I thought—"

"Thought what?" she snapped.

Matt was at a loss, but he was now getting angry. "Spill it."

"No personal conversations when we're on a case, Matt. We don't have time for it."

"I knew you were mad," he said, almost to himself, trying to figure out *why*. Thinking back to their last time together, before this case.

"Give the federal agent a badge."

"I just—shit." He went cold. How could he have missed it for so long? Damn. Damn.

She was upset about Catherine and her family stopping by unannounced. About him asking her to stay in the bedroom until he could get rid of them.

She laughed, but with no humor. "You just figured it out. Wow."

"Kara—"

"No, not having this conversation. We'll deal with all our baggage and bullshit when we find out who killed these women, okay?"

"We have time now, we talk now. If my parents taught me anything, it's never to go to bed angry."

"Lucky we're not married."

Was she just finding an excuse to walk away? When they had three days alone together in the San Juan Islands after solving their last major case six weeks ago, Matt was on top of the world. They'd come to an understanding. He'd told her mostly how he felt. She wasn't ready to hear that he loved her then, he knew that if he said it she'd bolt. The note…it just seemed she'd have more time to absorb it in writing. Hell, he didn't know. He'd never felt like this before, and he was thirty-eight.

Yet, he'd had to explain to her that he wasn't going to walk away just because of a few hurdles. That started with telling his boss. Not just because of federal rules regarding in-house relationships, but because Catherine suspected, and Tony needed to hear it from Matt. Tony wasn't happy, but there wasn't much he could do about a consensual relationship that Matt reported.

Tony liked Kara—she'd done an exemplary job for the task force. He simply told Matt *don't fuck up*.

Then last night—the sex—which, though amazing, lacked that connection with her that he was used to. She showed him she loved him, even if she couldn't say it. He wrote *I love you* because he wanted her to know that no matter what, everything was going to be okay *because* he loved her. That no matter what they faced, it was going to be okay because they had each other to lean on.

Matt knew that Kara didn't like being close to anyone, that the more she felt for him, the greater risk he had of her walking away. It was a balancing act with her, one he was more than willing to walk, but she had to talk. That was the only way he could know what she was thinking.

He had sensed that Kara was upset when Catherine and her family came over unplanned, but when he talked to her, she said it was fine.

And that was his biggest problem. It wasn't fine, and he had taken her at her word.

Of course it wasn't fine! She had to stay in your bedroom for an hour before you got rid of Catherine. He would have been pissed if he had to stay holed up someplace to avoid being seen with Kara.

"I'm sorry," he said.

"No. No, no, *no*. I'm not accepting an apology. You think there's nothing wrong."

"I told you I talked to Tony. We're discreet, but we don't have to hide our relationship." And Catherine already knew he'd been sleeping with Kara, so it wouldn't be a surprise. Matt could deal with Catherine's disapproval and judgment. Maybe that bothered Kara more than she'd let on.

"Yes we do! Do you think I want to be the topic of conversation? Do you think I want anyone on this team to think that you listen to me more than them? I knew I knew *I knew*!" She pounded her fist on the dashboard.

He hadn't seen her this agitated. Angry, yes, but she was definitely more upset than angry right now.

"I knew I should have walked away in Washington," she said.

"Don't say that."

"I was right. I knew it, but I didn't listen to myself."

"Because we're good together."

"I'm not doing this now."

"When? Dammit, Kara—"

"I need to get my head on straight, and if you're in my head, I can't. Just leave it. Leave it, Matt."

She was right, and she was wrong, but they only had five minutes before the freeway exit and they couldn't solve this in five minutes.

"For now."

But I'm not letting you walk away.

37

Matt dropped Kara off at the Hebert house where she'd left the rent-a-wreck, then he drove to the police station. He pushed all the problems with Kara aside and focused on the task at hand: convincing Chief Dubois to turn state's evidence.

If anyone knew that Dubois was talking to him, the cop would be in danger. Maybe his kid, too. Matt had already told Michael to call Ricky and tell him to be careful for the next few days. Matt hoped that no one went after Ricky—but he didn't know what Savannah had said to her ex-husband, or if she'd talked to anyone else.

Matt called Detective Andre Armand, who had given Jim the syringe that had killed Jean Paul LeBlanc. He hoped he had read the man right.

"Andre, this is Matt Costa. If you can't talk, yes and no answers are sufficient."

"Okay."

"I need to talk to Dubois alone. No one can know. In a place
no one will see us."

"All right. Thanks."

Andre hung up.

Dammit. Matt hated waiting.

He drove to the North Lake Hotel so no one saw him sitting
outside the police station. As soon as he pulled into the parking lot, he got a text.

He goes home for lunch every day between one and two.

Then Andre sent an address, which saved Matt the time of
looking it up.

It was quarter to one. Matt just might get himself shot, but
this was his best option—wait for Dubois at his house. He immediately started driving.

If they didn't find someone to turn state's evidence, they were
going to be here for weeks…months. Innocents would die. Winnie would be at risk.

The question Matt couldn't answer: how loyal was the chief
of police to Peter Landry and the Cormiers?

Dubois lived near downtown, but off a long, country road,
parallel to the river, with small houses set far apart. Nice area,
but not opulent and lavish like Landry's neighborhood.

Matt parked down the road, away from Dubois's property.
He didn't want anyone who might recognize his car to see it
parked in Dubois's driveway.

He crossed a field, walked behind a barn, then went up the
back stairs to Dubois's kitchen door.

It was locked.

He tried windows. Locked. The front door—it couldn't be
seen from the road since the house was set so far back. Locked.

He considered breaking in; dismissed the idea. Instead, he sat on the porch where he could see Dubois when he came home.

He'd wait.

Kara wanted to check out the Magnolia again, but she didn't trust that Savannah Trahan hadn't outed her, and she'd already been around town too much. Even if no one recognized her, seeing a strange blonde multiple times might stand out to an observant person. So she dispensed with a disguise, wore her basic "uniform" of jeans, black tank top and a lightweight blazer to cover her weapon, and parked partly hidden down the street from the Magnolia where she could see every vehicle that turned down the road.

Kara pulled out binoculars and fixed the lenses on the parking lot. Jean Paul's truck was in the parking lot. Winnie was there. She would have to wait. Waiting meant she had too much time to think, and she didn't want to think about her conversation with Matt.

He made her think too much. Feel too much. It was wholly frustrating.

Fortunately, she only had to wait ten minutes. At one fifteen that afternoon, Winnie left the Inn and walked to her truck.

Gray Cormier immediately followed her out.

Kara tensed. She was parked too far to see expressions and she couldn't tell if Winnie was in danger. They appeared to be yelling at each other.

Had Ricky called her already? Was he going to? Michael had thought he would.

Less than a minute after Cormier came out, he went back inside and Winnie drove off.

Kara waited until Winnie turned at the end of the street before she followed. Winnie headed through town, but drove past her house. She turned left, then right over the train tracks, heading deep into farmland. If she was going to Landry's farm, Kara wouldn't be able to follow.

When she saw a No Outlet sign at an intersection, Kara slowed down. She didn't want to spook the teen. And since there was no road out of wherever they were heading, Kara wasn't worried about losing her. The truck disappeared from view around a bend. Kara followed.

At the end of the road was a church—a small, white building set on a high foundation, surrounded by tall grass. A weed-choked gravel parking lot showed no cars, except for Winnie's truck. An old sign read St. Augustine Baptist Church. Under the sign was a hanging plaque, the kind you could pop out the plastic letters to change the words. It was missing many letters.

All wel o e

S vice Sunda 9

Was the church even open? It looked like it was maintained—the stairs had been replaced recently, the small windows looked clean—but the paint had seen better days.

Winnie wasn't in her truck. Kara parked next to it and got out. Looked around for a threat; saw no one. Walked up the stairs and checked the doors: they were locked.

Kara headed back down to Winnie's truck, then cautiously circled the church.

Behind the church was a cemetery, all the graves above ground in large stone mausoleums, gothic and creepy. Hundreds of old stone structures, some large enough to fit a family, with gargoyles and angels perched, watching. Others a single stone casket, like Snow White might have been in, but without the glass viewing window.

And Winnie. Sitting on the steps of a tall, narrow stone building with the name DAVIS etched in the stone on the top. An

angel with wide wings, as if about to embrace her, looked down
upon the crying teenager.

Kara walked over to her and sat down. She didn't say anything, then suddenly Winnie leaned over and hugged her.

Kara, intensely uncomfortable, hugged her back.

"I don't want to die," Winnie said.

"Good," Kara said.

"Ricky called me. He said to trust you. I don't know what
to do."

"Tell me everything."

Kara began to have second thoughts.

This wasn't the first time that she'd convinced a scared young
woman to do the right thing. The last time Kara had done it,
her informant was murdered.

I don't want to die...

Richard Dubois eyed Matt from his truck when he drove up
to his house. Matt watched him. The cop didn't get out for a
long minute. When he finally did, Matt stood, on alert.

He walked up the stairs without a word to Matt, unlocked
his door and went inside.

Matt cautiously followed.

Rich took off his utility belt, dropped it on the dining room
table and walked to the back of the house. Matt followed, stood
in the kitchen doorway. Rich opened the refrigerator, pulled out
a decanter of iced tea and poured himself a tall glass. Drank it.

"Want some, Costa?"

He almost declined, but Rich's tone sounded defeated. As if
he knew his days were numbered—either as a living man, or
a free man.

"Thank you."

He poured himself a second glass, got a fresh glass for Matt,
put it on the table. Rich sat down. So did Matt. Still cautious.
He sipped the tea.

They sat there in silence for a minute as Matt tried to figure out exactly what to say. He'd run through multiple scenarios while he waited for Rich, but he'd been expecting belligerence and animosity. Not resignation.

It was Rich who spoke first. "I had a call from my son today."

Matt tensed. Michael didn't think Ricky had any relationship with his father. They might have completely blown it talking to the kid.

"You don't understand," Rich said.

"Enlighten me."

"Ricky hasn't called me once since the day he left—the day after his high school graduation. Not once. Not on my birthday, not on Christmas. For two years, two months and twelve days, I have not heard from my son. I knew where he was. I called and left messages on his birthday. When I saw in the Tulane student newsletter that his ROTC squad had beat a record for a swamp hike. Just to hear his voice on voice mail. He never called me back, never acknowledged he received my messages. And today, he called me. All he said was 'Do the right thing, Dad.'"

There were tears in Rich's eyes. "I don't know that I can."

"Start at the beginning."

"I made a deal with the devil."

"And which devil is that?"

Rich laughed without humor.

"You know damn well, Agent Costa. Peter Landry. He ain't the only one, but he's probably the cruelest. I doubt you can stop them. They have friends in high places."

"Like Congress?"

Rich smiled. "Everywhere."

"I will stop them. I need you on record."

"You know they'll kill me. Then they'll kill my son."

"If you turn state's evidence, I can protect you both."

Rich didn't say anything.

Matt took a gamble, took out his cell phone and hit his recording app. "This is Special Agent in Charge Mathias Costa sitting with St. Augustine Police Chief Richard Dubois on Wednesday, August 23 at 1:22 p.m., in the residence of Chief Dubois, Broussard Parish, Louisiana."

He waited. A long minute later, Rich started talking. For more than an hour he spoke, telling Matt an increasingly sad and sorry tale of sex, violence, drugs and murder.

Rich outlined how he looked the other way for years when Preston Cormier was running drugs in town—at first, just minor violations. Then Peter Landry started buying up property, and approached him, before he was mayor. And Rich went along with it. He had bills, medical and personal. He had debt. He had no wife, but spent a lot of money at the Magnolia Inn because he wanted no-strings female companionship. He did things he wasn't proud of…and somehow the Cormiers knew.

By the time Peter Landry was mayor, Richard Dubois was his cop. Appointed him as police chief and Rich covered up a multitude of crimes.

He confessed everything, including the fact that Jean Paul LeBlanc was killed not because they were afraid he'd say anything about anyone's business, but because he'd killed Jake West, the only contact the Cormiers had to their supplier from Mexico. Without Jake, they had no one but a teenager.

"Who?" Matt feared he knew.

"Winnie LeBlanc. Jake had brought her along with him for the last year, paid her well because she knows the bayou, knows how to navigate the waters better than most, and isn't a threat to anyone. She's practically a little girl. With Jake dead, she's the only one they're going to deal with because they've seen her and haven't been stung."

"And Jean Paul killed Jake to free his cousin Winnie."

"Hell if I know. Probably. Or he could have been working for Tammy, she and Preston have been dancing around each other for years, cutting into each other's business. I really don't know. His death was punishment for him screwing things up, and as a sign to Tammy and Debra, in case he was told to kill Jake. Either way, he was out of the picture, and that's all Preston cared about."

"Who killed the seven women?"

Rich obviously didn't want to say, but he shrugged. "In for a penny, in for a pound," he muttered.

Matt waited. He would wait as long as it took to get the truth.

"I don't have firsthand knowledge as to who killed anyone. Only rumors. Except Nicki LeBlanc." He hesitated.

"Do not lie to me."

"I don't have to. I need to get something."

He got up. Matt grabbed his phone, put it in his breast pocket and followed, his hand on his gun.

Rich walked down the hall into a small room he used as his office. He removed a picture from the wall, revealing a safe. He turned the dial. It opened.

"Step away," Matt said.

Rich complied.

Keeping Rich in his peripheral vision, Matt glanced into the safe. There was a lot of cash, and a paper bag.

"The bag," Rich said. "The knife that killed Nicki LeBlanc. It has the killer's fingerprints and blood all over it."

Matt didn't make a move for the bag yet. He didn't want his back to Rich.

"Who killed her?" he asked.

"Peter Landry. She broke the cardinal rule. She outed him."

"Outed? Like being gay? Is that still an issue down here?"

Rich shrugged. "Among some people. But it was a problem for him because he was a pedophile. He liked teenage boys and he had Jerry clean up after him. Pay them off, give them drugs, whatever. But Nicki had a mouth on her, she taunted him when he couldn't perform and he killed her for it. I told him I got rid of the evidence, but in the back of my mind—I was angry.

Not just because he killed Nicki, but because he was responsible for Ethan's death. I'd known Ethan most his life. He was a good kid. Ricky's best friend." He paused, swallowed heavily. "Ethan was an addict because of Landry, because Landry—did things to him."

He rubbed a hand over his face. "Ricky told me Ethan was gay at the beginning of their senior year. I made a negative comment, about gays in general, and Ricky got mad. Said his best friend was gay and he didn't care and if I ever said anything around Ethan, he'd never forgive me. Ethan wasn't public about it, he had a girlfriend and all, but Ricky knew and I wanted my son's respect, so I didn't say anything. Then I learned about Ethan and Peter—and I might be old-fashioned. Hell, I'm an asshole. I didn't care much that Ethan was gay, even if I said shit, I guess to each his own, but Peter was twenty years older than the boy. And that made me mad. Just as mad as if Ethan was a sixteen-year-old girl that Peter was sniffing around."

Matt didn't have to read between the lines to understand exactly what happened.

"So you kept the murder weapon."

"Yes, I did. I didn't know if I'd ever use it against him, but I liked knowing I could."

"And the other women?"

"I don't know. I'm telling you the truth about that. I suspected Gray Cormier, but I don't have evidence. Jerry Guidry knows."

"Could Guidry have killed them?"

"Maybe. But Jerry and Gray are tight, and for all I know Jerry watched while Gray strangled them."

"Lily Baker wasn't strangled. She was shot in the head execution style and stuffed in a barrel."

"The body you found. In the river."

Matt didn't tell him that the evidence had been all but destroyed. "We're running ballistics. We know that she was pregnant."

"Pregnant?" He seemed surprised.

"Jean Paul knew where her body was dumped. He knew that she was pregnant. How would he know when her family didn't?"

Rich shrugged. "I didn't hear anything about that. I'm telling you the truth."

"She's an outlier."

"Lettie, Tanya, Hannah, Ginny—they all worked for the Cormiers. Running drugs up and down the bayou with Gray or Jake. I always thought they got mouthy or stole from them. Preston hates thieves. Or Peter thought they knew something that would get him or one of his associates in trouble. I don't know. I have nothing to lose telling you now, I just don't know who killed them. But Lily was always a little different. She was a looker. I mean, real pretty. And she was always trying to get clean—I think her friends sabotaged her."

"What do you mean?"

"What do I know about women? Not much, I'll tell you that. But Lily was pretty. She got the men who paid extra because they wanted a pretty girl to look at, to pretend she wanted to be there with them. She had regulars who came from out of town, tipped well. And she was always trying to clean up her act, would talk about going to school or finding a real job. The eternal optimist. I think they were jealous that she might make something of herself, free herself. So when she tried to get clean, they'd push her back into the pit."

"Are you suggesting that one of the girls at the Magnolia killed her?"

"No—I don't know who killed her, God's honest truth. Just that she wasn't like the others."

"Neither was Ernestine. She wasn't a prostitute, wasn't an addict."

"So sweet, so stupid. She can't keep a secret. She mentioned 'Mr. Beau' more than once, and that's when everyone knew that Hebert was trouble. The paranoia grew and Gray wanted her dead."

"Did Elijah Morel kill her?"

"I don't know. After we found out Ernestine was talking to Beau, Peter came to me. Said he was getting suspicious that one of his people was working for Tammy. He tasked me with finding the traitor. I've been going around and around in my head and I think it's Gray Cormier. I didn't tell Peter—I have no proof—but there've been a few problems here and there and Gray is the only one who has been party to every problem."

"If Gray was working for Tammy, why have her niece killed? Did she know?"

"I couldn't say. Tammy is cruel—she cut off a guy's pinky finger once for stealing from the till—but I've never known her to kill anyone."

Matt had more questions, but he needed to start pulling warrants, get Rich into protective custody, call in a team to keep an eye on Ricky at Tulane.

"What's happening tomorrow? At the farm Landry owns."

He looked surprised. "You found out about that?"

Matt didn't say anything.

"I don't know. Like I said, I never ask questions. I just did what they said and tried to keep my head down. Counting my days."

"For what?"

"Until I die."

Matt took the bag from the safe, looked inside. There was indeed a knife covered in dried blood. He said, "Are you going to tell them that you talked to me?"

"Only if they ask."

"Keep a low profile. Stand up, be the hero your son thought you were before you tore up the evidence he gave you about Cormier's drug dealing. Give an official statement and be prepared to testify in court. I might be able to keep you out of prison."

Matt left Rich standing in his den looking small and defeated.

He stepped out onto the porch and called Kara. She had texted him to call her ASAP.

"What do you know?"

"I have the plans from Winnie," she said. "We don't have a lot of time. Tomorrow night they leave after sunset, come back early morning before dawn, navigating the rivers and bayou all the way to and from the Gulf."

"Where are you?"

"She'll only help if we get Bonnie out of town. So, well, I'm driving a four-year-old to Curt Danville. He and his wife agreed to take her in for as long as we need. I'll be back in an hour."

"Where's Winnie?"

"She says she can't deviate from her schedule. She finished cleaning the rooms at the Magnolia, now she's heading to The Catfish to clean the bathrooms. I have to find a way to get eyes on her."

"Meet at Beau's when you get back. I—"

A gunshot went off.

"Matt? *Dammit, Matt!*"

"I'm here. Hold on." He ran into the house. Rich Dubois was slumped at his dining room table, his brains all over the ceiling. He turned his head away and told Kara, "Dubois just committed suicide."

38

Matt put the knife Dubois gave him in his car while he called the sheriff's department to report the shooting. No way was he bringing in SAPD. He called Michael and told him to get here pronto, then dialed his boss to tell him exactly what happened.

"You taped the conversation?" Tony asked.

"Yes. I'm sending you the recording now, just in case something happens."

"What? What could happen?"

"They could arrest me."

"No fucking way are they touching you. Shit—I'm sending the FBI in. Don't you dare get put into custody. These people are insane. He shot himself? You're positive?"

"Yes. Forensics will prove it." He told Tony exactly what happened. "I'm not sharing this recording with the sheriff—I have no idea if he's on the up and up, but his cousin manages the Magnolia Inn."

"Michael?"

"On his way."

"Kara?"

"Putting a child into protective custody."

"What are you telling the sheriff?"

"That Dubois and I met here because he wanted to talk to me outside of the office. I'll tell him everything Dubois said, except about the knife. I won't tell him I have a recording. I'm having Michael take the knife straight to Lafayette. It's our only evidence in the Nicki LeBlanc homicide."

"If you believe him."

"I believe him."

"Okay, I'm sending the FBI out, I'll have NOLA issue the order. I'll talk to my boss, play him the recording. Don't get arrested, and keep me in the loop."

"Roger that."

Two deputy vehicles pulled up and Matt met them next to Dubois's vehicle. He introduced himself, showed his ID and said, "I had just finished meeting with Chief Dubois and was leaving when I heard a gunshot. I ran back inside and found him at the dining room table, dead."

"Did you touch the body?"

"No."

"Stay here, sir." The deputies went inside. At least they seemed professional enough.

Michael pulled up next, while the cops were in the house. Matt had already told him what happened over the phone. He handed Michael his phone that had the recording, told him to exchange keys. "Give me your phone, then send a message that if anyone needs me, to call your number. Take my car all the way to FBI headquarters in Lafayette. Do not get pulled over. The knife that killed Nicki LeBlanc is in a paper bag in the trunk. Ask Dr. Lind and Ryder to process it immediately. Prints, blood. Dubois says Peter Landry killed her. I need confirmation ASAP. Be careful."

"I should stay with you—"

"Just go. My car is right down the street."

"You're the boss."

Michael left and the deputies came out. "Who was that?" one of them asked.

"My partner, Special Agent Harris. He's calling our boss, filling him in, so that I can answer any questions you have."

"I just called Sheriff Landry. He's going to want to talk to you. Wow, I can't believe the chief killed himself."

"You don't know that," the other deputy said.

"Shee-it, Paulie, his brain's on the ceiling!" He put his index finger under his chin and mimicked a gun and pulled the "trigger." "No doubt about it, I've seen it before."

Paulie turned to Matt. "What were you doing here?"

"I've been in St. Augustine since Monday morning working with the chief on a case."

"He called in the FBI?" Clearly, Paulie didn't believe that he would.

"No. I'd rather explain this once to the sheriff."

Paulie shrugged. "Suit yourself."

Matt looked at Michael's phone when it vibrated in his hand. Tony had texted: Danville is sending two agents to assist, and NOLA is on standby. Keep me informed.

Matt listened to the deputies talking about nothing important, and it was only five minutes later that the sheriff pulled up, along with another deputy.

Sheriff Landry was in his sixties and large all-around, at least six-foot-four and 250 pounds, with a thick graying mustache and a full head of gray hair under a cowboy hat.

Matt waited for the deputies to give their verbal report, then he introduced himself to the sheriff.

"Deputies say it appears that Rich killed himself. Do you concur?"

"Yes, sir. I had just left the house when I heard the gunshot."

"I'm going to take a look." He walked into the house, the stairs creaking under his weight. He was inside for a minute, came out and said, "Yep, looks like suicide. What were y'all talking about with Rich?"

"The murders of seven women in the parish."

"Hmm. I heard the FBI was in town, that you were interested in the murders. Surprised you didn't contact me."

"They were all within the St. Augustine jurisdiction, I was told. The one body found in the county was put under St. Augustine because it was a like crime."

"Detective Hebert has the case. Met with him?"

"Yes, sir, I did."

"Why do you think Rich killed himself?"

"I can't say, sir."

"Can't? Won't?"

Matt didn't know whether Sheriff Landry was a friend or a foe. He didn't want to give too much away, but he wasn't going to lie, either.

"Sheriff, I had come out here to the chief's house to speak to him away from his station. I felt he would be more open with me if we were alone."

"And was he?"

"In part."

"About?"

"Preston Cormier, his brother, Gray, and their drug business."

"Yep, we've never been able to get something to stick."

"I felt, and Rich concurred, that someone on his staff might be assisting them. I felt that the chief may have been compromised, and wanted to give him the opportunity to come clean."

Neither a lie nor the whole truth.

"And did he?"

"He implied that he may have looked the other way. I told him to think about it, and I would come back after I checked in with my boss to see how he wanted to proceed. I was leaving when I heard the gunshot."

"So you're the one who had iced tea with Rich in the kitchen?"

"Yes, sir."

"Friendly."

"I felt he was resigned that the truth would come out, and he wanted to get in front of it, but was concerned about repercussions."

"He wanted a deal."

"That was my impression, not what he said."

"Special agent in charge," Landry said. "That's the guy in charge. You're not from N'orlins."

"No, I'm from DC. I head the mobile response team."

"That RV I saw at the North Lake Hotel. I heard that was federal."

"Yes, it's back in Lafayette now. I would be happy to send you a copy of my report, or sit down and talk if you have any insight to share."

The sheriff was eyeing him. Matt still couldn't tell if he was working with Peter Landry or not. He needed to feel him out a bit.

"Are you related to the mayor, Peter Landry?"

"I'm sure back in the primordial ooze we shared a cell or two, but he's not my kin."

He didn't like Landry. But that didn't mean that he was clean.

"What happens to the police department now?" Matt asked. He was genuinely interested in the answer.

"The assistant chief will take over on an interim basis until the town council appoints another chief. Could be a week, could be a month."

"Who's the assistant chief?"

"Whoever Rich had designated."

One of the deputies said, "It's Jerry Guidry."

That wasn't good, Matt thought.

He said, "Is there any mechanism in place where you, Sheriff, can take over the police department on a temporary basis?"

"I suppose there is, but why would I do that?"

"Because one of the things that Chief Dubois said to me was that Jerry Guidry was a dirty cop. As of this moment—well, about twenty minutes ago when I talked to my boss—Jerry Guidry is under federal investigation for public corruption, abuse under the color of authority, sexual assault, and murder."

Matt stayed at the chief's house until the Lafayette agents arrived, then after he debriefed them, he left them with the deputies to deal with jurisdictional bullshit. He didn't care if they played hardball or gave everything to the sheriff's department.

He called Kara as soon as he got into Michael's car; she didn't answer. He then called Michael; he had delivered the knife and was now heading back to St. Augustine.

"Meet me at Beau's," Matt said. "We need a game plan for tomorrow—every idea you have, nothing's off-limits. We have to stop this shipment and protect Winnie LeBlanc."

"I just got off the phone with Ricky Dubois. His dad sent him a text message—had to have been right before he killed himself."

"What did it say?"

"'*I'm sorry I failed you. I've always been proud of you.*'"

"Shit. That poor kid."

"He's solid, he'll deal with it. When this is all over maybe I'll go see if I can do anything for him."

"You're a good man, Michael. Have you talked to Kara?"

"No. The little girl is in the FBI office with Curt. Kara left twenty minutes before I arrived. She must be nearly back to St. Augustine by now."

"She's calling me." Matt cut over to Kara. "Are you back already?"

"I just sent you my GPS location. Hurry." She ended the call.

Kara had seen the lights in her rearview mirror as soon as she exited the freeway in St. Augustine.

Fuck.

They were waiting for her. How did they know? Did they know that she'd taken Bonnie into protective custody? If so, Winnie was in immediate danger.

She saw Jerry Guidry getting out of his car. This was getting better and better.

She glanced around, but saw no one. He'd pulled her over near West Canal, the street of properties owned by Peter Landry. The business in front of her was boarded up.

She rolled down her window. Guidry said, "Ms. Quinn. Step out of the vehicle." She couldn't read his expression because he wore reflective sunglasses.

Keeping her hands visible, she said, "Officer Guidry, my name is *Detective* Kara Quinn. Los Angeles Police Department. I will show you my badge, it's in my pocket."

Whether he'd already known or not, she couldn't tell.

"You will not reach for anything. You will step out of the truck now."

Hurry up, Matt.

She was only marginally concerned about her safety. She was more worried about what she might do to Guidry that would get her into trouble, or if he had friends on the way.

Matt texted her back.

7 min

Seven minutes. She could stall for seven minutes, right?

"Officer, what is it you think I did?" She tried to smile, but he wasn't having it.

She itched to bolt. But she didn't.

"I don't know who you are, but you're no fucking cop."

He pulled open the door of the truck with one hand and grabbed her by the arm with the other. The only thing that prevented her from being pulled into the street was her seat belt.

He reached around and unlocked her belt. She elbowed him in the gut as he attempted to pull her out again. He grunted, then grabbed her neck and squeezed, pressing her head hard against the headrest.

"You fucking little bitch. You think no one noticed you in that hot little red glittery top, just because you were all dolled up?"

She mentally ran through all her outfits and where she'd been. *The Broiler. With Preston Cormier.*

"Who do you work for? You will tell me or so help me God I will break your fucking neck."

Against every instinct to fight him, she forced her body to relax and his grip on her neck loosened. She then jabbed her left elbow hard and high right under his sternum. He dropped his hands and staggered back with a bellow of pain, then she jumped out of the truck and put distance between her and Guidry. She looked for help, any open business. Across the street, several people were watching from behind the hardware store window, but no one came to assist.

He had a gun, but he hadn't drawn it yet, and she didn't want to get into a gunfight. Maybe he realized he had gone too far.

"Stay where you are," she told him as she ran to the far side of the truck. She pulled out her wallet, showed her badge and ID. "I'm a cop. I'm working with the FBI, and you're going to fucking stand back." Her voice was hoarse and she worked to control her breathing.

He stared at her badge. It was as if it all clicked at once—that she wasn't lying, that she really was a cop, that she really was working with the feds.

He straightened up and started back toward his patrol car. She didn't take her eyes off him. Right before he got back into his car, he said, "You're dead."

He drove off.

Kara didn't breathe until he was out of sight. Then she slid down to sit on her bumper, trying to calm down.

Matt squealed up behind her not a minute later. He jumped out of his car and ran to her. "Kara—what happened?"

She looked up at him. "Guidry pulled me over."

He was staring at her neck. "Did he do that to you? Dammit, did he have his hands around your neck?"

She didn't quite register what he said. She replayed the last seven minutes in her head and then said, "Yeah. He was trying to pull me out of the truck."

Matt pulled out his phone and took a picture. He showed it to her. Her neck was red in the shape of a hand. It was already starting to bruise.

"Well, shit," she said. "You know, maybe you should take some more, compare it with the strangulation victims. The only thing the fucking coroner did right was take pictures."

Matt made a call, not taking his eyes off hers. He looked angry, worried and relieved all at the same time. But mostly angry. "Sheriff Landry? This is Matt Costa. Officer Guidry just assaulted one of my people after she identified herself as a law enforcement officer. I want you to arrest him and keep him in jail until I can talk to him."

He listened to the sheriff, then said, "Thank you, sir." He turned to Kara. "You did identify yourself, right?"

"Twice."

He reached out and touched her cheek. She closed her eyes and allowed just this one small moment between them. "Thank you for coming so quickly."

"We need to go. I don't know how safe any of us are right now."

Kara glanced over to the hardware store; the sign on the door had been turned to read "closed" and no one stood in the window.

"It seems you developed a rapport with the sheriff."

"We'll call it a temporary partnership. I don't know whose side he's on, but so far, he's been cooperative. And I don't think he likes Peter Landry."

"The enemy of my enemy is my friend?"

"Something like that."

39

Matt followed Kara to the Hebert property, still worried about her. During the drive, he called in two SWAT-trained agents from NOLA to keep an eye on Winnie LeBlanc. Kara had told him where Guidry recognized her from—what she wore at The Broiler—and that he hadn't at first believed she was a cop, but was working for someone against the Cormiers.

When they arrived at Beau's house, Matt parked behind her and opened her door. She was sitting there, staring at nothing.

"Hey, you good?"

"Yeah. Sorry. Just running through everything that's happened this week seeing if I missed something. I'm worried about Winnie."

"I already have two agents from NOLA heading out. They'll be at her place in less than two hours. They'll be discreet."

"You did that?"

"Of course. She's an important witness. Plus, we need her—without Winnie, I don't know if we'll be able to get the warrant for the farm. We'll keep eyes on her throughout this process."

"Thank you."

Why did she thank him for doing his job?

Then she said, "If you don't mind, I'm going to take a shower. Give me twenty minutes?"

"Take all the time you need."

Matt watched Kara enter the small house. He wanted to go after her, but decided to give her some space. He didn't know if that was the right thing to do, but at that moment, Michael pulled up.

They entered the main house to the most amazing smell. Toni and Beau had spent all day cooking jambalaya. Matt's mouth literally watered.

"We have a lot to talk about," Beau said. "I invited my contact at the district attorney's office to come over and share what she knows. She may get fired, but now's the time to take a stand."

"Everything on the table," Matt agreed.

"Eat, first," Toni said. She was bustling around the kitchen and Beau was smoothly helping her, getting down bowls from a shelf, then slicing bread and pulling decanters from the refrigerator. "Y'all haven't stopped since you arrived, and that's not good for anyone, especially for your mind. Eat, sleep, you'll be able to think clearly."

"You're always right, Mimi," Beau said and kissed the top of her head.

A plump, attractive woman knocked on the wood frame. "Hello!"

Beau handed Michael a stack of plates, then went to greet his guest. "Addie, I'm glad you made it."

She put her briefcase down next to the door. "I don't think Alston noticed when I left. Richard's suicide really has thrown the parish into a tailspin." She walked over to Toni. "Mrs. Hebert, it is so good to finally meet you. I'm Addie Benoit."

"Benoit. Is your grandmother Mary Benoit? From Lake Pierre?"

"Yes, she is."

"My dear! I feel like we're kin already. Mary was my dear Carl's second cousin by way of the Rousseaus. We were at her wedding! My, that was a lifetime and a half ago, it seems. Then she up and divorced what was his name—Lloyd, I think. Well, I didn't like him much, not too bright." Toni tapped her head. "And she moved to N'orlins."

"Yes, scandalous—first divorce in our family. But she was very happy, raised my dad on her own, worked on a riverboat casino. She was a hoot. Dad was a lot more…conservative, shall we say. But he loved her."

"I was so sorry to hear she passed. What brought you back to Broussard Parish?"

"When I graduated from law school I applied to every parish in the state. This is the one that hired me."

"Divine intervention," Toni said with a smile, looking from Addie to Beau and back.

Beau turned to Michael and Matt. "Where's Kara?"

"Taking a shower," Matt said. He waited until Toni went back to the kitchen, then told everyone else about what Guidry did to Kara. "I called the sheriff, told him to arrest him, and to call me when he was in custody."

"Is she okay?" Michael asked.

"She's angry and upset. He left marks on her. I will see him in prison."

After dinner and cleanup, Beau had everyone meet across the driveway in his office.

Matt stood by the whiteboard. Kara had already updated it

with the new information they had—who was suspected of killing Nicki LeBlanc, the photo of Robert Abbott, the suicide of Rich Dubois. She'd also created a web of associations—the Cormiers, Landry, Steele and Guidry under the heading *Magnolia* and Tammy and Debra Martin under *Catfish*. Then she had Gray Cormier circled with arrows going to both headings.

Matt said, "We have a lot of information we didn't have when we arrived on Sunday." Matt and Kara had already brought everyone up to speed on what they'd learned from Dubois and Winnie respectively. "We have less than twenty-four hours to prepare. My boss is in the process of getting all the warrants we'll need to raid Landry's farm, but we have to sit on them until the shipment arrives. We have to catch them in the act. We'll have the joint task force assembled at the Lafayette office by noon tomorrow, and we're working on full surveillance of the farm via both drone and ground."

Beau looked impressed. "Didn't think you guys could act that fast."

"They came after mine," Matt said. "Jim is still in the hospital." He glanced at Kara and the bruises on her neck. "We have a clear mission—protect our informant and arrest the people on this list. The DEA is going to take lead on the Gulf angle—they'll track the boat that delivers the drugs and proceed accordingly. The Coast Guard has been alerted as well. They hope to get the main ship. But our responsibility is here, in St. Augustine."

"What about Sheriff Landry? The farm is technically outside town limits."

"I'm going to alert him at the same time as I give the go order. I'm not giving him advance warning. I don't think he's dirty like Dubois, but he could have deputies who are. We have to be careful, and I don't want to alert anyone at the farm that we're coming. Surprise gives us the advantage.

"Beau and Michael will be on the river," Matt continued.

"They're going to wait downstream for Winnie and Gray Cormier to come up from the Gulf, then follow at a distance. If she is in any danger, they'll act accordingly.

"FBI SWAT will be following my orders. Kara and I will wait for the delivery to arrive at the dock. As soon as Michael alerts us the boat is docked, we go in. We told Winnie to stay on the boat or dock—Michael and Beau will then bring her to safety. If it's not possible for her to remain behind, then my team will extract her. Winnie's safety is our number one priority. Questions?"

"How many people do we have?" Michael asked.

"Tonight? Us and the two agents watching Winnie. Tomorrow? Sixteen more between DEA and FBI, and that doesn't include the teams being sent to the Gulf."

Matt answered questions about the raid, then Beau asked, "How's Jim?"

"The MRI was good, but they want to hold him at least until tomorrow, do a follow-up MRI. His wrist was a clean break but he'll have a cast for a few weeks."

"What happened to the evidence in the barrel? Was it destroyed?"

"Not completely," Matt said. "Dr. Lind, the forensic anthropologist, was able to salvage many of the bones, including fetal bones. He's taking them to his lab at LSU. Better, they found the bullets and they appear undamaged. The bullets have been sent directly to the FBI lab at Quantico and we'll be running ballistics and matching with every known gun in the United States if we have to. But this is the first piece of solid physical evidence we have. The second is the knife I recovered from Dubois's safe this afternoon. That is at our mobile crime lab and Ryder and Jim are working on processing it."

"Jim?" Kara said. "You said he was still in the hospital. He'd better not leave."

"He is working via Zoom, walking Ryder through the process. Ryder has some experience with forensics, so it's not unfamiliar to him. As soon as he gets clear prints we'll hopefully match them to Landry and then I can get an arrest warrant."

Matt turned back to the board and said, "Kara, can I erase this web you have? I think we now understand the connections."

"Go ahead."

She was sitting on the couch, tapping her fingers on the armrest. She wasn't a still person, but she was attentive.

He replaced the information with the names of three LLCs. "Our white-collar expert, Agent Zack Heller, has been analyzing the LLCs that are controlled by Peter Landry. They are expertly structured and there is nothing illegal about them on the surface. However, property is the single best way to launder money. Considering the amount of product coming in and the money involved, their setup is extensive.

"Zack calls this an onion—there are layers of accounts, properties, businesses that are all legitimate, but as he peels back each one, he can trace them to their origins—and criminal connections. He's not done with the forensic audit, and probably will not be able to complete it until we have warrants for Landry's bank accounts, but he's not the only one involved.

"Seven years ago in New Orleans, one of Landry's partners, Derek O'Neill, was indicted for insurance fraud. O'Neill plead guilty, then said that none of his partners knew what he was doing. The FBI didn't believe him, but they found no evidence indicating that O'Neill's three partners were part of the racket. O'Neill went to prison and was killed. His wife received a two-million-dollar life insurance settlement. The NOLA office is following up with her and asking more questions, but that's a process as she's not under investigation at this point.

"The other two partners—Jasper Steele and Robert Abbott—are all over the LLC paperwork in different areas. Steele has control over the Magnolia Inn. Landry has control over Apex. We only recently learned about Abbott. We have determined that he is a so-called 'silent partner' but as Zack dug down, his name is on a key original document tying him to all of Landry's businesses. This is how we'll get them—if we can't get them on murder."

Kara said, "And Abbott is the ex-husband of Agent Trahan."

She was still angry about that, and Matt couldn't blame her. Matt said, "Agent Trahan has been relieved of duty and is currently on administrative leave pending investigation by the OPR. She won't have a job when this is over, and she might be going to prison. But that, again, is a process."

Addie said, "I've been working with Beau for the last few years trying to build a case against my boss, Alston Gary, the district attorney. It's been difficult. But I prepared a document listing every case he declined to prosecute, every offender he's let off and his reason—almost always lack of evidence—and they all have ties to the Cormiers. I'm hoping that will help in your investigation. I also documented serious legal errors that may get him disbarred, but as soon as I file that with the state attorney general and the state bar, I'll be fired. So I need to time it right."

"Reach out to Beau or me before you file. The FBI may be able to offer you cover."

"Thank you, Matt, I appreciate it. I'm ready, but figured your investigation is at a critical point and I don't want to alert Alston just yet."

"Addie," Matt said, "can you take the next two days off? Go to your parents' house maybe?"

"I'm staying here with Toni. Beau asked me to sit with her because she's worried about him." She paused. "I own a gun and know how to use it. I might look helpless, but I'm not."

"You don't look helpless," Matt said with a half smile. "We might need some legal work-around, so it'll be nice to have you close by." He turned to Kara. "Kara—you had a conversation with Winnie today."

"Yep. You pretty much said everything."

"Except—you said she recognized Robert Abbott."

Kara nodded. "He's a semi-regular at the Magnolia. I wanted to show his photo around, but I'm trying to stay off Guidry's radar."

Matt tensed. He wouldn't think about that cop right now.

"That corroborates what we know about his involvement with Landry's businesses. Steele is the only person on the official paperwork, but dig deeper and both Abbott and Landry come up," Matt said. "If we get Landry on murder, we can get warrants for all his other holdings. And then hopefully build a case against Steele and Abbott. But that's for after the raid."

"Who's this?" Addie asked, pointing to a photo.

"Robert Abbott and his family—wife, kids."

Addie turned her head, as if looking at the photo from a slightly different angle. "Is she from here? She's very pretty, very familiar."

"Her name is Elizabeth Anderson Abbott," Matt said after a quick glance at his notes. "Originally from South Carolina. They married six years ago, have twin daughters. She's twelve years younger than Abbott, who's forty. I don't have a lot on her, but she doesn't have a record or any known employment since her marriage, some family money it seems but that's a lower priority for us."

Matt stared at the picture. "I thought she looked familiar, too."

Suddenly, he knew why.

He pulled out Lily Baker's high school photo. Long blond hair, blue eyes— "Damn."

Kara groaned. "Well, fuck. He has a type. Notice something? Elizabeth… Lily…and his ex-wife. Long white-blond hair, blue eyes, very pretty."

Kara was right. The three women could have been sisters.

"I'm going to call Catherine," he said. He walked down the hall into Kara's room and closed the door.

Kara watched Matt leave the room. She could tell he was angry with himself over bringing Trahan onto their team and the fallout from that decision. "Well, I guess the party's over," she said to the others.

"You need to get some sleep," Michael told her. "You look like death warmed over." He reached out and lightly touched the bruises on her neck. "He's not getting away with this."

"I know."

"You okay?"

"I'm great."

He tilted his head and narrowed his deep brown eyes. "I can see."

Kara didn't want extra attention or sympathy. "I will sleep. I'll admit, all that food has made me lethargic."

Beau said, "I have a room for you, Addie. Michael, I hope your boss doesn't mind the couch in the living room? Unless he's going back to the hotel."

"Matt thinks it would be best for all of us to stick together. He'll be just fine on the couch. I'm not giving up the most comfortable bed I've slept on in my life."

Kara waved the three off as they left for the main house. She collapsed on the couch, truly exhausted. She was half-asleep when Matt came out ten minutes later.

"Did I miss something?" he asked.

"The leader walks away, everyone scatters. What did Catherine say?" Kara already suspected, but she wanted to hear it from Matt.

"She needs more information."

"But."

"But what?"

"You thought what I thought—that Abbott likes a certain type, he frequented the Magnolia, Lily was a prostitute, she turns up pregnant then dead."

"Yeah. I ran the details by Catherine and she still wants more information. However, Catherine suggested that the fact that Lily was a prostitute meant he could do things with her that his wife might not be willing to do. If Lily told him she was pregnant, he wouldn't let her keep the baby. It would impact his career, his life, destroy his marriage. He may have aspirations to higher office, though congressional staff can be just as powerful."

"And if she didn't want an abortion, he might kill her."

"As Catherine said, she can't make that determination without more evidence."

"Seven women, three killers." She paused. "I wonder if Crystal Landry would give him up."

"Abbott?"

"She would have seen him there."

"We'd tip our hand."

"Not now, but after all this goes down tomorrow. If we can place him there, place him with Lily—maybe she was a regular for him—and Crystal is already going to be reeling from us taking down Cormier's drug enterprise. Maybe she'll cooperate. Hell, we know she knows damn near everything, Matt. She's dirty either by remaining silent or being actively involved. If I was running a brothel? I'd have dirt on every man who walked through the door."

Winnie couldn't sleep. She was surprised that she actually missed Bonnie Mae. The house was too quiet—her mother had gone on a bender, and Winnie didn't know where she was, didn't even care. Probably shacking up with some scumbag swapping sex for drugs.

Tomorrow was going to be the day to end all days. Either she died or she was free. There was no middle ground.

Kara promised her that if anything happened, Bonnie would be taken care of. That she would be raised by good people, never to set foot again in St. Augustine.

"There are good people in St. Augustine, I know them," Win-

nie said, surprisingly melancholy. "I believe in them. But there's bad people, and everyone will know who Bonnie Mae came from. I don't want her around that. The drugs and drinking and stuff. I want her to have the freedom to do what she wants, not live in the shadow of her mother, or me."

"Nothing is going to happen to you, Winnie, but if lightning strikes you down, I will make sure that Bonnie is safe and loved. I promise."

That promise gave Winnie surprising peace. She'd given Kara pictures of her mom shooting up with Bonnie playing in the background, her mom passed out with a cigarette smoking on the couch. Her mom leaving pot and beer within reach of the kid. Just in case her mother tried to get Bonnie back. Loretta LeBlanc only cared about Bonnie because of the government check attached to her.

Winnie wasn't ready to be a mother, but she would do it, if she was all Bonnie had. She'd already been doing it since the day Nicki went back to the Magnolia only weeks after she gave birth.

Winnie finally had closed her eyes and started drifting off when she heard a noise downstairs. A crash, then someone swearing.

Damn you, Ma! she wanted to scream, but just rolled over and put a pillow over her head.

A minute later rough hands grabbed her, put a bag over her head and dragged her down the stairs.

She didn't have time to scream.

THURSDAY

40

Kara had been asleep for less than two hours when she heard her name.

"Kara. Kara, it's Matt."

She sat up.

The clock showed 1:07 a.m. Matt was standing in her doorway.

"Two men took Winnie from her house. My men said one of them looked to be Gray Cormier, but they couldn't be positive. They're on their way to the Gulf."

She jumped out of bed in underwear and a tank top, not mindful of her state of undress as she pulled on her jeans and holstered her gun before she was fully awake.

"This wasn't supposed to happen until tomorrow night! Why didn't your men stop it? Why didn't—no. Fuck no, Costa! You bastard! You let them take her?"

She hit him in the chest hard. He grabbed her wrist before she could hit him again.

"It was my call, Kara."

"I promised that she would be safe. I promised her!" She pulled her arm away from Matt.

"They're following the same plan as Winnie outlined to us, just a night early."

"Why did they grab her? They know she's working with us! They're going to kill her, Matt!" Kara couldn't believe that Matt let this happen. "You had men on her to prevent this."

"Kara, think clearly. The Cormiers told Winnie Thursday night, but this may have been their plan all along, or their suppliers arrived early."

"Which means they don't trust her. They're nervous because we're in town, but they don't trust Winnie."

"They need her."

"You don't *know that*. And if they do need her? They won't after they get the drugs."

Kara walked past him to the door. Matt followed her. She couldn't shake the deep fear that Winnie was in imminent danger.

"Beau and Michael just left. We're going to the farm. The agents are tracking Winnie, they'll tell us where she is. They're well trained. As soon as she's on the water, they'll alert Michael. Then it's up to him and Beau to track her on the river."

"Backup?"

"I've called it in, but SWAT hadn't planned to mobilize until tomorrow. Curt and NOLA are working on it, but it could be hours before we have anyone on-site. I may have to call in Sheriff Landry."

"This is fucked, Matt."

"Kara," Matt said. She turned to face him. "I will do everything in my power to protect Winnie. I had to make a split-second decision. She had already planned to go down to the Gulf with Cormier, she knows what's expected of her. When my men called, I told them to follow, not to intervene unless Winnie was in immediate danger."

"Nothing's going to matter if she dies," Kara said. But her anger at Matt faded. She would have made the same decision. She hated herself for it, but she would have made the same decision.

She had before.

And others had died.

She felt like a monster, using people as if the ends justified the means.

"I would have done the same thing," she whispered.

"Kara—" Matt reached for her.

She stepped away from him. "I'm okay," she lied and walked out.

While they drove to the farm, Matt talked to his DEA liaison. The DEA was nowhere near the expected exchange point, but could mobilize the Coast Guard quickly. They might not get the small boat, but would work to nail the supply ship, which was preferred.

"Did they know about our plan? Is that why they moved up twenty-four hours?"

"I don't think so."

"Savannah could have told them."

"She didn't."

"She could have told her ex-husband. Or he could have figured it out based on what she said or didn't say."

Matt was thinking. Let him. Kara hated corrupt cops of all stripes. She hoped Savannah Trahan went to prison. Would serve her right.

"She didn't know about *this* plan."

"But she knew we found the farm. That we were talking to Winnie."

Matt didn't respond. He had to be thinking the same thing.

"If anything happens to Winnie," Kara continued, "and I find out that Savannah Trahan outed her as our informant? I will kill her."

"Don't say that to me."

"I pushed Winnie. I told Michael to convince Ricky to call her. I put Bonnie into protective custody because that was the last hurdle, she couldn't say no if her niece was safe. I listened and pushed, convinced her this was her only option." Just like Sunny in Los Angeles. Sunny didn't want to help Kara take down the sweatshops. Sunny knew that she was putting her life on the line if she helped Kara. And still Kara pushed her, closed her case, caught the bad guys—and Sunny ended up dead.

Kara knew Winnie would be in danger, and she pushed her anyway.

"We're going to find her."

"If she's not already dead!" Kara didn't mean to yell at him, but she was tense and worried. She was angrier with herself than she was at Matt.

Thankfully, Matt didn't chastise her or tell her some platitude like it would work out or everything was fine, because he knew damn well that it wasn't fine. Nothing about the bad guys changing plans was ever *fine*.

Matt turned off South Lake Pierre Road and went along a farm road to the west. Beau and Matt had determined the best way to approach the farm on foot based on aerial maps and Beau's knowledge of the area. He parked his car at the end of the road. The house here was boarded up after being damaged in a storm. And though they couldn't see the Landry property from here, the abandoned house was directly across the road, a half mile as the crow flies.

They sat in the car for a minute while Matt checked his phone.

"Michael and Beau are on the river past the farmhouse, getting into position," he told Kara. "And the two SWAT agents just reported that the vehicle with Winnie stopped at Lake Pierre. Winnie and one man identified as Gray Cormier boarded a hard-sided motorboat and continued down the river from there."

"Is she okay?"

"She wasn't restrained," Matt said, "and was walking of her own volition. They need her to navigate, right? Until they return, she's safe."

What was Winnie thinking? That Kara had lied to her? Failed her? Was she scared? Did Cormier know Winnie was working with them? Did Winnie know that the FBI was tracking her?

Matt continued, "The second man, currently unidentified, is driving back north."

"Here? To the farm?"

"Don't know. I told the agents not to follow but to meet us here. We need the backup."

"We should get closer and identify the truck and who's driving. He's going to have to come up Lake Pierre Road, it's the fastest way to get back to St. Augustine."

Matt considered, then agreed with her. Kara was relieved. She didn't sit still well, and being worried about Winnie was not helping.

Matt turned off the dome light and opened his door. They got out, both dressed all in black. They wore Kevlar vests, turtlenecks—even though it was warm—and Kara had a black ski cap over her blond hair.

It took them five minutes of brisk walking to reach the road. The land was flat, but there was enough foliage to hide behind—bushes that grew thick out of the moist drainage ditch that paralleled the road.

Kara loved undercover work, but she didn't like working stealth. Too many things could go wrong, too many decisions had to be made in seconds. With undercover, she could talk her way out of almost any potentially dangerous situation; in a raid, talking rarely worked. If someone didn't immediately comply and had a weapon, you had to be willing to shoot. Often, the gunfire came as soon as the cops identified themselves.

Kara had killed in the line of duty. Each and every one had been justified. But she wouldn't forget any of them. She didn't regret her actions, but they still haunted her.

She didn't want to add another body to that count.

They could see headlights long before they heard the truck; they heard the truck long before it reached the driveway.

It passed by.

"Was that it?" Kara whispered.

"It matches the description."

"I couldn't see the driver. You?"

Matt shook his head.

A minute later, they saw more lights. When the car passed, it slowed—drove past the driveway, then turned down the road where Matt and Kara had parked.

"Backup," Matt said. "Stay put, let me know if anything changes. I'll get them up to speed."

Matt left and Kara watched. From this angle, all she could see was the light coming from the property—no buildings, no cars, no people, just an eerie glow in the middle of darkness.

Kara couldn't wait to finally put an end to this conspiracy.

And put a whole lot of people in jail.

Michael checked his watch. "How long to the Gulf from the lake?" he asked Beau.

They were hiding near Lake Pierre where the river dumped in. The river itself had several meandering curves, many split with growths of trees, vines hanging from many of the branches. It was creepy and beautiful at the same time. The new moon from last night had grown just a sliver, but the night was clear and bright with stars, so they stayed behind a clump of trees growing out of the murky water. He really hoped none of the dangling vines were actually snakes.

Michael had spotted four alligators sleeping on the banks. Fortunately, being cold-blooded animals, they wouldn't be disturbed by the boat, and even if they noticed the interlopers, Beau said they would likely ignore them.

Michael couldn't wait to tell Kara about the critters. Maybe he'd pick her up a stuffed gator at the airport on their way back to DC. She'd probably hit him with it, but it would be fun to tease her.

"If they know the route well, forty-five minutes to an hour," Beau told Michael. "So we'll be here for at least an hour and a half, probably two."

It was 1:45 now. He could easily fall asleep here on the boat—spending so much time on warships had him more at peace on the ocean than anywhere. The river here was just as relaxing, though Michael could do without the unending chatter of crickets and frogs.

"So, you and Addie."

"Excuse me?"

"Don't lie to me."

"There's nothing."

Michael laughed.

"Shh, you're going to wake those gators."

"You said they wouldn't care."

"Probably not, but start splashing around and they might think food. It's colder than daytime, but warm enough for them to be interested in eating."

A moment later, Beau responded to Michael's previous comment. "I haven't asked her out yet. We meet for breakfast once a week to talk about crime in St. Augustine, but we don't talk much about personal things. I didn't even know she was related to my grandfather."

"Second cousin a hundred times removed? I think you're safe."

"She's a good girl, Michael."

"She's in her thirties. Maybe forty."

"She's thirty-six. I mean, she's sweet. She goes to church. I haven't been in a church since, well, my Pop's funeral was the last time."

"Excuses, excuses. Beau, you're what, forty-two? You want to settle down, you need to start thinking about it. And you're ugly as sin. You should be damn lucky a smart girl like Addie Benoit likes you."

"Screw you."

"I know these things. Just ask her. If she says no, she says no. But she won't."

"What about you and Kara? You have a good rapport. I'm sure in your job you don't have a lot of time to cultivate relationships outside of work."

"She's with someone."

"Oh. Maybe she'll dump him."

"Maybe. I like Kara, she's a good partner, but we have fundamental differences and I don't know that we'd be able to reconcile them." He had found Kara intriguing and attractive when they first met, but he realized when they were working undercover in Patagonia that Matt was more than a little interested. And since being back in DC for the last six weeks, Michael accepted that there was something going on with them. They didn't flaunt their relationship, but Michael would have been an idiot not to see it.

"She has good instincts," Beau said. "I can see why she worked undercover for so long."

"Nearly killed her."

"Mimi likes her. Mimi is a good judge of character."

"That she is." Michael looked at his phone. "SWAT is with Matt. They're getting into position across from the farm."

"We have a long wait. I'm going to take twenty."

And like that, Beau was out. Typical, Michael thought with a grin.

He looked up to the sky. He could get used to this place.

He slapped his neck. Damn, he'd doused himself with bug spray and they still loved his tasty skin.

Maybe he wouldn't be moving down here anytime soon.

But he would visit Beau more often. He'd like that a lot.

He looked at his watch. It was 2:30.

Kara was glad that Matt had partnered her with Agent Donovan Hunter, and he with Agent Theo Trusseau. While she and Matt worked well together, Guidry laying hands on her had affected his judgment. She was glad he recognized that. One of the problems with being in an intimate relationship with your coworker in a dangerous job—military, law enforcement, fire—was that you might make decisions you wouldn't otherwise make, in order to protect them. Put yourself at risk, hesitate, do something wrong.

It was better to split and trust than have that emotional component to decision-making in the field.

His decision actually endeared him to her.

Hunter was a ten-year FBI veteran and had spent eight years in the Army. She felt ill-suited to be his partner. But the one thing she had on him was speed and size. Being small helped when you were crawling through tall grass.

Matt and Trusseau were on the north side of the farm; she and Hunter on the south side. The ground was damp and she was sticky and wet. Between sweating and the muck they crawled through, one whiff of her body told her she stunk to high heaven.

There were no fences, which made their life a bit easier, but Hunter was checking for wires and booby traps as they slowly made their way toward the buildings. It took time, but they had time. And having something to do helped Kara not think about

Winnie and the fear that must be going through her mind. Fear that they wouldn't know what happened to her. Fear that she was going to be killed. She hoped that Winnie didn't do anything rash, that she knew that Kara was watching over her. That she would save her.

Like she couldn't save Sunny.

It was 2:45.

Beau's internal clock woke him after sleeping hard and soundless for forty minutes. It was just after three and if everything went well at the exchange, Cormier and Winnie would be reaching the south end of Lake Pierre shortly. Then they'd cross the wide lake and head upstream on the river to take them to the farm. Right by Beau and Michael.

Beau started the motor, then let it idle.

"Why?" Michael asked.

"They won't be able to hear an idling motor over their own engine, but starting up has a distinct sound, and if I wait until they're closer, they might hear it."

"And that's why you outranked me."

"I outranked you because I had a college degree. You were always a better soldier."

Michael shook his head. "Everything I learned, I learned from you, buddy."

"Can't take a compliment, can you?"

"Sure I can. I'm a helluva lot better looking than you with your scrawny ass."

Beau laughed softly. He took out his binoculars and looked out past the mouth of the river into the dark lake beyond. Waited. Waited.

Waited.

"Showtime," he said several minutes later.

Michael texted Matt.

Possible target boat about to pass our location.

It was 3:20.

In her earpiece, Kara heard Matt's voice.

"Be alert, target approaching Agent Harris."

Hunter put his hand on her wrist. She looked at him. He held up two fingers, pointed east, toward the river.

She slowly turned her head. Not fifty feet from where they were lying in the grass watching the outbuildings, two men exited the house and were heading to the riverbank.

One of the men was talking, but Kara couldn't make out his words. Then they disappeared from view as they headed down to the dock.

Hunter said into his wrist microphone, "Two males approaching dock."

A moment later, Matt said, "Three confirmed in barn. Hold position."

Waiting was going to be the death of her.

It was 3:28.

Michael watched as the boat passed them only twenty feet away. He wasn't positive the trees would provide enough cover to avoid being seen.

As soon as Cormier passed, Beau steered the boat carefully out from the inlet, keeping far enough back to avoid detection, then suddenly stopped.

Cormier had stopped the boat on the north side of the inlet.

As they watched, Cormier picked up a sack from the deck and tossed it in the river. The sack was writhing and it hit the water with a thud and splash. Cormier laughed and sped up the boat, making a lot of noise.

One of the gators looked up from the shore. Then another.

Without thinking, Michael jumped into the water and swam

to where the sack had gone under, following the ripples in the water.

"Harris! Stop!"

Michael didn't stop. He reached the center of the ripples, drew in a deep breath and dove down headfirst into the murky water. He had no light, no gear, nothing but his instincts and training.

Burlap brushed against his fingers. He kicked once, grabbed as much of the sack as he could, and using all his strength, pulled it up while simultaneously turning and heading to the surface.

The sack was heavy, and it wasn't moving.

He broke through the surface and Beau was there with the boat.

"Fool, get in."

Michael grunted as he pulled the sack out of the water with one hand.

"Take it."

Beau reached down and picked up the sack, pulling it onto the boat. The outline of a body showed clearly. "Get the fuck in right now, sailor!"

Michael hoisted himself in on the opposite side, to avoid overturning the light boat.

Then he saw the last of the four alligators slide into the water from the bank where they had been sleeping.

Beau already had the sack opened and Michael's fears were realized: Winnie had been inside. Her hands and ankles were tied, her mouth duct taped, and her eyes were closed.

Beau pulled off the duct tape as an alligator butted the boat.

"Save her," Beau ordered Michael as he steered the boat away from the gators. "If it was any warmer, you'd both have been gator chum."

Michael didn't pay any mind to his old friend. He immediately started mouth-to-mouth resuscitation on Winnie, praying with each breath that she made it.

"Don't do this, God. Don't let her die." He breathed into her mouth four times, then pushed down on her chest four times. Gently but firmly.

She started coughing up water. Michael turned her to her side, then she puked. Michael let himself breathe normally.

"Dammit, girl, you scared me."

She looked small and terrified. Michael hugged her. "You're going to be okay, kid."

That bastard had used her to navigate through the treacherous bayou, pick up the drugs from their supplier, get them back safely...then tossed her overboard. Either they didn't trust her or were cleaning up knowing the feds were in town. Michael hoped Cormier spent the rest of his miserable life in prison.

Beau sent Matt the message that Winnie was safe.

It was 3:41 a.m.

Calm poured over Matt as his training took over.

He said to his team, "The package is secure. It's a go. Wait for my order."

He didn't need to tell anyone what happened to Winnie, Kara would learn soon enough what Cormier had done.

Matt was waiting for Beau's signal before they moved in.

They had a plan, and Matt would stick to it. As soon as Matt said go, Beau would call Sheriff Landry and ask for every available unit to assist the FBI at Peter Landry's farm. But Matt and his team would be on their own for at least ten minutes.

They had five confirmed targets on-site, plus Cormier.

Matt got the signal from Beau.

He counted to three.

"Go go go!" he said into his mic. He jumped up from his hiding spot and pulled down the cloth on his vest to reveal FBI in reflective letters. He pulled the cloth off Trusseau's back, Trusseau did the same for him.

They moved into the barn. Three men were already unloading two barrels that had been brought up from Cormier's boat.

Double-wrapped gallon-sized bags of pills. Thousands of blue pills. Fentanyl.

"FBI! Get down, get down, get down! Hands visible! Now!" Matt ordered.

None of the men resisted. They all put their hands up.

"Face down! Arms out. No sudden movements."

Matt covered Trusseau while he quickly zip-tied each man's wrists and ankles, then searched for weapons—all of them were carrying.

"Barn secure!" Matt said, standing by the door in case more men came in. "Delta Team, report!"

Kara's voice said, "Cormier's attempting to flee in the boat!"

"Don't engage! I'm coming!"

Kara and Hunter had moved down toward the dock as soon as Matt said go. They encountered a man coming up the ramp pushing a large barrel on a dolly. "FBI! Hands up!"

The man bolted toward the open space north of the property. "I got him," Hunter said. "Get Cormier."

She continued to run toward the dock, spotted Cormier at the edge frantically trying to untie the ropes that secured his boat to the dock. She was *not* going to let him get away.

"Cormier's attempting to flee on the boat!" she shouted into her mic.

She heard sirens in the distance and didn't know whether to be relieved or concerned. She half ran, half slid down the slippery slope toward the dock. Out of the corner of her eye she saw a man in black running from the barn. Matt. He was only thirty yards behind her.

Cormier had the ropes untied just before she reached the dock. He jumped in the boat and started the engine. She sprinted, slipped, caught herself and jumped on the boat just as he was backing out of the dock.

Matt hopped in right behind her.

"Gun!" she yelled as Cormier pulled on her and fired. Missed her, but Matt grunted.

"Matt—"

"I'm fine," he said, his voice twisted with pain.

She pulled her gun out as Cormier fired again, but the rocking of the boat had the bullet going wild. Cormier rushed her like a linebacker. She fired and knew she hit him, but he didn't stop. Adrenaline or drugs, he came at her. He tackled her and they both went over the edge into the water.

She went under, swallowing an awful-tasting gulp of water. Almost immediately, hands reached down and pulled her up and out of the water.

Matt had her on the boat in short order. She coughed, looked for her gun, saw it on the deck and picked it up. "Fuck! Where is he?"

"Help!" Cormier screamed. He was frantically swimming for the boat.

Matt turned the light toward him and tossed out a life preserver as he turned the motor to idle.

"Help!" Cormier cried. "Gators!"

Kara looked around, eyes wide. The light from the farm illuminated the water. She didn't see anything but the wake from the boat and Cormier splashing.

Then she saw something move. A splash. A ripple. She couldn't see anything beneath the surface, but then she saw more movement. A shadow. Another splash.

"Can you get to him?" she said to Matt. "Shit, I see two— three!" Three alligators. Could they climb into boats? She hoped not. But maybe they'd hit it from underneath. Force the boat to capsize. Would a bullet even stop them? Or just make them angrier?

Matt was steering the boat toward Cormier, who flailed in the water. Something hit them on the other side and Kara stifled a scream. She didn't want to be breakfast for a giant water lizard. She shivered.

"Gray!" she shouted. "Here!" She reached out her hand for the struggling man.

"Kara, don't!" Matt said.

She couldn't let Cormier just die like this—no matter who he was or who he'd killed.

His upper arm was bleeding; she had definitely shot him. His eyes were in full panic. He grabbed her wrist. Squeezed. She tried to pull him in, but he was heavy and wet. He twisted her wrist, not making any effort to climb on board, his face filled with terror and rage.

Matt grabbed Kara by the waist, holding her tight with his left arm to keep her from tumbling over after Cormier. He reached around her with his right hand and called out, "Grab my hand!"

But Cormier, whether in shock or pain or because he just wanted to bring Kara down with him, wouldn't let go of her wrist—and wouldn't take Matt's hand. If he continued to fight, the boat would capsize and they would all be at the mercy of the alligators.

"What's that! What's that?" Cormier shouted, frantic, desperate. He pulled at Kara, and she pulled back. Her wrist burned and her lungs ached.

Cormier screamed and Kara looked down into the eyes of an alligator only a few feet from her, in the water, every inch of its body below the surface except for the top of the head.

And another set of eyes, another alligator.

"Dammit, Kara, don't you dare go overboard!" Matt was saying as he fought to pull her back. Her arm throbbed, her chest ached from where Matt held her. The boat wobbled unsteady, and if it was any smaller it would have already turned upside down. Matt was balancing it somehow with his feet, pulling Kara toward the center. But still, Cormier wouldn't let go of her.

Cormier went underwater and Kara was falling with him.

Matt grunted and with all his strength held on to Kara. Her shoulder twisted and she screamed as she felt her body being yanked into the safety of the boat, and her arm being pulled in another direction, down into the water with Gray Cormier, as if she was being drawn and quartered.

Suddenly, her arm was released and she and Matt fell backward onto the bottom of the boat.

"Are you bit? Are you hurt?" Matt asked.

"Fuck fuck fuck!"

"Are you bleeding? Kara? Tell me what's wrong. I don't see blood, where are you hurt?"

"Shoulder," she said through clenched teeth. "Put it back. Put it back."

"Dislocated?"

"Yes. Just do it, make it fast—" Before she finished her sentence, Matt had cracked her shoulder back into place. Waves of pain and relief washed over her. She was sore, but she was in one piece.

"Matt—are you really okay? He shot you."

She stared at him, his dark eyes full of relief and rage and concern and...yes...love. She saw it there, held his eyes just for that moment, and saw it.

He leaned down and kissed her.

"Thank God you're okay."

"You were shot." She reached up with her good arm and touched his shoulder. Came away with blood on her fingers.

"Flesh wound. I promise. Hurts like hell, but barely grazed me."

There were lights and sirens in the distance as they sat up in the boat. Thrashing in the water—the alligators—suddenly stopped.

"What just happened?" she asked, clutching him. "Are they coming back?"

"Gators take their prey down to the river bottom, spin around until they're dead."

"Oh, God."

He held her. She couldn't stop shaking.

"I don't know that we'll be able to retrieve his body. I don't know if they leave it for a while or if they guard it. I'm not risking anyone on my team, but there may be wildlife experts in the parish who know what to do."

She didn't want to think about it. No one, not even an asshole like Gray Cormier, deserved to be eaten by alligators.

Matt turned her to look at him. "Are you okay? Really?"

She nodded. "Nothing that a hot shower, a shot of tequila and twelve hours of sleep can't fix."

41

Kara watched from the back of an ambulance as Matt explained the situation to Sheriff Landry.

A paramedic was checking her out as well as her partner Hunter. He'd apprehended the man he was chasing, but not without a scuffle that left a nasty gash on his forehead. They'd already bandaged up Matt's flesh wound—which, even though the bullet had gone all the way through his bicep, had to have hurt.

"You need an X-ray on your wrist," the paramedic was saying.

"It's not broken."

"You don't know that."

"Later," she said.

The sun was beginning to creep over the horizon. She wanted to be in bed before it was too bright, or she'd never get to sleep.

She needed sleep. A lot of it. She was exhausted. Maybe the sun wouldn't even keep her awake.

"Let her be," Hunter said. To her, he added, "You did good."

"He's dead. That's not good."

"His choice, not yours."

She saw Beau approaching and waved him over with her good arm.

"Winnie?" she asked.

"Michael took her to the hospital in Lafayette. Wanted to make sure she was safe and protected. He's not leaving her."

"What the hell happened?"

"Matt didn't tell you?"

"Just that you had her."

"That bastard Cormier tied her up, stuffed her in a sack and threw her off the boat in Gator Bay."

"What the hell is Gator Bay?"

"It's the wide spot of the river as it spills into Lake Pierre. Gators are known to nest there. She would have drowned, but the splashing woke the alligators on the shore and they slipped into the water."

"That is fucked," she said. She turned to Hunter. "Definitely his choice, in more ways than one."

"Not only his choice," Beau said, "but his fault. If he hadn't stirred up them gators downstream, they wouldn't have followed the boats back here."

She still felt ill at how Cormier died, but her guilt faded a bit.

"But Winnie's okay?" she asked Beau.

Beau squeezed her hand. "Michael saved her life."

"He's good at that."

Matt walked over. He didn't have to say anything, she saw it in his eyes. Just that moment of connection to tell her that he was there for her in every way.

He said, "Go home with Beau. I'm staying until the FBI and DEA arrive. We're looking at tens of thousands of pills."

"You don't have to tell me twice. Don't wake me until noon."

Matt said to Hunter, "You can crash in the hotel on the interstate, we have a couple rooms there."

"No, sir. I'll wait for my partner then head back home to my family."

"You have a family?" Kara asked.

"Excuse me?"

"Nothing." She didn't want to be responsible for a fellow cop, a cop with a family.

"My wife would love you. She's also a cop. In fact, maybe you can come over for dinner before you head back to DC. We'd like that."

Matt, who knew that she was uncomfortable in these kinds of situations, saved her by saying, "If we can, we will. Depends how fast we wrap things up and have to get back to Washington."

"You have my number."

He walked away to talk to his partner and Matt said to Kara, "Are you really okay?"

"Yeah. Better now that I know karma's both a bitch and my best friend."

"I told her about Winnie," Beau said. To Kara, he said, "I'll take you back to the house."

"Be alert," Matt said. "The sheriff is taking Peter Landry into custody right now, but we don't know where Jerry Guidry is— he's not at his house and he's not at the station. He might have left town, so we put an APB on him and flagged his passport."

Ten minutes later, Kara was glad to sit in Beau's truck. She sighed. "Tell me you didn't lie about Winnie and Michael."

"They're both good. I promise. He took her to the hospital just for his own peace of mind. GQ loves being the hero."

"He saved my life more than once. He never has to buy a beer as long as I'm around."

"It's over," Beau said.

"Almost."

"It's done. We broke the chain. The sheriff is taking over the police department for the time being. He might not be squeaky clean, but he's not involved in this shit, swore up and down he would fire any of his deputies who were involved. We'll have a new mayor—I think I have someone in mind who can help clean up the town. I was talking to Trusseau, who has some good candidates for police chief, someone the town will accept but who will be clean. It's good."

"Why not you, Beau?"

"I don't want to be in charge. Maybe temporarily, but not for the long haul."

She understood that. "The girls at the Magnolia are going to need help. And you still have Tammy and Debra Martin at The Fat Catfish. Take out the Cormiers, they're going to slither into their place."

"True, but it's going to take time and it's going to take resources, and after this week I think I can encourage Tammy to focus on illegal cigarettes and backroom poker games."

She laughed. "I think that's—" She hesitated then said, "Turn off the lights."

He did at the same time he asked, "Why?"

"Stop the car."

He complied.

"What's wrong?"

Something was off with the house.

They'd just turned off the main road and something caught her eye, but at first she didn't know what.

The lights. The wrong lights were on.

"Your grandmother always leaves a small light on in the kitchen, the porch light, and there's a night-light upstairs that illuminates the window at the top of the stairs."

"Okay. And?"

"All the lights are off, but the second house—they're on. I didn't leave them on when I left."

There was no other car in the driveway—just Toni's car and Addie's practical sedan. Kara said, "Turn off the dome light. You go to the house and check on Toni and Addie. I'm going to the war room."

"Wait for me."

"I'm just going to check it out. I can be stealthy when I want."

They quietly got out of the truck and walked down the driveway—Beau on the right, in the weeds so he didn't kick up gravel. Kara to the left.

She reached the small house. All the blinds were closed. She walked around to the bedroom. Tried the window she'd opened when she slept; it was still open. She quietly, carefully, removed the screen.

Her phone vibrated. She turned the light all the way down and read the message.

No one is in the main house.

She listened. Someone was pacing. She heard a female voice, thought it was Addie. Then a male voice said, "Just stop already."

She texted Beau.

I'm going in through the bedroom. Go back to the truck. Drive up, make noise. Anything. I think it's Guidry. Get him out of the house. I'll get Addie and Toni.

She got his thumbs-up. She wasn't one hundred percent positive it was Guidry in there, but someone was, and Guidry was the only one who hated Beau—and her—so much that he would hold two innocent people hostage.

She pulled herself up and over the windowsill, wincing at the pain in her wrist. Her shoulder was sore, but her wrist was severely sprained. She was glad she'd let the paramedic wrap it. She hated that it was her dominant hand. She could shoot with her left hand, she'd trained for it, but accuracy dropped—and she certainly wouldn't shoot when she had two innocents in the room.

The house wasn't a quiet home, and the wood floor creaked when she landed on the braided rug. She froze, listened.

Someone was still pacing.

Then it stopped.

She heard Beau's truck. Beau stopped and revved it as he turned off the ignition.

"Finally," Guidry said.

"Don't hurt him." That was Toni.

Kara saw red. For the second time this week, that bastard had terrorized Beau's grandmother.

"Shut up," Guidry said.

Kara stepped softly on the floor. It creaked again.

The front door opened. "Hebert!" Guidry called.

He sounded like he was standing on the small porch, door still open.

"What the hell are you doing here?" Beau sounded farther away, still near his truck.

"Waiting for you."

The sound of a gunshot, then another, and Addie screamed.

Beau knew his grandmother was in the house, he wouldn't return fire for fear of hitting her or Addie.

Kara had her gun out and ran into the living room. Toni was on the couch, Addie tied to the chair. Guidry was outside the door firing at Beau's truck. She didn't know if Beau was hit, she couldn't think about him right now.

Addie saw Kara run in. Kara placed her knife in Addie's hands and strode over to Guidry.

"Drop the gun!" Kara shouted. She was holding her gun in both hands, ignoring the pain in her right wrist. "Toni!

Get down!" She couldn't take her eyes off Guidry to see if she obeyed. Kara walked forward, positioning herself between Toni and Guidry.

Guidry whirled around. He looked drunk or stoned. He didn't drop the gun.

Kara fired. She was aiming center mass, but hit him in his shoulder. She fired again and hit his ear. Damn sprained wrist had her aim off, but he dropped the gun as he screamed in pain. She could have killed him. Right then, right there, stepped closer, shot him in the gut, the head, the balls. She wanted to.

But he was now unarmed. And she couldn't kill even this bastard in cold blood.

She walked over and kicked his gun away, rolled him over to his stomach and pulled his own cuffs from his belt. She handcuffed him as he blubbered in pain.

Then she kicked him in the balls. Just because. And it felt real good.

Beau ran in.

"Are you hurt?" she asked him.

"My truck is, I'm not. Addie—Mimi."

Addie had cut her ties and ran over to Toni, who had indeed dropped to the ground. Addie and Beau helped her up.

"Get me a fucking ambulance!" Guidry screamed. "You fucking bitch!"

Kara ignored him and focused on Toni. "Are you really okay?"

"I'm okay." She smiled shakily. "I knew I was a good judge of character."

Kara spontaneously hugged the old woman.

Matt stared at Jerry Guidry in the hospital bed. He'd lost a lot of blood and was well above the legal alcohol limit, which could have contributed to his precarious medical condition. But he'd survived, he was handcuffed to the bed, and tomorrow he'd be transferred to a prison hospital where he would stay until he could be arraigned.

He would never get out of prison. Matt would see to it.

But they had an offer for him. Matt was loath to give it, but Peter Landry had lawyered up, Preston Cormier had lawyered up, and they had nothing on Jasper Steele except Winnie's statement. That would not be enough for an indictment.

Guidry knew everything; Matt wanted to know everything.

"This is a one-time offer. I'm making it to you first, then I will make it to Preston Cormier, then to Peter Landry. If you don't talk, you'll be in the state pen. If you talk, you'll be in Club Fed. You might be a corrupt cop, but you're still a cop—and you won't survive in state."

"Fuck you."

"You have one minute."

Matt put the tape recorder on the nightstand.

"I want to know who killed each one of those girls and why. Start."

"I want it in writing."

"You'll get this recording. State pen, federal pen. Your choice. Talk."

Guidry only remained silent for a few seconds. Then he spoke.

"Lettie had a big mouth and started flapping it to Tammy that the girls weren't happy, and that wouldn't have been good for Jasper's business. Tammy was just waiting for an in to screw with Jasper."

"Meaning Jasper Steele?"

"Yeah. So Jasper told Gray to take care of her. He did."

"By 'take care of' you mean kill her?"

"Yeah."

"Nicki LeBlanc?"

Silence.

"I know Peter Landry killed her. I have the knife."

Guidry's eyes widened. "How the fuck?"

"Did Peter Landry stab Nicki LeBlanc to death out of rage? Because she taunted him?"

"Pretty much."

"But it was Peter Landry who killed her?"

"Yeah."

"She was killed where she was found. How did he get her out there?"

"I took her out. I didn't know he was going to kill her, for the record."

Matt didn't believe him, but let it slide.

"Tanya Ewing."

He shrugged.

"Speak for the record."

"I don't remember why, but PC—"

"Preston Cormier?"

"Yeah. He was pissed about something. Told his brother to take care of her. Probably skimming, I don't know. Tanya was going with Jake to the Gulf, probably had taken some pills for her idiot brother. Maybe was selling them herself, on the side. I don't really know why."

"But Gray Cormier killed her?"

"Yeah."

Matt had made sure that no one told Jerry Guidry what had happened to Gray Cormier. He didn't want him putting the blame on a dead man for all the murders.

"Hannah Silar?"

"That one's interesting."

"How?"

"Well, you know she was married, right?"

"Yes."

"Her husband was furious she was using again, taking johns, all that shit. He throttled her right in front of half the girls at the Magnolia. But they were wasted, barely remembered what happened, and all I did was drop her on the road. He paid me. I thought for sure Beau would pick him up for it, but you know, Beau had it in his head that I was the killer, which I thought was hilarious—and he didn't do shit. Asked Silar a few questions, didn't even follow up because he thought he knew the truth. He didn't know shit."

"He knew enough to call me."

"Whatever."

"Ginny Chaisson?" He intentionally skipped over Lily for now.

"Preston. And if he says otherwise, he's lying through his teeth. Ginny was his girl, and then she wanted out, and you don't walk away from PC."

"So he didn't know that Ginny was informing on him to Beau Hebert?" Matt asked.

By the look on Guidry's face, that was a big no.

"Bitch. She deserved worse than she got."

"Ernestine?"

"That was fucked. We knew she was talking to Beau, but she was Tammy's kin, so we couldn't touch her. And we thought, maybe she'd take out Tammy for us, you know? Give Beau something to nail her."

"Did you know Gray Cormier was playing both sides? Working for Tammy as well as his brother?" It was an educated guess on Matt's part, and he wasn't positive that it was true, but he might get better information out of Guidry if he turned on Cormier.

"No way," Guidry said.

"There's evidence that points to him feeding Tammy and Debra Martin information."

Matt let that sink in. He saw Guidry working through things in his head, maybe replaying them, thinking, then he said, "Fuck him. He told Elijah to kill Ernestine, but Elijah wouldn't do it. So Cormier killed her and Elijah started crying like a fucking baby. Couldn't have him going to Tammy with that information, she would have declared war, and that wouldn't be good for business. So Cormier framed him for it, shot him."

Matt pulled up a chair and sat down. "Lily Baker?"

"Can't believe you found her after all this time."

"I know who killed her. I need to prove it."

Guidry stared at him. "You never will. The guy is Teflon. Nothing sticks to him."

"He made a mistake. And whoever he hired to destroy the evidence in our crime lab? Didn't do a very good job."

"Good luck with that."

"Why are you scared of him?"

"I'm not. I couldn't care less. But you won't like it when someone gets away, so there's that. Look, I can't prove he did anything."

"Lily Baker was pregnant with Robert Abbott's baby. She refused to have an abortion. He killed her. Can't have a bastard kid when you're running a congressional office, maybe have your own aspirations for office. But he shot her, there's ballistics, and he sealed her in the barrel and dumped her in the river. Somebody helped him. Was it you?"

"How many years?"

"Excuse me?"

"How many years can you get off my sentence if I tell you who disposed of Lily's body?"

"I'm right about Abbott."

"Oh, yeah. When he found out Lily was preggers he lost it. Killed her right there in bed after he fucked her. Because you know, had to get his rocks off one last time. She probably thought he was going to leave his wife and take her away from all this." He laughed coldly.

"And then?"

"How many years?"

"How about I take the death penalty off the table."

"I didn't kill anybody."

"Accessory, accessory after the fact, aggravated kidnapping, assault on a peace officer, attempted murder of a peace officer…"

"Not death penalty cases."

"Life, possibility of parole."

"When?"

"Dammit, Jerry, no one is going to let you out of prison until you're gray and balding."

"I pick my prison."

"Maximum security, federal."

"Okay, but I get to pick it."

Matt had a lot of leeway here—he'd precleared it with the AUSA before he walked in. And as long as Guidry was behind bars, Matt didn't much care where he was. "Agreed."

"Crystal Landry and Jasper Steele put her in the barrel, hired Jean Paul LeBlanc to dump the barrel in the river."

"Did LeBlanc know her body was in the barrel?"

Guidry shrugged. "Maybe, maybe not. They told him it was contaminated drugs from a shipment, that PC told them to dump it. Don't know whether he believed it—probably, the guy had killed most of his brain cells with oxy. If you check, there's an identical barrel, without the lid, somewhere at the Magnolia. I don't remember what was originally in them."

Guidry shifted, looked pained and reached for the morphine drip. Matt grabbed his hand. "You will wait."

"Fucking prick."

Matt stared at him. He'd answered all the questions, and got more than he deserved. But Matt didn't want to let it go. He wanted to hurt this bastard for touching Kara. For putting marks on her. For being a dirty cop.

Then he let go of his wrist. Picked up his recorder and left.

42

Kara said goodbye to Toni Thursday afternoon. Toni handed her Tupperware with leftover jambalaya in it. "You don't eat enough," Toni said.

"I wish I could move in with you."

"You are welcome anytime, and I mean it."

She hugged the old woman and said, "I'll be back sometime. I don't know when, but I will be, and we'll have a nightcap together."

"I'll keep a light on for you."

Beau walked Kara out to where Michael was waiting for her at the car. He and Michael had already said their goodbyes. "You saved her life," Beau said.

"He was so drunk he couldn't hit the broadside of a barn." They both grinned that she'd picked up one of Beau's Southern expressions.

"How's your wrist?" he asked.

"Sore. It'll be fine. It's not broken."

"You didn't get an X-ray."

"I can tell. But I promised Matt I'd get an X-ray when we get back to Lafayette, just in case I'm wrong." She leaned forward, hugged him and whispered in his ear, "I'm not wrong."

He laughed, hugged her tightly. "Be safe, Kara Quinn. You're one of a kind."

She winked at him and climbed into the passenger seat. "You know good people," she told Michael as they drove off.

He glanced at her with an odd smile. "I certainly do."

Michael told her that Matt got a full confession from Guidry and knew who killed each of the girls. "But do we have enough evidence to arrest Robert Abbott?" she asked.

"He's working on it. Told me he'd meet us in Lafayette, if you want to participate."

"You know, I would say I want to be there and nail that jerk. But truly, I want to sleep. Does that make me a bad person?"

"It makes you normal."

"I also want to see Winnie. Can we do that? And then I'll get the stupid X-ray Matt wants."

"Actually, that was the plan."

"Great, my partner, plotting against me."

She reached down, dropped the passenger seat back and closed her eyes.

Forty minutes later Kara sat next to Winnie in her hospital bed. The girl looked gaunt, but she was alive. "Do I have to go through it all again?" Winnie asked. "I told the FBI agent and I told the police and I really don't want to explain what happened."

"I can read the reports." Winnie had been the liaison for Gray Cormier because she was the only one who had worked with the suppliers, through Jake West. Once the pills were onboard, and she thought she was home free, Cormier tied her up and put her in a burlap sack. He didn't know she was working with the FBI, just said that it was payback for her cousin fucking everything up by killing Jake—which was why Cormier thought the feds were there in the first place.

"Have you seen Bonnie?" Kara asked.

"No." She frowned. "I'm not ready to be a mother."

"Of course not, you're nineteen. I'm thirty and I'm not ready to be a mother." Kara had no desire to have kids, not with her job and lifestyle. Not now. And by the time she was ready, she'd probably be too old. And that was okay. There were plenty of kids who needed to be adopted, kids who had fucked-up parents. Kara might be good at that. Someday. In the distant future.

"Mr. Danville said no pressure, but he and his wife are real nice," Winnie said. "They said Bonnie and I can stay with them until I get settled. He even said he'd help me go to college, maybe like a community college. Help me with the paperwork so I can get it for free. I didn't even know I could go to college for free."

"There are a lot of programs out there. It's pretty cool if the Danvilles can help you navigate all that."

"Yeah. He's really nice. Like, um, genuine. Not like he wants anything. And, well, I guess his wife can't have her own kids and she said that Bonnie can stay, too. Like forever, so she doesn't have to go to foster care. Because he's like an FBI agent and stuff, and it makes it easier to skip a bunch of steps."

"How do you feel about that?"

"I like the kid a lot, I mean, I love her, she's my niece and she's a good kid, but I don't know how I can raise her, and my mother can't. She probably doesn't even know we're gone yet. I would just have to tell a judge what it was like at home and because my mother isn't Bonnie's mother, she doesn't have a lot of rights. I mean, unless she got herself cleaned up and proved to the court and all, that's what Mrs. Danville said, but I know that will never happen. They have a really nice house, and they're nice people, and Bonnie never has to know what her mother did or how she was born."

"I think it's a great idea."

Winnie smiled, relaxed. "I do, too. I was worried because she's my niece, people might think I needed to take responsibility for her. And I would—she's mine—but—"

"But nothing. You can be a part of her life, but you're nineteen, you're not her mother, you're her aunt. And the Danvilles are good people who can give her a home, an education, a family."

"They have two dogs."

"And dogs. A big plus." Kara had always wanted a dog, but with her hectic life she'd never got one. It wouldn't be fair to the animal.

"Good. I'm glad. Thank you. I mean it. I didn't believe you could help, that you even wanted to, but you did. And I appreciate it more than you can know."

Matt walked up to Robert Abbott's front door along with two uniformed officers. He'd considered making a splash to arrest him, waiting until tomorrow when Abbott was in the congressman's district office and calling the press to watch him haul the bastard away in handcuffs. But instead, he opted to take the man into custody as quickly and quietly as possible.

It hadn't taken him long to get the warrant. It was really a state case, but his boss Tony Greer had made the case to the AUSA that they should handle this federally because Abbott was a congressional staffer. The state could also file charges. Matt didn't really care who got the credit, as long as Abbott never saw the light of day again.

Elizabeth Abbott opened the door. "Yes, officers? How can I help you?"

She was a beautiful woman who looked a lot like Abbott's first wife, Savannah, and his prostitute mistress, Lily Baker. That would, hopefully, make the conviction even easier.

Not that it would go to trial. Matt suspected Abbott would plea once he knew the truth.

"Please step aside, ma'am. We have a warrant for the arrest of Robert Abbott."

The officers entered, Matt following behind them. "Where are your children?" he asked.

She looked stricken. "What's going on?"

"Where are your girls?" Matt repeated.

"Playing upstairs."

"Where is your husband?"

"His office." Her hand fluttered, vaguely pointing down the hall.

"This officer will take you to your girls and stay with you. I'll talk to you in a minute."

When she didn't immediately move, the female officer gently took her arm and steered her upstairs.

Matt walked down the hall to the closed double doors and entered without knocking. The second officer stood at the door.

"Elizabeth, I told you I was working," Abbott snapped before looking up to see Matt. "Excuse me?" He spotted the uniformed officer. "Who are you?"

Matt flipped open his badge. "Special Agent in Charge Mathias Costa."

"I know the SAC of NOLA, you're not him."

"No, I'm the SAC of the mobile response team, and I think you know that because your ex-wife gave you information that she shouldn't have given you."

Abbott didn't move.

"Agent Trahan has been suspended and is under investigation."

"I think there's a big misunderstanding here." Abbott gave him a wry smile. "I told Savannah not to redact my name, that I explained to Congressman Emerson about the situation years ago, how my old partner committed fraud. But she thought she was helping. I'm really sorry she got in trouble for it, but I didn't tell her to do that."

"I'm not here because Trahan has an ethics problem. I'm here with a warrant for your arrest."

"Okay, that's ridiculous. I didn't remove my name. I didn't do anything—I just explained that."

"Robert Abbott, you're under arrest for the murder of Lily Anne Baker and her unborn child." Louisiana had a specific law that made feticide a first-degree murder charge if done in the commission of a felony with the intent to kill the mother or the fetus. He was pleased because it would certainly help the case if this went to trial—that he killed Lily *because* she was pregnant would almost guarantee he'd spend the rest of his life in prison.

"I'm sorry, you can talk to my lawyer."

Matt read him his rights, all the while Abbott was talking over him.

"Do you understand your rights?"

"No."

"No, you don't understand your rights?"

"Yes! Stop! I didn't kill anybody. I'll come down to the police department and answer questions when my lawyer is present. You don't need to do this." He waved his hands around gesturing to nothing in particular.

"It might interest you to know that the Magnolia Inn has a security system that records everyone who goes in and out. It's behind the bar. Crystal Landry, the manager, had it there for her protection, though she never shared it before. And usually, she tapes over every month. Except four months ago when you came out of the, ahem, bedroom area with blood on your clothes and a gun in your hand. You put the gun down on the bar. I wish the tape had sound—it doesn't—but Crystal Landry *and* Jasper Steele each signed statements that you told them to, 'Take care of the whore.' And you walked out."

Matt was enjoying this far too much. "You should have taken the gun. It was Crystal's gun, and she put it in a paper bag and put the tape with it and said to Jasper, 'When he runs for Congress, he'll be in our pocket.' There is truly no honor among thieves."

Matt didn't like that both Crystal and Jasper were going to do minimal jail time because they were cooperating, but the Magnolia Inn was closing for good.

The officer walked over to Abbott and said, "Mr. Abbott, please stand up, turn around and put your hands behind your head."

As soon as Abbott was cuffed, Matt went upstairs to explain the situation to his wife.

He didn't like this part of the job as much as he enjoyed arresting a killer.

Matt went to Jim's hotel room to check on him. He'd been released that morning, but was staying until Saturday before flying back. Matt had a few things to wrap up here, and the doctor wanted to check on Jim one more time before letting him fly.

They sat across from each other on the hotel couches. Matt told Jim about everything that happened in St. Augustine.

"I would say I'm sorry I missed it, but it sounds harrowing."

"I didn't lose one of mine, so it's a win."

"How's my RV?"

"Dr. Lind and Ryder cleaned up the damage—it wasn't serious, just a mess." He filled him in on the status of the investigation and Abbott's arrest. "Dr. Lind is preparing Lily's remains so her family has something to bury. Give them closure."

"Good. Good." He closed his eyes and leaned back.

"I'll let you rest, just wanted to check in and tell you what happened."

When he reached the door, Jim asked, "How's Kara?"

"She wasn't seriously hurt—bruises but what else is new."

"I love that kid," Jim said.

Matt turned back to him. Grinned. "I don't think Kara would appreciate being called a kid."

As if Matt hadn't talked, Jim continued, "Maybe that's me being a father, maybe that's me being a friend, I don't know. But, Costa? You'd be an idiot if you don't stop her from sabotaging your relationship."

Matt was surprised.

"Get the shock off your face. You think that I didn't figure it out back in *March*? I wasn't positive, thought it might just be mutual attraction, the way you looked at each other. It was clinched in Friday Harbor when you were jealous of the bartender who was flirting with her, the dad of those two girls. I saw it, but then again, I've been around for a while, I pick up on these things. I'm not as clueless as people think I am."

"It's, um, complicated." Damn, he sounded like Kara.

"It's not complicated, Mathias. We've known each other for some time now, so I'm just going to speak freely. I don't know if there's one person for everyone. I know for me, it was my wife. Knew it the day I met her. I was head over heels for the rest of my life. She's been gone for five years and I don't regret our life together. I think about her every day. I grieve—and some days, it's worse than others. But I don't regret a day in the life I shared with her. I told her I loved her every night, kissed her before I went to work every morning, and wanted to make sure that if I died by some asshole's bullet, that she *knew* I loved her. That she *knew* she was the best thing that ever happened to me.

"You and I, Matt, we had good families. I'm one of eight kids. My parents argued and loved and were there for all of us. I know your parents are gone, but they were good parents, you've told me that."

"They were. I miss them."

"Kara didn't have any of that. She doesn't know what a good relationship is, doesn't even know what a bad relationship is. She is her job, but that's because she doesn't know anything else. She is so confident in the field—she's one of the best cops I've ever worked with. Not the most educated, not the most seasoned, and she bends rules as if she doesn't even know they're there. But her instincts are better than both of ours put together, and I don't say that lightly. Her compassion is endless, and it affects her."

Matt nodded. "She internalizes her cases. It makes her good, but it takes a toll."

"Yes. She needs you. She won't admit it now, but you're good for her."

I need her, too.

But he didn't say that. He didn't feel comfortable talking about their relationship with Jim, or anyone for that matter.

"She's going to push you hard, Matt. Push you away. Push you to get angry with her. Push you to give her an ultimatum, which she will *relish* because she hates ultimatums and that will give her the excuse she needs to walk. You can handle it—you can handle her. Because you and I both know she'll never be able to go back to Los Angeles—she would be too high-profile, too vulnerable to people she put away while working under-cover. And you know she'd never settle for a desk job. *Everyone* knows she can't go back—except Kara. And when she realizes the truth, it's going to destroy her—unless she has someone, un-less she has you, to hold her up."

"Kara will always have a spot on this team."

Jim threw his hands in the air. "That's not the point! She has put her entire identity into her role as an LAPD detective. Her home is there. Her sanctuary. Why do you think she hasn't found a place to live in DC?" He didn't wait for Matt to answer and continued. "It's because she has not accepted that she can't go back to LA. You have to show her there is a future."

Jim leaned back into the couch. "I wish I could drink. I'd love a beer about now, but the doc says not for a week."

The conversation was over. And Matt had a lot to think about.

"I'm glad you're okay."

"Me, too." He smiled. "I have a lot I want to do with the second half of my life."

FRIDAY

43

Kara was amused at how attached Jim was to his RV. He went over all the potential issues, how she needed to double-check that every door was secure and every piece of equipment was in its place. Against doctor's orders, he'd gone through the lab on Friday morning to make sure that Dr. Lind had documented everything that was damaged or missing. But in the end, he handed her the keys.

"I made it in less than two days," he said. "But if you need an extra day, that's fine. If you're tired, pull over."

"Ryder's coming with me. We have two drivers. Which is what you should have done."

"Ryder?"

"Yes. Don't you trust him?"

"Of course, but—well—just don't drive when tired. Remember, you have a million-dollar RV with you."

"Scare me more, please."

"You'll be fine. I trust you."

She hugged him. He still had a bandage on his head and his wrist was in a cast and a sling, and she had never been so happy to see someone moving around.

"Don't overdo it, okay?"

"Promise. I'm flying to Dallas tomorrow morning, going to spend my mandatory time off at home. My daughter is going to be a mother hen."

He sounded like he was looking forward to it.

"Call me, let me know how you're doing."

"I will. I'll be back in DC a week from Sunday. Maybe we can go to another ball game. My sister is always able to get good tickets."

She smiled. "I'd like that."

She climbed into the RV, securing her bag in the "personal" closet in the back. She wished she was driving alone, but Tony Greer had said no. She liked Ryder, of course, and he wasn't overly chatty, but she really wanted time by herself.

She needed the time to think. To not have to talk. To just listen to music and not think about the upcoming trial in LA that she had to prepare for, about what happened in St. Augustine and all the lives ruined, about corruption and violence and drugs and all the crap that happened in that beautiful little town.

She was glad she'd had time to say goodbye to Toni. Toni wanted her to visit again, and maybe Kara would.

Maybe.

But mostly, she needed to think about her and Matt and figure out how they were going to end this. Because it was tearing her up inside and she didn't want him to—couldn't let him— love her.

She didn't know if she even believed it.

But at least it was Ryder. He would let her brood and be miserable and not force conversation with her or try to fix everything like Michael.

Where was he? He was never late.

She pulled out her phone and called him. It went to voice mail. Well, shit.

"I'm here, the engine's running, and I'll forgive you for being late if you have coffee with you. Hint hint."

The passenger door opened and she looked over. "About—" She stared when Matt put two coffees into the cup holders, then climbed into the passenger seat.

"Where's Ryder?" she asked.

"He's flying back with Michael tomorrow."

"No."

He turned and looked at her. She tensed. She didn't like being under his scrutiny.

"Kara. We need this."

"No, we don't."

Eighteen hours on the road with Matt. They were going to kill each other.

"I love you."

She put her head on the steering wheel.

"You don't want to hear it. I've handled this wrong. I know that. I tried to do it your way, being discreet and quiet and sneaking around, but everyone knows."

"No."

"Jim told me to grow a pair and stop pretending. So I told Ryder and Michael last night that I was going to drive back with you so we could figure this out."

"Oh, God. Tell me you didn't."

"They knew. When I told Tony, for the record, he told me not to fuck up. But I did, I fucked it up, and you are too important to me. We can make this work, but we have to talk things through. Starting with what happened two weeks ago."

"What happened two weeks ago? When you kept me in your bedroom like you were embarrassed by me?"

"You know I'm not embarrassed of you. God, Kara, I love you, how can I be embarrassed? I asked you to stay because I thought that's what *you* wanted, that you didn't want to flaunt our relationship."

"Catherine knew about us since Friday Harbor and yet I was stuck in the bedroom for over an hour while you entertained her and her family. She's smart and educated and her husband is smart and educated and I'm just a cop."

"You're not *just* anything, Kara."

"I don't fit."

"If you don't fit, it's because you don't want to."

She shook her head, looked straight ahead, willing the tears that threatened to just *go away.*

"I might not even be here in two months. We have a hearing in October, and if everything goes well—"

"Kara, you have to accept that you may not be able to go back to Los Angeles."

"You don't know that." Her voice cracked.

"I want you on this team. But if you return to LA? I'll be there."

"You can't."

"I can do anything I damn well please. Do you think my career is more important than you?"

"Yes."

"You actually think that?" he said. Matt sounded furious. "Do you think I care more about my job than I do about you?"

"No. But your career *is* more important than me. Mine is more important than you. What we do—it *has* to be more important. You're a great cop, Matt. I'm a great cop. I know that—it's the one thing I've never doubted. I wouldn't let you give it up for me. I would never be able to forgive you, or forgive myself, no matter how good the sex is."

He didn't say anything for a minute. "The sex is damn good."

She almost smiled, but she still wanted to cry.

"But it's good because I love you," he said. "And I'm not planning to give up my career. I can go anywhere I want. I'm probably one of the few agents who can. So if you do end up going back to Los Angeles, I'll be there, working for the FBI."

"This team is good. You don't want to give it up. You can't."

"It's a compromise, but one we can both live with. Kara, why can't you accept that I have real and strong feelings for you? That I not only want you, but I need you?"

She didn't know. She just didn't know.

"Look, I'm not saying we take out a billboard and announce that we're in love. I'm saying we just move forward. Let things happen. No secrets. No hiding. Maintain professionalism while working. We've both proven we can do that. I never want you to feel the way you felt stuck in my bedroom. Ever. I will do anything to make amends for that. I was wrong."

"You don't admit you're wrong very often."

He smiled. "Because, like you, I'm rarely wrong."

She sighed. She didn't know what was going to happen.

"Kara, when we were in Friday Harbor, you said we'd take this one day at a time. I'm still okay with that, if that's what you want. But the days are going to be in the sunlight, not in the dark. We'll be discreet—our relationship is really no one else's business—but I want to take you to my favorite restaurant for dinner. I want to take you away for the weekend and have fun. I'm a workaholic—you are, too—but for the first time in my life, I look forward to my days off because I can spend them with you."

She didn't know how this was going to work, but she didn't feel as tense or worried as she had before.

She didn't know if she loved Matt. She couldn't think of a

time when she had been in love with anyone. She wasn't even sure she was capable of loving someone. What the hell was love anyway?

But the thought of letting him go pained her, and it had been the source of her conflict for the last few weeks. So maybe… maybe this was a start.

"Do you want to drive?" she asked.

"Is this a trick question?"

"Nope. I'm tired. You take the first leg." She slipped out of the driver's seat and stepped into the body of the RV to let Matt claim the controls.

He rose from the passenger seat, but he walked toward her. He could just barely stand in the center of the RV. He looked down at her. Touched her chin, her face, her hair. Then he kissed her.

"It's going to work, Kara." He then sat down, his legs hit the steering wheel and he swore. He adjusted the seat and said, "Shit, could you even reach the pedals?"

She buckled up, sipped her coffee. "So I'm short. Live with it."

She leaned back and let Matt take over.

And somehow, the stress fell away and she could breathe.

Maybe this was going to work out.

And for the first time, she really hoped it did.

★ ★ ★ ★ ★

ACKNOWLEDGMENTS

A few years ago, I was speaking to a writers group or a library group—I can't remember now—about my love of research. I've watched an autopsy live and in person; I've gone on ride-alongs; I've toured Quantico. I have more than a hundred books on everything from tracking people to cyberstalking.

I told the writers there that I was a great study. I did well in school largely because I knew how to study—I would read and absorb information the day before, then ace my test, and then promptly forget everything I learned.

Research for my books is basically the same as when I was in school—as soon as I'm done writing the book, I promptly forget everything I learned. So I'm always reading nonfiction if I think I can learn something for a future book, and I still go on "field trips" so I can talk to experts.

And still, I sometimes need to reach out to others when I need very specific information that I can't confirm on the internet.

For *Seven Girls Gone*, I reached out to a friend I've known for years who asked not to be named, but I had to shout "Thank You!" because without the history lesson about law and order in small-town Louisiana, I couldn't have written this book. *You know who you are.*

And my other Louisiana expert, Toni Causey, who helped me whenever I needed to brainstorm, when I got stuck and needed to talk things through, who introduced me to all the amazing truths about the Deep South, including telling me things I did *not* want to know about water moccasins. Thank you for everything, I love you. Yes, I did name Toni Hebert after you. I expect you'll be just like her when you're eighty-four.

There is no question too bizarre for arguably the most generous fellow author I know, Dr. Doug Lyle, my go-to person for all things medical. I had a lot of questions for this book, and I hope I got everything right. But if I didn't, know that it was me, not Doug, who made the mistake. Thank you so much for your continuing help and friendship! Doug writes terrific mysteries under the name D.P. Lyle.

Sometimes when I'm writing, I have a plot-critical question but no one to answer it. I have to rely on the internet. I stop everything and start typing into search engines. I found the Cary Company website and read everything I could about the barrels they sell, but I still didn't know if what I needed my barrel to do would work—or what size I would need. So I hit on the "chat" button and a real person came on. I explained to her that I was an author writing a book so my question might seem unusual...and she took it all in stride. Thank you, Charisma from the Cary Company! I would have been lost without you!

The story behind the story is long and involved—you can

find it on my website if you're interested—but it started with a question I asked readers many years ago about unsolved mysteries they were drawn to. As an avid reader of true crime, I was interested mostly in cases I wasn't aware of, and one reader mentioned the Jeff Davis 8—eight unsolved murders in the bayou. It was in the back of my mind for years, then I read a true crime book by Ethan Brown: *Murder in the Bayou*. One of the best researched and tragic true stories I've read. Though my book is completely different, I drew on the concept of the unsolved murders of prostitutes and the ravages of drug addiction, which Ethan highlighted in his book. I wanted to thank Ethan for his work on this tragic case, and I hope that someday, the killer—or killers—will pay for their crimes.

As always, there is far more to publishing a book than writing the book. I want to thank first and foremost my agent, Dan Conaway, who is always a calm voice of sanity in my life. And Chaim Lipskar, Dan's amazing assistant who is really more than an assistant, who I am both blessed and lucky to have on my team. Then everyone at MIRA—I have a terrific team. My editors, April Osborn and Dina Davis; publicists Justine Sha and Sophie James; the terrific art department who has delivered amazing covers for each and every book; and everyone else who works so hard to ensure that my books are out in the world where readers can find them. Thank you all.

I'm always thanking my family, but it never seems to be enough. They know when to leave me alone to write! What more can I ask? And to my readers: whether you've been with me from the beginning or just discovered me with this book, a sincere and grateful *thank you*. Without my readers, I wouldn't be able to do what I love most: tell stories.